A Monsoon Rising

BOOKS BY THEA GUANZON

THE HURRICANE WARS SERIES

The Hurricane Wars
A Monsoon Rising

A MONSOON RISING

A HURRICANE WARS NOVEL

THEA GUANZON

HARPER Voyager
An Imprint of HarperCollins*Publishers*

This is a work of fiction. Names, characters, places, and incidents are products of the author's imagination or are used fictitiously and are not to be construed as real. Any resemblance to actual events, locales, organizations, or persons, living or dead, is entirely coincidental.

FIRST EDITION

Endpaper illustration © Kelly Chong
Map illustration and part and chapter opener art © Virginia Allyn

Library of Congress Cataloging-in-Publication Data has been applied for.

ISBN 978-0-06-327730-4 (hardcover)
ISBN 978-0-06-341460-0 (international edition)

24 25 26 27 28 RTLO 10 9 8 7 6 5 4 3 2 1

To everyone who, honk-honk, loves the library

The Nenavar Dominion
Light Sever
Sedek-We
Belian
Storm God's Eye
Bukang-nabi
Iantas
Shadow Sever
Chal
Void Sever
Aktamasok
Vasiyas
House Silim
The Silklands
Irrawad
Lidagat
Eset

The Roof of Heaven
Port Samout
Eskaya
Ahimsa
Delanep
House Ossinast
Tepi Resok
North
W
E
S

PART I

CHAPTER ONE

A breeze that spoke of snowmelt in the Highlands tumbled across the barren plains and came whistling in through the lone window of the Regent's private hall. It crashed against the swirling plumes of shadow magic that drifted from stone to stone and was swallowed up by them, vanishing along with the daylight—everywhere save for one bright corner, where the sariman lay in a pool of sunbeams, pinned to the table by leather-gloved hands.

The bird struggled fitfully in the grip of its three captors, issuing a plaintive warble from its twisted golden beak. Its eyes went as round as copper pieces when a fourth Enchanter approached with a glass-barreled syringe, the cold glint of the hollow steel needle emerging from the darkness as its wielder walked into the nullification field.

Gaheris's Enchanters looked even more distressed than the sariman. It was no easy thing to feel one's magic drain away, to suddenly have a gap in the soul where the aether used to be. Even from where he stood at a safe distance, before his father's throne, Alaric's veins crawled with a memory so visceral that his gauntleted fingers twitched against the urge to open the Shadowgate, just to check if he still could.

"Cursed beast spends its every waking moment singing." The growl from the dagger-shaped throne threaded through the sariman's melodious wails. "Even if your time in Nenavar provided no clues as to how its traits can be utilized, did you at least learn how to make it shut up?"

Alaric thought of the amplifying configuration, the circle of wires and metalglass jars laid out on the Roof of Heaven's marble tiles. The molten cores of ruby blood suspended in sapphire rain magic.

He shook his head.

"Why did I even bother to ask?" The bitter disappointment on Gaheris's face, riddled with lines and scars and fissures, was much too clear. "You sailed southeast and discovered nothing. What is the *point* of you, Emperor?"

The sariman's song took on a higher pitch as the needle plunged into its jugular. It was a sound like a fistful of iron nails raked along porcelain, magnified seven times over, clawing at the pit of Alaric's stomach. But he couldn't let on that it affected him. Not in front of Gaheris.

The Regent looked like he'd aged a decade in the ten days since Kesath's imperial delegation returned from Nenavar and the bird was brought to him by Commodore Mathire. He was thinner and more haggard, deep circles carved into the weathered skin under the gray eyes that were so much like Alaric's own.

"Father, if the bird's singing keeps you up," Alaric ventured, aware that Gaheris took the sariman everywhere he went, "perhaps it can stay in this hall when you retire for the night."

"So that every loose-lipped scullery maid and dim-witted stable boy in the Citadel can blather on about this priceless advantage that we now possess?" Gaheris struck the armrest of his throne, and the tendrils of shadow surrounding him flared ever higher, fueled by his wrath. His paranoia. "You spout nonsense about my health when we should be discussing *your wife*."

Spooked by the Regent's outburst, the Enchanters hurried through the rest of their task, transferring the syringeful of sariman blood into a corked vial, applying herbal disinfectant to the extraction site, and ushering the beast back into its ornamental brass cage. They bowed to Gaheris, and then to Alaric, before fleeing the hall, the Shadowgate nipping at their heels.

"Attend to me, my son," Gaheris rumbled once he and Alaric were alone. "After the Moonless Dark, the Lightweaver's magic will have served its purpose. There will likewise be no further need for this pretense at peace with Nenavar. We must strike quickly to bring those islands into the Night Empire's fold. Therefore, once you and your wife have stopped the Void Sever, you will bring her here—under the guise of the provision in your marriage treaty stating that she must hold court at the Citadel from time to time."

"What if you haven't found a way to remove her magic by then?"

"There's still the sariman to keep her in check."

"You wish to hold her hostage," Alaric said dully.

"The Nenavarene will be more obliging with their Lachis'ka at our mercy, don't you think?" Gaheris smiled, a humorless stretch of parchment-thin lips. "If not, well, then we'll remind them how their dragons fared against our void cannons."

The ghastly images roiled through Alaric's mind. Talasyn stripped of the Lightweave, dragons dropping from the sky, their rot-covered corpses sinking beneath the Eversea. The

Shadow falling over the Dominion, Kesathese stormships turning a proud, millennia-old civilization into rubble, as they had all the Sardovian states.

"We wounded one dragon, and there are hundreds more." Alaric forced the words out through the taste of bile. "I'm not sure our Voidfell supply can—"

"You leave that to me and my Enchanters," Gaheris snapped. "Should we use it all up in the assault, there is more for the taking, alongside fresh aether crystals and Nenavar's other riches. Your only job, *Emperor*, is to bring your wife here." Then he paused, his mouth curling into a sneer. "Do not worry. She is of more use to us alive than dead, especially once I can better stomach her presence when she's not a Lightweaver anymore. I won't kill her." His next statement dripped with scorn. "I wouldn't do that to you."

"You were the one who insisted upon the marriage," Alaric replied, careful to show no emotion. No sign of faltering. "She means nothing to me."

"I should hope so," Gaheris said wryly. "She grew up on the Continent. She fought for Sardovia. There are deep ties there, and you *cannot* trust her."

Alaric had always known that. But to hear his father say it . . . It tore at something in his chest. He kept silent, enduring the ache.

"When she arrives for her coronation in a few days," Gaheris continued, "keep her under lock and key. We can't have her running around and finding out about the recent unrest. Inform the generals not to breathe a word, or their tongues will be nailed to the city gates."

The "recent unrest," as Gaheris called it, was a string of uprisings that had taken place in several towns across former Allfold territory. The Regent had been busy putting out those fires while Alaric was in Nenavar, his son's absence no doubt contributing to the Regent's annoyance. They'd been local revolts, though—too small in scale, too scattered, to amount to much.

"The Lightweaver won't risk breaking the peace on account of a few resistance fighters," Alaric protested. "She understands what's at stake."

The Void Sever was to be unleashed in a little under four months' time, spreading death, amethyst and roaring, all over this corner of Lir. A merging of light and shadow was the only way to stop it. Talasyn had promised to cooperate. She wouldn't . . .

"You told me once," said Gaheris, "that it was inadvisable to wager the future on a woman's heart. Neither will I hinge the safety of our people on such a capricious thing."

Alaric drew a breath and Gaheris slumped, infinitesimally, as though the weight of his own declaration was settling over him. As though a string stretched between them in that moment, pulled taut by years past. Father and son entangled.

"Remember your mother," Gaheris murmured. "Remember how she left us when the work got hard. When what she wanted didn't align with what Kesath needed in order to survive."

I will still work with you, Talasyn had said on the rooftop, her eyes blazing. *But you won't* ever *convince me that the Night Empire saved Sardovia from itself . . . Whatever better world you think you'll build, it will* always *be built on blood.*

"Yes," Alaric said hoarsely. "I remember."

"Good. Don't let your wife out of the Legion's sight during this upcoming visit," Gaheris warned. "She will help the resistance fighters the first chance she gets. Of that I am certain."

The eternal mountains of the Nenavar Dominion's Belian range carried the start of wet season on their craggy shoulders, iron-gray clouds heavy with the promise of rain looming over the viridian jungles that carpeted the lofty peaks. From the tallest summit, though, a colossal pillar of golden light shot up, breaking through the ashen skies, filling the misty air for miles around with a thunderous hymn like glass bells.

At the heart of that radiant column, amidst all the golden light and pulsing power, stood a woman. The brilliant glow distorted her features, but two things were sharply etched: the beads of fired clay adorning her smooth brow, and the sobbing infant in her arms, swaddled in embroidered cloths.

The magic flashed and then focused, revealing impressions of buildings, ladders, bridges—all of it carved out of cracked ochre dirt. All of it gathered close to form an arid city packed upon itself until it soared over the Great Steppe's sea of tallgrass and rabbitbrush.

The woman walked down a mudbrick path, slipping unnoticed through the apathetic crowds, holding the child tightly against her chest. She stopped in front of a building as drab and rust-hued as all the others and set her squirming burden down on its front steps.

"Everything will be all right," she whispered, stroking the back of the child's head. "You have to be strong, Alunsina."

Talasyn leaned forward for a closer look at the woman's face, but this scene was woven only from aether and memory. It vanished when the Lightweave did, and Talasyn stumbled backward, out of the sandstone fountain, no longer buffeted by the waves of her magic's nexus point. When she hit the rocky ground ass-first, she shouted a crude expletive at the pain that jolted through her hips and spine—an expletive that was quickly followed by a splinter of lightning that silhouetted the gnarled tops of the grandfather trees, a peal of thunder from the heavens, and then rain.

She got to her feet with a groan. The drizzle sluiced down

her braided hair and into her eyes as she tried to make sense of what she'd seen. Of what aetherspace had shown her.

That had been the day she was abandoned at the orphanage in the rammed-earth city of Hornbill's Head. That woman—those beads had marked her as a servant of the Nenavarene court. The words she'd spoken had been carried to Talasyn in a dream before, in the hollow of a grandfather tree.

Indusa, Talasyn remembered, was the name of the nursemaid tasked with accompanying her to the Dawn Isles, where they were supposed to wait out the Nenavarene civil war, safe with Talasyn's mother's people.

Yet Indusa had taken Talasyn in the completely opposite direction. Northwest, to the Continent, to the Sardovian Allfold's most impoverished state.

Why? Had they gotten lost? Talasyn had been told that two royal guards also boarded the airship that ferried them away from the Dominion capital while civil war raged below—where had they been in that memory? And why had Indusa left the heir to the Dragon Throne in such a desolate place?

Talasyn glared at the empty fountain in the middle of the Belian shrine's overgrown courtyard, willing the Light Sever to flow from its dragon-shaped spouts once again. She was desperate to chase this new lead, this thread in the enigmatic tapestry that was her past. But the fountain was still, save for the patter of rain darkening its stone.

After Alaric's fleet had faded out of sight in the Dominion skies, Talasyn had waited only a few days before scampering off to the Lightweaver shrine, reveling in the newfound freedom she'd gained from standing up to Urduja. She'd been encamped here for almost a sennight, aethermancing and exploring and fielding concerned messenger eagles from her father back in Eskaya. This was the first time that the nexus point had discharged since she'd arrived. It did not look likely to do so again before she had to leave, and it was frustrating.

At least the Light Sever had shown her something *useful*, instead of all the memories that she'd spent her waking hours trying to banish to no avail. Hazy images and phantom sensations from her wedding night, hungry lips on her bare skin, clothing shoved out of the way, a flush to the column of a pale throat, a hoarse voice in the dark of her bedroom, strong hands urging her higher, holding her closer—

A twig snapped behind her.

She whirled around. Months ago, something like this had happened, someone sneaking up on her as she stared at the fountain, under cover of late evening, and she'd flown at Alaric in a blinding rage. They'd fought, light against shadow, his silver eyes gleaming in the aether sparks.

But the Night Emperor was in Kesath. The man looking at her now, from across a respectful distance, was Yanme Rapat, the border patrol officer who had apprehended her and Alaric the first time she'd stepped foot in these ruins. What felt like a lifetime had passed since then.

Rapat saluted. The gilded lotus blossoms embedded in his brass-plate cuirass caught rivulets of rain. "Your Grace." He hesitated, then corrected himself. "Your Majesty."

Talasyn's skin crawled, but she waved off his unspoken apology. "I was the Lachis'ka before I was the Night Empress." Was she even already the Night Empress? Technically, her husband had to crown her first, didn't he?

Her husband. Gods. Of all the ways to think of Alaric Ossinast.

"Before you were either of those things, you were my prisoner." The kaptan's tone was rueful. "I'm truly—"

"You were doing your duty," Talasyn hastened to assure him. It was because of this man that she'd been reunited with her remaining family, after all. "But what are you doing *here*?" Suspicion crept in, along with the same old anger at Urduja for never leaving her well enough alone. "Did my grandmother send you?"

"Not today." Rapat gestured vaguely in the direction of the sandstone fountain. "Your mother, the Lady Hanan, visited this place frequently, Lachis'ka. I sometimes come here to remember, and to mourn."

While Talasyn felt *some* chagrin for jumping to unflattering conclusions about his motives, this was swiftly replaced by the nervous excitement bubbling through her veins. "Did you know my mother well? Were you friends?"

"Her late highness was very lonely in Eskaya," said Rapat. "She detested politics and had no patience for . . . all the formalities and maneuvering. I was one of her few confidants."

Talasyn hung on Rapat's every word. At her grandmother's court in the Roof of Heaven, Hanan Ivralis's very name seemed to be taboo. Whenever Talasyn attempted to bring up the past in conversation, nobles changed the subject and servants ran away. Talking to Elagbi about it was out of the question as well—her father was haunted by the civil war and his wife's death. The mere mention of any of it brought such pain to his kind eyes, and Talasyn had no wish to distress him. Not when they'd only so recently found each other.

Perhaps Rapat could finally provide the connection she sought. Still, she was confused. "Were you often at court then, Kaptan?"

The question had barely left her lips before she recalled something that Prince Elagbi had told her the night they met in the garrison's interrogation chamber. *Yanme Rapat is a good man. A fine soldier, if still smarting a bit from his demotion nineteen years ago.*

Rapat flashed a thin smile and rubbed a hand over his

closely shorn head. "I am now a kaptan in the border regiments. I *was* the Huktera general in command of Eskaya's defenses. It was my task to prevent Sintan Silim's rebels from gaining a foothold in the capital, and I failed."

Talasyn's brow creased. "But the rebels were eventually defeated, weren't they?"

"Through your father's doing, not mine," said Rapat. "I made many tactical mistakes that necessitated the Zahiya-lachis's evacuation—and yours. It was because of my inadequacies that you were lost to us for so long. I can only be grateful that Queen Urduja deigned to show mercy."

There was something hollow in the way he said that last part, something not quite sincere behind his eyes. Not treacherous, but *bitter.* Talasyn couldn't fault him for it, and not just because her own relationship with her grandmother had been strained since their confrontation the morning after Talasyn's wedding.

It's a bad thing to rule through fear, she found herself thinking. *It's a bad thing to punish those who are loyal to you.*

"But I am intruding," Rapat said. "I shall take my leave."

"No, wait—"

There was so much else that Talasyn wanted to ask him. About Hanan, about how Hanan had been manipulated by her brother-in-law, Sintan, to send warships to the Northwest Continent. But Rapat now appeared deeply conscious that he had divulged too much information.

"I insist, Your Grace," he said. "You are Lady Hanan's daughter. You have more right to this place than I do." He saluted again, and Talasyn watched him walk away, a lump in her throat. The grandfather trees swayed in the wet breeze.

However, just before he disappeared into the cavernous mouth of one of the many crumbling hallways that bordered the courtyard, Rapat stopped in his tracks, his armored frame rife with tension. He looked back at Talasyn, his expression solemn, almost poignant.

"Lachis'ka." Rapat spoke quietly, but the words echoed in this place of stone and leaves and lurking magic, a grave undercurrent beneath the raindrops, punctuated by the occasional rumble of thunder. "I have sworn my life, service, and fealty to the Dragon Throne, but I would be no friend of Lady Hanan's if I didn't tell you that there was no love lost between her and Queen Urduja. The Zahiya-lachis was most displeased by Lady Hanan's refusal to be named her heir, and Lady Hanan in turn did not wish for you to be declared as such before you were old enough to choose for yourself. So—take that as you will."

Talasyn's nape prickled. Rapat's words sounded like a warning, and more questions came rushing to the tip of her tongue. Before she could give voice to any of them, however, he was gone.

As she turned to pack up her campsite, the world suddenly swam before her eyes. The Belian ruins melted away into—

—deep blue waters, gliding below as though seen from the air in the midst of flight—

—a hand, knotted and gnarled with age, clinging to a jagged, snowy ridge—

Thunder burst through the heavens anew, and Talasyn gave a start. The images fell away, the stone courtyard brought back in all its clarity.

What *was* that?

It wasn't the first time she'd had visions. Back when she was a helmsman in the Sardovian regiments, she'd seen the Nenavarene dragons and Urduja's crown long before laying eyes on them in the flesh as an adult. Long before she learned who she really was, she'd dreamed of Eskaya, and Indusa, and her mother saying goodbye.

She hadn't known what those glimpses meant when she had them. Nor did she know what these new visions meant now.

Talasyn looked at the empty fountain. She felt helpless and bewildered. She longed to stay here until the Light Sever activated again and she could find more answers.

But if she didn't leave *now*, she was going to be late for her meeting.

CHAPTER TWO

The training hall rang with the guttural shriek of the Shadowgate, summoned from aetherspace in the form of talons—the small curved knives resembling raptor claws that were often a Kesathese soldier's last resort in close quarters, when crossbow bolts had been depleted and swords and spears had been knocked aside. With a talon in each hand, Alaric and Sevraim met in the middle of the hall, slashing and parrying, ever on the alert for a weak spot in the other's defenses.

Alaric found sparring with Sevraim rather predictable for the most part, as they'd been at it since they were children. Today, however, the lanky, mahogany-skinned legionnaire had adopted a new tactic to throw him off balance: running his mouth about Alaric's wife.

"You've slowed down, Your Majesty," Sevraim panted as he slid beneath the arc of Alaric's strike. "Has marriage dulled the Night Emperor's lethal edge?"

Alaric rolled his eyes. The sole of his boot connected with Sevraim's midriff, sending the other man flying across the floor. Sevraim landed on his back with a grunt and hurled one of his knives at Alaric, who sidestepped the inky projectile with ease.

Alaric stalked toward his fallen opponent, idly flicking his own talons from one gauntleted knuckle to the next. Sevraim lay sprawled on the floor, seemingly oblivious to the harm looming in his immediate future, an irreverent grin spread across his face.

"Are you missing your pretty bride?" he suggested. "Counting the minutes until you see her again? Not that I blame you. A most fascinating girl, Talasyn. Or should I say, Alunsina Ivralis. I can see why you—"

Alaric went in for the kill. Sevraim sprang to his feet, blocking with his remaining talon as he conjured a new one in his empty hand and tried to drive it between Alaric's ribs. But his opponent had been expecting this, and he spun around, trapped Sevraim in a headlock, and fit a shadow-spun blade against his throat.

Sevraim was unfazed. "Will the children be Shadowforged or Lightweavers, do you think?" he asked brightly. "It warms the cockles of my cold, cold heart to picture a pint-sized prince brightening these gloomy halls. Then again, His Majesty's firstborn could be a daughter, so you'll need to keep trying—"

He broke off when the talon's crescent-shaped edge was wordlessly pushed closer to his neck. "All right, I yield!" Sevraim called out, shoulders shaking with silent laughter, the black knives in his hands disappearing in wisps of smoke as he batted Alaric's arms away. "So much for my new distraction technique."

"I'd hardly call that a *technique*." Alaric banished his own weapons and strode over to one end of the hall. Grabbing a washcloth from the nearby rack, he dipped it into a barrel of rainwater before scrubbing the sweat from his brow.

Sevraim was soon beside him. "Well, you can't blame me

for trying to rattle you. You've been in a mood since we returned. Even more so than usual." Forgoing the washcloths entirely, he dunked his head into the barrel.

A vein at Alaric's temple twitched. Not only was the water indubitably fouled, but he *was* rattled, more than he would ever let on. Since sailing away from Nenavar, he'd been haunted by that last glimpse of Talasyn, standing on the front steps of the Roof of Heaven, watching him go. Right now, she was most likely preparing for the three-day airship voyage to Kesath, for her coronation as his empress. The prospect of seeing her again, not in the hot jungles of Nenavar but on the Continent, where the echoes of their war still hung in the air, made him feel *strange*.

It certainly didn't help that Sevraim had brought up the issue of progeny. Once, that notion would have repelled Alaric, but now it only elicited intrusive memories of his wedding night. How easy it would have been to hold Talasyn closer, to press deeper and . . .

We shouldn't have done this, she'd told him then, her chestnut-brown hair a mess and her lips still swollen from his kisses. The faint, lush scent of her release lingering, and his spend on her slim fingers.

Jaw clenched, Alaric fought back the memory. Talasyn had made herself clear in that regard at least. He buried his tumultuous emotions before he could give name to them. There was a matter that he had to take care of before her ship made landfall.

"There's something that we need to discuss," he said when Sevraim resurfaced from the depths of the barrel.

For all his cavalier ways, Sevraim understood when his commander meant business. He ran a washcloth through his soaked hair, then waited, canny and alert.

"My father—" Alaric's mouth snapped shut. They were

alone in the training hall, but one could never be too careful within the walls of the Citadel. He lowered his voice. "My father has acquired a sariman from Nenavar. Commodore Mathire captured it without my knowledge while we were searching the archipelago for traces of the Sardovian remnant."

"Those odd little birds that cut us off from the Shadowgate?" Sevraim scratched his head, perplexed. "I *hate* those birds. What does Regent Gaheris want with it?"

Alaric watched Sevraim's face carefully. Ever since he'd walked out of his father's hall that morning, Alaric had been gauging the situation, weighing the dangers. Revealing what he knew was treasonous, and it put them both at risk. If he'd underestimated the extent of Sevraim's loyalty to Gaheris, then everything would come crashing down. Practically a lifetime of knowing each other, fighting side by side, defying death together—it would all be put to the test in this moment.

But he had no choice. Only two Kesathese had been in that atrium when Ishan Vaikar explained how Dominion Enchanters suspended sariman blood in the Rainspring so they could manipulate its effects. Alaric had to make sure that this knowledge never reached Gaheris's ears.

Alaric still believed that the Night Empire was the way forward. It would restore order and stability to the Continent and keep the Shadowforged safe from all who would destroy them. When it came to *that*, Alaric and his father were in accord.

But Gaheris looked to a better future from where he sat in the shackles of the past. He believed that war was the only option. And even though Alaric knew that he couldn't trust Talasyn, he had to figure out a way to secure the Night Empire while not destroying her and the Dominion in the process.

He needed to buy time.

It took Alaric a worrying amount of effort to keep his expression neutral, his tone steady. "Regent Gaheris thinks the sariman could hold the key to removing Talasyn's magic. Permanently."

Sevraim arched a brow, but gave nothing away.

"It's imprudent to antagonize the Nenavarene," Alaric said quickly. "The trade agreement and the mutual defense treaty that come with the marriage alliance are far more beneficial to Kesath than anything that we can hope to gain from another conflict so soon after the Hurricane Wars. My father is a wise man, but in this case I believe that his hatred for Lightweavers has made him reckless. Understandably so, but reckless nonetheless."

"And what of *your* opinion of Lightweavers?" Sevraim asked.

Alaric nearly blanched. He reined it in at the last possible second.

Upon closer inspection, he could see that the glint in Sevraim's eyes was playful rather than malicious. Yet Alaric knew that, as a combatant, Sevraim had a knack for drawing the enemy out and striking hard when they slipped into complacency. It wouldn't do to rest easy just yet.

"Light magic is a plague on the world," Alaric replied, echoing the words his father had spoken so many times. "But Talasyn's bloodline grants us access to Nenavar, and we need her power. For now. Until the Moonless Dark."

The words were heavy on his tongue. He felt as though he were lying. He couldn't tell Sevraim that, as abhorrent as he knew the Lightweave to be, it filled him with a bone-deep ache to imagine Talasyn permanently losing her connection to it. Losing the magic that set fire to her eyes and lit her skin from within and had come close to killing him on more than a few occasions, yet that had also merged with his to create something that had never before been seen in all of Lir.

Something that was theirs alone.

Sevraim studied him for an unsettlingly long while. At last, he shrugged, as though they'd been discussing nothing of importance. "I wish our esteemed Regent luck on his new project, but I have no idea how his Enchanters can pull it off, considering that the sarimans cancel aethermancy."

The weight that Alaric had been carrying since he first heard lilting birdsong echoing through his father's darkened hall finally began to lift. "You have no idea?" he repeated, hardly daring to believe it.

"Not in the slightest." Sevraim smiled, brilliant and sharp. "The Nenavarene didn't explain anything about those creatures to us, did they? They just keep them in cages as a safeguard against aethermancers."

Alaric swallowed. They were sixteen again, stumbling back to the Citadel after their first taste of rose myrtle and rice wine, and Sevraim was loudly swearing on his life, slurring promises to Alaric that he wouldn't tell Gaheris. This was a far more serious matter than two schoolboys carousing out of bounds, but Sevraim hadn't betrayed him then, and the atmosphere in the training hall was the same now—solidarity.

And rebellion.

It's what's best for Kesath, Alaric told himself. *We can't afford to start another war.*

That didn't stop the guilt from gnawing at him, nor the adrenaline rush that was so much like what he'd felt on that rare night of defiance he had allowed himself as a child. But it was with the gratitude of years that he agreed with Sevraim's statement.

"No. They never explained it to us."

*

Lidagat, the southernmost of the Dominion's seven main islands, was a realm of lakes connected by the odd strip of field and jungle and airship grid here and there. The lakes were said to have formed from the tears of a dragon—more specifically, Bakun the World-Eater, who wept when his mortal love, Iyaram, the first Zahiya-lachis, reached the end of her life. Once he had shed all his tears, Bakun took to the skies and wrought vengeance on the world that had caused him such sorrow.

Talasyn was thinking about this legend as she sat in a private room on the top floor of a teahouse, looking out the window. She was in Eset, Lidagat's second-largest city. Like all the other settlements on the island, Eset had sprouted out of a lake; its wooden buildings, with their vibrantly painted, upturned roofs, stood on stilts that rose above the water and were linked by grand bridges that arched like hills. The teahouse was no exception, and the room that Talasyn had rented provided a sweeping view of the rippling waves beneath, as gray as the thundering sky above.

Chin propped up on one hand, ignoring the tea and sweets on the table before her, Talasyn peered out the window into the lake's depths. She imagined Bakun taking wing long ago, a serpentine leviathan caught in a whirlwind of fury and heartbreak, unhinging his great jaws wide enough to crush Lir's eighth moon between his devastatingly sharp teeth.

According to legend, this was also how the rare gemstone vulana came to Nenavar. It was harder than diamonds, brighter than moissanite, and said to be the pieces of the eighth moon that had dripped from Bakun's maw and fallen onto the islands.

Talasyn held up her free hand, fingers splayed out against dark water and darker clouds, brow furrowing at the sight of her wedding ring, where the vulana stone gleamed like a star plucked from the heavens, embedded in a band of gold.

Alaric had a matching stone on his ring, for all that he was ignorant of its significance.

"You shouldn't care whether it's significant to him or not," Talasyn chided herself out loud.

The room's bamboo door slid open, causing her to jump.

After latching the door, the brown-cloaked new arrival tugged her hood away from her face, revealing graying curls and a patch of steel and copper on a leather strap where her left eye should have been.

Talasyn sprang to her feet and saluted, an instinctive gesture borne of years of training.

"No need for that." Ideth Vela hurriedly motioned for her to sit back down. "You're not my soldier anymore. In fact, I should be saluting *you*."

"Please don't," Talasyn said, with feeling.

It was the first time she had seen Vela since the wedding, and a sledgehammer's blow of guilt momentarily stole the breath from her lungs. If Vela were to ever find out what Talasyn had done with Alaric—

Composure. That was the first step to Vela never finding out. Talasyn had to keep her composure.

"How is everyone?" Talasyn asked, feeling a glimmer of pride at how normal she sounded, and not at all like a foolish girl driven to the height of treachery by ungovernable lust.

"Surviving." The Amirante sat across from Talasyn, her bronze features drawn. Talasyn had sent word yesterday, and Vela must have left the isles of Sigwad in the dead of night to avoid being spotted by Nenavarene patrols, then hidden somewhere here in Lidagat until it was time to meet.

Clearly in no mood to linger on the niceties, Vela immediately changed the subject. "That young lord who relayed your message and brought me here—are you sure that he can be trusted? On the way over, he was very"—her lip curled in disdain—"chatty."

"Surakwel Mantes owes me a debt of the self," Talasyn explained. "There is no love lost between him and the Night Empire, and he in fact petitioned Queen Urduja to help the Allfold during the Hurricane Wars." *Also,* she thought, *he and Alaric tried to kill each other the first time they met.* "We can trust him."

"Very well." The Amirante poured the teapot's virulently green vanilla-pine concoction into their two cups. "Speaking of your grandmother, I'm surprised you were able to steal away from her in broad daylight."

"The Zahiya-lachis has no more say on my comings and goings." Gods, but it felt *amazing* to give voice to that fact. Talasyn felt no remorse at all that she was breaking her promise to Urduja to not contact the Sardovians; what her grandmother didn't know wouldn't hurt her. "I've taken up residence at Iantas. I run my own household now."

"That's right. Because you're a married woman . . ." Vela's remaining eye fixed upon her with a hard gaze. "A married woman who will soon be the Night Empress."

Talasyn occupied herself with spooning generous dollops of honey into her tea. To take the edge off the bitter-leaf-water taste that she would probably always detest, yes, but also so that she wouldn't fidget under Vela's scrutiny.

Someone knocked on the door. Vela and Talasyn exchanged sharp glances, rose to their feet, and approached the sound cautiously, fingers flexing to aethermance.

While Vela took up position by the adjacent wall, well away from the immediate line of sight, Talasyn unfastened the latch, niceties on the tip of her tongue in case it was a teahouse attendant, magic surging through her veins in case she and the

Amirante had been found out. She slid the rectangular bamboo panel open and—

—a pair of walnut-brown eyes blinked back at her.

"You're supposed to be keeping watch!" Talasyn hissed, hauling Surakwel Mantes into the room by his collar. Behind them, an equally exasperated-looking Vela secured the door once again.

"Group of minor lords passing through Eset—they spotted me." Surakwel made a beeline for the tea, helping himself to an extra cup. "I told them I'm meeting a friend, which is surely less suspicious than skulking around in the corridor by myself." He regarded the two women expectantly from beneath a fringe of shaggy brown hair. "So what were we talking about?"

Vela appeared severely unimpressed by this new development, but she wasted no more time once she and Talasyn had joined Surakwel at the table. "Repairs and modifications on our vessels here in the Dominion are going slowly," she told them. "It's no easy task synthesizing Nenavarene with Sardovian tech, but we're getting there."

"It's not enough," Talasyn said quietly. "We need the Huktera fleet, but the Dominion court will revolt if Queen Urduja outright breaks the treaty with Kesath for a venture with such an uncertain outcome. We'll need numbers on our side to convince them. We need more allies."

"Precisely. Which is why I've started sending envoys to other nations again," Vela told her. "My best spies and politicians, who can be counted on to infiltrate discreetly and broker deals with the right people, those who won't rat us out to Kesath. Of course, they're at a disadvantage because we can't reveal where we're hiding, but it's worth a shot. And they have time, considering that we can't make our move until *after* the Moonless Dark."

"Isn't it dangerous, though?" Talasyn asked. "If Queen Urduja finds out . . ."

"Nothing about this is safe." Vela sipped her tea sparingly. "But I think there's a reason why the Nenavarene no longer patrol the waters southwest of the Storm God's Eye. I think your grandmother fully expects me to use this time to rally sympathetic nations to the Sardovian cause so that she can use the additional troops as leverage to convince her court to go to war." She gave Talasyn a searching look over the porcelain rim of her cup. "You need to use this time wisely as well. Along with your new role."

Surakwel had thus far been showing proper Nenavarene male deference in letting the women speak without interruption, but at the mention of Talasyn's "new role," he cried out, "How can you *stand* it, Lachis'ka? Being married to that—that figurehead of all evil—"

"It's because of Talasyn's marriage into the Night Empire that we might actually be able to liberate the Continent from it," Vela reminded him.

"Still!" Surakwel rounded on Talasyn. "Aren't you ever tempted to drive a blade through Alaric Ossinast's heart while he lies in your bed?"

"In my defense," said Talasyn, "he's only ever lain in my bed once." *Before I kicked him out of it, after we did something that I swear I will never tell another living soul.* "But I'll let you know where we're at with the stabbing in due time."

The breeze picked up, stirring the edges of their cloaks and the gauzy curtains that framed the window. Eset's sea of weathervanes spun frantically as the black clouds that had been haunting the sky all afternoon made good on their promise and a heavy rain came pouring down, water on water, the lake churning around the stilts that held the city above it.

"You leave for Kesath tomorrow, don't you, Lachis'ka?" said Surakwel.

"Yes," Talasyn replied. "There's a storm coming. It will be a rough journey in this weather."

"A storm indeed." Vela stared out over the lake. Whatever stared back at her—whatever she saw in the charcoal swirl of waves and lightning—made her draw a breath.

"After the Moonless Dark, Talasyn," she repeated. "Be ready."

Talasyn could only nod. The waters of Eset boiled within their banks and a cold wind swept through her heart.

CHAPTER THREE

He was wearing his mask when they met again.

Talasyn descended the ramp of the diplomatic schooner that had borne her from Kesath's shoreline to its capital city, then stopped to look around. They were high up on one of the docks that spiraled from the Citadel's control tower in long strips, like the arms of an octopus. The coolness of the spring air lanced through her bones, a foreign sensation after her long absence from the Northwest Continent.

She had only ever seen the Citadel in maps before. A few years ago, in a fit of desperation, Ideth Vela and the rest of the Sardovian Allfold's War Council had toyed with the idea of rescuing their soldiers from its prisons, but they'd nixed any such plans when it became clear what they would be up against.

Now that she was walking above the Citadel with her grandmother, her father, her lady-in-waiting Jie, and their royal guards, the Lachis-dalo, Talasyn could understand why Vela had changed her mind.

This was one great military stronghold rather than a living, breathing city. A series of starkly cut stone buildings and bare courtyards were tucked away behind thick walls lined with sentry towers and ballista platforms. Unlike Nenavarene settlements, where the skies were filled with ships cutting one another off and racing for prime spots on landing grids, here sleek vessels bearing House Ossinast's chimera on their sails drifted through the air at a sedate pace, in carefully controlled lanes. Beyond the walls was nothing but barren fields and stormship hangars, stretching onward to the horizon.

"Haven't been here five minutes and I'm already depressed," Jie grumbled as she, along with the rest of the Nenavarene delegation, trailed after Talasyn.

"Be quiet," Queen Urduja hissed. Talasyn heard Prince Elagbi chuckle before he, too, was shushed by his mother.

In all honesty, Talasyn was inclined to agree with her lady-in-waiting, but Alaric's tall, broad figure, standing stock-still a few feet away to receive her, demanded all of her attention. He was in his battle regalia: spiked pauldrons and clawed gauntlets, chainmail tunic and belted cuirass, a mix of black like night and crimson like blood. Strands of wavy dark hair fell across his pale brow. His gray eyes regarded her blankly above the obsidian half-mask bearing a carven design of snarling wolf's teeth.

Behind him were Sevraim and two identically armored figures. The Shadowforged twins. The Thing and the Other Thing, as she called them in the privacy of her head.

Talasyn had no idea what Alaric was thinking as she crossed the distance between them on legs that she had to will to remain steady. It felt as though the walkway, built of metal grids that stretched high above the city that was not a city, threatened to shatter with every step she took.

When she came to a stop in front of him, he inched closer until she was forced to look up to see his face.

"Lachis'ka," he murmured.

It had been a fortnight since she'd last heard his voice. Time had not in the least diminished its effect on her. Those deep, rich tones of honey mead and oak, lent a muffled, smoky quality by his mask, sent an unwelcome thrill somersaulting through her stomach.

"Emperor," Talasyn replied as calmly as she could manage.

Alaric tilted his head up for a brief moment, idly perusing the heavens. "You brought your warships," he remarked, acting for all the world as if he could see the outriggers and moth coracles hovering over the Eversea that she'd left behind at the Kesathese port, instead of doubtless having been briefed on their presence by the harbor guards. "Perhaps I should take offense."

"You're the one meeting me in full armor," Talasyn pointed out.

"We were training. You arrived earlier than expected." He glanced at her companions over the top of her head. "Queen Urduja. Prince Elagbi. Welcome."

"What am I, sour goat-liver soup?" Jie asked in a whisper that carried, and Talasyn had to hastily fight back a snort.

Alaric turned on his heel and led the way to the control tower, the Nenavarene delegation following him—rather like a gaggle of finely dressed ducklings, Talasyn observed with some amusement.

But it was an amusement that was quick to fade when the two identical legionnaires wedged themselves on either side of her while they walked.

Unlike the helms of most of the Shadowforged, including Sevraim, the winged design of the twins' helms exposed wide patches of their faces. They were light skinned like Alaric, with long raven-black hair bound high on their heads and fawn-colored eyes that were narrowed at Talasyn in dislike. The last time she had encountered them was at the battle of Lasthaven, where they'd been heartily trying to kill her and she them. Without the adrenaline of combat blotting out all the little details, Talasyn finally noticed the subtle difference between the twins: the one on her right—whom she decided was the Thing today—had a small beauty mark on her cheek.

"Hello, little Lightweaver," the Thing said with a sneer. "Or should I start calling you *Princess*?"

"She cleans up so well, doesn't she?" the Other Thing opined from Talasyn's left. "I almost didn't recognize her."

"Oh, I'd know that smell anywhere," the Thing said airily. "Smells like Sardovian scum."

There were squawks of outrage from Jie and Elagbi, as well as a noticeable stirring among the Lachis-dalo. Before any of them could exacerbate the situation by coming to her defense, as the twins clearly wanted, Talasyn spoke, her head held high.

"I am the Nenavarene Lachis'ka, not a princess." She stared straight ahead, at Alaric's back. He had tensed somewhat. "You will address me as 'Your Grace,' and after my coronation as the Night Empress, you will call me 'Your Majesty.'"

A stunned silence fell over the group, punctuated only by the sound of footsteps slowing on the metal walkway. Talasyn braced herself for retribution, the magic in her veins simmering to life at this great height. Gods, if her attackers tried to push her off—

Sevraim guffawed, as loud as a crack of thunder. "Oh, well *done*, Lachis'ka!" He looked over his shoulder, waving a gauntleted hand at the twin on Talasyn's right, the one with the beauty mark. "This is Ileis." He then indicated the twin on Talasyn's left. "That's Nisene. And I have *never* seen anyone shut them up that fast." He playfully elbowed Alaric. "Isn't it amazing, Your Majesty?"

The Night Emperor ignored him. "Talasyn," he said without turning around. "Come here."

He was giving her a convenient excuse to get away from the twins. Still, she bristled at his high-handedness and opened her mouth to take him to task for it—

"Walk with your husband, Lachis'ka," Queen Urduja said from behind her. The warning was implicit in her regal tone: Talasyn couldn't afford to make any more of a scene than she had already gotten swept up in.

Talasyn pushed past Ileis and Nisene, the weight of their resentful gazes boring into her nape. Perhaps there was *some* benefit to be had in reigning over her former enemies after all. She wouldn't deny that she felt a surge of satisfaction at having gotten the last word with the reminder that the Shadowforged Legion would soon be her subjects. It made marrying Alaric almost worthwhile.

She hurried over to his side and tucked her hand into the crook of the elbow that he held out to her. Her fingers closed around a scaled leather armguard stretched over solid muscle, and it rose up to engulf her—the memory of how his bare arms had felt beneath her wandering hands. She was going to burst out of her skin at any moment, and she couldn't help but sneak glances at his inscrutable profile as they entered the dimly lit corridors of the Citadel. How in the name of all the gods and the ancestors was he so *calm*?

Then again, they had agreed that the kiss in the Belian amphitheater and all else that happened in her bed had meant nothing. Alaric was merely staying true to his word. It meant nothing because it *was* nothing, and so he was treating it as though it were nothing, which it was. And she should, too.

"Are you attempting to cut off my circulation, Your Grace?" His low rumble broke through her reverie.

"Sorry." She loosened her constricting grip on his arm.

Alaric fell silent. His gray eyes flickered to her and lingered a beat too long before darting away again. Was he thinking about their wedding night as well? For him, was it also the ghost that walked between them, the invisible current that trembled with their respective awareness of each other?

Clear your mind, Talasyn scolded herself. She hadn't sailed all the way to Kesath just to be crowned the Night Empress. Once they had a moment alone, she needed to ask Alaric if he'd found Khaede. He had promised to look for her friend in the Citadel's prisons—and if Khaede *was* here, then Talasyn wasn't leaving without her.

She needed all her wits in order to pull that off.

In the end, the Nenavarene contingent was shown to a suite of interconnected rooms, where they were expected to stay until Talasyn's coronation the next afternoon. Aside from the bedchambers, there was a dining room and a lounge, all sporting black stone, large mantelpieces, and polished but simple furniture, with the odd ancient tapestry here and there. Queen Urduja's brows had already nearly disappeared into her hairline by the time Alaric stated, as they stood in the circular lounge at the conclusion of the short-lived tour, that all meals would be brought to them by the servants.

"You will not be dining with us, Your Majesty?" the Zahiya-lachis inquired.

"My schedule does not permit, Harlikaan," he replied, dryly polite. "However, there will be a gala tomorrow, after the coronation. We will take our meal together then."

Urduja nodded, slightly mollified that not *all* semblance of hospitality was lost in this strange new world.

Alaric exited the lounge without another word, leaving Talasyn staring at the empty space where he'd been. In all her stress-filled imaginings of what their reunion would be like, she hadn't expected it to be this . . . anticlimactic. She was *bothered.* And annoyed with him.

She stomped over to a table laden with wine and an assortment of small plates, where Jie and Elagbi were helping themselves.

Jie bit into skewered cubes of grilled duck's blood and chewed tentatively, then made a face. "It's bland!" she exclaimed, aghast.

Elagbi squinted mournfully at the remnants of the vegetable roll between his fingers. "The bean sprouts are soggy, and the dressing is most uninspired."

"It will be up to Her Grace to introduce the finer points of Dominion cuisine to the Night Emperor's court," Jie declared.

Talasyn blinked at them, her cheeks bulging around a piece of egg-dipped sticky rice cake. They stared at her and she shrugged as she swallowed, then reached for the plate of vinegar-cured prawns and sea-grapes without the slightest hint of remorse. Food was food, after all.

She eventually had to stop eating because Queen Urduja beckoned her over to the lounge's sole window. Talasyn went reluctantly; they had more or less been ignoring each other since the fight that had earned her some measure of freedom within Nenavar's borders, but she should have known that such a state of affairs was too good to last.

"I have never before left the Nenavar Dominion," the Zahiya-lachis said, as though it were a point of pride—which it probably was for her. She was speaking in Sailor's Common. "So far, I am not impressed by what I find. A most shabby domain."

Talasyn wanted to tell her grandmother that there was beauty only hours away. That it would become clear the moment one saw them why the snow-laden Highlands were called the Spine of the World. She longed to say that it was spring and the canyons of the Heartland would be teeming with silver-blue rivers, its gorges bedecked in greenery and its meadows covered in flowers.

But all of this belonged to a Sardovia that no longer existed, and so instead she pointed out, "You only have to endure it until the day after tomorrow, Harlikaan."

"Indeed." Urduja extended a slim arm dripping with silk and gemstones to indicate several spots with one stiletto-coned finger. "You will need some fountains there, there, and there. A promenade connecting the various buildings would not go amiss—perhaps with some flowering trees."

"I don't think beauty ranks very high on the Night Empire's list of priorities," Talasyn remarked.

"It should. The masses appreciate a bit of flair. This city is the heart of your empire, yes? You need to keep its inhabitants happy, and to do *that*, you need to make it livable."

"It's not really *my* empire—" Talasyn started to protest, but Urduja cut her off with an impatient shake of her head.

"There's no use thinking like that anymore, Alunsina. The chips have fallen into place. No one knows what the future holds, but for now"—the Zahiya-lachis gestured to the skyline once more, this time sweeping her hand as if to encompass it in its entirety—"the Night Emperor is yours, his lands are yours, his *power* is yours. It's time for you to rule."

"You're sounding awfully enthusiastic about this." Talasyn narrowed her eyes at her grandmother. "You *like* the idea of having a granddaughter on the Kesathese throne."

"And why shouldn't I?" countered Urduja. "What matriarch would object to her house gaining more influence, more prestige? '*We will become a major player on the world stage*'—you told me so yourself, the day after your wedding."

This won't last forever. The Night Empire will *fall,* Talasyn wanted to argue, but at that moment Urduja folded her hands together, her right forefinger tapping on the curve of her left hand's knuckles with painstaking deliberation.

Talasyn froze, recognizing the warning gesture for what it was. She glanced around the lounge, bringing her awareness of every inch of it to the forefront.

Every inch of its *architecture*, to be exact.

The curved walls. The elliptically arched roof. Certain rooms in the Roof of Heaven were also built like this, engineered to deliver sound to a focal point . . .

Urduja's finger ceased its tapping and stretched out to languidly indicate an enormous ebony-wood mantelpiece that occupied a portion of the wall from floor to ceiling.

It was large enough to conceal the entrance to another chamber, where someone could listen to the conversations in the lounge.

How had Urduja known . . . ?

"I account for everything," the Zahiya-lachis reminded her, lowering her voice as she switched to the Nenavarene tongue just in case, echoing words that she had said a fortnight ago, "and so I am caught unprepared by nothing."

It dawned on Talasyn that Urduja had sought to lull whoever was listening into a false sense of complacency by making them think that the Dominion was content to revel in their newfound position and to occupy themselves with superficial matters such as redecorating—rather than hiding the last bastion of the Sardovian Allfold within their borders.

"It also does not escape me," added Urduja, "that your husband has put us up in this dingy corner wing, isolated from the rest of the Citadel." She kept her tone light. To make any potential eavesdroppers believe the topic was still frivolous, even if they couldn't understand the words. "Which implies he wants to limit his people's exposure to you, and *that*, in turn, means there's either something he doesn't want you to know, or he has no true interest in a lasting alliance, or both."

Talasyn's stomach hurt. Was it the questionable vegetable roll? No—this was a different kind of pain. It spread to her extremities, leaving her numb.

What Urduja was saying made perfect sense, but it shouldn't matter to Talasyn that Alaric had hidden motives. So did she.

Combined with the chilly reception he'd just given her, though, the realization stung.

She was going to betray him. That had always been the plan. Now she just had to be wary that he had something up his sleeve as well, but the bigger picture remained unchanged. It *should* be unchanged. And yet—

What's going on with me? Why do I feel hurt?

Maybe it really *was* food poisoning.

"What should I do?" Talasyn asked.

Urduja patted her arm. "Keep your head down, and keep it clear. At your coronation tomorrow, I shall be at my most charming and sociable and will find out what I can—or, at the very least, get a handle on the general feel of things."

"If your intuition is right, then the Kesathese aren't going to be all that talkative," Talasyn said.

The Zahiya-lachis smirked. "I do love a challenge."

Don't you ever grow tired, Talasyn wished she could ask her grandmother, *of always being two steps ahead of everyone else?* She couldn't imagine what it was like to have to live that way. But it was time to start learning.

Night in Kesath was a rolling darkness under a blanket of star-speckled clouds and a bitter wind. Talasyn peered out from the lone panel of metalglass in her chambers, taking in the lightless Citadel that stretched below her in swaths of never-ending, nearly solid black. Hers was the only window burning at this late hour, when not even the bright glow of the fire lamp on her bedside table could dispel the oppressive shadows.

In her mind's eye she was flying in a wasp coracle, its striped sails emblazoned with the Allfold phoenix. She steered it over the Citadel, over all the other settlements on the vast Kesathese plains, eventually clearing the cliffs until she glided down into what had formerly been the Sardovian Hinterland. On and on she went, over the Great Steppe, where she'd grown up, and above the spine of the Highlands, where Khaede and Sol had gotten married and he had fallen in battle only hours later. And after the mountains came the Heartland, that place of last stands, its cities now splintered into pieces by the Night Empire's stormships. The same empire that had now spread to cover the whole Continent.

Talasyn pressed her palm to the window. The chill of metal-glass against her bare skin brought her back from the ruins of Sardovia, back into this room.

Guilt, her constant companion lately, clawed at her soul like an animal. After all this time, she had returned to the Continent—married to the man who had been instrumental in destroying most of it.

I had to, she told her reflection as it stared back at her accusingly in the dark glass. *This way, everyone gets to live.*

Except for Gaheris.

She couldn't actually do anything to him for now. Nenavar needed to stay in Kesath's good graces to stop the Voidfell. But afterwards she could look forward to finding a way to get to the Regent, to kill him, and in doing so help the Sardovian remnant reclaim their lost homelands.

After—she could believe in an after.

CHAPTER FOUR

Though Urduja was well versed in the art of keeping her own counsel, the way her right eyebrow threatened to prematurely join the ancestors in the Sky Above the Sky made it easy for Talasyn to discern that the Zahiya-lachis found it more than passing strange that drinks were served *before* the coronation.

It was the anticipation of refreshment that kept the Nenavarene court moderately well behaved during important ceremonies; Talasyn believed that as firmly as she also believed that the Kesathese needed copious amounts of liquor to get through *this* one.

None of the black-and-silver-clad officers in this cavernous hall wanted her to be the Night Empress. To be fair, neither did the Night Emperor himself. But at least Alaric had so far refrained from huddling in corners with his cohorts, muttering into his wineglass and darting occasional glances at her that ran the gamut from suspicious to resentful.

It took all of Talasyn's self-control to stop from returning the officers' dark looks in kind. The Hurricane Wars were as fresh in her memory as it was in theirs. She was surrounded by former enemies, stuffed into an impractical dress that was a swirl of black and red, layered skirts and ribboned train flowing from a structured bodice with an asymmetric neckline and wrist-length sleeves. It was a dress that made her feel ridiculous, that was not at all conducive to fighting or running away. She would have happily done either.

Black and red. The colors of Alaric's battle regalia. She wasn't sure if the color choice was mere coincidence or if Urduja and the dressmaker were in cahoots to stage some elaborate joke. She wondered how Alaric felt about it, but his granite-carved features were as unreadable as always as the two of them stood around nursing lychee wine and accepting clipped congratulations and insincere plaudits from various guests.

It wasn't as big a gathering as one might have expected for such a landmark ceremony. Only some commodores and generals, and even fewer regional governors, were in attendance, lending credence to Urduja's theory that Alaric wanted to limit interaction between his people and the Nenavarene.

"Your father has not seen fit to grace us with his presence?" Talasyn asked Alaric after their latest well-wisher had walked away. Not that she particularly cared what Gaheris chose to do, but the fact that he was not present for his daughter-in-law's coronation was suspicious. And if she were being truly honest, she had to admit that she was impatient to lay eyes on the man at last, to see what he looked like in the flesh, this shadowy specter of every Sardovian child's nightmare, this architect of all the destruction that had plagued the land for years.

"He has retired from the public eye," Alaric replied. "Your grandmother, on the other hand, appears to be enjoying herself quite thoroughly."

Talasyn followed his line of sight to where the Zahiya-lachis was holding court amidst the regional governors, but she said nothing.

"They're building diplomatic relations," he explained, "in order to facilitate the lucrative flow of commerce."

"You mean that each one of them is sucking up to her in the hopes that she'll prioritize importing his region's products."

"Not only that. Each region is also vying for that much-coveted first direct trading route to Nenavar."

"The capital would claim that, surely?"

"Perhaps not." He scratched at his jaw, appearing a little self-conscious. "It's something I've been working on. A robust national economy would necessitate diverting focus from the center instead of leaving other regions out in the cold. That, I believe, was one of the problems of the Sardovian Allfold: the majority of trade dealings benefited only the Heartland, while other states languished."

Talasyn stayed quiet. Stricken. There hadn't been much employment to be found in Hornbill's Head, or elsewhere on the Great Steppe. Most people with skills and some education had made their way south, leaving those bleak grasslands behind forever.

"Things are going to change," Alaric vowed, as though he'd correctly deciphered the look on her face. "I—*we* will make it better. You're my empress, and you'll rule by my side."

A chance to change things. To distribute what wealth there was and make sure that no child would have to grow up the way she did, that no one would have to suffer as she'd suffered. Alaric held it out to her so tentatively, this future. The ambient noises in the hall melted away and it was only the two of them on the verge of . . . *something*. Something that called to mind promise, and a far horizon.

But it all came crashing down quickly when she remembered

what it had cost. The future that Alaric envisioned—a Continent where Kesath was in full control—was only possible because of the war she and her comrades had lost. What so many of them had died for.

And now he was hiding something from her, something that potentially threatened Nenavar and the impending Sardovian attack that she was hiding from *him.*

They couldn't trust each other. She would do well to never forget that. She had to put things back the way they used to be before the Belian amphitheater, before the wedding night.

"Is that before or after we murder every dissenter on the Continent?" Talasyn asked with false brightness. "*After* would be more convenient, I think. That way, there'll be no one to stop us from doing whatever we want. It's for the greater good in any case, isn't it?"

Alaric's gray eyes turned as hard as flint. "The Nenavarene have certainly trained you in sarcasm. It doesn't suit you, my lady."

She met his gaze boldly. *We are our nations' blades.*

"How unfortunate, seeing as I hold your opinion in the highest esteem," she drawled, just to rile him up, and he . . . stormed off.

To an outside observer, it probably would have looked as though the Night Emperor had merely walked over to the entryway to greet the generals who had just arrived. Only Talasyn knew that she'd gotten under his skin and he'd seized the first convenient excuse to get as far away from her as possible.

She couldn't exult in her petty triumph at his hasty retreat for too long—because now she was standing awkwardly by herself. Talasyn spun on her heel with the intent of finding either Elagbi or Jie, but she stopped short, her fingers tightening around the stem of her wineglass as she came face to face with the bushy-bearded Kesathese officer who had crept up behind her. The absolute *last* person she'd wanted to encounter in the Citadel.

"Lachis'ka," greeted Commodore Darius, the former Sardovian coxswain who had betrayed the Allfold in the final months of the Hurricane Wars. "Or should I say—Empress."

The last that Talasyn had heard of Darius, she and Alaric had been hiking up to the ruins of the Lightweaver shrine and he'd made some snippy reference to the man's new rank. It was Darius's reward for passing information to the Kesathese on the Sardovian Allfold's defenses in the Heartland, as well as for telling them about Talasyn and providing the map to the Light Sever in Nenavar.

She could find no trace of the kindly coxswain who had led her fourteen-year-old self away from the rubble of Hornbill's Head, the same person whom Ideth Vela had once trusted with her life. Neither was there even the slightest glimpse of the frightened, despairing veteran outside the Amirante's office bringing news of the Highlands' surrender and whispering that they were all going to die. Darius was wearing a spotless, smartly tailored dress uniform, his eyes cool and his manner professional, and it was as though he and Talasyn had never met before.

But that didn't stop her from daydreaming about plunging a light-woven dagger into his chest. Or maybe chopping his head off with an axe . . .

She found her voice at last. "I guess *Empress* is a step up from when you were addressing me as *helmsman*," Talasyn said, rather ungraciously, but she figured that she was entitled.

"Several steps up," Darius agreed. "Although I never pegged you for the type to lord a new rank over others."

"Indeed, there's no telling what people can be capable of, Commodore."

Darius beckoned a serving-girl over and plucked a goblet of plum brandy from her tray before sending her on her way. He peered into the depths of the goblet, swirling its contents around. "There's no telling how the need to survive can change people, either," he said solemnly. "Hate me all you like, but some of us don't have a royal heritage in a far-off land to fall back on."

"The Amirante would have died for you," Talasyn hissed.

"That's the most ridiculous thing I've heard." He let out a quiet, disparaging chuckle. "Ideth would have died for Sardovia, yes. She would have died to defeat the Night Empire. But not for me or for you. We were chess pieces in her war, purely expendable. Why else would she send a young girl across the sea to look for a Light Sever, all alone and in unfriendly territory? But"—and here he looked up at her and gave a shrug—"it all worked out in the end for the two of us, didn't it?"

Talasyn wondered if she could get away with throwing her barely drunk wine in his face. One quick glance around the hall was enough to make her decide against it, though. A few Kesathese officers were avidly watching her and Darius; it was clear that they were anticipating a scene between their emperor's new consort and the man who'd sold out her side of the war.

Like steppe vultures circling a sick muskox, she thought with disgust.

But the Nenavarene had prepared her for this. She had never been so grateful for her time in the Dominion court as she was now. Drawing herself up a little straighter, she offered Darius the frosty, enigmatic smile that Queen Urduja was so, so good at. "I *am* rather content with my lot."

Darius's beard twitched, his upper lip curling. "And I suspect that Ideth Vela hasn't died for Sardovia yet, for that matter."

Talasyn kept utterly still and blank-faced. It was a sheer feat of self-control, hastily walled over the panic that unfurled from the depths of her soul and numbed every part of her being. *This* was the greatest danger, what she and everyone else in on it had failed to account for in all their desperate grasping for a lifeline, for a way forward. Darius knew the Amirante well. He had been her right hand for a decade. He was well acquainted with her resourcefulness and determination, with every trick up her sleeve.

He knew that Vela would never have gone down easy.

Talasyn was overwhelmed by the urge to vomit up the few drops of wine that she'd been able to bring herself to sip thus far. She was spared from actually having to do so by her father swooping in, smoothly taking her by the arm, and leading her away from Darius.

"Goodness, what was Ossinast thinking, leaving you in the lurch like that," Prince Elagbi grumbled. "The least that he could have done was escort you to me or to your grandmother first. I suppose that you must introduce social graces to his court in addition to better cuisine." He shot her a sideways glance of deep concern. "I hope that I didn't overstep, my dear—you looked so uncomfortable chatting with that man. Who was he, by the by? Shall I call him out?"

"I'll tell you everything later, Amya," Talasyn assured him faintly.

Her Grace Alunsina Ivralis of the Nenavar Dominion was crowned the Night Empress of Kesath while a light spring rain fell from the skies above the capital. Sheltered from the drizzle by the roof that hung over the grand balcony of the Citadel, from which streamed black-and-silver banners bearing the chimera crest of House Ossinast, Talasyn knelt before her husband. The blood-and-midnight train of her dress was splayed across the polished obsidian tiles as he held up her crown.

The crown was another cause for anger. It had been hammered out of platinum mined from the former Sardovian Hinterland, where the only deposits on the Continent were found, and it was studded with pearls from the Coast, as well as with Heartland rubies. The crown was downright *plain* by Nenavarene standards, but it was a powerful symbol of the Night Empire's total conquest of this corner of Lir. A slender thing, it was dwarfed in Alaric's black-gloved hands as he raised it above Talasyn's head with everyone watching—from Kesathese High Command and the Dominion representatives on the balcony with them to the scores of soldiers and legionnaires spread throughout the vast plaza in precise rows, raindrops spattering their dress uniforms and black armor.

Her knees were starting to twinge. She silently urged Alaric to get on with it.

"Do you swear to govern the people of the Night Empire in accordance with our laws and customs and the tenets of our gods?" he asked, his stony eyes never leaving her face.

"I swear it." Her declaration rang through the air, calm and steady despite the fact that she was speaking in front of those who numbered among her most despised foes. The Sardovian Amirante was alive and well in Nenavar, gathering allies. There was a way forward, and knowing that gave her composure. She would cooperate for now because one day Kesath would fall.

"Do you swear fealty to my crown and obedience to my will for as long as we are bound in matrimony?"

This was the part that she especially didn't like. "I swear it." A vaguely belligerent note crept into her tone as she came dangerously close to rolling her eyes. *Obedience to his will*—she'd show him!

The line of Alaric's mouth curved upward in a faint smirk, as though he knew *exactly* what she was thinking, and for the briefest second something companionable passed between them, as though their quarrel had never taken place. His voice was noticeably gentler as he segued into the final lines of the oath. "Will you stay by my side?" he asked. Framed by obsidian buildings and rain and silver chimeras on black banners blowing in the wind, he added, "Will you stand with me against my enemies and help me build my empire?"

"I will," Talasyn said over a racing heartbeat, through the chill of the knowledge that she was lying.

He placed the crown on her head, released it, and let his hands drift down her face, his silk-clad fingers brushing against her cheekbones. Fleeting, soft, most probably accidental touches, but her pulse skipped all the same.

She was looking up at him, and so was one of the first to see it—in the heavens, over his shoulder, the stormship emerging from behind thick gray rainclouds. It plunged into a swift descent over the Citadel, lightning cannons extended outward in firing position to fringe its convex underbelly like hundreds of metallic limbs. Painted over a wide section of the translucent metalglass panels comprising its elliptical hull, shining bright orange even in the weak daylight, was the Sardovian phoenix.

To her shock, Talasyn recognized the *Chiton*, one of the three Allfold stormships that had survived Lasthaven and the only one that hadn't made it to the Storm God's Eye in Nenavar. Like everybody else, she'd assumed that the *Chiton* had either been destroyed by Kesathese search parties or escaped to the other side of the world. But here it was now, a dread colossus above her, moving at reckless speed toward the coronation venue, which had devolved into roaring chaos.

Alaric hauled Talasyn to her feet and shoved her away from the balcony railing, toward the Nenavarene contingent.

The lightning then came in waves, spilling from the *Chiton*'s cannons in bluish-white streaks that swept through air and buildings and bodies with searing fury. As Alaric cast an inky shield to protect himself from the onslaught, Talasyn's eyes met her father's in the shadow of the stormship, and she broke into a run, no thought left to her but to get him and Jie and Urduja to safety. She had almost reached her delegation, she was only a few more steps away from the Lachis-dalo, who were reaching out to drag her into their protective circle and usher the Nenavarene nobles indoors, when the space in front of her erupted in a blinding barrage of lightning streams.

The floor disintegrated, and she was falling, along with a rain of broken stone that had once been the balcony.

A golden dagger appeared in Talasyn's hand, and she plunged it into a crumbling column within her reach. The radiant blade sent up flecks of obsidian like black sparks as it gouged a deep path down the column, stopping her fall five feet above the ground, while she clung to the hilt for dear life.

Amidst the debris, a grappling hook summoned from the Shadowgate sank into the column next to hers. The crackling midnight rope it was attached to quickly shortened until Alaric was dangling on its length slightly below her.

"Jump!"

Alaric so rarely raised his voice that Talasyn immediately obeyed without thinking. She dropped to the plaza floor and he followed, landing beside her as another tidal wave of lightning bolts shattered the columns they'd been clinging to scant seconds ago.

Lying on her stomach, Talasyn looked around wildly. Wasp coracles were spewing out of the stormship's hangars, firing crossbow bolts at anything that moved. Most of the plaza's surrounding anti-aircraft towers had been obliterated by the initial lightning wave, and Kesathese soldiers and Shadowforged legionnaires alike were scrambling to take up defensive positions behind pillars and doorways and crumbled sections of roof.

A rebellion. Talasyn pieced her scattered thoughts together. There was a rebellion on the Continent. The Sardovians had not simply rolled over and accepted Kesath's rule.

But it was a suicide mission. Once the Citadel rallied its own airships, its own stormships, which would be at any moment now, the Sardovians would be crushed—and with them the *Chiton*, the most valuable weapon that they could ever have at their disposal. What was the objective here?

And was Khaede with them?

She sat up as Alaric scrambled to his knees. They'd both lost their crowns. "My family" was all that she could choke out over the din of battle.

"I saw them get indoors right before the balcony collapsed. My men will watch over them." He wove a knife from the Shadowgate and brought it down over her skirts.

"*What are you doing?*" she shrieked as he slashed at the silken material, ripping off the underlayers, hacking at the edges, cutting away the voluminous train. She would have kicked him if not for the fact that she did *not* want to disrupt the delicate, perilous dance of the whispering blade gliding so close to her bare legs.

"Making it easier for you to run." Satisfied with his handiwork, Alaric stood up—just in time to face the ground force of Sardovians swarming out of a battered shallop that had landed in the middle of the plaza under cover of the *Chiton*'s lightning.

They were a ragtag bunch who wore no discernible uniform save for orange-and-yellow armbands. Some carried crossbows and others were armed with swords, but a good majority wielded only farming implements. Talasyn couldn't save them all, but she had to try. If she could just find a way, without blowing her cover, to let them know that they had to retreat—

if she could just tell them to not waste the stormship, to wait for the Amirante—

A ceramic object with rounded sides and a conical base was hurled into the space between her and Alaric. It was instinct, simple and unthinking, as though the war had never left her bones, that enabled Talasyn to fling herself away in the nick of time. The shell exploded as soon as it hit the ground, with a bang that thundered in her ears as the world dissolved into clay shards and quicklime and sulfur.

Talasyn couldn't even check on Alaric, because a wasp coracle swooped down low before the dust could settle, reeling off a volley of crossbow bolts in her direction.

What the—

The helmsman nestled in the vessel's well was slightly familiar to Talasyn, but he clearly didn't recognize her. She wove a shield and held it in front of her, hoping that the display of light magic would jog his memory. But he kept on coming, and she ran to find more cover. The iron bolts bounced harmlessly off her aethermanced defense, catching one of the Shadowforged legionnaires barricading a doorway unaware.

He collapsed, one bolt through his chest and another through his abdomen. The hem of Talasyn's slashed skirts brushed against his corpse as she sped past to crouch behind a pile of debris. His fellow legionnaires unleashed their magic with a vengeance, crafting javelins of shadow energy that flew through the air and tore the wasp coracle and its helmsman to pieces.

Talasyn fought back a wave of nausea. The sane thing to do was to stay put, stay with the Legion. But she couldn't just hunker down and let more Sardovians die. She had bargained and begged, trained in politics and in aethermancy, shut herself off from everything she'd ever known, and pledged her troth to her sworn foe so that no one else would have to die.

And she couldn't let her husband get himself killed, either. She scanned the plaza until she saw him, fighting in seamless formation with Sevraim, Ileis, and Nisene. Alaric was disheveled, his fine clothes soot-stained, but he was in one piece and that was what mattered, in a way that went beyond the treaty and the need to stop the Voidfell. A way that was too dangerous to acknowledge, and Talasyn certainly wasn't going to dwell on it *now*, because she saw Hiras a little further away.

Hiras. The young cadet whom Talasyn had saved from the Legion at the battle of Lasthaven. She hadn't even realized that he'd gotten left behind in the mass retreat. He'd grown like a weed since then. The gangly and pockmarked young man had currently taken up a defensive position with four other rebels between two pillars, a wall behind them.

The *Chiton* sent another barrage of lightning into the plaza, and Talasyn seized the opportunity to run to Hiras while the Kesathese were distracted. White-hot currents zapped at her heels as she wove between broken stone and broken bodies, and finally she made it to the wall that ran along behind the little group of rebels and she was calling Hiras's name . . .

He whirled around, along with the four other Sardovians. Beneath a shock of russet hair, his brown eyes widened in recognition. She opened her mouth to tell them to escape while they still could, or to ask about Khaede, she couldn't decide—

—and in that split-second of hesitation Hiras's boyish features twisted in fury.

"There she is!"

He raised his crossbow, aiming it at Talasyn's head while his companions charged at her, brandishing pickaxes and hunting knives.

"There's the traitor! *Kill her!*"

CHAPTER FIVE

Time slowed to a crawl, the click of the crossbow's trigger reverberating through the space between Talasyn's heartbeats. A curved, spike-tipped sword materialized in her hand, and she swung it in a wide arc, slicing the iron bolt Hiras shot at her in half. Epiphany sank in, like the chill of a fever from which no relief can ever be found.

The helmsman steering the wasp coracle from earlier *had* recognized her. The Sardovians who'd been left behind on the Continent had learned of her marriage to Alaric, but they didn't know about the deal that Ideth Vela made with the Nenavar Dominion. They assumed that Talasyn had betrayed them.

They wanted her dead.

"Wait!" Talasyn cried out as Hiras's comrades converged on her. She summoned a shield to block the hunting knives, and her light-spun blade loped the head off one pickaxe. Her maneuvers were purely defensive, her aethermancy muted. She couldn't hurt any of her assailants. Their names eluded her, but up close they were all familiar. She had fought at their side and shared barracks and meals in mess halls with them, united by a common cause. "Wait," she tried again, when they'd backed her against the wall and the man with the remaining functional pickaxe was digging its point into her shield, looking for an opening in the already weak magic, "please, you don't understand—"

"What I *understand*"—spittle flew from the man's lips—"is that you were our Lightweaver, but now you're the Night Emperor's whore. And the two of you will be dead soon enough."

His fist slammed into her cheek, over the blazing edge of her shield. He had a farmworker's brawny build, and as Talasyn's neck twisted to the side with the force of the blow, her vision blurred from the agonizing pain. Sword and shield flickered out of existence as she sagged against the wall, sinking to the ground, ears ringing, her mind a fog, no defenses left. The rebels lunged with their weapons from all sides all at once, and there was no way out, except—

To be most useful, the Lightweave needed to be honed into tools reflecting the wielder's intent. The mind had to be sharp so that the magic could be sharper still, whether the intent was to spare or to destroy. But sometimes the mind knew only desperation, knew only to save the body.

An eruption of golden radiance seared the battle-torn air, washing over the four rebels as swiftly as day washed into a room the moment the curtains were drawn back. Four silhouettes, freezing where they stood. Devoured by flashes of sun and aether, their blackened forms illuminated from within.

It's coming from me, Talasyn realized in a daze. Her magic was blazing forth from her veins, gathering around her at the same time that it engulfed those it had marked as her foes. It whirled and raged, outlining with each actinic pulse the contours of bones, the skeletons of grimaces. The rebels' screaming split the air, and her eyes filled with tears. Four silhouettes, crumbling to the ground, burned into her memory. Adding to all her other sins.

The Lightweave left dark spots in her vision after it had ebbed. The ringing in her skull subsided, but the world remained vaguely blurred through her wet gaze. Hiras was trembling at the sight of his fallen comrades, at how their blistered skin had peeled all the way to ashen bone. Eaten away by light.

"*Why?*" The plaintive note in his scratchy voice made him sound less like a soldier and Talasyn's would-be killer and more like the child he had never been, the boy growing up in the shadow of the hurricanes. "You were supposed to—to *save* us . . ."

He raised the crossbow again, sobbing, and Talasyn could only stare up at him through her own tears, her back to the wall, the plaza filled with smoke and the last currents of lightning fizzling out as the *Chiton* exhausted the Tempestroad in its cannons. It was the end of the line, for the stormship and for her, because she *couldn't* kill Hiras, there was no way . . .

Then a snarl of fury, issued from between bared teeth, a shriek of aether as the Shadowgate was opened, the swirl of a tattered formal cape, as Alaric leapt in front of her, swinging his war scythe at the crossbow in Hiras's hands.

Hiras let out a panicked cry as his weapon was cut in half. He dodged Alaric's next strike, moving to the side, but his fear eventually rooted him to the spot. Talasyn saw them both in profile. Hiras shook like a leaf in the wind, and there was nothing but icy rage in the Night Emperor's silver eyes as he brought the scythe down on the rebel's head.

"*Alaric, don't!*" Talasyn screamed.

Alaric froze. The scythe vanished, a mere hair's breadth from making contact with its target. He turned to look at her fully.

A rebel's sword rose behind him.

And because Alaric's back was to this new assailant, because it was too late for anything else, because they needed him alive—

—because *she* needed him alive—

Talasyn used the last vestiges of her strength to fashion a spear from the Lightweave. She hurled it at the Sardovian rebel sneaking up on Alaric. The blade sank into the man's chest and the life faded from his eyes, and he fell to the ground at the same time that Hiras was tackled by two helmed figures in black armor. Out of the path of a Shadowforged throwing knife.

"We have to leave one alive for questioning!" Sevraim yelled at the weapon's source as he helped Ileis pin Hiras to the ground. "*Honestly.*"

Standing a few feet away, Nisene shot him a rude gesture. In the sky above her, beyond the *Chiton*'s hull, five squadrons of Kesathese wolf coracles closed in on the plaza, along with the grim specter of a Night Empire stormship.

Hiras was lying on his stomach; Ileis and Sevraim were practically sitting on him, twisting his arms behind his back.

I should kill him.

The words pierced through the haze that was Talasyn's mind. Hiras would prefer that brief moment of agony to days at the hands of Kesathese interrogators. It would be a kindness.

And what's one more?

"Do it," he said through clenched teeth, and at first Talasyn thought that he was speaking to her.

But Hiras had turned his head to look up at the *Chiton.*

"Do it," he repeated, his bitter gaze fixed on that dread silhouette like a deep-sea creature risen to the heavens. "For everything we have lost."

The Sardovian stormship, its Squallfast-imbued aether hearts glowing a brilliant, venomous green, *plunged*, away from the oncoming Kesathese fleet and down toward the plaza. Thousands of tons of steel frame and metalglass panels swooping down upon them all. Large enough to flatten a quarter of the Citadel, large enough that it was too late to run.

Talasyn finally saw the rebels' plan in its entirety. All of the Night Empire's political and military leadership had turned up for her coronation. Everyone on board the *Chiton* would die, yes, but they'd take House Ossinast, Kesathese High Command, and the Shadowforged Legion down with them.

And there was nothing anyone could do to stop the assault. Legionnaires cast their inky shields over their heads, bracing themselves, while military officers and their subordinates abandoned the fight and fled to whatever paltry cover they could find in the surrounding buildings, which would soon all be smashed into dust. Talasyn stood too slowly, too shakily, as Alaric ran to her, wild-eyed.

She would have called out to him, would have told him to either shield or get inside, to protect himself, but the words evaporated halfway up her throat, lost in the screaming all around her, in the certainty of death, in the daylight fading and the *Chiton* diving down.

Darkness erupted from the northeast. A few towers in that direction had been demolished by the lightning waves, leaving Talasyn with a clear view of one of the Citadel's drab stone buildings. It was quivering at the very foundations as the Shadowgate poured forth from the openings in its roof.

The magic was so thick that it initially seemed as though the building was on fire from within. But all the black smoke soon swept toward the falling stormship, in a tidal wave of night, and took on the hazy shape of chimeras, those creatures on Kesath's imperial seal that were long gone from the Continent but today had been brought back to phantom life. Obsidian energy from aetherspace twisted into eel-like bodies that unleashed the guttural shriek of the Shadowgate with lions' maned heads and galloped through the air on antelopes' hooves. The chimeras filled the sky, all black smoke and nightmare, a feat of aethermancy that Talasyn would never have believed possible if she had not been witnessing it herself.

Alaric reached her at the same time that the stampede of inky chimeras consumed the Sardovian stormship. He pressed her up against the wall, covering her with his body as a rain of metalglass and steel blanketed the plaza. As the Shadowgate tore the *Chiton* apart.

Overwhelmed with relief, Alaric stared at the wall while his father's magic raged above the capital. He didn't have to look around to know what was happening; the chimeras would be winding around the stormship, ripping through its hull and devouring everything—*everyone*—within. Unleashing such power was not without cost, but it was a necessary sacrifice. Today the Citadel would not fall.

Alaric felt Talasyn take a shaky gasp of breath against him, and he hunched further down, further into her, stirred by an instinctive protectiveness that was all he had to give for now. He was rattled by how close she'd come to getting killed—by her former countrymen, no less. He could barely comprehend that she had saved his life, that she had killed a former comrade in order to do so. He was struck by anguish at how he and his people had been sitting ducks, wholly unprepared for a surviving Sardovian stormship.

Just as the Citadel had been unprepared for the attack of the Sunstead Lightweavers all those years ago.

Alaric watched dust stream down the wall as he caged Talasyn in his arms the way his mother had held him while his father bled and his grandfather died somewhere beyond the bolted door, in this very city where war and ruin were raging anew. *This is why we have to keep fighting,* he thought over the cacophony of twisting steel and shattering metalglass and imploding aether hearts. *Everything can be snatched away in the blink of an eye. It will never stop.*

All around us are enemies.

The wrenching sobs sounded as though they were coming from a long way off, despite the fact that the sitting room in which the Nenavarene contingent was barricaded wasn't anywhere near large enough to account for such a distance.

Talasyn worried—vaguely, somewhere deep under layers of numbness and fading adrenaline—that the sobs were coming from *her*, but upon taking stock of her surroundings, she saw that Jie was hunched over in the adjacent armchair, weeping violently, while Elagbi patted her back in a befuddled attempt at consolation. He kept glancing over at Talasyn as though he couldn't believe that she was alive. It had been awful, earlier, when Alaric brought her to Elagbi and the Dominion prince had wrapped his arms around her and cried into her neck. Now Jie was the one having a breakdown.

"What kind of country is this?" the poor girl wailed, trembling from head to toe. "Ancestors, I want to go home!"

In an old life, Talasyn would have been bewildered and quite possibly downright annoyed by all this carrying on, but now she knew something of what people were like when they had been brought up in luxury rather than in wartime. Moreover, Jie was only sixteen. To be that young, to hail from that sort of background, and to be so abruptly confronted by the sort of violence that could erupt outside of the Dominion's harmonious isles must be hard to bear.

Urduja *had* seen war, however, and she was quick to take matters into her no-nonsense hands. "Chin up, Lady Jie. This is just like court politics back in Nenavar, with different factions vying for power—albeit using more barbaric methods. You are the Night Empress's lady-in-waiting. If you are to survive this new game, you have to be strong."

Jie blew daintily into a silk kerchief. "I'll . . ."—she hiccupped, eyes watery and red—"I'll try, Harlikaan."

Talasyn would have taken umbrage at how callously her grandmother had written off the Allfold's struggle to reclaim their homeland, but she was having difficulty feeling much of anything. She was dimly aware that she was in shock. Everything sounded a bit muffled to her ears, and she couldn't stop fixating on her hands, couldn't stop thinking about what those hands had done earlier. All the people they had killed.

"Lady Jie is not far off the mark," Elagbi pointed out. "We must set sail for the Dominion as soon as possible. We can't stay here. Who knows when more fighting will erupt?"

"I fully intend on us leaving within the hour," said Urduja. "While I do believe that the rebels risked everything for a gamble that didn't pay off, there's no telling what else can happen on these strange shores. However, there *is* one upside to this dreadful situation—it lays to rest any Kesathese concerns over whether there is any lingering fellowship between Alunsina and the Allfold."

That's not my name, Talasyn thought with a faded ember of mutiny. Alunsina Ivralis was the Night Empress, the traitor. She didn't want to be her. She wanted to go back to the days when Hiras was telling jokes around forest campfires.

Gods, Hiras . . . They'd dragged him away once the dust had settled. He was probably in the bowels of the Citadel's prison now, awaiting his fate along with the other surviving rebels. He wasn't much older than Jie.

Hearing voices behind the door and the sound of unbolting, the Lachis-dalo stationed inside the room reached for their weapons, relaxing only marginally when Alaric entered.

"Ah, Your Majesty, there you are," said Urduja. "If you would be so good as to clear us to sail, we'd like to leave post-haste. I'm sure you understand, given the situation—"

"Which has been contained," Alaric tersely interrupted. "The coronation gala has been postponed to later tonight, but it *will* be held, and I need Talasyn in attendance. You may leave in the morning."

"Preposterous!" Elagbi thundered. "Have my daughter be paraded around only hours after a deadly attack took place? I won't allow it."

"The alternative," Alaric retorted, "is for *my wife* to make her way to the docks when our interrogators have yet to extract any useful information on rebel movement and our sky patrols haven't finished their search for more enemy ships. I would much rather not give the Sardovians the opportunity to ambush your convoy. There is currently no safer place in Kesath than the Citadel."

"Then I must have been mistaken," said Elagbi, "and it is some *other* city with a center lying in ruins."

At this display of cutting sarcasm, Alaric shot Talasyn a pointed look. "Now I know where you get it from."

He didn't bother explaining what he meant to the other people in the room. Instead, he went on to counter the Dominion prince's argument. "Only the plaza complex was destroyed, and you saw how efficiently we dealt with those who destroyed it. You saw my father's power. There is no reason to cancel the gala."

"So that's the plan, is it?" Urduja huffed, guessing his intent, seeing ahead and through as always. "You wish to celebrate not only your new empress but also your victory over the rebels and the fall of a Sardovian stormship?"

"It rather takes away from the message, having the guest of honor turn tail and flee back home," Alaric said by way of confirmation. "It is also in Nenavar's best interests to show the Continent that she and Kesath are united in the face of all dangers."

He approached Talasyn where she sat. It was only then that she noticed that he was holding her crown, dangling from one black-gloved hand at his side. The platinum surface was slightly scuffed, and one of the rubies had a barely perceptible crack. When he held it out to her, she stared blankly at him. With a frown, he placed it on her lap with care.

Then he knelt before her so that they were almost eye level, his gaze lingering on her bruised cheek with an intensity that was both wrathful and startlingly possessive. His lips were set in a stern line, and his fingers clutched the chair's armrest, grazing her elbow. The lips that she had kissed, the fingers that had been inside her . . .

The Sardovians she had killed to save herself.

The Sardovian she had killed to save *him*.

I am the Night Emperor's whore, she thought bleakly. Her former comrade had called her that, before he died, and it was true. She was a traitor.

"Why did you run to them?" Alaric asked quietly. "Nisene said she saw you."

Think. She had to think. Talasyn forced her sluggish mind to come up with a passable excuse, and it felt too long—it felt like ages before she spoke. "There wasn't anything logical about it. I just—I knew them. From before. And I wanted to get them to stop. I couldn't believe it when they started attacking me. I wasn't being rational."

A maze of half-truths, which all amounted to a lie. She could have taken a page from Jie's book and wept with uneasy relief when Alaric seemed to accept her explanation.

"And now we know," he said, "that Sardovia will stop at nothing to destroy us both. But you have my hand and therefore my protection, and there is no need to fear. Come to the gala tonight. You will be safe."

Talasyn nodded slowly. What else could she do? It helped with her cover.

"Was this what you were hiding from us?" she asked. "A rebellion?"

A muscle worked in his jaw. "Yes. There have been a few small uprisings scattered throughout the Continent, but all quickly contained. We didn't know until today, though, that they had organized. Or that they had a stormship."

What would the Nenavarene Lachis'ka say? The one who'd been born to rule, who had no need to allay her husband's suspicions? "This was a security threat." She forced the words out through a throat clogged with thorny bramble. "And you kept it a secret from my delegation because . . ."

"My father didn't trust you." Alaric looked away briefly. "*I* didn't trust you. But you saved my life today." He met her gaze again, and this time his own was open. "Everyone saw you use light magic to kill your attackers, as well as the rebel sneaking up on me."

"He wouldn't have been able to sneak up on you if I hadn't distracted you." Why was she arguing with him? Perhaps because some fury from him would make her feel better, would usher the two of them back to a place that she understood. Perhaps because nothing was worse than having gained his trust—at the expense of the Sardovian lives she'd taken.

Alaric shrugged. "You said it yourself—you knew them, you weren't being rational. But it doesn't change what today's events showed us." Earnestness was written all over his face. "We are stronger together, Talasyn."

You shouldn't trust me, she wanted to scream.

But if he didn't, so many would have died for nothing.

And if he had been less quick on his feet, less adept with

his magic, even for just a second—if a lightning strike or a crossbow bolt had hit true, if *she* had been too slow in striking that sword-wielding rebel down—Alaric would have been one of the Shadowforged dead today. The near-miss made her confront a question she'd been avoiding.

If in the end he had to die so that the Allfold could triumph, could she let it happen? Could she be the one to land the killing blow if it came to that?

The answer should have been obvious. It *had* been obvious months ago, before everything that had happened since. But now, gazing down at her husband, the grime of battle clinging to his pale features, which were soft with the solemnity of his promise, Talasyn realized that she was no longer so sure. And she was running out of time to figure it out.

"Khaede." She clung to the name as though it were a lifeline. It burned on her tongue like damnation. "Have you found her? Or was she—" *On the stormship, or in one of the wasp coracles, or there on the ground—*

"I'll keep looking," Alaric said.

It wasn't until he was at the door, about to leave the room, that Talasyn managed to break out of her stupor somewhat. She hurried over to him, ignoring Jie's and her family's dumbfounded expressions. There was one question burning in her mind. She needed to know the answer.

"Alaric." Talasyn caught his arm. He looked back at her blankly. "The rebel with the crossbow—why didn't you kill him?"

His gray eyes lingered on her hand on his sleeve, then drifted to her face. "Because you told me not to."

CHAPTER SIX

By nightfall, Talasyn's shock had mostly worn off and the next steps that were within her capabilities had taken shape in her mind. She would learn where exactly Hiras and the other rebels were being held and what the security measures were. She would meet with Vela upon her return to Nenavar, armed with all the data needed to coordinate a rescue mission. Then she would camp out at the Belian shrine for as long as possible, missing no chance to commune with the Light Sever whenever it activated.

Her aethermancy was the only thing that had a hope of countering such a display of Shadowgate as had come from Gaheris. Talasyn had no idea how she would even begin learning an equivalent skill, but she would make do, she would blunder through, as she always had.

But first, she had to endure the gala.

Her coronation dress was a lost cause, so Jie had strapped her into another Nenavarene contraption of stiff ice-blue abaca fiber and embroidered silver trim, studded with pearls to match her dented crown. It dipped appallingly low in the back, but she found consolation in remembering that she would be seated for most of the event—even though she would be sitting beside Alaric, in the middle of one of the long banquet tables full of his officers.

The overall mood was festive. Or as festive as Kesath could get, anyway. The generals congratulated one another on successfully holding the plaza. They sang the Night Emperor's praises and the Regent's, proclaiming the might of shadow magic over and over. They toasted the *Chiton*'s destruction. As Talasyn maintained the most neutral expression that she could muster, her insides turned over with bile, the food like cardboard in her mouth.

The Kesathese did not mourn their dead, she noticed. They seemed to accept that everyone who fell on the battlefield earlier had simply been doing their duty. Well, she couldn't say that it wasn't the same for the Allfold. They'd willingly sacrificed a stormship and everyone on board. And even before that, in the thick of the war . . .

Talasyn remembered Sol, the life gone from his blue-black eyes, the *Summerwind*'s deck spattered with his blood. There had been no time to mourn him as they fled, his death being just one of many, barely a footnote in the grand scheme of things.

And thinking about Sol naturally led her to think about Khaede, whom Alaric hadn't been able to find, who was either dead or not. If not, then Khaede must have delivered her child, Sol's child, by now, if she hadn't miscarried. Khaede could be alive and well somewhere, with her baby, or she could be one of those crushed beneath today's rubble. Or her ship could have been shot down during the Sardovians' retreat from the Continent and her bones were being picked clean by the creatures of the deep. Talasyn didn't know, and it was starting to look more and more likely that she would never know.

Khaede wasn't a footnote; she was a story without an ending.

Talasyn tried to watch the evening's entertainment, if only to distract herself from spiraling. At the northern end of the hall was an orchestra of bronze gongs and reed pipes and boat-shaped rosewood xylophones, and moving to the deep and rousing beat these instruments struck were dancers in chain-link attire, cavorting and cartwheeling along the aisles between the tables. They twirled burning staves through the air and breathed plumes of fire, a clever mimicry of aethermancy achieved by fuel mists and precision. Talasyn was struck by how ghastly it was, all this merrymaking in the same city where the Shadowgate had ripped an entire shipload of people to shreds that very afternoon.

Her gaze met Darius's at another table. He inclined his head in a quick bow that contained a hint of apology. Her lips struggled not to twist into a scowl as she realized that he assumed they really were allies now. Now that the Sardovians had tried to kill her and the Kesathese had witnessed her kill *them*.

It was apparently a notion shared by the officers at Talasyn's table. Commodore Mathire, who had only ever been stern or threatening during the marriage negotiations, was all deferential smiles as she encouraged Talasyn to try the fermented plums. When Talasyn ate only a spoonful—and only to be polite—the commodore clucked her tongue in sympathy. "I suppose these Sardovian rats can put a damper on *anyone's* appetite. Have no fear, Empress. They'll never bother you again."

One of the generals chortled. "Even if they do, Her Majesty will easily put them in their place."

"To be sure." Mathire's smile turned almost lupine in the glow of the flickering fires. "Shadow and light have long been at odds, and for good reason, but today has shown us that much can be achieved by working in concert."

"Enough." Alaric broke the gloomy silence he'd sunk into at

Talasyn's side. "My consort has had a long day. Let her dine in peace." He was looking at Mathire with something like anger, an anger that puzzled Talasyn, that was quite disproportionate to the apparent cause—the commodore's disruption of her meal.

"Of course, Emperor Alaric." Mathire's smile faded a little, but never truly left.

Before Talasyn could even wonder at this strange interaction, there was a swirl of black amidst the dancers and their red-gold streams of flame. One of the Shadowforged Legion had entered the hall, made his way to Alaric, and was murmuring in his ear. Talasyn was close enough to hear the man say, "Your Majesty, the Regent wishes to see you."

Alaric waited for the legionnaire to leave, then pressed a black-gloved hand against Talasyn's shoulder in a fleeting, feather-soft touch. "You'll be all right?" he inquired.

She almost bit through her tongue to stop from begging—no, *ordering*—him not to leave her alone in this chamber of wolves, but it wasn't as though she would ever take precedence over Gaheris in Alaric's head. And perhaps his departure was a blessing in disguise: without him breathing down her neck, perhaps she could set in motion her plan to extract information.

"I'll be fine," she told him. "Of course you must go to your father when he asks for you."

A slight flush rose to the top of Alaric's cheeks. She had once called him his father's dog, and she herself was uncertain as to whether her latest implication of such was accidental or not. Maybe she was lashing out to feel a little bit less helpless, maybe he deserved it, and maybe she stared after him a little too long when he got up and walked away.

Even though Gaheris's private hall was only a handful of buildings away—a ten-minute stroll, at most—it might as well have been a world away from the gala. Everything in the hall was silent, dimly lit. The caged sariman slept on its perch, in bars of moonlight, its golden-plumed head tucked beneath one iridescent wing missing several feathers.

There were no shadows this evening. Gaheris usually filled his hall with magic, to muffle the highly sensitive conversations that took place within, but even he needed time to recover after aethermancing an entire stormship into dust.

Alaric sank to one knee before the dagger-shaped throne, waiting for judgment.

"You know what this means, don't you?" Gaheris's voice was painfully raspy through heaves of threadbare breaths. Alaric's heart ached to see his father so gravely weakened—because of *him*. His failure. "Either Ideth Vela is alive somewhere on the Continent, or someone else has stepped up. We have a full-blown insurgency on our hands."

"Yes, Father," said Alaric.

"I'm curious," drawled Gaheris. "What would you have done if I hadn't been there today?"

Alaric swallowed. "It was unusually cloudy, and the rebels used it to cover their approach. A tactic that will work only once, because we will be more vigilant in the future—"

"There would have been no future if not for me. You were *staggeringly* incompetent." Gaheris sat a little straighter, as though his rage gave him new strength to tap into. "You were so incompetent that the Lightweaver had to save your skin, after your magic faltered instead of cutting down an enemy. This is in addition to all your shortcomings in dealing with the whole Nenavar mess. What is the *matter* with you lately?"

"I apologize." Alaric's response was automatic. The field of combat had been thick with legionnaires, and there was no use wondering which of them had reported to his father. It could have been anyone aside from Sevraim, Ileis, and Nisene—and he wasn't even certain about the twins.

What are you, then? Talasyn's jeering tone rose from the depths of his memory. *Emperor in name alone?*

But whoever reported it clearly hadn't noticed that Talasyn was the one who'd stayed Alaric's hand, for Gaheris made no mention of such a thing.

This was where rebellions began. In the little cracks that people slipped through.

The thought snaked up from a shuttered corner in Alaric's mind, perilous yet somehow oddly tempting. As though he could give in to it and then his failures would matter a little less.

"And now our people's view of the Lightweaver has softened," Gaheris muttered. "The worst possible outcome from this crisis."

"She killed several of her former comrades today," Alaric pointed out. "They threatened her and her family. And she chose my life over that rebel's—"

"That is nothing to be proud of. If a *Lightweaver* had to come to your rescue, you should have just died."

It hurt, of course. Like a knife from out of nowhere, slipped between the ribs. But Alaric persisted. "Be that as it may, doesn't this prove that the Lachis'ka's allegiance is no longer with the Allfold? Perhaps she is truly willing to work with Kesath."

"Perhaps," Gaheris begrudgingly conceded.

"So—there might be no need to continue the experiments with the sariman—"

Alaric knew that he'd made a mistake as soon as the words left his lips. The Regent's eyes darkened, then flashed silver.

The shadows rose.

It shouldn't have been possible. Not after all the magic that Gaheris had expended earlier that day.

But wrath was a powerful fuel.

"How quickly my son forgets the lessons of the past," the Regent growled. "You would have Kesath work with the same magic that once sought to destroy it. You would place your faith in the same breed of aethermancer that killed your grandfather. Rather than striking first, you would leave our realm vulnerable to the whims of the Dragon Queen."

Alaric hung his head.

"You weren't ready, after all. It's a shame. What the Night Empire could become with a capable ruler . . ." Gaheris trailed off, features twisting in disgust.

So why don't you *take over again, if I'm doing such a poor job of it?* Alaric thought, in a burst of sudden defiance. *Ah. That's right—you never will, because you don't want people to know how much the Shadowgate has aged you, and you see assassins everywhere.*

Caught off-guard by his own insolence, no matter how secret it was, he lowered his gaze to the floor.

"I have let you get away with far too much for far too long," the Regent concluded. "Your wife will have to preside over her coronation banquet without you. Now . . . rise and face me, boy."

Alaric got to his feet, steeling himself for what was to come. A hollow sense of despair washed over him as he realized that *this* was why he'd initially been let off the hook when he returned from Nenavar a fortnight ago. Gaheris had been saving the punishment for the most humiliating moment that it could be inflicted—with Alaric's new empress and her family in the Citadel, wondering along with his officers where he'd gone off to during an important celebration. On a night that marked a triumph and a turning point of his reign, he would slink back to his chambers alone and heavily injured, like a street dog hit by a cart.

His father was reminding him of his place. And there was

nothing that Alaric could do about it as the shadows enveloped him.

Nothing except stand tall and rely on his pride to suppress his cries amidst waves of debilitating pain, tendrils of magic lashing at his skin, his eyes gazing upon only darkness, swirling with flecks of aether like the ghosts of stars in some black night. He could do nothing except ride it out, breathe out each current of agony as it seared into the marrow of his bones.

And yet there was a part of him that seemed to experience all this from far away. Some tiny part of him had left his body and was wrapped in sunlight, sheltered somewhere spun from memory, a place where Talasyn carded her fingers through his hair as he lay atop her, the gentlest touch he'd ever known.

As the pain heightened, this sunlit place grew larger—

—and when the next shadow-whip cracked against a fresh wound in his back—

—when his knees threatened to give out at the renewed onslaught—

Alaric seized control of his father's magic and, arms slicing through the air, sent the shadows roaring toward the throne.

He had no idea how he did it. He wasn't even fully aware that he'd done it until the dust settled and the waves of attacking darkness parted from Gaheris's form to reveal that the Regent had managed to cast a shield before he was consumed.

Through the haze of lingering anguish that ripped into his nerves like knives, Alaric dimly registered the smile of twisted delight on Gaheris's face.

"Pain is instructive," Gaheris whispered. "Do you understand now how it brings out the best in you? Not even I can bend someone else's aethermancy to my will. You brim with raw power, child of darkness. I will see that you learn how to harness it properly—that you learn how to *rule* properly—so that you may always keep our people safe."

Something warm and wet was streaming down Alaric's cheek. At first, he assumed that he'd started crying from the physical toll, but when he blinked his lashes became tangled in something too sticky to be tears. He was bleeding from a cut on his head. The hall swam before his eyes.

"F-father," he heard himself stammer out. "I can't—"

"You will," said Gaheris. Black fumes of magical energy gathered around him once more, preparing for the next strike. "You are my son. Your grandsire watches from the willows. You will endure this and prove worthy of our family's legacy."

And the Shadowgate swept over Alaric once more, and he could no longer hold back a scream as his torment began anew.

CHAPTER SEVEN

The Hurricane Wars had shaped Talasyn in more ways than one. The most glaring way, in her opinion, was her tendency to be deeply suspicious when things were going well.

Because it was almost *too* easy, wasn't it? And she had her Nenavarene companions to thank for that, whether they knew it or not.

At first, it was frighteningly awkward in the wake of Alaric's departure. Every once in a while, the Kesathese officers' questioning gazes slid to the empty seat beside her, containing no leader to take cues from. The obvious implication was that the Night Emperor thought so little of his political marriage that he had no compunctions about abandoning his wife at a feast purportedly held in her honor.

This was a uniquely excruciating brand of humiliation, to be sure, but Talasyn would rather have scooped out the World-Father's earwax than let on that any of it affected her. As she sat straight, holding her head high beneath the weight of her new crown, Urduja and Elagbi and Jie eventually came to the rescue. There was nothing quite like the Nenavarene at their most charming, and the tension was lessened somewhat as the three of them worked together to draw even the most taciturn diners at their table into lighthearted, perfectly appropriate suppertime conversation. After that, it was only a matter of waiting for the opportunity to present itself once the officers had relaxed and the liquor had loosened their tongues.

Talasyn didn't make her move until Mathire was distracted. Although the Dominion nobles had run rings around the commodore during negotiations, making plain that her talent was in brute political force rather than cunning, Talasyn still didn't trust that secretive little smile from earlier. Some instinct cultivated during the months under Urduja's tutelage warned her not to play games with Mathire. Therefore, it wasn't until the other woman was embroiled in discussion with some other commodores that Talasyn turned to the general sitting beside her.

"You cannot imagine my relief, General Vim"—Talasyn marshaled her snootiest Lachis'ka airs, praying that he wouldn't see through them—"to learn that all the surviving rebels from today's attack have been apprehended. It is commendable how swiftly, how *bravely* your men acted in the face of such an emergency."

Talasyn could hear Urduja's voice in her head as she watched the general's chest puff out with pride. *If you have no strong pieces on the board, then play to your opponent's weaknesses. Ego is usually the most reliable path to someone's downfall.*

This was one of the many tidbits of wisdom that the Zahiya-lachis was forever spouting during all those long, drawn-out lessons in her salon at the Roof of Heaven. Talasyn was glad that she'd been paying attention that particular day.

"Indeed, the stars will never set on the Night Empire," General Vim proclaimed, taking another swig of brandy. His grin was broad, his cheeks were flushed, his guard was down.

"The Allfold set sail for the Citadel believing that they had the upper hand—now they languish in our cells."

Underneath the table, Talasyn's fingers laced into her skirts, gripping the fabric so tightly that one of the pearls came loose. She leaned toward Vim, widening her eyes in a picture of innocence. "And we are absolutely certain that they'll stay there?" She let her voice tremble from anticipation, let this arrogant man in his cups mistake her tone as fear.

"Not to worry, Empress Alunsina." Vim grabbed a table napkin and patted at the crumbs on his walruslike mustache. "The eastern wing of the prison is so heavily fortified with ballista platforms and sentry towers that the Legion doesn't even need to patrol it. It's right by a mess hall, too, so at any given time there are scores of the Night Empire's finest soldiers who will come running at the first sign of disturbance."

Talasyn smiled. "I'm glad to hear it, General."

It really was too easy to loosen their tongues, but the nebulous dread in Talasyn's gut refused to abate until the whole onerous affair came to an end and she and her delegation left the hall, accompanied only by their guards and Nordaye, Alaric's aide. She recognized him as the one who had poured the wine on board the stormship during Kesath's sweep of Nenavar.

Quietly mousing along ahead of the group, Nordaye had, in Alaric's absence, been tasked with showing the Night Empress back to her quarters. The aide was short and skinny, with brown hair cut in the shape of an inverted winnowing basket and a perpetual downtrodden look on his face. He was the most forgettable young man Talasyn had ever encountered—a trait that apparently fixed him in Urduja's mind as a spy, for the Zahiya-lachis kept her voice painstakingly low as she walked behind him with Talasyn and Elagbi, clutching their arms.

"It is odd that the Regent does not show himself to us," Urduja mused in Nenavarene. "Quitting the business of governance does not render one incapable of greeting his new family, surely. A private audience, at the very least. Although I should think that he would have quite liked to celebrate his victory against the rebels with his people!"

"He is ill, I believe," said Elagbi. "I overheard a few officers inquiring with one another after his health. No one seems to know the true state of things, and such secrecy is usually only employed to prevent causing a panic."

"That might be why Alaric took the throne," Talasyn ventured. "A nation postwar is vulnerable—even more so with an ailing leader."

"You're learning." Urduja squeezed her arm. "But the simplest answer is often a ruse, is it not? Or the surface of a vast root system."

Talasyn bit her lip, considering the situation. "Even if Gaheris *is* ill, his influence has far from waned. We all saw how quickly Alaric left to answer his summons. I think the Regent has found a way to quell fears about the Kesathese sovereign's physical condition while still ruling from the shadows."

And that means I was right to call Alaric his father's puppet, and to tell Vela that Gaheris is the real power in the Night Empire.

"I would certainly tire of my reign not being wholly my own." Urduja's tone was casual and yet not—an airiness grounded in intent. "One can only marvel at Emperor Alaric's sense of filial piety."

Talasyn didn't have the patience to puzzle out her grandmother's words. She knew only that she wanted to talk to Alaric. To demand where he'd gone off to and why he hadn't come back.

There was a melodious giggle up ahead. Nordaye had gone as red as a ripe tomato, from the base of his neck to the roots of his winnowing-basket hair. Jie, who appeared to have fully recovered from her earlier distress, was strolling beside him, fluttering her lashes and looking far too pleased with her handiwork.

"Lady Jie, stop torturing that poor boy," Urduja barked. "Come *here*, you silly siseng-goose."

Nordaye recovered in enough time to direct them to their wing of the residential building. After bidding goodnight to Urduja, Elagbi, and Jie—when it was just her and Nordaye standing outside her chambers—Talasyn put her plan into motion.

She fixed Nordaye with her steeliest glare, one that she had learned from Urduja. The aide started shaking in his boots.

"Take me to my husband," Talasyn commanded.

Nordaye was too much of a wilting flower to put up a fight. He escorted her deep into the heart of the fortress and then vanished so swiftly that he might as well have been a spectral. But Sevraim was a different story.

"Absolutely not, Empress." The masked legionnaire stood, arms crossed and feet slightly apart, beneath the severe archway that led to Alaric's suite of rooms.

"Who are you?" Talasyn asked waspishly.

There was a squawk from behind the obsidian helm. "It's me! It's Sevraim!"

She already knew that, but she hadn't been able to resist. "Well, then, let me through."

"I *can't.* His Majesty isn't even in yet."

"So I'll wait."

"You can't just waltz into the Night Emperor's bedroom unattended—"

She shoved past him. "You can abandon your post to keep watch over me in his chambers—where, as his wife, I have every right to be—or you can try and stop me from going in by raising your blade to your new empress. It's your choice."

"Have it your way," Sevraim peevishly replied. "But I warn you, if His Majesty demands my head for this, I *will* be seeking political asylum in Nenavar!"

"That's a risk I'll have to take," Talasyn shot back.

There were five doors on each side of the hallway she'd marched into. She paused.

"Third one on the right," Sevraim grunted.

And Talasyn stepped into an austerely furnished bedroom that was, very obviously, Alaric's.

It smelled like him.

She had never developed the habit of associating certain scents with certain people. In Hornbill's Head, everyone had smelled like the Great Steppe, dusty and sunbaked, and the Sardovian regiments had used the same kind of standard-issue lathers. Among the Nenavarene court, the mix of various perfumes and oils was too confusing to try to make sense of—and it was downright cloying on occasion, to the point that she would sometimes sneeze in a crowded hall.

Alaric, though, was different. Talasyn just hadn't realized how much until she entered a room she'd never been in before and knew instantly that it was his because of the scents that hung in the air. There was the warm fragrance of sweet myrrh in his soap, mingled with juniper berries and the spice of the sandalwood water that he splashed on after shaving, as well as a hint of honey from his pomade. Underscoring all of these, also, was the slightly acidic tang of coffee, the earthiness of leather, and traces of vellum and ink.

She spent ages standing in the middle of the room, agonizing over whether it was more proper to sit at his desk or to remain on her feet while waiting for him. She also didn't know whether she was here to be mad at him for abandoning her at the gala or to squeeze more information out of him. She still hadn't decided what tack to take by the time Alaric stumbled in.

Their eyes met, then widened in sync as the door slammed shut. There was a gash on his forehead. His shoulders sagged and his body dipped forward in the beginnings of a slow, terrible collapse.

Talasyn hurried over to Alaric, bracing him in her arms before he could hit the floor. "You're injured!"

"Your powers of observation are—" His sentence cut off into a sharp hiss as he pressed one gloved hand over his ribs.

Burdened by her dress and heeled shoes, it took some effort to haul him onto the bed, but she finally succeeded. His face was a worrying gray at the edges against the black sheets, and his fine tunic was soaked through with—with blood—

She wrestled the tunic and his formal gloves off him, her heart clenching in sympathy as he grunted with each jolting movement, and sat down beside his sprawled form. Now he was bare from the waist up, but she couldn't afford to be embarrassed; all of her attention was on the bruises and lacerations marring his skin like some gruesome star chart.

"What happened?" she demanded, vehemence leaching into her tone. These weren't battle wounds. He'd had to have stayed still for them to be this concentrated. And she recognized the telltale jagged edges left by the Shadowgate. "Who did this to you?"

Alaric turned his head to the side, avoiding her gaze, his lips clamped shut.

"Tell me." Talasyn put her hand against his cheek, urging his eyes back to hers. "Or I'll go to your guards and ask them instead."

"*Don't.*" Within the depths of his pupils, sparks of silver aether flashed. But this stirring of magic brought on by an abrupt surge of emotion vanished just as quickly as it had appeared, its wielder utterly sapped of strength, his pride running aground on her stubbornness. "It was my father," he said hoarsely. Every word sounded ripped from his throat. "In punishment for my shortcomings—" He shuddered with a fresh spasm of pain, eyelids twitching as he closed them, long lashes fluttering against the tops of wan cheeks. "A lesson."

Talasyn had known, of course, that Gaheris was cruel, but it had never before occurred to her that this cruelty would extend to his son. *This is how he keeps him chained.* The epiphany brought with it a rush of nausea. That the Master of the Shadowforged Legion did not fight back told her this had been going on for a long time. It had been *ingrained* in him to not fight back.

She reached out to scrub some of the blood off his face with the pad of her thumb, and her stomach twisted when he flinched at her touch. She thought about the orphanage keepers and how they'd made a game of hitting her and the other children, how she'd snuck out on her own as soon as she was able.

Alaric's mother had left. He'd had nowhere to run.

"I'll tell Sevraim to call for a healer," Talasyn announced, getting to her feet.

"He already offered to. I told him to get lost." Alaric's large fingers clamped around her wrist, dragging her back down. "No one else can see." She hesitated, unconvinced and worried sick. He added, his tone uneven and his grip on her tightening, "Don't, Talasyn."

His blatant panic forestalled all argument. A leader could not appear vulnerable to his people. Not so soon after a war. His thumb brushed across the inside of her wrist in fretful strokes, and her free hand moved as though of its own accord, wrapping around his, squeezing in reassurance as she asked, "Do you have any bandages, then? I can—"

"Leave it," Alaric told her through clenched teeth. "I'll take care of myself."

"You're in no condition—"

"I can manage—"

"No, you *can't!*"

He gave a start at her raised tone, his powerful body twitching as though it longed to curl in on itself in a protective ball. Thoroughly chastened, she cradled his cheek, the walls that she had so carefully built around herself in his presence crashing down. "Alaric," she pleaded, "let me help you."

"You shouldn't even be here." Despite his rough, strained words, he leaned into her touch with a quiet desperation that made up her mind for her.

"I am, anyway," she retorted. "You're not getting rid of me that easily."

He opened his eyes and suddenly she was staring into the liquid silver of them, glazed over with terror and anguish. Perspiration dotted his brow. It was several long moments before he spoke again. She could see various decisions playing out across his conflicted features and, above it all, the yearning for comfort. For relief from his suffering.

"My back's worse off," he admitted.

Talasyn bit her tongue to keep from scolding him for taking his sweet time telling her. She helped him roll over onto his side, and then she had to stifle a gasp at the sight. Gaheris's magic had lashed at him with tendrils of thorns and heat. The striated wounds crisscrossed down his spine, weeping drops of scarlet on singed skin. How had Alaric survived this? How could *anyone* have survived this? What kind of father would do this to his son?

Later, she thought. She could ask questions later. For now, she had to concentrate on the daunting task at hand.

CHAPTER EIGHT

There was a tea set on the desk, and Talasyn brewed some valerian root that she rummaged from the herb chest. Alaric would be pretty out of it, but it would help with the pain, and he drank from the cup that she held to his lips willingly enough—albeit with a somewhat disgruntled expression that spoke volumes about her tea-making abilities, or lack thereof. She also found bandages, washcloths, and a truly foul-smelling pot of herbal salve in the bathroom, and she lugged these into his chambers along with a bucket of hot, soapy water.

The next hour passed mostly in silence, in stillness, punctuated by faint ripples as she dipped the cloths into the bucket to clean his wounds, and by his harsh intakes of breath as she gingerly spread the salve over them.

She had done this before for many others during the war, in those grimy trenches and razed forests where the healers were too far away or all dead, but it was a new thing with him. It was almost an act of revelation, to be able to slowly map him out like this, unlike the frenzied touches of their wedding night. Her fingers pressed into his broad back, learning the strength of his sinews and where the hurt began.

When she turned him over to work on the injuries to his chest and abdomen, she found herself tracing the remnants of a much older wound—the pinkish, knotted line of skin right below the edge of his clavicle, all that was left from when she'd stabbed him the night they met.

Alaric wasn't so dazed that he failed to notice where her attention had drifted. "Don't tell me you're feeling guilty after all this time," he said flatly, and yet there was an edge of bitterness to his comment. He'd gone all stiff, the way she had when he fell silent after she told him about her early life in the slums. The way she had reacted when she assumed that he was pitying her.

It's not pity for you that I feel, he'd said back then. *Rather, anger on your behalf.*

How she yearned to echo those words to the proud, broken man lying before her now. But to do so would mean acknowledging the part that he hadn't said out loud. She had no idea how he would respond to her giving voice to the inconvenient truth that they were more alike than was sane to admit when it came to the things that they carried.

They were alike in another way, too. There was a long, faded line of white on her left arm from the only cut that had left an imprint out of the many shallow ones that his war scythe had inflicted during that first battle. It was hardly visible unless one knew to look for it, but it was her own permanent reminder of that night.

"Of course I don't feel guilty for defending myself from you," Talasyn muttered. She soaked another washcloth in the now-lukewarm water and resumed tending to him.

And it was—different—with him looking at her while she worked. More dangerous, with the rise and fall of his sculpted chest beneath her hands as she mopped up the blood and applied the dressings, cautiously navigating a labyrinth of wisteria bruises on moon-kissed skin. It was even worse when necessity dictated that her ministrations move lower down his body and his defined abdomen contracted slightly at her every touch.

It brought back memories of how her fingers had slipped under his shirt and skated along these same muscles while he kissed her neck. Memories of what she would find if she went even lower still, past that dusting of dark hair bracketed between his lean hips.

You horrible girl, some aghast inner voice chided. *The man is covered in bandages and you're thinking about his—*

Cringing, Talasyn darted a furtive look at Alaric's face. Her heart slammed against the bones of her rib cage when she saw that he was already peering down at her through half-lidded eyes.

Upon closer inspection, though, she saw that his gaze was unfocused, probably from the valerian root. She cursed inwardly, realizing that she should have treated his head injury first. She scooted further up the bed and dabbed at the gash on his brow.

"It's not as deep as I feared," she assessed, bandaging it as best as she could, "but if your head aches or you feel faint at any point over the next few days, you really should consult a healer."

His charcoal gaze studied her drowsily from beneath the careful motions of her hand. "Is that a command, Empress?"

She lifted her chin stubbornly even as she flushed at her new title. At the raspy, teasing way in which it was drawled. "Yes, it is. I can't hold back the Voidfell without you."

"I've survived worse than this."

She wiped away the bloodstains on his sharp cheeks and his long nose, and then the ones located lower still, at the side of his mouth. Her stomach roiled. "Why did your father do this?"

"I disappointed him." It was a blunt, honest answer. One that Alaric would never have willingly given if he weren't under the effect of anesthetic tea and dizzy from blood loss. His lips brushed whisper-soft against Talasyn's thumb as he spoke. "The attack nearly succeeded because I was unprepared. I was weak. That rebel I didn't kill . . . Someone saw and told my father."

Talasyn listened, stricken. He'd only spared Hiras because she'd begged him to. No matter what she did, someone always got hurt. She was trapped in a labyrinth. She couldn't see the way forward.

Alaric relinquished the last of his defenses with a sigh, the planes of his chest heaving slightly. "I'm—*tired.* I suppose it was naive to hope that the fighting would end after Lasthaven . . ."

The war isn't over. Talasyn's fingers twisted into the bloodstained washcloth. *Not while there are things still left to fight for, and people to fight for them.*

Against your father.

Against you.

A sense of wrongness ate at her for harboring these thoughts of her inevitable betrayal in this place of silk sheets and lamplight, when he was soft-eyed and vulnerable, laid up in linen bandages, confessions spilling from that usually stern mouth.

At a loss for how to react, Talasyn seized hold of the practical. She rose to her feet with the intention of putting away the used cloths and the bucket, but Alaric grabbed her elbow, despair surging from him in waves, and pulled her to him. She let out an indignant squeak as she found herself sprawled on top of his bare chest, her nose inches from his. She held still, careful not to disturb the bandages, and his hand darted from her elbow to her lower back, exposed by the cut of her blue dress, his warm fingers trailing static charges along the base of her spine. She hadn't realized that she was so sensitive there.

"Don't go," he murmured hoarsely, fitfully, a man caught in a fever-dream. "I won't bring up the rebels again. I won't breathe another word. Just—don't leave me, Tala." The name he had first called her on their wedding night sent a mess of starlit recollections swirling through her at the same time that it caught in his throat, along with what he said next. "Please."

Talasyn stared into the hollow desolation in Alaric's gray eyes, the utter defeat. She knew this loneliness. She understood it in the marrow of her bones. "I was going to clean up, that's all," she whispered. "I'm not leaving. It's just—the bucket and—"

"Forget the bucket," he told her, a hint of his usual imperiousness breaking through the valerian fog. "Stay here."

"All right." Not her wittiest moment, but it was difficult to think when she was pressed up against his solid body, his hand on the small of her back. "I'll stay."

He looked like he didn't believe her, and it pierced her heart. She wondered if this was a common occurrence: Alaric crawling back to his chambers after Gaheris's punishments and nursing his injuries while he dreamed of not being alone.

Talasyn suddenly wanted nothing more than to assure Alaric of her presence. She sank fully against his form, holding him down with her weight, burying her face in the side of his neck in a chaste imitation of what he had done to her once, in another bed.

"I'm here," she vowed into his smooth, overheated skin. "I'm not going anywhere."

A sound between a groan and a hitch of breath caught in his throat. The hand on the small of her back rubbed compulsively, tracing the notches of her spine, and his arm tightened around her. His other hand tangled in her hair.

"I couldn't kill that rebel." It was a choked, bewildered rumble in her ear. "One word from you and I let my guard down. I couldn't kill *you*, either, all those times before . . . What am I, if I'm not a weapon? What have you done to me?"

It shouldn't have mattered what he was saying, trapped as his consciousness was in valerian dregs. But there was a kernel of truth in his bleak questions. This time the voice that crept into Talasyn's head was not Urduja's, although it was definitely telling her what Urduja would have taken away from the situation.

He cares what you think. It was Talasyn's own inner voice, from some dark part of her. *You can use this.*

She blocked it out, this epiphany. She focused only on Alaric, on how his words reminded her of the orphanage at Hornbill's Head, the keepers' brutal fists, how they'd spat out that she and the other children would never amount to anything more than the bottom-dwellers they'd been born as. Her body was melting against her will into Alaric's arms, rationality giving way to the urge to comfort. To do for someone else what nobody had ever done for her.

"You're not just a weapon," she mumbled into his neck. "You have a sweet tooth and sometimes you make me laugh. I tell you things that I've never told anyone else." The very air seemed to spin golden with each surge of memory, aether humming between their forms. "You helped me with my magic. You tackled me out of the way of that void bolt. Today you made sure I could run and fight. All of these things—they're not what a weapon is, or does. You're so much more than a weapon. You could be more."

She meant it, she acknowledged to herself, their past interactions blurring together. It caused a sensation that felt like surrendering, there in the hollows of her heart. She meant every word.

Alaric's fingers tightened in her hair, a gentle tugging that lifted her head from the crook of his neck. She blinked down at his pale, anguished features, her pulse quickening as it was caught in the stormy undertow lurking in the haze-ridden depths of his dark eyes.

"Be kind to me, wife," he said.

It was a gruff entreaty wrapped up in a voice like smoke, all gravel and valerian, curling halfway between yearning and madness. She froze at being called *that*, but then a not altogether unpleasant shiver rippled through her veins as his palm slid along her hair, cupping her nape, exerting just enough pressure to urge her lower.

Talasyn let herself be moved, just as she had done at the Roof of Heaven, in that place of sunlight and snow-white plumerias. Here and now, however, there was no Sevraim to interrupt them as her mouth slanted over his and the world went—*soft*. Like summer rain.

It was a bad idea. It would always be a bad idea. But Alaric's lips pressed against hers with quiet hunger, his hands were hot and heavy on her, and his callused fingers curled around the back of her neck, tracing staticky patterns on her spine. He smelled like herbs and sweat, and he was so broad beneath her, offering a taste of an end to loneliness. She surrendered, relaxing in his strong arms, unthinkingly chasing his mouth with her own.

Then he went still.

Am I doing it wrong? In a burst of panic, Talasyn broke the kiss in order to cautiously check on Alaric. His eyes were closed, his breathing even, the line of his mouth slack.

He was asleep.

"You're an asshole," she snapped. It echoed through the quiet, lamplit room, but he didn't so much as stir.

Despite her annoyance, perhaps there was some tenderness in her touch as she reached down to brush strands of his wavy black hair away from his bandaged forehead. She allowed herself this one small gesture, because no one would ever know. *Especially* him.

Talasyn was awakened by the sound of a Shadow Sever, a faint, sputtering screech, like icefall.

She bolted to a sitting position in Alaric's bed and peered out the open window into the distance, where the Shadowgate billowed in plumes of smoke at the stark gray edges of the Citadel.

Alaric's chambers overlooked the building from which the horde of inky chimeras had spewed forth the day before. From its rooftop, a black ship was taking to the air, and it wasn't long before it glided in the direction of the active Sever. Amidst the slew of legionnaires on the deck, Talasyn could make out a stooped, dark-robed figure with fingers as pale and brittle as twigs clutching the railing.

Gaheris.

It had to be. The Shadowforged circled him protectively, all of them facing outward. Before Talasyn could get a closer look, they cast a dome of obsidian magic, obscuring the entire deck from view.

The emaciated figure remained burned into her mind long after the ship had become a speck sailing past the Citadel's walls. Talasyn had seen aethergraphs of Gaheris from before the Hurricane Wars, then no more after that. She now saw why. The change in the Night Emperor from those earlier images to this wraithlike Regent was alarming. The might of Gaheris's aethermancy and the frailty of his physical form were incongruous.

Alaric stirred beside her.

His brow was knitted even in sleep, speaking to the immense pain that he was in. One look at the multitude of bandages she'd done her best with was enough to ignite an ember of fury within her, to have her clenching her fists. She should have hurled a light-woven dagger into his father's chest while she'd had the chance. She should—

—be leaving now.

Her gaze had happened to slide over the clock on the nightstand, only to zero back in on it with disbelief. Her delegation was supposed to set sail for Nenavar in two hours, and any minute now Jie would be wandering into her room to help her get ready. If Jie found the Lachis'ka missing from a bed that hadn't been slept in at all, the day after a devastating attack . . .

Scrambling off Alaric's mattress, Talasyn had never moved so fast in her life, but she *also* had never before been stopped from moving so fast, with Alaric lacing their fingers together as soon as her hand brushed against his.

"Where're you going?" he mumbled into his pillow, eyes still shut. He ran his thumb over the back of her hand in a drowsy caress.

Was this her heart, this racing thing? Her cheeks turning warm, her stomach caught in free fall like a coracle mid-spin—could she still blame the vegetable roll from yesterday?

"Back to Nenavar," Talasyn whispered. It somehow felt like the hardest thing she'd ever had to say. She extricated her hand from his as gently as she could. "I'll—I'll see you there?"

"All right." His voice was small. Almost boyish. He sounded forlorn and resigned, and she had no idea whether he was dreaming or not. Whether he would remember this exchange upon waking. "See you."

Talasyn padded quietly out of the room. She didn't look back, afraid that what she'd find would make her want to stay.

CHAPTER NINE

"Emperor Alaric, forgive me, but I don't understand."

The unctuous, nasal tone sank barbs into the base of Alaric's skull, threatening a headache far worse than any that his father's lesson a few days ago could have inflicted. When he looked up from the map of the Continent's former Sardovian territories that he and Kesathese High Command were poring over, he was frowning at the officer who had spoken.

"And what nuances of rice distribution are *so* esoteric to you, Commodore Lisu?" he demanded.

Slender and pointy-faced, with spiked black hair and skin the color of hemlock wood and eyes like darkened amber, Lisu was the youngest member of High Command—a position he had achieved through a blend of sheer cunning and leveraging of his family's influence.

In the past, Alaric's sentiments toward Lisu had amounted to nothing more than fleeting contempt. Now that Alaric had ascended to the throne and was forced to work closely with the commodore on a regular basis, however, he was fairly certain that he loathed the man.

If the feeling was mutual, Lisu made no show of it, ducking

his head in a slight bow. "I merely wish clarification, Your Majesty, as to why we are distributing rice when we should be focusing on matters of national security. The insurgents—"

"—can be tracked down and dealt with at the same time that we feed our people," Alaric countered. "One of the many advantages of having thousands of soldiers is that we are able to delegate tasks, Commodore. Not to mention that a starving populace will be more likely to side with these rebels."

Lisu was unperturbed by Alaric's reprimand, a vaguely conciliatory smile flashing across his thin lips. "While I defer to His Majesty's judgment, of course, surely it is within the bounds of duty that I attempt to verify that such a judgment remains unclouded by . . . more recent allegiances."

Alaric glanced around the table. The nine other members of High Command sat still, gazes lowered deferentially. He wondered which of them had connived with Lisu to test him like this. His eyes hardened as they darted to Commodore Mathire, who was a foregone conclusion; she had delivered the sariman to Gaheris behind Alaric's back, and during the gala she'd had no scruples about amusing herself with that grand statement that shadow and light would work together, knowing full well that Gaheris and his Enchanters were scheming to take away Talasyn's magic.

But Alaric couldn't discount *any* of the officers present. They all had their own ambitions, and he knew that they doubted his ability to lead Kesath into a new age. His choice of wife had only made matters worse.

He nearly gave a start when another officer spoke—to rush to Talasyn's defense.

"Damn shame that your common sense has yet to catch up with that borderline treasonous tongue of yours!" General Vim barked at Commodore Lisu. "Or were you cowering in some little hidey-hole during the attack? Because the *rest* of us witnessed it, plain as day, when Empress Alunsina slaughtered the insurgents with her magic!"

Vim was a bumbling lout on his best day, but Alaric had never felt better disposed toward him than now. Especially when more than a few officers looked like they might actually agree with the general's statement.

Alaric pressed his advantage. "The Night Empress is as bound by the terms of the marriage treaty as I am," he told the room at large. "While she may have once fought for the Allfold, she gave that up when she reclaimed her birthright as the Nenavarene Lachis'ka, and I do believe that any lingering loyalty she might have had to them vanished when they tried to kill her. In addition, she swore before all of you that she would stand with me against my enemies, and it has been made abundantly clear to her what will happen to the Dominion should she renege on that vow. You may trust in *her* common sense, if nothing else."

He felt uneasy discussing Talasyn so callously, as though she were a chess piece, but it did the trick and some officers nodded along, Vim the most eagerly. Lisu appeared somewhat incensed that he'd been made the butt of the joke, but Alaric simply considered that a bonus.

The Night Emperor steered his council back to the logistics of providing sacks of rice to the territories whose fields had been destroyed during the war, but it wasn't long before he was once again interrupted. This time, the culprit was Nordaye, who timidly shuffled into the meeting chamber looking nothing short of terrified.

"I gave strict orders that I was not to be disturbed," Alaric said coolly.

"Yes, Your Majesty. Apologies, Your Majesty." There was a slight tremble in the aide's voice, but he otherwise refrained from dissolving into a puddle of nerves. "However, you instructed us to treat all messages from or pertaining to the Nenavar Dominion as first priority regardless of the circumstances. A messenger eagle has arrived, sir."

Alaric left the room at a brisk pace, telling himself that he was simply in a hurry to get back to business. In a way, this was true, because he didn't wish to give High Command the opportunity to gossip and scheme for a second longer than necessary, but he was *also* eager to hear from Talasyn, who was the only person on Lir who could possibly be sending him letters via the Nenavarene messenger birds.

No, not eager . . . curious. Yes, that was it. He was *curious*. He wondered what she could possibly want. That was all. Nothing more.

A few days ago, he'd woken up to find her gone, along with her retinue. Thanks to the valerian root, he had only the haziest recollections of her tending his wounds. But he'd been talkative; he remembered that much at least, how words slipped easily past his lips at each touch of her gentle hands. He was certain that he'd told her the reason for his father's punishment at some point, before the night had fully blurred into oblivion.

A horrific possibility occurred to Alaric. What if this message wasn't even from Talasyn? What if something had happened to her on the journey southeast? Another rebel attack—

He walked faster, heart pounding.

The Citadel's rookery was a tower attached to the High Command building. This domed edifice was honeycombed with holes that let in air and sunlight and through which the skuas of the Kesathese regiments and the ravens of House Ossinast could come and go as they pleased or as communiqués demanded. Inside, the high walls were dotted with craggy ledges tufted with dozens of nests, and most of the space from floor to ceiling was crisscrossed by wooden beams where the birds could perch.

It was a rare commotion that greeted Alaric when he strode in. Over the course of the tower's long history, the ravens and the skuas had arrived at a begrudging coexistence, but today feathers were flying. A Nenavarene eagle had landed in their midst, and now its wickedly curved talons were wrapped around one of the lowermost perches, a roll of parchment tied to one leg. Several ravens and skuas surrounded it in a whirl of glossy black and dusky brown plumage, cawing and screeching, beating their wings in warning.

The lone eagle was ready for a fight. It was almost the size of a small canoe, easily dwarfing its opponents. The white feathers cresting its head flared out as it moved its neck in snakelike motions. Snakelike, too, were the hisses that it emitted, adding to the deafening cacophony that echoed off stone and wood. Its blue-gray eyes surveyed the other birds with a raptor's deadly intent.

Nordaye rushed forward, making shooing noises and waving his arms. The ravens and the skuas scattered, gliding all the way up to the ledges, but the eagle—with the murderous rage typical of Nenavarene beasts, from the dragons to the damn cows—*lunged.*

Nordaye recoiled with a shrill scream, narrowly managing to avoid being disemboweled by the large, powerful beak. The eagle flapped its enormous wings as though about to fly at the aide and peck him to death, but Alaric wisely chose that moment to draw near. The bird went still, cocking its maned head, staring at him. Threads of silver aether flashed within its black pupils, like lightning in the night.

Then it held out its leg and waited with an air of general impatience while Alaric retrieved the message it had carried across the Eversea.

My lord, Talasyn had scrawled on the parchment, in the clumsy Sailor's Common of one unused to corresponding in that alphabet. Her upbringing would have offered her precious little opportunity to write, perhaps just enough to get by. *I am writing because there will be three eclipses next month, in quick succession, and it will be a good time for His Majesty to come to Nenavar for an extended stay as we prepare for the Moonless Dark. I have taken up residence at the castle at Iantas, and it is well equipped to receive you and your household.* Some ink stains followed, as though she'd held the stylus over the parchment for a beat too long, torn about what to scribble next, and then: *I hope you are feeling better.*

She'd signed it with her birth name. *Alunsina Ivralis.* Alaric frowned as he studied the unfamiliar shape of it, a screen slid between them to obscure her from his sight, just like when he'd met her as the Lachis'ka in the Roof of Heaven's throne hall after the Hurricane Wars.

The letter was stilted. Formal. Had her grandmother told her what to write? Had she told her family what Gaheris had done to him? Prince Elagbi seemed harmless enough, but it was a given that Queen Urduja would file it away as ammunition.

Talasyn wouldn't have been inclined to keep it a secret from her grandmother and her father had Alaric asked her to, anyway. Their marriage was purely a strategic maneuver, one in which both their courts would happily seize any opportunity to gain the upper hand, and that was simply the way of it. He didn't need their alliance to be anything more than that.

He only wished that he felt a little less vulnerable. A little less bereft.

"Write back to the Night Empress," he instructed Nordaye. "Tell her that I will join her at Iantas in a month's time." He noticed that the eagle had now fixed its keen gaze on the skua nests above, where plump, fuzzy, straw-colored chicks were blithely chirping away, and he added, "You'd better feed her messenger first, though."

Nordaye gulped, turning as white as a sheet.

From a ramshackle assortment of nipah-palm huts, time had turned the Sardovian encampment in the Storm God's Eye into a suggestion of a city. There were pastured animals and a communal longhouse at the very center, and most of the buildings now sported upper levels. But the hulking shell of the *Nautilus* still reigned supreme, casting a shadow over everything in the moonlight.

Talasyn had been too impatient to arrange for a clandestine meeting such as the one that took place in Lidagat. She'd sailed to the Storm God's Eye on Surakwel's yacht almost as soon as she returned to Nenavar and contacted him. Then she'd ordered the young lord to wait on the beach while she trekked through the mangroves alone. She needed to talk to Vela, just the two of them.

She'd sent one of the castle eagles ahead of the yacht; Vela was waiting for her at the edge of the settlement. The Amirante gave a brisk nod as Talasyn approached.

Talasyn proceeded to discuss her sighting of Gaheris—leaving the exact details vague—as well as her encounter with Darius and the presence of a resistance movement. Vela bore the news of Darius with her usual stoicism, but it was no easy task to describe the look that came over her face at the mention of the resistance. It was the exhaustion of someone who had been hiding in the mangrove swamps of the Storm God's Eye for the last several months. It was the relief of someone learning that she and her cause hadn't been forgotten by the people left behind.

Talasyn was loath to watch that softness vanish, but she had no choice. She couldn't put it off anymore. "There's something else that you should know, Amirante. The resistance attacked during my coronation." Vela's features froze, and Talasyn had to duck her head as she relayed the whole sorry tale, fear and shame eating away at her with every word. One of the three remaining Sardovian stormships gone. Dozens of rebels dead, five by her own hand, and Hiras and the rest captured. The losses were too harrowing to encompass in simple words.

"But we can break the prisoners out," Talasyn hurriedly continued when Vela said nothing. "I learned that they're being kept in the eastern wing. It's heavily guarded, but there are no Shadowforged patrolling within, and it's beside a mess hall, so I was thinking that we could sneak in through the kitchen cellars—"

"Talasyn." The Amirante held up a hand. "It wasn't your fault. There was nothing that you could have done, and you had to save yourself. And if you'd let Alaric Ossinast die that day, *we* would all be dead, come the Moonless Dark."

"I can make up for it," Talasyn said desperately. "I'll join the rescue attempt—"

"There will be no rescue attempt," said Vela. "Not on my end. We need to conserve all of our resources, and Kesath cannot know that I am alive and well in Nenavar until we make our move."

Talasyn couldn't believe what she was hearing. "But Hiras and the others, they're being tortured even as we speak," she protested. "We can't just let it *happen*."

"It's unfortunate, but our hands are tied. Surely you must understand that, deep down." It was jarring how much Vela reminded Talasyn of Urduja in this moment. Cold and resolute. Unyielding. "Their suffering won't be in vain, and neither will the deaths at the plaza, because each fallen rebel helped you gain the Night Empire's trust. They will all be avenged when we reclaim the Continent."

We were chess pieces in her war, Talasyn remembered Darius saying. *Purely expendable.*

But she *did* understand Vela's point of view, didn't she? Pulling off a prison breakout would be a logistical and strategic nightmare. She'd only been pushing for it to make herself feel better. She hadn't considered how much she would be asking of Vela, how grave the risk would be to Sardovia's survival.

So she swallowed her retorts and her pleas to save Hiras and the other captives. And she knew full well that her silence damned them all, a burden that she would carry for the rest of her days.

There was something else she had to talk to Vela about.

"Amirante," she began tentatively, "about Alaric . . ."

The way Vela's right eye flashed would have made any soldier shake in their boots. But Talasyn was no longer a soldier—Vela had said so herself—and she plunged ahead. "He was about to kill Hiras, but I begged him not to, and he didn't. And his father tortured him for it. With shadow magic." She hadn't told anyone else this. It felt wrong to reveal Alaric's secret now. But Vela might have some insight. "His body was covered in wounds. Gaheris is cruel even to him, and . . ."

She trailed off, because the Amirante looked—*unsurprised.*

"I know what his father does to him," said Vela, and Talasyn reeled. "Apart from the Severs, pain is how Kesath's Shadowforged tap into their aethermancy and grow stronger. You asked me once why I didn't join the Shadowforged Legion, and I told you that I didn't want to be the person that it would have required me to become. So I kept my abilities a secret." She heaved a sigh at Talasyn's stunned nod. "The *whole* truth is this: I'd been a helmsman for about a year when the Shadowgate first poured forth from my fingertips. I went to the Citadel to inform the Legion, as Kesathese law required.

"Gaheris and Alaric were sparring in one of the courtyards, and I stopped to watch. This was several years before the Hurricane Wars, and Alaric couldn't have been older than ten. A child facing the Night Emperor at the height of his power. I watched as Gaheris's magic overwhelmed his son. I watched as he yelled at Alaric to get up and fight like a man. And the crown prince did. Blood was running down his shirt, and it looked like his arm was broken, but he wasn't even crying. Just bracing for more." Vela was speaking in a near-whisper now, as though still aghast at the memory even after all these years.

Talasyn could see it, a little boy who had not yet grown into his sharp features, relentlessly assaulted by his father again and again in the midst of that drab gray city of unforgiving stone. She thought about the person that boy had become—her husband, with his sullen silences and occasional wry remarks, with his moments of gentleness that Gaheris had failed to stamp out. She thought about his cold anger, how he never raised his voice even when he was frustrated—such a strange thing to her once, but now she understood why.

Be kind to me, Alaric had said. He'd been at her mercy, broken and bruised and the valerian ensuring that he had no defenses left, and that was what he'd asked of her.

Be kind to me.

"Right then and there, I decided that I wanted to be no part of that," Vela solemnly concluded. "I left the Citadel and went back to my post, and I aethermanced only in secret, never revealing to anyone that I, too, was Shadowforged—until the day I defected and used my magic against the soldiers chasing us."

"Why didn't you tell me the whole story before?" Talasyn couldn't quite keep the accusation out of her tone. She was reminded too much of Elagbi and Urduja withholding information about the Voidfell from her, a fresh cut over an old scar.

"What good would it have done?" Vela countered. "That boy grew up to become the Master of the Shadowforged Legion, defeating all the others in trials that lasted for days. He finished his father's war—or so he thinks—with little remorse. Regardless of how horribly he is mistreated, he is what Gaheris has made him. What would be the use of having sympathy for—" Whatever she saw on Talasyn's face made her abruptly break off. "*Do* you have sympathy for him?" she demanded.

"N-no," Talasyn stammered. An inner voice screamed at her for the lie that it was, hollowing her out from within. "But since he didn't kill Hiras, and given how Gaheris treats him, I was thinking that maybe—maybe he could be brought over to *our* side."

She had never really given any thought to how ludicrous such a statement would sound. It hung between her and Vela awkwardly, her secret hope laid bare. So secret that she hadn't even been able to admit it to herself until now.

Vela stared at her with nothing short of horror. "Do you honestly believe that a moment of humanity can overcome a lifetime of conditioning? That the Night Emperor will choose *us* over Kesath?"

Talasyn couldn't bear to disappoint the Amirante. The woman who had taken her in, who had held Sardovia together for so long. Who was keeping the possibility of its continued survival alive still. The night in Alaric's bedroom felt so far away, drowned out by harsh reality, by the burbling of the mangrove swamp and the aether flares.

But she had to at least try to make her case.

"He—he cares what I think," she said. "He's searching for Khaede at my request. He was telling me about his plans to . . . to improve the economy . . ." Oh, that was weak. Vela blinked, and Talasyn had never felt more stupid. "If I can just, I don't know, convince him—"

"Listen to me." Vela gripped Talasyn's hand, tightly enough to hurt. "No matter what Alaric Ossinast says, no matter what understanding the two of you have reached, or might reach in the days to come, he will never go against his father's wishes. His loyalty is to Kesath, as yours should be to Sardovia. Once he discovers that you—that *we*—have been playing him for a fool, he will not hesitate to kill you, as he tried to do the first time you met, and the next couple of times after. He can never find out, not until the final hour when it's too late for him to do anything about it, or the consequences will be disastrous for all of us. Talasyn, *please* be careful."

PART II

CHAPTER TEN

One month later

"What are the chances," Sevraim drawled, "that this is some kind of ambush in the making?"

He was lounging against the railings on the deck of a black Kesathese shallop gliding over the islands of Nenavar on fumes of emerald-green wind magic. He had threatened to throw a fit if Alaric made him wear his helm in this humid weather, and so his bare face was tipped up to the tropical sun, his eyes half shut in languid contentment.

From where he stood at the airship's prow, Alaric shot Sevraim a glare that spoke warning in volumes, but the latter was undaunted. "Do think about it," he went on. "We were supposed to meet the Lachis'ka in Iantas, but Dominion coracles intercepted us, and now we're following them somewhere else, all while our stormship is at their mercy, docked at *their* port. It's suspicious."

The legionnaire's words were belied by his teasing grin. Alaric couldn't resist pointing out, "It's going to be *your* problem if your suspicions turn out to be correct, you know."

"A bodyguard's work is never done," Sevraim agreed. "His Majesty ought to grant me a title."

"On top of all the other names I already call you?"

Sevraim threw back his head and let out a guffaw that was even more spirited than usual. Alaric could blame neither him nor the shallop's crew, who looked over in amusement, as they would never have done within the borders of the Night Empire. There was a certain lightness in being here in Nenavar—the crisp blue skies and balmy winds, the glowing sands and gilded cities and rainforests as thick as storm clouds—after the cold and damp of a Kesathese spring.

It would have been picturesque, if not for the . . . *audience.*

The previous times Alaric had sailed over this archipelago had either been at ungodly hours or when civilian airships were grounded for security reasons. It was afternoon now, however, and the Dominion had apparently come to the conclusion that Alaric wouldn't do anything as gauche as shoot down random Nenavarene vessels when he was married to their Lachis'ka.

Granted, the Iantas squadron of moth coracles, with their opalescent hulls and winglike sails and bronze cannons, was sufficient to deter other airships from gliding too close. But it didn't stop the people on the assortment of dugouts, pleasure yachts, and cargo freighters from gawking at Alaric even as they kept a wide berth. He could see a great number of them whispering among themselves as their ships, with sails in a rainbow of colors and emblems fluttering in the breeze, darted along hopelessly disorganized lanes, cutting one another off, racing forward with neither rhyme nor reason.

Alaric was glad for the wolf's-snarl mask that granted the illusion of armor to protect against Nenavarene gossip, but he also wondered if he would be better off without it. He wasn't difficult to spot, even from this distance. Curiosity and apprehension colored the commonfolk's faces while they tried to reconcile this monstrous image with their Lachis'ka's consort.

And speaking of Talasyn . . .

Her face filtered into his thoughts like sunlight through a window. He frowned at the fluttering sensation in his chest. Though it had happened every time he thought of her in the last month, it remained odd to him all the same.

Alaric chalked up his discomfort to nerves. He was anxious, certainly, about his father's plans. There was still time to dissuade Gaheris, especially since Kesathese experiments with the sariman had yet to yield any promising results, but Alaric was also worried about how Talasyn would react if she ever found out.

She would never believe that he'd had nothing to do with the experiments. And even if the gods smiled upon him and he managed to keep it from her, it was still an immense betrayal, stealing that sariman from its native shores and subjecting it to such cruelty. But there was a way to make amends. There had to be. He just had to find it.

So many things were up in the air. So many possible paths the future could take—most of them disastrous. But at the center of it all was the present moment, his nervousness at the prospect of seeing her again. The former enemy who had saved him on the battlefield. The first person to ever tend to him after his father's lessons. The wife he kept dreaming about in a blurred vision of freckles and golden eyes and gentle hands.

After a while—after several more terrified looks from passing airships—Alaric came to a decision. He removed his mask and handed it to one of the crew, for storage with the rest of his personal effects. The mask was a lethal promise to the Sardovian Allfold, but a true alliance with the Nenavarene could not stem from fear.

Also, the rush of fresh air fanning over his newly bare face was a relief in the sweltering heat, although he would never admit it to Sevraim.

The moth coracles holding up the vanguard eventually pulled into a swift descent, with the rest of the convoy following, over Vasiyas, centermost of the seven main islands—and the island where the Void Sever was located. A sense of foreboding slowly began to prickle at Alaric's spine. The Voidfell had flared up earlier that day, its amethyst glow illuminating the dawn. He had seen it as his stormship approached Nenavarene waters. Had something happened to Talasyn? Had she gotten caught up in the outburst somehow? Was *that* why his ship had been rerouted?

Alaric was numb by the time the convoy docked near a dense grove of coconut palms at the outskirts of a small village. The landing grid already contained several moth coracles but was mostly occupied by an outrigger warship that dwarfed the Kesathese shallop. A member of Talasyn's royal guard—distinguishable from the other soldiers milling about by her bulky armor molded to resemble dragon bones—was waiting on the ground. Once Alaric had disembarked, she closed a spike-knuckled, gauntleted fist over her chest in the characteristic Dominion salute.

"Where is she?" Alaric demanded, fear constricting the inside of his chest.

The woman arched a brow at his tone—a subtle reminder that, for the Nenavarene, Alaric was a consort within their matriarchal system *before* he was the Night Emperor of Kesath. She was almost his height, and her dark hair was pulled back severely from her square-jawed face. "The Lachis'ka has instructed me to bring you to her, Your Majesty. I am Nalam Gao, kaptan of Her Grace's Lachis-dalo, at your service."

Alaric and Sevraim followed Gao past the coconut palms and into the village, which was little more than a collection of huts with tall, steeply pitched straw roofs and walls fashioned from geometric-patterned bamboo mats woven together. The village had looked rather ordinary from the landing grid, but as they ventured further in, past the first few dwellings, it soon became apparent that something had gone horribly wrong.

It was the smell that hit Alaric first. A pervading rankness of sulfur and infection, haunted by a sickly sweet undercurrent. He knew it immediately; it was the stench of battle's aftermath, as pungent as though the dead were festering in the heat of a Continental summertime. Made much, much worse by Nenavar's humidity.

However, no combat had taken place in this little village. Its inhabitants had been running away. Their remains littered the dirt road winding between the huts. Chickens, pigs, goats, and humans, all desiccated husks of their former selves, charred black as though they'd been rotting for sennights, fallen over one another in the grisly aftermath of a futile stampede. Not a single blade of green grass remained; not on the roadside, not in the fenced backyards where fruits had blackened on the vine and flowers had shriveled in their beds.

In the distance was the sound of wailing.

"The crater where the Voidfell is located lies only a few kilometers to the north," Gao quietly explained. "It activated shortly before sunrise, roaring through the villagers' fields and then their homes. The Lachis'ka sailed from Iantas as soon as we heard. No one was expecting it. The scale of this conflagration, this far off from the sevenfold lunar eclipse, is unprecedented. I'm afraid that it's a sign of things to come."

This year promises to be the worst one yet, Queen Urduja had told Alaric. Only two months from now, the Void Sever would have grown only more and more volatile, affecting a wider and wider area, until it crossed the Eversea and subjected the Continent to the same fate as this village.

Trailing after Gao along a bend in the road, Alaric finally saw his wife. With the Lachis-dalo and other Dominion soldiers hanging back to form a secure perimeter, the survivors had gathered in the village square and Talasyn was in their midst, speaking softly to them as they wept and wrung their hands and tried in vain to console their crying children. Dressed in a cotton smock and breeches, her chestnut braid draped over one shoulder, she hardly looked the part of royalty, but there was no mistaking how the equally bedraggled people clustered around her, hanging on her every word, watching her every move with both hope and despair on their faces.

Those at the edge of the crowd noticed Alaric first. Word of his appearance then spread like a wave, the turning heads, the widened eyes, the harsh intakes of breath. He wanted to reassure them that . . . that *what*? That he meant no harm? Wouldn't his fleet have done this, and more, had Urduja Silim not offered up the heir to her throne in marriage? Hadn't his father's stormships already inflicted death and destruction on the many civilian settlements of the Continent?

What right did Alaric have to promise these people that they were safe with him around?

But when Talasyn spotted him across the sea of villagers, her countenance showed none of the anger, none of the fear. Something soft and tentative broke across her features, and he was walking toward her before he even realized it, caught in a waking dream. Somewhere at the edges, the Nenavarene scurried aside and tugged one another out of his way, as though he carried the plague, but he knew only her.

He came to a stop in front of her and had no idea what to do next. She stared up at him as though they hadn't seen each other in years.

"How are—" he started to ask.

"I thought—" she said at the same time.

They faltered into silence. The tips of Alaric's ears burned as he gestured for her to go ahead.

"I thought it would be better to have you brought here," Talasyn mumbled, "rather than have you wait around in Iantas suspecting that you were going to get ambushed."

He resolved never to let her find out what Sevraim had japed about earlier. He nodded instead.

Talasyn's brow furrowed slightly at the villagers' wary expressions. Then she squared her shoulders and looped her arm through Alaric's. *A show of unity*, he realized, almost dazed by her sudden touch. By the feel of her tucked against his side.

She addressed the villagers in the Dominion tongue, all flowing syllables and lilt. Alaric caught his name, as well as *Iantas*, but not much else. And he watched as the audience's wariness transformed into cautious optimism that grew the more Talasyn spoke. A few even cheered.

"What did you tell them?" Alaric asked out of the corner of his mouth.

"I said that *we*"—Talasyn's grip tightened on his arm—"insist that they reside with us at Iantas, where they shall want for nothing, until their fields are arable again. And I also promised that you and I will do everything in our power to stop the Voidfell on the night of reckoning."

Talasyn put her soldiers to work. The Lachis-dalo and the coracle helmsmen and the crew of Iantas's lone warship were all dispatched to help the villagers pack up their personal effects and bury their dead. The animal corpses could be taken care of later by the battalion that would be sent to clean up, but over twenty people had died and Talasyn wasn't about to force their bereaved families to evacuate without the proper rites being observed.

They had to move fast, though. There was no telling when the Voidfell would flare up again.

Kaptan Gao had more than a few reservations about the survivors transferring to Iantas. "Your Grace, shouldn't the Zahiya-lachis be consulted first?" she asked as Talasyn bustled past her with a shovel.

"What for?" Talasyn shot back, hardly breaking stride. "The castle was ceded to my husband as my dowry, so it's ours to do with as we please."

Besides, she'd already sent an aetherwave transmission to the Roof of Heaven, and no one had come out here to join her from there. The silence probably meant that she had her grandmother's blessing to deal with this situation by herself.

Alaric and Sevraim had retreated to the northern edge of the village. Talasyn approached to find the two of them wordlessly studying the brown-black expanse of sugarcane fields spread out before them, gone to rot. On the horizon, wreathed in clouds, was the imposing, roughly cone-shaped silhouette of Aktamasok—the Dragon's Fang, the ancient volcano that spewed out void magic instead of ash and lava. Its rugged slopes were a deep coal-tar hue, with no sign of the rich foliage that carpeted other Nenavarene peaks.

And now that lifelessness had spread, decimating the land that was the village's main source of income and wiping out their livestock.

"Here." Talasyn thrust the shovel at Sevraim. "They're digging graves. Go and help."

For once, the legionnaire had no witty remarks. He took the shovel from her and left to do as she instructed, and she replaced him at Alaric's side.

"Are you angry?" Talasyn ventured. "That I'm bringing the villagers to the castle?" It was technically *his* castle, after all.

Alaric's gaze flickered to her, irises flashing silver in the places where they caught the sunlight. "I'm not angry."

"Annoyed, then."

"No. You're doing the right thing. The fair thing." He nodded toward the ruined fields to emphasize his point. "Compared to what they've suffered, us being a little crowded at the castle is of no consequence."

She hadn't realized until then how badly she'd been hoping that he would agree with her decision. *There's a heart there, somewhere,* she mused as her own twinged with a poignant ache. *Maybe the Amirante is wrong. Maybe he can still—*

"How can I be of assistance?" There was a piercing note of earnestness in Alaric's tone. "What do you need me to do?"

Be on my side at the very end.

Talasyn swallowed. She forced herself into the present, into the sea of death, into the shadow of the Dragon's Fang.

"Come on." She turned away from him, away from things she could never say, and back to the task at hand. "We need to help load the ship."

Although the hundred surviving villagers could theoretically squeeze into the Iantas warship, there were their rattan baskets and bulging cloth packs to consider, as well as the livestock that had managed to outrun the Voidfell's wrath.

Talasyn solved the problem by decreeing that half of the luggage and a few of the animals would be stored on the Night Emperor's shallop for the duration of the journey.

"We'll tip over," Sevraim opined as he stood on the landing grid and watched with an air of unbridled skepticism while a Kesathese crewman timidly led a sun buffalo up the ramp. "I'm not sure if we'll even be able to launch."

"It'll be fine." Alaric wasn't all that convinced either, but with a rattan basket filled with damp laundry clutched in one arm and a disgruntled chicken tucked under the other, he had no patience for trying to allay Sevraim's fears. "Stop complaining and help me with . . . this."

Sevraim took the orange-and-white chicken. He glanced up at Talasyn on the deck of the Nenavarene warship; she was hauling packs into the cargo hold and barking orders at her men in the same breath. "Our new empress is rather bossy for someone so short."

The color drained from Alaric's face as the memory of his wedding night blazed to the forefront of his mind with all the force of a punch to the gut. He knew just *how* bossy Talasyn could be; he had firsthand experience—

"And now I've just been shat on," Sevraim grumbled. The chicken nestled in his sleeves issued a satisfied little cluck.

Alaric followed Sevraim up the ramp and onto the shallop's deck, where he navigated a careful path through the maze of luggage and farm animals until he found a place to sit—on a pile of rattan baskets, beside the tethered sun buffalo. Talasyn joined him a few minutes later, plopping down beside him with an exhausted huff.

"My ship's full," she said in response to his questioning look. At the sound of her voice, the sun buffalo lowed softly, and Talasyn laughed. "Well, *this* is familiar."

The sun buffalo was half the size of the swamp buffalo, its wild, semi-aquatic cousin that had chased Alaric and Talasyn through the Belian jungle in a murderous rage. Instead of the colossal and sickle-shaped horns of that beast, the sun buffalo's horns were slanted daggers pulled back flat against its broad skull. The swamp buffalo's red eyes would lock onto its target with eerie menace, but this tame relative regarded its surroundings with an affable mien, happily chewing on its cud as the shallop lifted into the air.

Alaric spent the next half-hour staring at his booted feet. The silence between him and Talasyn had become suffocating, punctuated only by the hum of wind magic, the footsteps and brisk communication of the crew, the steady clucking of myriad chickens, and the occasional goatish bray. He yearned to talk to her, but what *could* he say to his wife of political convenience, a wife he had already inconveniently orgasmed with? A wife he had let tend his injuries and to whom he had revealed his deepest secrets when he should have been keeping her at arm's length?

He couldn't even take any cues from Sevraim; the infinitely more socially adept legionnaire was all the way across the deck, sunk into a state of complete and utter despondency as chickens and ducks pecked at him.

"I'm glad it didn't scar," Talasyn blurted out.

Her fists had been curled in her lap, and when Alaric turned to her, she brought one hand up to her forehead, indicating the spot where his father's magic had cut him.

It stung, the reminder that she'd seen him at his lowest, his most humiliated. He thought about all the other scars on his body, all the times that his failures had left a permanent mark. Had she been disgusted by them, that night in his chambers? Who wouldn't be?

"Yes, a husband grizzled with battle scars might be a point of pride on the Continent, but it's not quite all the rage here in the Dominion," he remarked in caustic words dredged up from the dark within him that had no place here in these sun-drenched heavens, next to a girl lit from within.

Talasyn blinked, her pink lips parting in confusion. It couldn't have been clearer that such a sentiment had never crossed her mind, and Alaric fought back a stab of regret. He braced himself for her ire, for yet another heated quarrel.

She crossed her arms and—*looked* at him. "Those weren't battle wounds."

He grimaced. She wasn't allowing him to sink into self-pity, but neither was she letting him off the hook for thinking so poorly of her. He could appreciate that, and even be grateful for it, but it was still hard to force out the "I apologize" that eventually emerged, half choked.

"Thank you," Talasyn said stiffly.

"Thank *you*," he countered in a rush, desperate to make her forget his surliness of moments prior, "for what you did at the Citadel. I hope that I wasn't too difficult a patient. If I said or did anything foolish—"

"You don't *remember*?"

"Not much after the valerian," he admitted. Her nose scrunched up and he continued, with some alarm, "Was I untoward in any way?"

She looked *incensed*, and he started to panic, thinking he'd somehow made things worse, but it must have only been a trick of the light, for her expression was quick to smoothen and she shook her head.

"No," Talasyn mumbled. "You were no more cantankerous than usual."

Alaric's lips gave a reluctant twitch. "What you did," he repeated, overcome by the sense of vague affection that he only ever felt around her, "that was more than anyone else ever . . ."

She bit her lip, her features crumpling with a pained sorrow that went far too deep for what she knew of his situation. Then she placed her hand over his, where it lay on the strips of woven rattan between them. He was struck dumb by the gentleness of the gesture, by how each touch of her slim fingers burned right through the leather of his gauntlets.

"Alaric," she began, and his heart soared at the sound of his name in her voice. *Yes, what is it?* every drop of blood in his body seemed to ask, one finger lifting as though of its own accord to curl around hers, *What is it, anything—*

A crewman beat the gong mounted on the quarterdeck by the ship's wheel, releasing a metallic bellow that thoroughly shattered the moment while signaling the beginning of the descent.

Talasyn stood up and, after wrestling his whirling mind into some semblance of order, so did Alaric. They clutched the railing for balance as the shallop pulled into a slow dive ahead of the warship, approaching a small island just off the Vasiyas coastline. Iantas's shores of quartz and coral sand gleamed snow-white against the azure waters of the Eversea. At its center, surrounded by stately coconut palms, was the eponymous castle of pink-veined granite, bristling with spires and pointed arches and flying buttresses. The riotous facade resembled an ocean's worth of spiny murex shells clumped together, laden with carvings of dancing nature spirits and opalescent mother-of-pearl windowpanes.

Talasyn flashed Alaric a small, hopeful smile. "Pretty, isn't it?"

Strands of chestnut hair had spilled loose from her braid and were blowing in the wind. The sun brought out the gold in her eyes and danced atop the freckles on her softly rounded cheeks. He was looking at her when he said, "Yes."

CHAPTER ELEVEN

The halls of Iantas were narrow, their stained-glass windows shedding jeweled light on the sparkling mineral veins running through the granite walls. The tapestries were woven mostly in shades of gold, plum, and cobalt, while the oil paintings depicted storm-tossed seascapes and the dragons that lurked beneath the currents.

Talasyn vastly preferred it to the Roof of Heaven's overstated grandeur, but she couldn't deny that it had been rather lonely with just Jie and the Lachis-dalo and the comparatively small number of servants for company. That was no longer the case. With the arrival of the refugees, the castle resounded with footsteps and voices. Even the vegetable gardens outside rang with the commotion of attendants trying to place dozens of farm animals all at once.

She busied herself with getting the villagers settled in while the Kesathese contingent was shown to their rooms. Running her own household was not as difficult as she'd previously feared; she simply had to think of it in terms of the army, with everyone having their role.

The sun had begun to inch toward the horizon when Talasyn

finally retreated to her quarters—or, to be more accurate, the quarters that she shared with her husband. A husband who didn't even remember kissing her a month ago. Her hand shook a little against the bronze-wrought bedroom door, but she determinedly pushed it open.

Alaric turned to face her at the sound of her entrance. He was standing by the sliding glass panels that led out to the balcony, and he had changed out of his armor. The gauntlets were gone, too, and the light of the late afternoon sun bounced off the vulana stone on his ring finger, the one that matched hers.

"Sorry about this," she said, a touch too loudly. "Things are different here in Nenavar. People will talk if we have separate chambers. But if you're truly uncomfortable—"

"Are *you*?" he asked, in that low and solemn rumble of his that always had the peculiar effect of making her want to crawl out of her skin, for reasons that weren't entirely too terrible.

"It's all right." In the name of all the gods and the ancestors, why did she sound so *faint*? "The bed's big enough."

Both their gazes snapped to the object in question. The canopied mattress could easily accommodate five people, and it was furnished with a mountain of plump eiderdown pillows, wine-colored silk sheets, and damask hangings trimmed in gold. Talasyn tried to suppress her blush—how many nights had she lain there all by herself, wide awake, her mind wandering to the kisses that she and Alaric had shared and the way his large hands had fumbled over her body?

"I'm not to sleep on the floor, then?" He quirked an eyebrow at her.

Her embarrassment faded, replaced by guilt. Given what she now knew of his past, it had been the height of cruelty to make him spend the night in such discomfort when she herself had not been blameless. *This is your home,* she wanted to tell him. *This is safe harbor from your father. No one will harm you here.* But what came out instead was the first sentence that she could string together in her flustered headspace: "You're always welcome in this bed."

It was only when Alaric drew a sharp inhale that Talasyn was struck by the double meaning of her statement. She had to get out of here before she made an even bigger fool out of herself. She—

She stayed where she was as Alaric closed the distance between them. He carefully tucked stray strands of windswept hair behind her ear, his expression losing a bit of its usual guarded edge.

"I didn't get to finish my question earlier," he mumbled. "How have you been?"

"You didn't write me back," Talasyn blurted out.

She could have kicked herself. Of all the issues to bring up.

He frowned. "Did you not receive—"

"I got the letter your aide wrote for you," she said, dying a thousand deaths. It had bothered her on and off in the past month, certainly, but it was a juvenile concern in the grand scheme of things.

It was his fault. He was too close. She couldn't think.

Alaric's fingers cradled the side of her face. His thumb brushed across her cheek, similar to how he'd run it along the back of her hand that morning in his bedroom. "I'll respond personally. Next time."

"Who says there'll be a next time?" she challenged with a huff. "I hate writing letters, I never had to until I was proclaimed the Lachis'ka, so they always come out all awkward—"

He chucked her under the chin. The way he had at the Belian shrine. Everything about this moment carried echoes of *before,* painted in a new light.

"I thought Queen Urduja might have told you what to write," he admitted. "I assumed you told her about—about what my father—"

"I didn't," she said quickly.

But she *had* told Vela.

Guilt again, rolling through her in waves.

Talasyn tried to step back. Tried to step away from Alaric and this jumble of emotions, this labyrinth. But she found herself frozen in place as relief softened his features, taking away the years. The corner of his mouth, mere inches from hers, lifted in what was almost a smile.

"Write to me again, Tala." There was a teasing lilt to his tone. "I'll write back. I promise. We'll endure your awkwardness together."

Her spark of annoyance was eclipsed by how close he was, close enough to kiss. And maybe she *should* kiss him, to erase some of that smugness . . .

Talons scrabbled against glass, and they sprang apart.

A messenger eagle was hovering over the balcony, attempting to gain entrance. Talasyn slid open the panels, and the smell of the ocean wafted into the room as the raptor perched on her arm.

She noted the dragon-embossed seal on the scroll tied to its leg. "*This* letter is from my grandmother."

Alaric had retreated as far away from the eagle as the room would allow. "One of these almost made a meal of Kesath's next generation of messenger skuas."

"That was my personal bird, and you should have fed him as soon as he arrived," Talasyn informed him, loosening the knots that held the scroll fast to Urduja's eagle. "Pakwan flew overnight to get my letter to you. He must have been famished."

"Pakwan." Alaric sounded out the unfamiliar Nenavarene syllables with the same Continental accent that Talasyn was practicing so earnestly to rid herself of, and she nearly grinned.

"It means 'watermelon.'" She began to unroll the missive, wondering what Urduja wanted.

"You named a deadly bird of prey 'Watermelon,'" Alaric deadpanned.

"I was hungry when the falconer said I could name him . . ." Talasyn trailed off as she read the Zahiya-lachis's elegant, flowing script. Then she looked up at Alaric with wide eyes. "My grandmother and my father are joining us for supper tonight."

The diplomatic schooner from the Roof of Heaven made landfall on Iantas together with the purple-hued drape of dusk, its multitude of blue-and-gold sails rippling in wind-tossed harmony with the swaying tops of the coconut palms. Queen Urduja and Prince Elagbi disembarked and, arm in arm over the white sands, mingled with the villagers who had come out to the landing grid to receive them, asking after their welfare, commiserating with their losses.

Talasyn observed it all, standing at Alaric's side, from where they stood at the castle entrance. If there was one thing she couldn't fault her grandmother for, it was how she treated her people. The Zahiya-lachis would never be warm—she had her son to compensate for her in that area—but she always listened to the commonfolk's concerns and tirelessly sought solutions for them. The Nenavarene revered her for it.

But even if Urduja had been a cruel or absent ruler, the Nenavarene had to revere her anyway. For she was blessed by the ancestors, who watched over the Dominion from their great ships in the Sky Above the Sky.

Talasyn had not grown up in Nenavar. Though she had picked up the habit of calling on the ancestors when she was cross, she felt no spiritual connection to them. She hardly even believed in the Continent's gods; there'd been precious little room for faith in the slums and gutters of Hornbill's Head.

Still, Urduja's regal bearing, the way her white hair and silver dress and the gemstones she was covered in glimmered beneath the faint stars, against the crashing surf—it all contributed to the illusion of divinity. And with his golden robes and golden dragon circlet, Elagbi was the sun to his mother's moon as he escorted her up the stone path to where Alaric and Talasyn were waiting.

"How long does it take these two to get ready for the day?" Alaric asked Talasyn out of the corner of his mouth. "Your father takes longer than the Zahiya-lachis, I'd wager."

Thus it was that, when the Night Empress greeted her family and bade them welcome to her and her husband's demesne, she was struggling not to *laugh*.

Elagbi's easygoing confusion and Urduja's frozen outrage at her granddaughter's lack of composure did not help Talasyn regain control in the slightest. As she and Alaric led the way to Iantas's dining room, her hand tucked into the crook of his elbow, she sank her nails into his arm in an attempt to ground herself and he nudged her in admonishment.

"Kindly do not pinch me, Lachis'ka."

"It's *your* fault," she retorted through stifled laughter. "Don't make me sic my eagle on you."

"Please, no." His lips twitched. "Anything but Watermelon."

Talasyn *choked*. But before long she could feel Urduja staring holes into her back, and that was enough to sober her.

In the dining room, the food was laid out in communal dishes on banana leaves that bedecked the glossy, maroon-toned narra table, with attendants at the ready. Both Jie and Sevraim had made themselves scarce, neither wanting to intrude on what was technically a family meal, and so it was only the four royals who sat down—Urduja and Elagbi side by side, Alaric and Talasyn across from them.

A stilted silence reigned supreme. The sound of sloshing

liquids as the attendants poured water and wine into their goblets echoed through the cavernous room, all the way up to the high vaulted ceiling.

"It's good that the two of you are getting along," Urduja finally said, ladling pale cubes of freshly caught mackerel cured in palm vinegar onto her plate. "This alliance could certainly benefit from some amicability between its two key components."

Talasyn had enough experience with Nenavarene double-speak to know that Urduja was subtly warning her, just as Vela had. Reminding her of what was at stake, of the fact that her marriage could only ever be strategic in nature and nothing more.

It stung, although she wasn't too keen on figuring out exactly why. She glowered at each scoop of rice that she doled out onto her plate.

Alaric, for his part, seemed to be in no hurry to respond, either. It wasn't until they'd begun eating that Elagbi made another attempt at conversation. "There is an eclipse tomorrow night, is there not? Will Their Majesties be training here at Iantas?"

"Yes, down by the beach," said Talasyn. "Daya Vaikar and her Enchanters will be present as well. They have a new amplifying configuration that they're eager to test."

"I should very much like to observe." Elagbi shot a beseeching glance at Urduja. "What do you think of sailing back to Sedek-We the day after tomorrow instead, Harlikaan?"

"*I*," said the Zahiya-lachis, "have several councils to attend in Eskaya. It would be better to have you there as well, but—you're free to do as you please."

"Wonderful!" Elagbi beamed. "Then I am Their Majesties' guest for the next two days."

Talasyn fought back a snicker at Elagbi's obliviousness to Urduja's pointed hint, while Alaric looked mildly scandalized that his father-in-law had invited himself to stay at someone else's home. But it was simply a norm among Nenavarene families, and he and the Dominion prince *were* family, whether anyone liked it or not. Talasyn bumped her knee against his under the table. His features smoothed into a polite mask.

"We are honored to host you, Your Highness," Alaric told Elagbi. "Should you require anything to make your stay more comfortable, please don't hesitate to let us know."

"I am the picture of an undemanding houseguest," Elagbi declared. "The Lachis'ka can well attest to that."

"It's true." Talasyn smiled at her father. His occasional visits, whenever he could tear himself away from his duties, had alleviated her sense of isolation the past month, and she was happy to be able to spend more time with him.

Urduja caught Talasyn's eye. "Since you have your hands full, Alunsina, I'll instruct the tailor not to drop by until next sennight."

"The tailor?" Alaric repeated, and Talasyn cringed as she realized that, with everything that had happened that day, she'd forgotten to tell him.

"We're hosting a ball here at Iantas after the Moonless Dark," she supplied. "A masquerade, to celebrate the Voidfell's defeat. The tailor will be paying a visit to take His Majesty's measurements and discuss options."

Alaric blanched as though the array of colorful, jewel-encrusted attire worn by Nenavarene men was flashing through his mind in a parade of horrors. "I *have* clothes."

"None suitable for the costume event in question," said Urduja. "As the Lachis'ka's consort, your ensemble needs to complement hers. It's tradition, I'm afraid, Emperor Alaric."

Alaric gave Talasyn a hard look. She ducked her head. She sympathized with him, but there was an uphill road to gaining the Dominion's acceptance and they had to pick their battles.

"You can't wear black or any other dark colors to the masquerade," she muttered. "Or else the court will think that you aren't happy that we stopped Dead Season—that you don't share in their joy. So that rules out your entire wardrobe."

She held her breath, nervous that he would argue, effectively dispelling the Dragon Queen's notion that they were *getting along*, but in the end Alaric just shrugged.

"Far be it from me to go against my empress's wishes." He lifted his goblet to her in a droll parody of a toast, still trying—wasn't it just like him—to get a rise out of her even when he was acquiescing. "Let your tailor do his worst, then."

He was still debating, long after the meal had ended and he'd retired upstairs to give Talasyn more time alone with her family, whether or not saving the world as he knew it was worth being dressed by a people as garish as the Nenavarene.

Alaric deeply hoped that feathers wouldn't be part of the equation.

He was in bed, careful to occupy only one side of it, by the time Talasyn entered the royal chambers—or, well, *stormed* into the royal chambers. She was pouting, and it was oddly adorable, but he wasn't about to tell her that.

"Where does she get off, insinuating that I don't know what I'm doing!" she burst out.

Alaric hazarded a guess. "Queen Urduja has reservations about us housing the villagers, I take it?"

"Yes, right before she left she said that it would have been easier to ship them to the transient homesteads on Delanep that are reserved for such a purpose." Talasyn stomped over to the vanity and tugged her hair loose from its braid with a fierceness that made Alaric wince. "But what's so difficult about *this*? Iantas has enough room and enough supplies!"

"It does," Alaric said evenly.

"She's just annoyed that I took the initiative instead of consulting her first—" Talasyn broke off, as though it was sinking in for the first time that Alaric was in her bed. Her cheeks flushed bright pink. "I need to wash up."

Then she all but *ran* to her dressing room, and he was left staring at a closed door.

Alaric closed his eyes, slumping against the headboard with an utter despair that was shameful for the Master of the Shadowforged Legion to exhibit. Living with Talasyn, having her constantly in his orbit—how was he to get through this visit unscathed? They would either kill each other or end up kissing again, and it would prove disastrous either way. Their alliance and all the murkiness surrounding it was complicated enough without adding trysts to the mix.

The solution is simple, a snide inner voice told him. *Simply do* not *kiss her.*

He could do that, surely. He hadn't kissed her at all since their wedding night, and he hadn't kissed her during that charged moment earlier, so he was *clearly* capable of some modicum of self-control.

His eyes flew open and homed in on the door to her dressing room as a horrifying possibility occurred to him. What if she marched out of there in nearly sheer robes like those she'd worn *that* night? He'd jump off the balcony. He truly would.

Alaric's fears, as it turned out, were unfounded. Talasyn emerged in a baggy nightshirt and loose sleep trousers, and he almost collapsed from crushing relief.

However, when she extinguished the fire lamps and gingerly

tucked herself in under the covers on her side of the bed, the smell of custard-flower soap lingering on clean, warm skin wafted over to him in the moonlight-tinted darkness, triggering an animalistic twitch of interest low in his belly.

"Goodnight," Talasyn said in a small voice, through silk sheets.

"Goodnight," Alaric echoed.

Doubtful, he thought.

CHAPTER TWELVE

Talasyn was awake. She knew that she was awake. Her eyes were open in the morning light that streamed into the bedroom.

But she couldn't move. She was flat on her back on the mattress, her rigid limbs locked in place.

The chimeras were eating her alive.

Creatures of silver aether and midnight smoke gnawed at her flesh with inky teeth, their eel-like bodies wrapping around her arms and legs. They stripped her skin from her bones; they gulped her down, piece by piece.

Talasyn screamed—or tried to. Not a single drop of sound emerged from her bursting lungs, even as she strained with all her might. She couldn't move, she couldn't scream, she couldn't aethermance.

There was a figure looming in the corner. The darkness emanated from him, in rivers, and her gaze traveled up to his face. She expected Gaheris's wizened features, expected the Regent to have crept into her room under cover of night.

But the gray eyes that looked back at her were Alaric's. He smiled as his magic devoured her whole.

She screamed again. It came out as a rattle of sound, pushed through a throat gone dry with fear. And suddenly she was bolting upright, freed from the shackles of paralysis, of that waking nightmare. There was no trace of the shadows that she'd seen and felt so vividly, or of the figure that had summoned them.

Through the pounding of her heart, through the horror falling away, she became aware of something else: her bladder clamored to be relieved.

It was a shock, her bare soles thudding against the cold floor. She stumbled to the bathroom on leaden legs. Her mind was all fogged up; that was her only justification, really, for not remembering that she was no longer alone in Iantas's royal chambers until she walked in on Alaric in her—*their*—bathroom.

He was hunched over the sink, clad in nothing but a towel wrapped around his lean hips, his black hair damp and his jaw slathered in the creamy white suds of his shaving soap.

"Why didn't you bolt the door?" Talasyn demanded, suddenly fully awake. For all her bluster, though, she couldn't quite stop herself from gawking at his bare chest. At the beads of water pooled in the hollow of his collarbones, and the expanse of pale skin and chiseled musculature, riddled with silvery scars. At the smattering of dark hair that dusted a tantalizing path from his navel to what lay hidden under the towel.

"I forgot," Alaric grunted, lowering the steel-bladed razor from his face. His expression was as cool and haughty as usual, but it carried shades of the ruthlessness from her nightmare, and she nearly shrank back.

Then his gaze flickered over her and darkened to soot, and it hit her that the fabric of her nightshirt was perhaps a little too thin. She crossed her arms over her chest, trying to be casual, but it was too late, of course. Their shared embarrassment suffused the air.

"I—um—nature calls," she faltered.

"By all means." He was careful not to let their bodies touch as he skirted around her in the doorway. Some wicked part of her keened in regret.

Talasyn spent the whole morning with her father on a grassy hill that lay to the west of the castle. It overlooked the beach and had the added benefit of being nowhere near Alaric. In the dappled shade of leafy coconut palms, she and Elagbi picnicked and played casongkâ, a game of count-and-capture. It was played with tokens in the form of tiny cowrie shells and an elongated wooden board with two rows of cup-shaped holes called *houses*, bracketed by the larger holes that served as each player's *field*. The objective was to plant more tokens in one's field than the opponent did in his by scooping up all the cowrie shells in one house and distributing them piece by piece to the other houses in a clockwise direction, each player's turn ending whenever the last shell landed in an empty hole. The game came to a close once all the houses were empty.

Casongkâ required precise calculation and careful observation—rather like dealing with the Dominion court, Talasyn thought. She was absolute rubbish at the game, and she was fairly certain that Elagbi was cheating on more than one occasion, but she was thankful for the opportunity to focus on something other than her shirtless husband, who didn't even remember kissing her. Whose magic had devoured her in her nightmare earlier. When it came to him, her fear and her desire were tangled together, a vicious web.

Elagbi had just claimed another victory, Talasyn vehemently protesting all the while, when excited cries in the distance drew their attention. A dragon had broken the wave-tossed surface of the Eversea while several of the villagers' children frolicked on the beach.

It was an old one, with clouded blue eyes set in a grizzled, horned head. Its fire-orange scales were crusted with barnacles and a multitude of scars, from centuries of battle against saw-toothed sharks and colossal squid and whatever else the ocean hid. As the children cheered and clapped their hands in delight, it waded into the turquoise shallows on clumsy reptilian fore-limbs, chiropteran wings tucked against its slithering flanks like a ship's sails, an eruption of sand and saltwater blossoming with every motion.

Once the dragon reached the shore, it lay down and closed its eyes. Talasyn would have suspected that it had died, if not for its breath stirring nearby ribbons of water, bringing them to a boil. The lower half of its body curled and twitched in rhythm with the tide.

"They spend most of their time in the deeps, but they like to bask when the sun's out," said Elagbi. "It will probably sleep there for hours."

"Even with those ruffians around?" Talasyn gestured to the children who had now swarmed the dragon and were clambering up its many coils and prodding at its folded wings.

Elagbi laughed. "What are mayflies to a leviathan? And the children are Nenavarene, so it will never harm them."

Indeed, the dragon gave no indication that it was in the least bit bothered by the small humans' antics. It slumbered on, and Talasyn was about to race down the hill for a closer look when her father gave a sigh.

"They all vanished during the civil war," he said. "Retreated beneath the waves. In all those long months, not a single dragon was spotted basking on the shore or gliding through the heavens. Their disappearance was an ill omen. We thought they had left us forever, and it was no more than what we deserved for tearing the nation apart."

In the past, Talasyn had refrained from asking too many

questions about the Nenavarene civil war, mindful of Elagbi's pain, careful not to stoke the flames of Urduja's wrath. But there was freedom to be found here in Iantas, two hours away from the Roof of Heaven and the Zahiya-lachis's watchful gaze, where brilliant sun on snow-white sand burned away all secrets, where fresh, salt-laced breezes softened the hurt.

Once the rebellion had surrendered after Elagbi killed their leader, his elder brother Sintan, Urduja had ordered all memory of her traitorous firstborn expunged. A sennight ago, however, while exploring Iantas's library, Talasyn had stumbled upon a portrait miniature hidden in a drawer—Elagbi and Sintan as teenagers, in stiff poses and even stiffer formal attire. In contrast to the dark curls of the youthful Elagbi, Sintan's hair had been a lighter shade of brown, and his eyes had been Urduja's, jet-black and calculating.

Talasyn had felt a chilling sense of unease at the sight of this younger version of her uncle, a boy who had grown up to want her dead. And she had the sneaking suspicion that it was Elagbi who had stored the portrait miniature in the drawer, keeping it safe from Urduja's purge.

"Amya." Talasyn leaned forward, over the casongkâ board. "Why did Sintan do it?"

Elagbi's features crumpled, and Talasyn regretted the question immediately. But it was too late to take it back. It hung heavy in the air.

"You must understand, my dear," Elagbi said in a hoarse whisper, looking off into the distance, "my brother and I were very close when we were children. We had only each other. He was terribly intelligent, and possessed such a strong sense of righteousness—a bit aloof, but he always protected me and told me bedtime stories when we were children.

"He was, however, a completely different person in the end. There was a seed that took root in his mind as he grew older, as he learned about lands across the sea where men could rule. Sintan became convinced that *he* should be the rightful heir to the Dominion throne. He used that burning intellect of his to quietly amass supporters from the more power-hungry noble houses who felt they did not have Queen Urduja's favor, and he plotted and schemed—"

"And manipulated my mother," Talasyn said dully.

Tears leaked from the corners of Elagbi's eyes. "My poor Hanan. What did she know of these kinds of games? Sintan told her about the plight of the Lightweavers on the Continent, and of course she agreed to help. I should—" He scrubbed at his wet cheeks with the back of a shaking hand. "I should never have brought her here. She wasn't happy. She refused to be named the Lachis'ka because she had no interest in politics, and yet she became a pawn anyway."

Talasyn's own tears burned in her throat. Sintan had been crafty, making it appear as though Hanan Ivralis had acted on her own in sending the flotilla to the Continent. When no one from that flotilla returned, Sintan and his allies had used their deaths as a pretext to depose Urduja. Hanan had later succumbed to an illness, imprisoned in her room while the capital was under siege, and Talasyn had been spirited out of Nenavar three days later.

It was too late for Talasyn to seek vengeance for her mother. Elagbi had already done that when his sword plunged into Sintan's heart on the limestone bluffs of the Roof of Heaven, in the final battle of the civil war. Elagbi had been doing his duty to the country and to the memory of his late wife, but keeping that portrait miniature against Urduja's wishes meant that he'd loved his brother, too.

"What I can't figure out," Elagbi said once he'd regained some composure, "is how Sintan got to Indusa." Talasyn gave him a curious look and he bent over the casongkâ board, scooping cowrie shells from the fields and redistributing them to the houses, setting up the game anew. "The memory you saw in the Light Sever last month . . . I've been thinking about it ever since you told me. I believe that your nursemaid was sympathetic to Sintan's cause and she found a way to give the Lachis-dalo escorts the slip and bring you to the Continent. It's the only possible explanation as to why she left you at the orphanage. Left the Nenavar Dominion without an heir."

"She could have just killed me. It would have been quicker for her." At Talasyn's curt statement, Elagbi froze and looked so much like he was about to burst into tears again that she hastily added, "I'm very glad she didn't, though."

"As am I." The last token fell from Elagbi's palm, shell clattering against wood. "I have tried discussing this with Queen Urduja, but she shut me down. According to Her Majesty, there's no use troubling ourselves over the past—not when the people who have the answers are either dead or gone. I suspect that she would rather forget the whole affair if she could. I cannot find it in my heart to blame her for that."

I can, Talasyn thought mutinously. While Urduja may have been wounded by her firstborn's betrayal, she certainly felt no similar sorrow over her daughter-in-law's passing. There had been no love lost between her and Hanan, as Kaptan Rapat had said at the Lightweaver shrine.

To her chagrin, though, Talasyn could see the wisdom in the Zahiya-lachis's resolve to look only to the future. They all had quite enough on their plates when it came to *that.*

"Ah," Elagbi said after a while, "I see our dragon has garnered more curious spectators."

"If you're distracting me so you'll win again . . ." Following his line of sight, Talasyn trailed off.

Alaric and Sevraim were on the beach, their gazes transfixed on the dragon even as they kept a wary distance. The children had long since scattered, probably spooked by the two Shadowforged's presence.

In unspoken agreement, Elagbi and Talasyn abandoned their game and headed down to the beach. There was no telling how the dragon would react to these outsiders from a nation that had injured one of its brethren months ago.

Sevraim bounded up to them. "Your Highness! Care for a rematch?"

"There's a board up on the hill," said Elagbi. "But I wouldn't want to tear you away from your sightseeing, Master Sevraim."

Talasyn arched a brow at the legionnaire. "*You* play casongkâ?"

"Learned how after supper last night." Sevraim pointed at Elagbi. "And soundly trounced this man, might I add."

"Because you were making up your own rules!" the prince cried, aggrieved.

Elagbi and Sevraim started bickering, Talasyn all but forgotten. She left them to it and let herself be pulled into Alaric's orbit.

Echoes of her nightmare crept up on her as she looked at him while he gazed at the dragon. There was something about the way his face was turned to her in profile. He had his father's sharp cheekbones and long nose. The same haughty gray eyes. The resemblance was enough to bring her up short, to shackle her again in the paralysis of earlier that morning.

Suddenly, in a great upheaval of orange scales, the old dragon rolled onto its back. Mountains of wet sand rose and fell, and leathery wings stretched out through fleeting tidal waves of Eversea shallows that drenched the four people on the shore before receding.

It happened so fast. Before she knew it, Talasyn's clothes were clinging to her skin and she was blinking at Alaric's blurry form through wet, salt-stung eyes. Somewhere behind her, Sevraim and Elagbi were groaning with laughter, but she saw only Alaric as her vision cleared. His black hair was plastered to his forehead, the shock on his features softening them.

She remembered the mud, how it had flattened his hair in this same way, how offended he'd looked as he emerged from the pond, spitting out dirt. Right before the swamp buffalo chased them through the jungle.

The heaviness in her chest eased, the nightmare dissipating along the crest of the snicker that bubbled out of her throat. He shot her an admonishing glare, which only made her snicker harder.

"You don't look any less comical right now, you know," he informed her snippily.

"Trust me," she said, "it's funnier when it's you."

Alaric rolled his eyes. Then they strayed to the dragon again, as though directed there by some compulsion. The beast continued to doze, blissfully oblivious to its audience, the vast road of its underbelly soaking up the sun.

Talasyn belatedly realized that Alaric had never seen a dragon up close before. His expression was uncharacteristically open—with wonder, and a trace of regret.

"I didn't give the order to fire that day," he said quietly. "Mathire panicked."

It hung between them, the memory of that copper dragon crashing into the Eversea below the Kesathese fleet, screaming in pain as the black rot of the Voidfell bloomed over its left wing. Talasyn felt that same old anger build inside her.

"I don't know if it makes a difference, that I didn't give the order," Alaric continued, "but it won't happen again. I swear it."

If Mathire hadn't fired the void cannon at the dragon, Talasyn thought, it was highly possible that there would have been a skirmish between the Kesathese fleet and the Dominion warships stationed at Port Samout. All the dragons would have risen from the ocean to defend the Nenavarene, and nothing could have stopped them, not until they'd taken down all the Night Empire's vessels or they'd all died, whichever came first.

It would have been a bloodbath.

Better that things had turned out like this, with the rest of the dragons unscathed, with Kesath oblivious, thinking they had the upper hand.

Talasyn had to learn to look at the bigger picture, as Vela and Urduja did. She took a deep breath and let her anger go.

Alaric seemed to be waiting for some kind of response from her. She couldn't offer forgiveness, and she truly had no idea if it made a difference whether he'd ordered Mathire to fire or not—but she *could* change the subject.

"Would you like to pet it?" she asked, gesturing to the dragon.

His reply was immediate. "No, thank you."

"Scared?" she goaded him.

"Smart," he tersely corrected.

She smirked. "What if I dared you?"

He exhaled. The wrinkle between his brows suggested that she was about to give him a migraine, if she hadn't already.

Undeterred, Talasyn grabbed her husband's arm with both hands and tugged him toward the dragon. In truth, this had the potential to be the worst idea she'd ever had, but she wanted to rattle him, in some petty approximation of vengeance. And she was also curious as to what would happen. If the Ahimsan Enchanters could experiment on the Night Emperor, surely so could his wife.

Still . . .

"I'd better go first," she declared.

The wrinkle in his brow deepening, Alaric's lips twisted into a scowl. "Talasyn, if anything happens to you—"

Her hand came to rest on the beast's flank.

There were no two ways about it: dragons *stank*. They smelled of what they ate—fish and squid, blubber and carrion, with pungent notes of decomposing seaweed and the musk of burning fields. Up close, it would have been enough to make Talasyn gag if not for the feel of the creature against her palm grounding her.

The hard orange scales were surprisingly smooth to the touch, except for the ridge in the middle of each one and the triangular seams where they overlapped one another. The heat given off by the scales was just shy of unbearable; that split-second before one snatched one's fingers back from a boiling pot, spun out into forever. The dragon seemed to almost lean into Talasyn's touch as it slept, its hide swelling and contracting against her with every somnolent breath. Aether flowed from its form and into hers, then looped back, a pulsating, endless tide of magic. Fire that gave off light, the sun's light that stoked a brushfire.

With her free hand, Talasyn wordlessly urged Alaric's wrist toward the dragon. His palm flattened beside hers on the scaled reptilian flank, their fingers brushing. And aether flowed from him and into him as well. The shadows cast by the sun, the volcanic fire raging in the dark beneath the earth.

Everything was connected. Their hearts and the leviathan's beat together with the waves. The same light of eternal summer that bent off the edge of Alaric's slight smile poured into Talasyn's eyes.

The dragon *snored*, long and low, the barbels on its snout twitching.

Talasyn laughed. Alaric's gaze warmed.

"Almost as loud as you," he remarked.

"How dare you, I do *not* snore—"

"Tell that to my sleepless nights."

He said it so dryly that she laughed again. There it was once more, that cautious hope, stirring beneath the sun, reveling in the *one* difference that she was certain of. He wasn't his father.

Alaric reached out to brush some sand off her shoulder. Talasyn made a pretense of batting his hand away, but her fingers lingered over his. She glanced up the shore, where Elagbi was hanging back with Sevraim.

Elagbi was staring at her and Alaric. He looked—*worried.*

CHAPTER THIRTEEN

Alaric could still smell the dragon long after it had slunk back into the Eversea. By the time night fell over Nenavar, he could still feel traces of dragonfire against his skin, mingling with the ghost of Talasyn's touch.

In a few minutes, the night would bring with it the first eclipse of the month. The shores of the tiny island bustled with activity.

In Kesath, outdoor aethermancy training tended to garner its fair share of spectators, all of whom afforded the Shadow-forged Legion the respect that was their due by observing quietly, careful to keep an appropriate distance and to refrain from doing anything that could be considered a distraction.

As Alaric found out, much to his displeasure, that was *not* the case in Iantas. The villagers and the castle staff had trooped out to the beach in full force. There was a bonfire. People passed around bottles of distilled coconut liquor and, for the younger ones and the teetotalers, the coconuts themselves, the tops lopped off to reveal creamy white flesh and sweet, clear juice to be imbibed through bamboo straws.

At first, the intrigued crowd gathered closely around the

Ahimsan Enchanters, who were arranging the jars and wires on the moonlit sands, but they good-naturedly retreated further up the shore after some words from an amused-sounding Talasyn. It was a far cry from the Dominion court's fear of only months ago—the gazes straying every so often to the sariman cages as though they were protective talismans, the panicked screams when Alaric channeled the Shadowgate at the banquet.

"People are afraid of what they don't know," Talasyn said, noticing his bewilderment. "They know us now. They know that our magic will stop the Voidfell. So they've come to accept us, I think."

Alaric had a feeling that it went beyond that. It was plain to him, in the light of the flickering fire and the seven moons, that the Nenavarene regarded their Lachis'ka with fondness. And for good reason. Not only had Talasyn opened her home to those in need without hesitation, but the two days that Alaric had spent on this island thus far had been enough for him to see that she treated the servants kindly and as equals. It was no difficult thing to accept someone like her.

"Your Majesties!" Sevraim wandered over to them with a somewhat unsteady gait, holding out a bottle. "May I tempt you?"

"Why are you drinking on duty?" Alaric growled.

The legionnaire pouted. "There's nothing to protect you from here, and it's an insult to the Lachis'ka's hospitality to assume otherwise." He waved the bottle under the aforementioned Lachis'ka's nose in offering, and even Alaric could smell the potent burn of fermented coconut sap from where he stood.

Talasyn paled slightly and took a step back. Not sparing a second thought for the oddness of her reaction, reacting purely on some nebulous primal instinct, Alaric darted between her and Sevraim, baring his teeth at the other man.

Sevraim fled. Perhaps he was drunk, or perhaps it was the first time in a long while that Alaric had responded to his antics with anything more than grudging tolerance; whatever the case, the legionnaire beat a hasty retreat toward the safety of the bonfire, stumbling all the while.

When Alaric turned to his wife, whatever anxiety had gripped her appeared to have passed, but he still needed to check. "Is everything—"

"I'm fine," Talasyn interrupted. "It's—I just don't like the smell of that particular liquor."

While her reasoning made sense, it was starting to occur to Alaric that he had never actually seen her take anything more than sparing sips of wine, not once finishing a glass. At supper last night she'd drunk only water. Before he could delve into the matter, though, Ishan Vaikar beckoned them over to the amplifying configuration.

"I'm really rather pleased with this!" True to her word, the daya was practically bouncing up and down in glee, as much as her prosthetic leg would allow her to on the soft sand. "We had the idea to increase the area of effect by adding a few strands of the Tempestroad to the aether cores. It's produced promising results, thanks to the ability of lightning and thunder to travel. If we are successful, Their Majesties' eclipse magic should be able to wholly surround the chasm from which the Voidfell springs! But," she said, beaming at them, "let's start with this strip of beach first."

Alaric eyed the jars dubiously. They held the shining, molten combinations of sariman blood and rain magic that he had first seen in the Roof of Heaven's atrium. This time, however, something was different. This time the ruby-flecked sapphire cores were marbled with the white heat of the Tempestroad, and they crackled unnervingly within the crystalline walls that caged them.

Talasyn's thoughts were clearly running along a similar vein to his. "Is it safe?" she asked Ishan.

"It wasn't initially," Ishan replied with great cheer. "Almost blew my assistant's fingers off. Worse than firecrackers! However, I believe we've figured out the proper dilution."

Talasyn glanced at Alaric with a small, wry smile. "It was nice knowing you."

"Likewise," he quipped.

The Ahimsan Enchanters first wanted to test if Talasyn could cast eclipse magic with another Shadowforged. Thus, as Lir's seventh moon turned blood-red, Sevraim gamely threw a knife at her.

It was a shadow-smithed knife. Slender and deadly, weightless like the air through which it sliced. It spun toward Talasyn, its path erratic, the edge of its dark blade rippling with the silver threads of aetherspace.

Instead of shielding, she conjured a blazing sword and slashed at the knife as it spiraled within inches of her chest. Shadow split into two at the onslaught of light and then vanished. Rather than being enveloped by a black-and-gold sphere of combined magic, Talasyn was left holding her radiant blade, meeting Sevraim's gaze over the fiery haze of it.

No barrier. Not even beneath the eclipse.

The legionnaire threw up his hands good-naturedly. "Looks like your wife only knows how to cast the light-and-shadow shield with *you*," he told an intently watching Alaric.

"Very curious indeed," muttered Ishan. "Something in the blood, no doubt. Though whether House Ossinast or Ivralis, I couldn't say."

Talasyn couldn't say, either. But as Alaric stepped forward and faced her within the amplifying configuration, she was all too aware of the odd sense of relief running through her. Relief that the shield remained something that was theirs alone.

Afterwards, Talasyn would wonder what it had looked like from afar, that veil of Lightweave and Shadowgate unfurling from the water's edge, stretching and arching until it contained the beach and everyone on it within its shimmering sphere. The aether cores blazed and crackled within their jars, and Lir's moons danced on in the heavens above, their seventh sister half shrouded in crimson.

"Wonderful, wonderful!" Ishan had her arms outstretched along with the other Enchanters, carefully controlling the energy that surged through the incandescent wires linking one jar to the next. "Let's see how long we can keep this up!"

It was the first time that people other than Alaric were inside the light-and-shadow sphere with Talasyn. Ishan was close enough for her instructions to be heard over the roar of magic, but it was impossible to make out what the spectators further away from the waterline were saying. With the barrier dulling the moon's rays, with ribbons of Shadowgate obfuscating the bonfire, she could see the other Nenavarene only in brief flashes of aether as they looked around in awe. She caught a glimpse of the boyish fascination on Elagbi's face before the Lightweave shifted and he was gone from her sight.

Alaric, though, was right beside her. She saw him all too clearly, his eyes gleaming an ice-bright silver, his form tangled in nets of chiaroscuro, as ethereal as a dream that she might have once had.

"Talasyn, you're not focusing," he snapped, thoroughly shattering the illusion of dreaminess.

She scowled, irritated with him all over again, but she dutifully shut out all distractions. The magic that poured from her fingertips took on more solid shape and soared through the veil on the crests of the amplifiers. Sand whirled around her feet, stirred by an unnatural wind.

The last time Talasyn had cast the barrier with Alaric within the amplifying configuration had been in the Roof of Heaven's atrium, when it had felt like her magic was taking wing, becoming greater than the sum of its parts. Here and now on Iantas's beach, with the aether cores modified to project the barrier over a greater distance, it was the same but also—*different.* The longer Talasyn aethermanced, the more something seemed to open up inside her, beneath her heart, along her spine.

She couldn't let anyone down; she had no choice but to ride it out, this sensation that was like dread but not quite, this feeling of something being awakened. Sweat beaded at her temple, and a quick glance at Alaric—his complexion sallow, his jaw clenched—revealed that he was doing no better.

And soon some critical point was reached and the jars burst. One after the other, their wires shorting out, the world blurring into glass shards and rain and lightning. Startled, Talasyn's concentration broke and the light-and-shadow barrier collapsed in on itself, dissolving into wisps and then nothingness as the Enchanters redirected the mass of burst aether cores into the ocean before anyone could get hurt.

"Not as stable as I thought," Ishan grumbled. "But it held for half an hour, so we are getting somewhere. Only a few more minor adjustments . . ." She trailed off in a renewed surge of alarm. "Your Grace? You're shaking—"

Talasyn was burning up. Had it really been just thirty minutes? It had felt much longer. Her throat was parched and every inch of her body was on fire. *Heatstroke,* she thought groggily. Like the relentless summers on the Great Steppe. Too much light, too much warmth. She took a step toward the waterline with some hazy thought of drowning herself in the

Eversea. She would do anything for even a moment's relief, but the treacherous sand shifted under her feet and she couldn't correct, she was falling—

And Alaric was catching her. Strong arms wrapped around her, hauling her up against a broad, hard frame. The relief was instantaneous everywhere his skin touched hers, her fevered brow to the hollow of his throat, his bare hands on her shoulder and the small of her back. It spread, this cooling, the roar of light receding.

And Alaric was shaking, too. No, he was *shivering.* His teeth were chattering and he was ice-cold. Talasyn burrowed deeper against his chest, tightening her own grip on him, no thought left to her but to offer him some measure of comfort. Her left hand slipped underneath the hem of his shirt, palm flat on the heaving muscles of his abdomen. His tremors abated and his breathing evened out at the same time as hers.

Talasyn blinked up at the eclipse over Alaric's shoulder, at a loss as to how to rationalize what had transpired. The world came rushing back in all its chaos—people crowding around them and voicing concern . . . Ahimsan Enchanters yelling at everyone to steer clear of the broken glass that littered the sand and reflected the starlight in their jagged edges . . . the waves crashing against the shore.

Elagbi shoved his way to the front of the throng and grabbed Talasyn by the arm, gently pulling her out of Alaric's grasp. "My dear, what happened?" He held her by the shoulders, scrutinizing her from head to toe. "Are you ill?"

"Hot," Talasyn croaked. "I felt too hot."

She looked at Alaric. "Cold, for me," he said. "Like—like winter in the mountains."

If it had been as intense a sensation as she'd felt, and yet he'd somehow found the strength to steady her . . .

But the Shadowforged were used to pain. Vela had told her

that. Talasyn was seized by the urge to throw her arms around Alaric again, and for a horrible moment she resented her father for tugging her away.

Ishan was outright scratching her head. Talasyn felt a familiar twinge of guilt at being the source of all the daya's problems for as long as they'd known each other.

"Eclipse magic, amplifiers—this is all new terrain in Enchantment. There is no existing literature," Ishan said at last. "It's possible that the configuration we devised has affected Their Majesties' aethermancy on an internal level."

"And no one saw fit to inform me of such a risk?" Alaric's tone was sheer, quiet fury. It made Talasyn think of the seawater bubbling around the dragon's snout earlier that day. The surface rippling that was a paltry hint of the inferno from which it sprang. "In all this time that I have been submitting to these experiments, no one deemed it advisable to *warn* me that my magic would be altered?"

Ishan seemed rather taken aback at being chastised by a man, but she recovered and drew herself up straighter. "I cannot preemptively inform you of risks that I was not aware of, Emperor Alaric. As I said, this is still very new to us as well."

"And yet you had the temerity to act as though you knew what you were doing," he hissed. "Shadow magic is what stands between my people and the threats at our door. If my aethermancy is compromised in any way, I can't protect them. If the Lachis'ka and I are killed by these contraptions of yours, all of our plans will have been for nothing. We have foolishly placed it all in the hands of a—"

"My lord." Talasyn clutched at his sleeve before he could call one of the most powerful nobles in the Dominion a charlatan, or worse. When Alaric transferred his glare to her, she could see the fear that lurked behind its virulence, and she could understand where it came from. But the situation needed to be defused, and she tried to think of something to say, tried to paste an expression on her face that wasn't alarm.

Before she could manage either, he shrugged off her grip and stalked away.

Alaric stormed up the sweeping granite stairs. The Shadowgate crackled from his fingertips, chipping the marble banister. At least he could still do *that*.

He had no idea what the plan was. He knew only that he never wanted to feel anything like that ever again.

Not the cold that had made him believe he was dying, and not the way Talasyn's touch had channeled warmth into his veins like salvation.

Because she was *not* his salvation, she was the wielder of a dangerous age-old magic that had nearly destroyed his country, and what had he been *thinking*, letting her and her cohorts manipulate the very fabric of his aethermancy, as unintentional as it purportedly was?

He had been too complacent. He had let her get too close. She would be his undoing. Light and shadow couldn't exist together without one destroying the other.

"Alaric!"

Talasyn was chasing him up the stairs, taking them two at a time. He stopped begrudgingly and waited as she caught her breath a step below him.

"Look." She swallowed. He watched the butterfly-wing pulse of her throat and thought about how alone they were in the stairwell. "What the amplifying configuration did to our aethermancy, I know it bothers you—"

"An understatement—"

"—but it affected *my* aethermancy as well. We have to keep on going. It's still our best chance at stopping the Voidfell."

"*We* are the best chance to stop the Voidfell," he said. "That's why we can't risk our own lives before the time comes."

"It was temporary. We're both fine," she argued. Then she noticed the shadow-gouged cracks in the banister, and her hands clenched into fists. "You can't just go around demolishing things! Someone will have to fix that—"

Alaric was torn between a bitter laugh and a disbelieving groan. *Never runs out of fight, this one.* No matter the situation, his wife's claws always came out eventually.

But maybe that was what he needed right now.

He needed to quell the anxiety and frustration building up inside him, and he needed to check that his magic had not been compromised.

For what was he without the Shadowgate? How could he lead and protect the Night Empire without it?

You're not just a weapon. Talasyn had told him that. He hazily remembered her words, spoken softly in the lamplight while she held him. *You could be more.*

He fought back a shiver that had nothing to do with that strange chill from before. New wisps of shadow magic leaked from his fingers clutching the banister. The marble splintered at the onslaught.

"What are you going to do about it?" Alaric asked quietly.

Talasyn's eyes narrowed. In recognition, and in challenge.

"I," Sevraim announced, "am too drunk for this." He kicked at the moonlit sand. "Much too drunk."

"Shut up, Sevraim," Alaric and Talasyn chorused. They'd taken up position a few feet from each other, shielded from prying eyes by a thick wall of coconut palms. The lunar eclipse was over and the other residents of Iantas had retreated indoors. The castle's spiny silhouette was riddled with dark windows.

"The Lachis'ka needs to improve her focus," Alaric drawled.

"She's still so easily distracted. No amount of amplifying configurations can fix *that*."

"And the Night Emperor needs to be knocked down a peg or two," Talasyn spat.

"It's very confusing because you both sound like you're talking to me, but you just keep staring at each other," Sevraim said mournfully, shuffling to Alaric's side.

It wasn't long before the night air blazed with magic. An ever-transmuting assortment of shadow-spun weapons crashed into a light-woven shield in rapid succession and with startling ferocity, the three combatants' complicated footwork kicking up clouds of white sand with each sinking step.

Talasyn was fairly certain that things would be going better for her if she were to fight back. But she wasn't *allowed* to. The point was to keep up her shield, come what may.

Which meant that Alaric and Sevraim were attacking her one after the other, using a different weapon each time, and she could do nothing but dig her bare soles into the sand and do her very best to not let her only defense falter even as her teeth rang with the force of their blows.

"Good show, Lachis'ka!" Sevraim called out with a grin after Talasyn had fended off his shadow-sword. "His Majesty is simply too much of a worrywart, if you ask me."

"No one asked you," Alaric snapped. "No talking." He flung a dark spear at Talasyn, who ducked behind her shield easily enough, shadow vanishing the moment it hit the golden barrier, but then Alaric was suddenly to her left, conjuring a second spear and hurling it at her unguarded flank.

She twisted in the nick of time, her shield intercepting the new projectile before it could run her through, but then *both* her opponents charged, from opposite directions. Talasyn instinctively pushed back against Sevraim and his axe, causing him to stumble, but doing so left her with no opportunity to brace herself for Alaric's strike. Her shield flickered out of existence as it caught the brunt of his double-edged, wavelike kalis blade. His silver eyes widened and he scrambled to draw his arm back, but it was too late. She yelped at the kalis's icy bite on her hip bone, cold enough to burn.

Alaric banished his weapon, his gaze fixed on the blood welling up on the strip of skin between Talasyn's breastband and breeches. He stepped forward as though to reach for her, but then appeared to think better of it, swallowing.

"Get a healer," he told Sevraim.

"It's not that bad," Talasyn protested, stopping the legionnaire before he could dutifully make his way back to the castle. "If we stop for every little scrape, we'll never get anything done."

Alaric glared at her, and she at him in abject puzzlement. They'd fought against each other during a *war*, both of them inflicting their fair share of cuts and bruises. How was this any different? And it had been *his* idea to spar in the first place.

"Fine," he bit out. "Next time let your aethermancy do the work for you. When in a tight spot, modify your shield rather than physically dodge or block."

She nodded. She could do that. They resumed training, with the two Shadowforged's attacks more simultaneous than not, and she focused on altering her shield whenever necessary—from the teardrop-shaped war shields of the Continent to the forked rectangles of Nenavar, adjusting for different weapons, different angles. It was a bit of an excruciating process, Alaric and Sevraim showing her no mercy, but she gradually found her rhythm beneath the seven moons.

And there was relief, too—relief that her aethermancy still worked as it should. Relief that was mirrored on Alaric's face.

It was going to be all right. It had just been a passing spell. Some quirk of the amplifiers.

Sevraim eventually fell back, and Alaric and Talasyn locked into a precise, deadly dance of swirling darkness and shifting light. He drove her all the way to the waterline, where the ocean lapped at her toes as she blocked his furious strikes. He was relentless, forcing her to move faster and faster until her arms were sore and her breath emerged in harsh bursts and all she could see was him, windswept black hair and broad shoulders and shadows against gleaming sand and moon-razed saltwater.

Given their closeness, it was all too easy for her to spot the moment a glint of cunning sparked in the silver depths of his eyes. The sword in his hands melted into a bullhook on a chain, and with a flick of his wrist the darkly crackling coils wrapped around her shield, rendering her immobile as the hook's lethally sharp arrowhead point flew at her face in one smooth thrust.

Talasyn's desperation echoed in her magic, her shield doubling in size and bursting free of the inky chain. Her arm bearing the shield swung up wildly, and the edge of it smashed into Alaric's cheek.

He reeled back, the Shadowgate vanishing as his blood spattered the shallows.

A hoarse shout rent the air. Talasyn barely even registered the fact that it had come from her; she was too busy banishing the Lightweave and hurrying over to Alaric, seawater sloshing at her ankles, alarm spreading through her like wildfire.

"Are you—" She clutched at the side of his neck, giving him no choice but to turn his face toward her, and her heart dropped into her stomach at the sight of the crimson gash that ran along the edge of his cheekbone.

But they had fought a war against each other. Why was it so different this time? What was this regret, this urge to call for a healer like he almost had when he cut her hip?

If we don't want to hurt each other, she thought, *then where does that leave us?*

What is the way forward?

Alaric's brow furrowed at her touch. His hand came to rest over hers where it clasped his neck. Talasyn's pulse skipped a beat at skin on skin, at his fingers curling against hers.

He squeezed her wrist, and she had the impression that there was something compulsive about the gesture, something starved—but then he was peeling her hand away from his neck with an alacrity that made it clear that the gentle pressure of moments ago had been nothing more than an accident.

"An inventive maneuver," he said, "but hardly the point of our exercise."

She turned her nose up at him as much as she could given the several inches he lorded over her. "You cheated."

Alaric wiped the back of his left hand over his cheek, pale knuckles coming away smeared red, but the worst of the bleeding had stopped, much to Talasyn's relief. "I was testing you," he rumbled. "I'd venture to say that *you* cheated, as a matter of fact—unless you really are planning on punching the Voidfell with your shield."

Talasyn would have gladly continued their bickering, if not for the fact that she had finally noticed that the hand Alaric had used to pry hers away from his neck still hadn't let go. Their fingers remained intertwined at her side. He realized it a beat after she did, and for one blistering second he looked enraged—at her? At himself? He tried to wrench his hand away.

But she tightened her own grip, refusing to release him. The prolonged contact seemed to break through his defenses, laying bare the fatigue that had finally caught up with him. With them both. All the fight left his broad frame, and in response something like surrender rippled through her as well. They were each other's mirrors, beneath the seven moons.

"You were burning up earlier," he whispered. "I reached out to you, and for a moment you were like the dragon. Nothing but flame against my skin."

She saw the fear then, fear that he had tried to hide before—not for himself, but for her. She reached out and touched his shoulder, and he melted, as though she really were fire, sinking his head toward her hand.

"I'm all right. Because of *you*." Talasyn dragged her fingers down the muscled cords of Alaric's bare arm. "As soon as you touched me, it drew out the fever. It felt . . ."

Like someone stopping her fall. Like the end of a long journey home. She didn't know how to put it into words, these emotions that were bigger than her body, that ran deeper than her magic, that soared higher than the Sky Above the Sky.

"I felt it, too." Alaric reached for her fingers before she could lift them away from his arm. "The light inside you, it poured into me. Banishing the cold."

Both her hands were held by him now. He was all that she could see, etched in moonlight against the surf.

"I'm not sure what this means for us. For our magic," Talasyn said. "But I think—I think, maybe, we can protect each other."

Alaric closed his eyes briefly, looking almost pained by this sentiment. "You don't know how badly I want to believe that, Talasyn. But we can't run from what we are. Our history was one of war long before you and I ever met. Look what happened tonight—look at the consequences of light and shadow working together." His gaze darted away as though he couldn't stand the sight of her. "The toll it takes."

She wanted to argue with him. She wanted to bring up the sense of oneness they'd felt with the dragon, how it had showed that even opposing forces could be connected. She wanted to remind him that he was the one who'd said they were stronger together.

But another war was on the horizon, unbeknownst to him. His doubts breathed life back into her own, her skin still crawling with the memory of the inferno from earlier—of how their combined magic had nearly destroyed them both.

She had to look at the bigger picture. She would have to give him up to the Allfold when the time came. There was no other way this could end.

They couldn't protect each other. That had been Talasyn of the Great Steppe talking, the orphaned street rat who lived on dreams of what could be. She was Alunsina Ivralis now, and millions of lives were at stake.

Let him go, urged her sanity.

And yet her hands stayed where they were, clasped in his. He didn't pull away, either. She couldn't move. She was helpless in the face of all this yearning for what she couldn't even name.

I don't know what I want.

I know what Vela and Urduja want. I know what's best for Sardovia and Nenavar.

But I didn't know—no one told me—it would be this hard.

If Alaric just looked at her, though . . . if he would just say something . . . that might be enough to make it all make sense.

But he stayed silent, refusing to meet her gaze, and Talasyn's heart sank. He would never choose her over Kesath. And she wasn't strong enough to fight for this alone.

A soft moan shattered the moment. Sevraim was lying face down on the sand, several feet away. They'd forgotten all about him.

"Don't mind me, Your Majesties," he slurred pitifully. "Just trying to stop my world from spinning while you work through whatever *that* is."

CHAPTER FOURTEEN

"Are you positively certain that you don't need me to stay?"

It was early afternoon of the following day, and out on Iantas's sand-swept airship grid, Elagbi was peering at Talasyn with unabashed concern in the shadow of the diplomatic schooner that would bring him back to Eskaya. "I can, you know. Your grandmother will understand."

"I don't actually believe that she will." Talasyn grinned to soften the quip. "But I'm going to be fine, Amya. There's no call to neglect your responsibilities in the capital on my account."

"I am simply worried. With your husband in such a foul mood . . ." Elagbi's gaze darted to the castle windows, as though he expected Alaric to pop up at any moment like a dour wraith.

Talasyn scoffed. "The Night Emperor's moods are always foul. I can handle him, I promise."

Only after Elagbi had said his goodbyes and boarded the schooner, and after the schooner had become a palm-sized silhouette above the horizon, did Talasyn allow her shoulders to slump. It was going to be unbearable now that Elagbi had left. Alaric had slept in his study last night, and he'd barricaded himself in there most of today as well, emerging only for meals, where he glowered at his plate in lieu of saying a word.

Talasyn couldn't even blame him. The situation got murkier and murkier whenever they were around each other. She was scared of all the things he made her feel, and *he* was clearly not happy caring about her well-being and her opinions. There was also this new aspect of their magic to consider: light and shadow feeding off each other even as they remained diametrical opposites, patching over the weakness that each one had inflicted on the other.

So tangled a web. Perhaps it was for the best that they kept at a distance for now.

The beginning of a new sennight brought the royal tailor to Iantas. His name was Belrok and he was in his mid-forties, slim, cocoa-skinned, and bedecked in what was quite possibly the flashiest getup Alaric had ever laid eyes on. Aside from the striped blue-and-pink trim on its sleeves, his moss-colored tunic was embellished with gecko patterns in silver thread that put even Urduja's most ostentatious dress to shame. The crystal-studded gold sash around his waist glittered so copiously that Alaric couldn't even look at it in direct sunlight for fear of going blind.

Like all Nenavarene men, Belrok loved jewelry. Several gem-encrusted rings sparkled as they moved through the air on the ridges of the fingers that he was tapping on the armrest of his chair after Alaric had submitted to the indignity of his measurements being taken by a couple of assistants, who were now flanking the tailor in his seat, jotting down notes on rolls of parchment.

"I am sorry, Emperor Alaric, but a plain formal jacket simply will not do," Belrok was saying, having no qualms whatsoever about letting his exasperation show. "The Lachis'ka's couturier has been gracious enough to send me her design and it is positively *lavish.* You would look like a butler next to your wife, Your Majesty. I am afraid that I simply cannot allow it."

A nerve twitched under Alaric's left eye. "Very well," he stiffly conceded, "as long as it is within the bounds of good taste."

"Of *course.*" The tailor sounded offended. "Now, let us discuss concept. Your masquerade costume must strike a delicate balance between complementing the Lachis'ka's attire and not stealing her thunder, so to speak. Would you rather personify the resplendence of the peacock, the raw power of the tiger, the virility of the stag—"

"This was a mistake."

"Perhaps the ill temper of the swamp buffalo?" Belrok fired back. "The obstinacy of the common ass?"

Alaric smirked. "I'll have to abstain from those last two options, Belrok. I wouldn't want to steal *your* thunder."

The two men argued, sniped, and glared at each other for the remainder of the meeting. By the time they settled on a design and Belrok had exited in an icy huff, along with his assistants, Alaric was in the blackest of moods. He prowled the castle in search of Talasyn, fully prepared to rant about the tailor; after all the concessions she'd wrung out of him in the course of this damnable acquaintance, the least she could do was put up with it when he complained.

A servant directed him to the gardens in halting Sailor's Common, and soon he was walking out into that place of bright light and hibiscus blossoms. Suddenly, he stopped in his tracks. Talasyn had guests.

Beneath the graceful arched roof of a seashell-flecked pavilion, his wife was having tea with Jie and a gaggle of Dominion noblewomen. Alaric recognized Niamha Langsoune, the Daya of Catanduc, who had boarded his stormship armed with a proposal of marriage to the Nenavarene Lachis'ka months ago. The others' names and titles escaped him, but their elaborately painted faces were familiar enough that he knew they'd either been guests at his wedding or spectators to the banquet duel with Surakwel Mantes. Most probably both.

The stream of dainty giggles and chatter tapered off when they caught sight of him. The nobles rose and curtsied, then wasted no time in whispering among themselves and casting speculative looks as Talasyn hurried to where he was hovering at the garden entrance, ill at ease over being the object of so much feminine scrutiny.

"Yes, what is it?" she inquired, politely enough, given that they'd spent the days since the eclipse avoiding each other whenever possible, aside from meals and training.

Alaric stared down at her, disconcerted. He could hardly bellyache about the tailor *now*. His mind raced until it stumbled on a viable excuse. "I was wondering if Sevraim and I might put the courtyard to use. With your permission."

"Sparring? You don't need my permission for that," Talasyn said. "This is your residence as much as it is mine."

"Still. I thought I should ask." He cleared his throat. "Thank you."

She looked thoroughly mystified, but changed the subject. "Before you go—Daya Vaikar sent word that she and her Enchanters still haven't finished the new amplifier modifications. So you and I will have to make do by ourselves during tonight's eclipse."

"Very well," said Alaric. "I will give Nenavar no cause to accuse Kesath of reneging on the treaty, despite their recent incompetence."

"Your generosity is boundless and noted," Talasyn sniped.

Alaric spun on his heel and left. He found Sevraim in the kitchens and all but dragged him to the courtyard.

"But, Your Majesty, why?" the legionnaire whined. "I was helping shell these lovely little pili nuts and the cooks promised I could sneak a bite here and there. It is also *much* too warm to spar. Where is this coming—"

"Shut up, Sevraim."

The four nobles had ostensibly come to pay their respects, but Talasyn had lived in the Dominion long enough to know better. News of the Night Emperor finally taking up residence at Iantas had spread, and this courtesy visit was a thinly veiled excuse to gossip. Talasyn's guests wasted no time in getting back to it once she returned to the pavilion after Alaric's departure.

"Is black all the rage on the Continent, Your Grace?" inquired Bairung Matono, whose bronze skin was covered in the runic bottle-green tattoos that were the tradition of her island. "Emperor Alaric's wardrobe is rather . . . dull."

"Beyond Nenavarene waters, not all civilizations prioritize aesthetic as we do, Lady Bairung," Talasyn replied carefully.

"Fashion sense or lack thereof aside," said Harjanti of Sabtang, her plump frame draped in rich orange stitchwork fabrics with diamond-and-chevron patterns set in metallic silver thread, "His Majesty is not all that bad-looking, for an outsider."

Jie shrieked with laughter, playfully shoving her cousin, who shoved her back in a moment of girlish camaraderie that completely belied their fine clothes and lofty status.

"You and your consort *must* visit the Silklands, Lachis'ka," Oryal enthused. She was the only child of Ito Wempuq, the rajan who had given Alaric such a hard time during the engagement banquet. "The fire trees are currently showing their monsoon colors. It would be my honor to host you."

Although she had her father's rich umber hair, chopped to chin length in blunt waves, Oryal was as thin as Wempuq was portly, as soft-spoken as he was boisterous, and apparently as welcoming to the Night Empire as he was not. Talasyn flashed her a tentative smile. "That would be lovely, if time permits."

"*Honestly*, Oryal." Niamha Langsoune rolled her eyes. "Did it ever occur to you that Her Grace and His Majesty might want some time to themselves? They *did* just get married." She was being a good ally as always, slyly offering Talasyn an opportunity to wriggle out of any possible commitments, but the implication made Talasyn want to throw herself off a cliff.

Oryal huffed. "It was merely a suggestion, Daya Langsoune. Too much time alone together can be positively disastrous for a husband and wife. We can't *all* be Harjanti and Praset."

The other noblewomen tittered while Harjanti gasped in mock outrage. The blatant affection that the daya of Sabtang and her spouse showed for each other was a source of amusement among the Dominion court, whose marriages were usually strategic alliances rather than the natural outcome of anything so passé as feelings. Talasyn, however, couldn't help but remember how happy and in tune Harjanti and Praset were at her engagement banquet, how they'd worked together to help smooth over an awkward situation.

"It is not too difficult a task, making a man fall in love. Husbands included," Bairung said airily. "Daya Langsoune, show the Lachis'ka your favorite technique."

Jie, Oryal, and Harjanti *shrieked*. Niamha shook a dainty fist at Bairung, but quickly straightened up in her seat and cleared her throat with aplomb. The merriment reached a fever pitch. Talasyn's head was starting to hurt.

"It's quite simple, really, Your Grace," said Niamha. "First, a vague smile, like you have a secret, then you peer up at him through your lashes instead of directly meeting his gaze"—she demonstrated—"and you blink slowly, a bit exaggeratedly, and he melts at your feet with a flutter of your lashes—"

The others were doubled over, clutching one another in mirth. Talasyn, on the other hand, was at her wit's end. "Pardon me, my lady, why are you teaching me how to *flirt*?" she burst out.

"Because men are so much more malleable when they follow their blood," Niamha smoothly replied. "You don't have to go around setting anyone afire with lust, but it's amazing what a sprinkling of pretty manners can achieve." She smirked. "Who knows, you might convince His Majesty to stop wearing black."

Her last remark was said as a joke, and the other noblewomen treated it as such, but she held Talasyn's gaze long enough to make it clear that this was nothing less than a lesson. They needed Alaric Ossinast to be as malleable as they could make him. In light of what was to come.

But Talasyn wasn't about to go off seducing the Night Emperor anytime soon. "And what have *you* managed to convince Lord Surakwel of, Daya Langsoune?" she shot back, turning the tables on the other woman.

At the mention of Surakwel Mantes, Niamha paled while everyone else quite positively perished from laughter.

Oryal was the first to resurrect, wiping tears from her eyes. "Ah, Surakwel. The only man immune to Niamha's powers."

Talasyn wasn't so sure about that. Surakwel had named his yacht after Niamha. And the look on his face when Talasyn asked him about it as they sailed to the Storm God's Eye had spoken volumes.

Back when Talasyn had been fighting to survive Hornbill's Head and then fighting to survive a war, there was precious little time to think about romance. But now that life was softer, *easier*, she was noticing much more often what she had never had. She'd never been the cause of an expression like Surakwel's, and no one had ever looked at her the way Praset looked at Harjanti. Wistfulness rippled across the surface of her heart.

The echoes of that sentiment lingered long after her guests had taken their leave and Jie had run off to send letters back home. When a servant informed Talasyn that Alaric and Sevraim were still sparring, a mixture of curiosity and restlessness led her to ascend the stairs to a secluded tower room overlooking the courtyard.

She gingerly peered out the window. The open courtyard nestled within the granite walls of Iantas was ablaze with the Shadowgate as Alaric and Sevraim, coming at each other again and again, effortlessly switched from swords to daggers to spears. They'd both shed their heavier outer layers; Alaric was down to a sleeveless black undershirt and his usual trousers and boots. Talasyn had seen him wearing less, but she'd been too busy tending his wounds to pay much attention.

Now, however, there was nothing to stop her from looking to her heart's content.

There was not an ounce of softness on him that she could see—or *feel*, her traitorous inner voice reminded her. He had been pure muscle every time he pressed against her, every inch of his body honed into a weapon. A weapon that he was putting to good use as he fended Sevraim off, ducking beneath the arcs of the legionnaire's blows and retaliating with lethal grace.

It was only then that Talasyn realized how much Alaric held back whenever he sparred with her. This was nothing like their sessions. The two Shadowforged gave each other no quarter and fought like they were going for the kill. Sweat-damp strands of Alaric's dark hair were plastered to his bare neck, his cheeks were flushed red, and there was a wildness in his silver eyes.

The taut sinews cording his pale arms shifted with every thrust and parry, and his teeth were bared in a near-feral snarl as he came within an inch of slicing Sevraim's head clean off his shoulders.

Talasyn swallowed. Her husband was a dangerous man. Watching him like this, it was so easy to revert to her old ways and think of him as a monster.

So what did it say about *her*, then, that a familiar heat was pooling low in her abdomen, seeping beneath her legs?

Memories of her wedding night flooded through Talasyn's system, each one so strong that the phantom sensations whispered across her skin. Alaric's lips crushed to hers, his large hand palming her breast, his hardness rubbing against her thigh. She remembered, too, the burning intensity in his gaze, the husky timbre of his voice.

My wet little wife.

Talasyn stepped back from the window, knees knocking together beneath her skirts. Slowly, unsteadily, she made her way to a chaise lounge in the corner and sat down, no longer able to remain upright. Hot. She felt too hot, too consumed by thoughts of Alaric Ossinast, her nerve endings scraped raw by the ghosts of touch. She closed her eyes in an attempt to meditate, to calm and center herself, but the darkness only brought him into sharper relief. She could almost smell him, all sandalwood and juniper and smoke. She could almost hear his harsh, ragged pants in her ear. As though he were there with her.

It was an act of surrender, this hiking up of her skirts. Talasyn couldn't believe what she was about to do. But her body was on edge, crying out for relief, and it was best not to think about it. She was so tired of thinking. Of living on her constant refrain of *I can't* and her fears for the future.

I'm so lonely. She whispered it into the secret universe of her mind, where no one else would ever know. A lone tear of burning shame welled up in the corner of her eye and she blinked it away as her fingers slipped beneath the band of her undergarments. And began to move.

The eclipse came and the light-and-shadow shield went up over the Eversea. It had been Sevraim's brilliant idea to have Iantas's warship fire one void cannon after another at Alaric and Talasyn while they stood on the deck of one of the castle fleet's smaller vessels. The pleasure yacht was currently encased in a glimmering sphere of black and gold against which amethyst bolts slammed in vain as it hovered in the air, the conflagration reflected like flickering fireworks in the dark and restless waters below.

It was a good exercise. The threat of getting zapped with death magic was all it took for Talasyn to never let her concentration wane, even as she aethermanced by the side of the man she'd fantasized about while touching herself earlier that afternoon.

However, it was still taxing, especially without the help of the amplifiers. Once the last void cannon had been fired and summarily repelled, her legs refused to hold her up any longer, and she collapsed flat on her back, on a cold bed of teak and nails.

Alaric landed beside her with a groan. The two of them lay panting, bathed in sweat. The Eclipse of the Third filled Talasyn's eyes with its scarlet glow.

When the burning came, she met it with dread but no surprise. Her body had been expecting it, even though her mind had hoped it wouldn't happen. It spread through her, this heat like needles, and she knew without a doubt that this was how they'd all felt when they died—everyone she'd ever killed. This was her punishment. Her reckoning.

She reached for Alaric, because she was a coward. His ice-cold fingers laced with hers, soothing the inferno at the same time that his skin gradually warmed.

"It happened again. Even without the amplifiers," Talasyn said when she was well enough to speak. "Is it—does this mean that it will *always* happen from now on?"

"I don't know." Alaric sounded as confused as she was. Defeated. Tired. "Perhaps it happens only in the aftermath of casting the light-and-shadow shield. Or perhaps it's caused by the eclipse. Either way, it's certainly an effect of the amplifiers. And if it's permanent . . ."

"I hope not. We can't be with each other *every* eclipse from now on."

And after I betray you, you will probably rather die than touch me again, she added silently, pain stabbing at her heart anew.

The warship returned to the docks, leaving them alone above the open sea. Talasyn hadn't wanted to risk anyone else, so she'd steered the yacht away from the island herself. Now it was time to head back.

She sat up, fully intending to sail for shore, but something about the look on Alaric's face as he glanced over at her made her pause. Even if he *was* still carrying a grudge against the Dominion, and consequently *her*, for messing with his aethermancy—

He cares what you think.

There it was again. That dark inner voice. She couldn't put it aside as she'd done before. There might never be another opportunity like this, when it was just the two of them with no distractions, with no one around to interrupt.

She couldn't break out Hiras and the other prisoners, but she could still try to help them.

"About the rebels who were captured after the Citadel attack—" It was such a risky subject that she nearly lost her nerve at the clenching of his sharp jaw. "Have you been able to get any information out of them?"

"Nothing particularly useful." Alaric regarded her warily. "They're all low-ranking foot soldiers, which I believe was an intentional strategy, given that they never intended to escape. It's guerrilla warfare, with a lot of different groups at different bases that move around."

"Then maybe it would be all right to stop the interrogations," Talasyn said. The *torture* was what she really meant.

"They tried to *kill* you." He said this so slowly, so deliberately, as though she were stupid, that heat came rushing to her cheeks.

"I know they tried to kill me, I was there," she snapped. "But you said it yourself: they're foot soldiers, and there's nothing important they can tell you. Forcing them to give up information they don't possess is just causing those people unnecessary suffering."

Alaric got to his feet. He stalked over to the ship's guardrail and gripped it so tightly with both hands that Talasyn suspected he was imagining taking her by the shoulders and giving her a good shake. "Why do you still care what happens to them? They may have been your comrades in the past, but that doesn't excuse their present actions."

"Because they were only following orders, as I did once," Talasyn said. "Vengeance isn't justice—I told you that before, didn't I?"

"I remember." Alaric stared down moodily at the waters below, rippling in the moonlight, reflecting the yacht's Squallfast fumes in whorls of emerald green.

"Besides," she added, struck by a burst of sudden inspiration, "it hardly endears you to your subjects. It's no secret what Kesath does to Sardovian captives, but this could be an opportunity to show that your reign is different from your father's, that *you* are capable of extending mercy."

He scoffed. "If there is no punishment, then *more* aspiring rebels will come out of the woodwork. If I relent on this matter of national security, people will see only that I am not as strong as my father, that I cannot defend our homeland as he did."

"The same father who hurts you?"

Talasyn clapped a hand over her mouth as soon as these words spilled out, but of course it was too late to take them back. She hadn't meant to say it like that, to bring it all out in the open so callously. She hadn't meant to make her husband's shoulders tense, as if he were warding off a low blow that had come out of nowhere. "Alaric, I'm s—"

"Don't pity me," he hissed before she could finish apologizing. "I refuse to be the scapegoat for your ignorance in the ways of Kesath. Pain is instructive, and what you call mercy is nothing more than weakness. And casting my father in this light amounts to treason—"

"T-treason?" she sputtered. "Against whom? *You* are the Night Emperor." She closed the distance between them, stepping into his space, forcing him to look at her. "You are the Night Emperor," she repeated, her words unfolding with the sound of the waves below, "and you told me at my coronation that you wanted to change things for the better. So when do you start?"

He swallowed, and for a moment everything about him was a cornered animal. He seemed almost afraid of her. Or of what she could get him to do.

"Very well," he finally said in clipped tones. "I'll send a message to the Citadel to cease the interrogation process." And then his expression darkened, showing her that the animal had teeth. "However, if this decision ends up compromising Kesath in any way—"

"Yes, yes, I know. I will take my former comrades' place in the torture chambers."

Talasyn was being sarcastic, and yet not. There was a very real possibility of that happening.

But Alaric blinked. "Don't be ridiculous," he snapped. "I would never let—"

He broke off in abject frustration, then looked away.

In the act of sharply turning his neck, he grunted out an expletive and froze.

Alaric almost never cursed. Talasyn studied him intently. The tips of his ears were reddening, as though with embarrassment.

She put two and two together. He'd been sleeping in his study all this time, and that particular room of the castle didn't even have a couch.

"Can you please just sleep in the bed tonight?" she demanded.

He shook his head. Slowly, determinedly, pushing the act out through obviously sore muscles.

"We need to be well rested and at our best for the third eclipse this month," said Talasyn. "It's the last one before the Moonless Dark. There will be no more opportunities to fine-tune the amplifiers. Imagine jeopardizing that on account of a stiff neck—"

"Fine."

"And furthermore—oh." She stopped short. "I'm not used to you actually agreeing with me."

"And I'm not used to someone nagging me until I give in," Alaric muttered. "But we must all make sacrifices."

He insisted on steering the yacht to shore, and Talasyn had the feeling that it was his pride requiring him to prove that he could, that his stiff neck hadn't put him completely out of commission.

She would have protested, but with Alaric, as with the Nenavarene court, it was all about picking one's battles. Still, she couldn't resist sticking her tongue out at him as soon as his back was turned to sail them home.

CHAPTER FIFTEEN

He dreamed of her.

In truth, it could have been anyone because he couldn't see a face, but all he could do was feel, and it felt like her, soft skin stretched over wiry muscles, molten sunlight in his arms. She was saying his name over and over again, her every touch as soothing as safe harbor in a storm, as gentle as forgiveness. She returned his kisses eagerly, as though they lived in a world where there had never been a war and he was wanted and adored—and that was how he realized he was dreaming.

Alaric opened his eyes to pale morning light filtering in through the gaps between the curtains. Reality settled over him in gradual splinters of sight and sensation that slowly coalesced into a complete picture. At some point during the night, or perhaps the early hours of dawn, he and Talasyn had met in the middle of the mattress. He had pulled her to him so that her back was against his chest and he was curled around her, one arm clamped around her waist while the other had slanted upward and his hand cupped her breast through her nightshirt. At some point, his dream had spilled over into the waking world and he was hard against her buttocks, thrusting haphazardly against her.

Alaric knew that he should stop. He should disentangle himself from Talasyn and flee to his side of the bed. But he was too groggy for common sense, too frustrated from his unfinished dream, too lost in the feeling.

And Talasyn was moving as well. Moving *with* him, shifting her hips for a better, more perfect angle. She let out a breathy little moan, murmured something nonsensical, and the sounds pierced his heart at the same time that they brought him back to sanity. This was wrong. She was clearly still asleep, tangled up in a dream of someone far kinder than he was. He made to release her, but the moment his grip around her waist loosened she clutched at his arm, her blunt nails digging into his bicep, holding him in place. She craned her neck to look at him, long enough for him to see that her eyes were open and her lips were parted, before she turned away to hide her face in the pillow as she rubbed herself all over him.

Caught in her spell, he dipped his head forward, his lips grazing the slope of her neck. She arched against his chest, one hand reaching back to tug at his hair. Her nipple peaked through the thin fabric beneath the pad of his thumb and blood roared in his ears. *He* had done that, she had *let* him, and the sun had fully risen now, panels of amber illuminating the curtains, shafts of bright gold streaming into the room and over the bed where he and Talasyn rocked together in this fumbling imitation of sex. But no matter how clumsy it was, no matter how that one lingering rational part of him screamed that he shouldn't be doing this, it was still all so amazing and new and he was *almost there*—

Alaric lifted his hand from his wife's waist and wrapped it

loosely around the back of her neck. Her flushed skin warmed the cool metal of the wedding band on his finger. "Would that you were always *this* obedient," he growled.

Talasyn elbowed him in the stomach. Hard. "Fuck you."

Even though she'd quite literally knocked the breath out of his lungs, he couldn't suppress a grin. He plucked at her breast in retaliation and she yelped, squirming against him in just the right way, just the best way. He buried his nose in her hair, inhaling the scent of mangoes and promise jasmines, his hips snapping against her, bringing him closer to the edge—

"Stop." She moaned it into the pillow, ragged and overwhelmed. "Alaric, we have to stop."

His hands fell away from her immediately. The rest of him was a little slower on the uptake, but eventually he sprang to the edge of the bed, the sudden loss of her bringing with it some semblance of wakefulness.

Talasyn shuddered and her back, still turned to him, twitched with heaving breaths. It almost sounded as though she was crying. Alaric could only stare at her dumbly until the fog of lust clouding his senses abated and cold realization set in.

His proud, strong wife, curled in on herself, looking so small and shattered over the sheets. The air rife with each panicked gasp that she took. Her confusion was almost tangible, cutting him as deeply as despair.

This was *his* fault. He was the one who'd been giving her his rage and the cold shoulder, only to not be able to keep his hands to himself in the end, even though he knew better. Even though the stolen sariman sang within the Citadel. Even as the Kesathese fleet prepared to invade Nenavar.

Talasyn had told him that she thought they could protect each other. She had said it so wide-eyed, in the moonlight. In reality, she should be protecting herself from *him*.

He destroyed everything he touched.

Self-loathing ate at him. He got out of bed and holed up in the bathroom, both to collect himself and to give Talasyn what privacy he could. As he splashed cold water on his face, he contemplated how best to discuss with her what had happened. If they even should.

What would he tell her, though?

This was another mistake. We have to stop making those—possibly.

You took away the loneliness, even for just a little while—no.

This was why I didn't want to share the bed. It's really your *fault for insisting*—bad idea. He didn't have a death wish.

The correct thing to say was still eluding him by the time he returned to their chambers. He would let Talasyn take the lead, he decided, and go from there.

It turned out, however, to be a moot point. Her side of the bed was empty. He couldn't hear her moving around in her dressing room, but its door was open, as though she'd left in a rush.

Alaric didn't think much of it at first, not even when Sevraim was the only one who broke fast with him in the dining room. It was understandable that Talasyn would want some space after what happened. But when he didn't see her all morning and neither she nor her lady-in-waiting showed up for lunch, his restraint cracked.

"Where is your mistress?" he demanded of the blue-and-gold-liveried attendant serving him and Sevraim.

Starting at being addressed so suddenly, the man almost dropped a platter of omelets stuffed with goat meat and scallions. "I . . . don't know, Your Majesty. Her Grace set sail shortly after sunrise."

"She *left*?"

The attendant gulped at the frost that had leached into the

Night Emperor's tone. "Lady Jie might have an inkling where the Lachis'ka went. I shall fetch her at once."

Meanwhile, Sevraim was stuffing his face with freshly caught oysters on the half-shell, studded with flecks of the first shipment of Kesathese peppercorns. To Alaric's great annoyance, he was *still* stuffing his face with them when Jie strolled in fifteen minutes later.

"Emperor Alaric." The lady-in-waiting dipped into a perfunctory curtsy. "The Lachis'ka has departed for the Lightweaver shrine on Belian. She will return in a sennight, in time for the next eclipse."

"And no one thought to inform me?" Alaric gritted out.

Sevraim stopped chewing, staring at him with wide eyes while Jie's lowered to the floor. Not in deference, but petulance.

"I am informing His Majesty now," she muttered.

No one in Kesath would have *dared.* Alaric had to take several deep breaths so that he could respond calmly. "Lady Jie, this castle was ceded to me as the Lachis'ka's dowry, was it not?" This earned him a sullen nod. "It is therefore *my* household, despite being on Nenavarene soil, and it is only appropriate that I be informed of the comings and goings, especially when they pertain to *my* consort. Surely this is not too difficult a request."

To his utter disbelief, the impertinent teenager took a deep breath of her own, as though *she* was the one who found him exasperating and was struggling to control *her* temper.

"I understand, Emperor Alaric," she sang out, with a smile as chipper as it was false. "I shall endeavor to keep you up to date from now on."

Then she flounced out of the room, her pert nose in the air.

Alaric picked up his fork and stabbed an omelet with it. "I long for the Continent."

"*I* don't," said Sevraim. "That was wildly entertaining."

Alaric would have normally admonished Sevraim—or shot him a cutting glare, at the very least—but today his heart wasn't in it. He ate slowly, all the while aware that Sevraim was watching him.

"If it's hard that she left without telling you," the legionnaire said at last, hesitantly, "if it reminds you of—"

"It's not that." The words settled like a lie on Alaric's tongue even though the circumstances *were* different, far more so than anyone else could have ever imagined. No one—not Gaheris, not even Sevraim—knew that Alaric had spoken to his mother the night she fled Kesath. No one knew that Sancia Ossinast had begged him to come with her and he'd refused.

He'd refused and she'd left anyway. And although it wasn't the same, Talasyn's abrupt departure after he'd done something wrong in her eyes made him feel like that boy again, running after someone who would never look back, who would never return.

At dusk a skua flew in through the window of Alaric's study with a message from his stormship at the Nenavarene harbor: Lisu's frigate had made port and he was on his way to Iantas.

Alaric received the commodore in his study, taking a twisted satisfaction in how badly the tropical heat had affected the other man during the shallop journey from Port Samout and the short walk from Iantas's docks to the castle. There were beads of sweat in Lisu's spiked hair and damp patches all over his travel attire, and not even his perpetually urbane expression could disguise his discomfort as he saluted.

"At ease, Commodore," Alaric drawled. "To what do I owe the pleasure?"

"I'm here to escort a Nenavarene trade shipment to Kesath, Your Majesty. In case of pirates, you know. The Regent bid me drop by your lovely home away from home and send his regards."

So you're here to snoop on my father's behalf, Alaric thought with disgust. "Remind me—do we have so little faith in Nenavar's ability to defend her own cargo freighters?"

"It's more that we wish to leave nothing up to chance when it comes to fresh aether hearts for the Night Empire," said Lisu. "And mangoes, of course. Our people simply can't get enough of *those*."

Urduja had sent Alaric her numbers a few days ago. She'd been far more generous with the mangoes than the aether crystals, and he wasn't sure how that made him feel. On the one hand, Kesath needed more crystals to protect itself. On the other, a *lack* of crystals would delay his father's plans for Nenavar.

"I have also come by knowledge," Lisu continued, "of your interest in a certain Sardovian helmsman, Emperor Alaric. A friend of your wife's, no doubt."

Alaric's jaw clenched. Lisu had many informants and it had only been a matter of time. "It was one of the things I promised in exchange for her cooperation—to learn if this rebel was in our prisons. But my men couldn't find anything in our records."

"Because this Khaede escaped before she could be processed," said Lisu. "She and a handful of other Allfold soldiers broke out of their internment camp in the hours following the battle of Lasthaven. They were able to commandeer some coracles, but she was separated from them during the chase, and that was the last her companions saw of her.

"The other escapees eventually made their way to the mountains and found what at the time was the fledgling resistance. Someone who was aware of the story participated in the attack on the Citadel and was captured." Lisu flashed a thin smile. "You see, Your Majesty, when you set sail for Nenavar a fortnight ago, I thought I'd try my hand at interrogation. I already knew that you were looking for someone, and I earnestly wished to help. How fortunate that I managed to acquire this information."

"Thank you for your assistance," Alaric said through gritted teeth. "Is it too much to assume that you will rest content in having provided an invaluable service to the throne?"

"It is my honor, of course," Lisu replied without missing a beat, "but I believe that I would be of even more invaluable service to His Majesty should I be given command of a void ironclad once we have more of those in production."

In other words, once the Night Empire had seized control of the Void Sever. Once Talasyn had been stripped of her powers and the Shadow had fallen on the Nenavar Dominion.

Alaric fought to not let a sudden burst of nausea get the best of him. "Very well," he told Lisu. "The next void ironclad to be manufactured is yours."

The commodore had the nerve to look grateful rather than triumphant. "A wise decision, Your Majesty, I assure you."

"We can hope." Alaric glanced out the window, beyond which the moons had risen and the stars glimmered over the dark Eversea. "Shall I have the servants prepare a room for you?"

Lisu shook his head. "I'll retire to port, Emperor Alaric. I don't wish to trouble your household any further."

Thank the gods for small mercies.

Alaric couldn't dismiss Lisu fast enough. However, once he was alone again in his study, neither could he sit still or focus on work or reading.

Talasyn wouldn't be back for six more days. He could use that time to get his head on straight and figure out next steps, but he also needed to not be *here*, where her absence haunted the hallways. Where he wouldn't be consumed by the feeling of being left.

Alaric set down the stylus that had been hovering aimlessly over a pile of documents for the last several minutes as an idea occurred to him.

He knew where to go. Where to find the strength, peace, and resolve that he had been missing of late.

He needed a Shadow Sever.

CHAPTER SIXTEEN

Amidst the spiraling stone of the Belian ruins, within the jungle's dense green embrace, a man took shape, spun into existence by the Light Sever's golden threads. He had Urduja Silim's jet-black eyes, shrewd and intent beneath the dragon circlet adorning his thick brown hair. He walked into a room woven from aether and memory, giving a curt nod to the woman who was already inside, rocking a gilded cradle.

"The warships sail for the Northwest Continent tomorrow. At sunrise, as you requested," he told her. "Will you really be able to hold off any pursuers?"

"Yes." The woman looked like Talasyn, but she spoke with a confidence that Talasyn could never hope to match. Her Nenavarene was rough, heavily accented. Her eyes flashed gold, and even though this was only a memory, the Light Sever's threads gathered around her. Recognizing her for what she was. "Sunrise is my time. I can contain the Grand Magindam's fleet within Port Samout."

"If you hurt anyone, even accidentally," the man warned, "the dragons might attack."

"You were very clear about the risks when you first approached me." She gazed down at the cradle. "All I ask, Sintan, is that if anything happens to me, you keep my daughter safe."

Prince Sintan's eyes softened. "I'll protect Alunsina with my life. I swear it, my sister." He paused. "Of course, she would be much safer if she were officially Queen Urduja's heir."

"I want her to choose for herself," said Hanan Ivralis, with a stubbornness that this time Talasyn knew all too well.

Talasyn watched as her mother reached into the cradle. She felt a hand pat her own cheek, through the veil of years.

The scene shifted. It was the same room, but war raged outside the windows in flashes of amethyst and plumes of smoke. Hanan lay in bed, much thinner than in the previous memory, her sallow face slick with perspiration.

"Let me hold her," she croaked.

The nursemaid with the clay beads on her brow—Indusa—silently held out a squirming bundle wrapped in embroidered cloths. Hanan took her daughter in her arms and pressed their foreheads together.

"I will always be with you," she whispered fiercely. The same words that Talasyn had once heard in a dream. "We will find each other again."

The Light Sever vanished as quickly as it had flared to life. Talasyn clung to the golden threads as hard as she could, hungry for more of the past, but in the end she was left alone, kneeling in the middle of the empty fountain, tears streaming down her face.

Afternoon found her in the amphitheater, with ribbons of light magic spilling from the tips of her fingers as she stretched out an arm beneath the iron-gray sky.

She'd gotten all her crying out of the way as quickly as she could. Somewhere in the back of her mind, she suspected that it would be nice to wallow, even just once, but that was a luxury better reserved for those who didn't have everyone else's fate in their hands. Now she was focused only on aethermancing again.

The Light Sever had flared last night as well. It had actually been doing so rather frequently in the past month, as though aetherspace itself was restless in the lead-up to the Voidfell's great eruption. Talasyn had communed with it several times before Alaric arrived at Iantas; she'd refined her shielding—if not her focus, apparently—and had even managed to craft the light-woven version of the black whips that he employed in combat so often. Since then she'd moved on to attempting to mirror another Shadowforged technique, but she was turning out to be far less successful at it.

As she stood in the middle of this sunken, ancient sparring ground the day after leaving Iantas in a panic, she was thinking about Gaheris's chimeras, how they had filled the world. She was trying for what felt like the thousandth time to coax a counter to that out of herself.

But, as always, her magic thinned and flickered and was unsteady. It didn't know what she wanted, and she herself was at a loss. A great wave? A towering wall, like the ones Hanan Ivralis had reportedly used to cage the Dominion fleet until its breakaway ships had fled from sight? Anytime she pushed herself and created a surge of light bigger than her body, she lost control of it.

It hardly helped matters that she was training in the very spot where she and Alaric had first kissed. Talasyn had come out to the amphitheater for a change of pace, but this had clearly been a bad idea. Thoughts of her gloomy husband intruded with every other breath that she took. He was the one who'd taught her how to breathe, for meditation and for aethermancing, and thus not even this act was free of him.

But at least he wasn't around this time, and that meant she could avoid doing anything stupid. At least for a few more days.

Talasyn brought her arm down and began ascending the stone steps that led out of the amphitheater. Her plan was to retreat to the courtyard where the Light Sever was located, back beneath the roof of the grandfather trees. Halfway up, however, she stopped in her tracks at the sound of wings.

A messenger eagle landed a couple of steps above her, holding out one leg bearing a roll of parchment as it issued a high-pitched, whistling call.

"Hello to you, too." Talasyn rubbed the sweet spot on Pakwan's head, between its frill of brown-and-white feathers. There was blood on the raptor's beak, the remnants of a grisly meal that it had probably hunted on the way to Talasyn's location, but it leaned into her touch with puppylike affection before she drew her hand back to extricate the rolled-up message.

It was a frantically scribbled note from Jie. Talasyn read the contents in disbelief.

Alaric had sailed his shallop to the Dominion's lone Shadow Sever on Chal earlier that morning, leaving Sevraim and its crew behind. Once there, he'd sent away the Nenavarene moth coracles that had guided him. And now there was a storm brewing to the northwest.

I tried to warn him, Lachis'ka, Jie had written, *but he wouldn't listen to me.*

Inwardly cursing the Night Emperor for being all kinds of a fool, Talasyn shoved the message into her pocket. "*Uwila*," she told Pakwan, the command to fly home.

The eagle chirped in farewell and took wing, but Talasyn was already running to her campsite.

There she packed up her gear, then hurried out of the shrine and down Belian's steep slope. These days she docked her moth coracle on a ledge where the trees had been cleared out by lightning-induced wildfire a few sennights prior. It was closer to the ruins than the traditional landing grid at Rapat's garrison, but she still couldn't get there fast enough, barely taking a breath as she scrambled into the airship's well and buckled the leather harness securing her to the helmsman's seat.

Talasyn fiddled with the aetherwave transceiver, pulling levers and turning dials until she patched through to the communications tower at Iantas. She reeled off her instructions—that she would handle fetching her erstwhile consort, that a rescue team should be sent if they hadn't returned in two days. That was enough time, she figured, for the weather to calm. She didn't want to endanger anybody else.

One of the Nenavarene archipelago's seven main islands, Chal bore the brunt of the storms coming in from the northwest during wet season. The range of limestone cliffs where the Shadow Sever was located directly faced the Eversea, with no mountains to shield it. It *was* the shield, and it was the worst possible place to be when the monsoon unleashed its wrath.

Alaric was an idiot. A soon-to-be *dead* idiot, if Talasyn couldn't get to him in time.

She disengaged from the Iantas frequency before the officer-in-charge could get a word in edgewise. That was the best way to get people to do what she wanted, she'd learned. As she steered her coracle over the treetops, she tried to make contact with the Kesathese shallop's aetherwave as well, although she wasn't particularly surprised when there was no response. That would have been too easy.

Thirty minutes of gliding brought Talasyn within sight of the Eversea and the pillars of black clouds gathering over the water on the horizon. There were no other airships in the sky;

everyone else in the Dominion had hunkered down, bracing for the worst. It was all eerily still, too. No breeze, no birdsong, as though the world was holding its breath.

The coracle's aether hearts whined and whirred, spitting out emerald-green fumes as Talasyn accelerated. She streaked through the air in her opalescent ship, its finned blue-and-gold sails fluttering over jungles and rivers and villages whose roofs were a patchwork of colors and patterns. All the while the pillar of clouds drew closer, becoming thicker and darker and increasingly flecked with lightning.

Talasyn raced the storm, hoping to get to Alaric before it made landfall, but her efforts were futile. It was already drizzling when she crossed the channel between Sedek-We and Chal. She hastily tugged at the running rigs to fold up the sails, but still her coracle was nearly knocked off course by a gust of wind. She sailed over the narrow, sword-shaped strip of green that was Chal and began her descent, which was like diving into silver mist, rain spattering against wooden hull and metalglass sidescuttles and retracted canvas fins. Up ahead the black clouds washed over the shoreline and the world went dark with a howling that she felt reflected in her heart, in her bloodstream, all the way to the tips of her toes.

Rain and wind. Everything was pelting rain and roaring wind, slicing into her skin. But the Nenavarene *alindari* had been built for weather far more vicious than what the Continent's magic could ever achieve, and it plowed through, rolling with the current, slipping into the safer spaces between. Talasyn ignited the vessel's fire lamps to light her way through the fog; she could see only an assortment of vague silhouettes on the beach below, but that was better than nothing. Finally she broke past the low-hanging clouds and it was all spread out before her, white sand and forested cliffs and the Eversea's crashing waves.

She rolled her eyes when she spotted the Kesathese shallop docked several feet away from the rising waterline. At least Alaric had possessed enough sense to secure it to the mooring with ropes, but one would think that it should have occurred to him to wonder why his was the only ship at port.

Honestly, she wasn't much smarter, chasing after him, although there was some small consolation to be found in the good sense *she* had to dock her coracle atop the cliffs and lash it to a sturdy tree trunk.

Already drenched to the bone, her braid tossed this way and that by the biting gale, Talasyn shouldered her pack of supplies and inhaled slowly, the improvements in her aethermancy about to be put to the test once more. She had practiced this at the Belian ruins and along Iantas's granite-shell facade, but never from so great a height. She broke into a run—and leapt right off the edge of the cliff, every churn of the Eversea below promising dark death by water, by momentum.

As she fell, Talasyn first wove the lily-shaped grapnel with its crown of hooks. She hurled it, still attached to her hand by an ever-lengthening chain of light, toward the cliff face. The golden barbs dug in and the coils folded and she was yanked up onto the craggy limestone, where she soon found her footing in a passable imitation of how Alaric had stopped his own plunge when the balcony crumbled under them back at the Citadel. She had studied her memories of that carefully and she had asked the Light Sever to show her how, but a part of her still couldn't believe that it had actually worked. The storm continued to build as she rappelled down the cliff, her magic singing in her hands, in a feat of concentration not helped in the least by how treacherous limestone was in the rain. Every time her knees and elbows and the soles of her boots slid off the wet surface her heart caught in her throat.

Finally she made it all the way down and sank into the

damp and darkening sand of Chal's westernmost shore. The gray heavens growled with thunder and spat out a ceaseless downpour. The waves rolled in like the spines of dragons and loomed up like seesawing towers, agitated by the same bitter wind that bent the beach's coconut palms nearly in half and threatened to blow Talasyn away as she scrambled over the rocks that led to the Shadow Sever's cave.

Bukang-nabi, the Nenavarene called it. The Mouth of Night, where the Shadowgate came seeping in from aetherspace as plumes of steam rising out of cracks in the earth rather than as the eruptions of smoke that shot up into the skies of the Continent.

True to its name, the Mouth's entrance resembled a gaping, jagged maw at the base of the cliff, carved out by the ocean beating against the limestone over a span of thousands of years. The Eversea gurgled into it, forming rapids over its boulders and stalagmites, and Talasyn cursed her husband to hell and back while she navigated the treacherous path inside, trying to cling to cave walls that were far too slippery. Another row of turbulent waves dashed against the rocks, coating her rain-soaked body in salty sea spray, as though adding insult to injury.

Although the interior of the Mouth was shielded from the sky's wrath, conditions there weren't much better. The flood fed the swelling river and Talasyn had to watch her step on the narrow juts of stone serving as its banks. The gale whistled down the tunnel, raking at her spine, and the already meager daylight faded as she ventured deeper.

"Alaric!" Her call echoed around her in the gloom, but it was soon swallowed up by the torrents, by the song of wind on stone. She tried again and again, but there was no response.

This subterranean river was unpredictable, especially during the monsoon. It was the main reason she'd been in such a rush to get to the Mouth. What if he had already drowned? The mere thought set off an ache inside her. As she inched along the water's edge, she couldn't escape from the images that plagued the dark behind her eyes, images of that pale skin turned blue and those black locks tangled up in seaweed, his strong warrior's body unresponsive, bloated, dashed against the rocks, never to exist in the same room as hers again.

Something crept up Talasyn's throat, something that pinched behind the bridge of her nose and felt dangerously like tears. Gods. Crying for her Kesathese husband was a new low. She shook her head to clear the feeling, and that was when the unthinkable happened.

She slipped.

Her left leg gave out from under her and she fell into the freezing-cold river. It reached only up to her chest, but a surge barreled through the cave before she could right herself, and she was swept away.

CHAPTER SEVENTEEN

Saltwater rushed into Talasyn's lungs and stung her eyes. She did not know how to swim. There hadn't been so much as a pond on the Great Steppe. She was helpless in the face of the flood that carried her deeper and deeper into the Mouth, the world a rush of wet and ice and sparks of failing magic as she tried to conjure another grappling hook or anything else that could help her fight against the current.

But her aethermancy was no match for the fear and panic that gripped her, for the swift and violent waters that bore her. She was tumbled along the twists and turns of the cave and eventually down a brief cascade that deposited her into a deep, dark lake, where she kicked and flailed, desperately, to no avail. She was breathing water, she was sinking, she was fading, she was—

—being seized by an arm in a bruising grip and hauled up onto damp land.

Amidst rain-flecked shafts of wan daylight poking through cracks in the limestone ceiling high overhead, Talasyn barely had a moment to register Alaric's irate chiseled features before she doubled over, retching out the briny ocean in her lungs.

The sound of her every cough and heave was magnified within the grotto she'd ended up in. It was an age before she could breathe normally again, and by that point she was all but crumpled on the ground, with Alaric kneeling beside her, still holding on to her arm. Although he was quick to let go as soon as her gaze flickered to his bare hand on her skin.

He was *also* quick to start chastising her.

"This," he said, the flash of silver in his irises a testament to the anger lurking behind his cool, clipped tones, "is the most asinine thing that you have ever done."

"*M-me?*" Talasyn sputtered, sitting up. "You're the one who flew off to the seaside even though Jie told you there was a weather warning! The storms here are *not* like the ones we get on the Continent—the natural ones, anyway—and you could have died—"

"Says the girl I had to fish out of the lake. Unless surviving drowning is one of your many talents?"

Her mouth twisted. Alaric had established a cozy campsite on a rock shelf, but . . . She glanced at the waterline, which was steadily rising as more of the Eversea flowed in. "We might *both* drown, come to think of it."

"Hence, the most asinine thing you've ever done," he repeated with an annoyed impatience that set her teeth on edge.

No—actually, her teeth were chattering. The adrenaline had worn off and a bone-gnawing chill took its place.

Talasyn crossed her arms over her chest in a futile bid for warmth. Every inch of her trembled in her wet clothes, in her flooded shoes. Alaric shuffled behind her and she tried to ask him what he was doing, but she was shaking too hard to speak. The only sound she could make was a strangled little squeak as he threw his arms around her, tugging her against him. Why was he always *doing* that, just grabbing her and settling her however he pleased, and why was she always *letting* him?

Her back was flush to his broad chest and his thighs bracketed hers, and she gradually became aware that her trusty leather pack wasn't separating their bodies. She'd lost it in the river, along with rations and a firestarter and other essential supplies. In that moment, though, it seemed so fleeting a concern. She greedily clung to him, savoring the heat that he emitted despite the unwelcome rush of memories brought on by their close proximity.

Memories of how they'd melted against each other in a position almost exactly like this, in their bed the previous morning.

Memories of how she'd touched herself while imagining the feel of him, all alone in that tower room after watching him spar. How quickly she'd crested then, so unlike those fumbling climbs capped off by small, ultimately unsatisfying releases that she'd been accustomed to those rare times she took matters into her own hands in the years before they met.

As she continued to shiver, his large palms roamed briskly over her wrists, her arms, her abdomen, her sternum, her hips. Rubbing warmth everywhere he could reach. His warmth wasn't anything like the burning that the Lightweave sent through her veins whenever she aethermanced; rather, it was a cozy kind of heat, like applewood smoke from a cheerful hearth in the depths of a Sardovian winter. Talasyn fought against the temptation to close her eyes because that would have made it too real. Because that would have made her savor it. Because the comfort that Alaric could give her was just as terrifying as the pleasure. Just as forbidden.

"You'll catch a fever." He sounded so, *so* grumpy that her traitorous heart gave a twinge. "We need to get you out of these clothes."

They both went still. His unfortunate choice of words hung in the air like the storm clouds in the world aboveground, and Talasyn was suffused with an entirely different kind of heat—

she could have burnt an egg on her face with it and that would have been no great shock.

Alaric gently released her and stood up, then walked over to where the rock shelf met the grotto wall. He rooted around in his pack until he found a clean black tunic, which he tossed in her general direction. Talasyn caught the garment and saw that he was very markedly not moving even an inch, but facing away from her as though it was the most important thing he would ever do in this life.

Someone made of sterner stuff would have jumped back into the lake rather than disrobe with Alaric Ossinast only a few feet away. However, Talasyn was far too miserable in her sopping-wet attire and she couldn't change out of it fast enough.

The hem of his tunic ended a scant inch above her knees. She was swimming in it, but the fabric was luxuriously soft and above all *dry*. She rolled the sleeves up to her elbows—because the wide, silver-embroidered cuffs dangled well past her hands otherwise—and she pulled off her boots, shaking the water out of them. Then she worked on her hair, wringing the bedraggled braid between her fingers.

"You can turn around now," she said.

Alaric was slow to do so, and even then he didn't quite look directly at her. The lighting was abysmal, but Talasyn could almost swear that his sharp cheeks and the tips of his ears had darkened a shade, as though flushed.

Yet he was his usual infuriating self when he asked, "So, what exactly is the plan, oh great rescuer?"

"We could start with not being assholes, for one," she hissed, "but I suspect that such restraint is far beyond your capabilities."

He shrugged. "I do not believe it attainable for you, either."

She flicked her braid at him, droplets of water streaking through the air like the most ineffectual throwing knives in the history of Lir. He smirked as he stepped aside to avoid them.

"Well, what was *your* plan before I arrived?" she groused.

"Wait it out." He gestured to the lake. "This was all dry land and pathways to other caverns earlier this morning. I was communing with the Shadow Sever when the water rushed in. It should recede when the tide ebbs in a few hours."

Talasyn shook her head. "This is a storm surge, not high tide. It can last days. And there's no guarantee that the water won't continue to rise." When he didn't say anything, she reiterated, annoyed, "Jie *tried* to tell you that it was dangerous, but you didn't listen."

"Neither did you, and now you're here with me."

While Talasyn was quietly seething at that retort, Alaric sat down, casting a skeptical gaze around their surroundings. "No small wonder the ancient Shadowforged left Nenavar, what with their lone nexus point flooding every time the weather acts up."

"That and the sarimans." She sat as far away from him as the rock shelf would allow. His features hardened at the mention of the birds, which she chalked up to the same general unease at the very concept of them that she, too, felt on occasion.

He changed the subject, looking up at the grotto ceiling and its cracks of daylight, its overhang of stalactites. "We can aethermance, smash through there, if the flood worsens. Or if we run out of food and water."

"Do you *have* enough food and water? I lost my pack." Would he even deign to share? She fought down the panic, a leftover from her childhood. Surely he wouldn't let her starve, he needed her to face the Voidfell and to maintain Kesath's foothold in Nenavar. But what if . . .

Talasyn's stomach rumbled, an echo of her distress. Alaric clapped a hand over his mouth, a soft chuckle escaping him, and there was an undercurrent of regret to her mortification, regret because she had yet to see what he looked like when he was smiling and she was so unabashedly curious.

He nudged his pack toward her. "Help yourself."

She inspected the food squirreled away in straw baskets, cushioned by banana leaves. Steamed rice cakes, slabs of creamy white sun buffalo cheese, smoked venison, and whole salted duck eggs, their shells dyed a bright magenta hue so that kitchens all over Nenavar could distinguish them from fresh ones that hadn't spent sennights curing in clay and charcoal paste. Talasyn estimated that it would all last three days between her and Alaric, rivaling what she'd brought to Belian.

"You really were set on staying here a while," she remarked.

"Communing with the Shadow Sever seemed a much better use of my time than sitting around waiting for you to come back."

There was a note of accusation in his voice despite his cool facade. Unwilling to explain, Talasyn busied herself with methodically peeling a salted egg, the beetroot dye staining her fingers.

The longer she said nothing, the more her silence appeared to irk her husband. He leaned back, crossing his arms. "You always were the type to run," he drawled. "From me on the Highlands ice. Back to your quarters whenever we argued at the Roof of Heaven. In hindsight, I've no idea why I assumed we could discuss yesterday's situation like adults."

"There is nothing to discuss!" Talasyn snapped. "We were both half-asleep, and that's *all*. We can just forget it."

"Like all those other times?"

"*Yes.*"

"I fail to understand why you couldn't have told me that to my face—"

"I'm telling you now, you dolt—"

"—instead of sailing off to the other end of the country after the fact, like a coward—"

"Why, did I hurt His Majesty's feelings?"

Talasyn had spat it out with the thoughtlessness of reflex. Just pure venomous retaliation, just another volley in the never-ending war that they had been waging solely against each other since the night they met.

But the way Alaric's shoulders went tense, as though she'd struck him, made her stomach drop.

"*Were* your feelings really—" she started to ask, but he cut her off.

"It's male pride," he said coolly. "It's not good for our egos when the lady flees after the tryst."

Talasyn narrowed her eyes. An unpeeled portion of eggshell cracked in her fist. *And just how many ladies have lingered in your bed?* she nearly asked, before stopping herself in the nick of time. She shouldn't care at all.

"Your ego could stand to be whittled down a bit," she huffed, "so as far as I'm concerned, I've done humankind a service."

"As you say." He was uncaring, unaffected, as he casually leaned over to retrieve a salted egg from the pack.

She hated herself for wanting that encounter to have meant more to him, even though it was for the best that it didn't. She hated the ugly thing that clawed at her chest as she thought about the women before her. His past shouldn't matter; *he* should hardly even matter, outside of the role he would play in her endgame.

And yet Talasyn kept circling back to that night in his chambers, how he'd been so broken, how he'd asked her to be kind. How sweetly he'd kissed her.

But he didn't even *remember* the kiss—and even if he did, it would still be of no consequence, like all else they'd done together.

It was just physical attraction. They were both just lonely.

After their meal, he offered her one of the four waterskins that he'd lugged from Iantas. She took a hearty swig, then set it under one of the leaks in the limestone ceiling to be replenished by the rain.

Then there was nothing left to do but wait.

The rock shelf where Alaric and Talasyn were encamped was the only spot of somewhat dry land left in the whole grotto. He should have been grateful for it, but he spent the next few hours cursing its very existence.

It was far too small. Only a little bigger than the bed at Iantas, it didn't provide him with enough room to get away from her.

Come to think of it, a whole island's worth of space wouldn't have been enough. Because she was wearing his tunic.

He'd already known that the sight wouldn't do him any favors, which was why he'd initially avoided letting his gaze linger on her. She had looked rumpled and adorable at first glance, and then, as time passed, he started noticing the finer details in the grotto's dim light—how the sleeve slipped off her shoulder when she moved a certain way, revealing her graceful collarbone, and how the hem rode up her shapely thighs, exposing more and more of those long legs that would one day be his undoing.

Now she was more dangerous than adorable, and he didn't know how much more he could take, torn between shaking her for putting herself in danger with some harebrained notion of rescuing him and kissing her senseless for . . . for being *her*. For being his exasperating wife who looked so good in his clothes.

The same wife that his father was expecting him to betray after the Moonless Dark.

"I have something to tell you," he announced. Better now

before they forgot yet again what they were supposed to be to each other.

She turned to him, giving him her full attention. It would have been easier to avert his gaze as he relayed the news about Khaede that Lisu had brought him, but that was the coward's way out. He was the Night Emperor and this was on his hands. Difficult choices were made in wartime, and he was no rightful ruler if he didn't own every single one.

Alaric forced himself to maintain eye contact, to watch as Talasyn's expression shifted to shock and then to a slow-simmering anger. He watched her take a slow inhale, the Lightweave swirling in her irises in the same way that it must be moving beneath her skin, searching for a target.

He prepared to defend himself from her magic. He prepared for her to shout at him.

Instead, she burst into tears.

There was nothing gradual or delicate about it. Talasyn approached crying the way she did everything else—her whole heart in it, never halfway. She tucked her knees to her chest, sobs wracking her slim frame, and before Alaric was even fully aware of his actions he was beside her, putting an arm around her shoulders.

Compassion will be your downfall, whispered his father's voice in his head.

She raised her head over her folded arms. Her wet freckles shone in the subterranean light. She looked so vulnerable that self-loathing roiled through him, sudden and acrid and harsh. In that moment he was starkly reminded of how young she was. Too young to have lost a war, too young to bear the fate of an entire civilization, too young to be burdened with his broken pieces.

Unable to stop himself, he lifted a hand to her jaw and brushed away the tears dripping from the curve of it like rain.

He wasn't wearing his gauntlets and he felt it all so keenly—the heat of her tears, the silkiness of her skin, the fragile structure of the bones beneath.

Suddenly her fingers dug into his wrist, and it hit him that she was crying not from sorrow but from pure, crushing relief.

"Khaede's alive," she croaked. "She's—there was no better helmsman during the war. If she found a coracle, then she outflew your men and she's alive. She and her baby are alive."

Alaric couldn't bear to tell her that the odds of that were minimal. He also didn't know how he would feel if she were right. That would make Khaede one of the many enemies of the state still at large.

His conflict must have been blatant, or perhaps Talasyn could read him far too well these days. She clutched at his sleeves, but then, just as he thought she was going to pull him closer, she pushed him away.

"Don't act like you care," she bit out, still crying. "How dare you hold me while you think about how inconvenient it is that my friend survived—"

"Of course I care," he snapped. "I bargained away command of one of the next generation of invincible warships in exchange for that information, so there is *clearly* some part of me that cares, Talasyn—"

She blew her nose on the sleeve of the borrowed tunic, cutting him off. "If she ever turns up," she said sullenly, "what I want still stands. She and her child will stay here in Nenavar, under my protection."

"That was already a given. But I'm glad that you've been so comfortable making demands of me as of late."

Talasyn hiccupped. "Can I demand that you shut your mouth?"

Alaric frowned at her. "Only if you stop crying."

*

She didn't listen to him. She rarely had before, and she wasn't about to start making a habit of it now.

Talasyn wept her heart out over the rippling black lake, the salt of her tears mingling with the raindrops that trickled in from the limestone ceiling. At some point after the war, she'd locked Khaede up in a corner room in her mind, peeking in only occasionally; a defense mechanism, so she could keep her focus, so she wouldn't go mad with going over all the worst-case scenarios.

Now the door had been blown wide open, though, and Talasyn let it all out. All the guilt and the terror and the hope. Once she started crying, she couldn't seem to stop. This was the wallowing. This was the breaking point she'd been so afraid to hit.

If Alaric had tried to reach for her again, she would have clawed his eyes out. At least he knew her well enough not to even try—and wasn't that a sad thing? Wasn't that another cause for crying, that no one in this new life understood her as much as her sworn enemy did? He was a wraith at the edges of her blurry vision, standing around awkwardly while she soaked his borrowed tunic in tears and snot. And finally, *finally*, she was collapsing against the wall of the rock shelf, spent and strangely at peace.

He was at her side in an instant, raising a waterskin to her parched lips. She took grudging sips from it, then closed her aching eyes. In the darkness behind them, she felt Alaric run his knuckles along the inside of her wrist as he lowered the waterskin.

It was a diffident offering of comfort. Perhaps it was even entirely accidental. But her heart held on to it all the same.

I'm exhausted. The thought cut her in all its simplicity. She kept her eyes shut as his touch lingered, then drifted away. Briefly, she wondered what it would be like to live in a world where she was allowed to take his hand.

CHAPTER EIGHTEEN

Once she had gotten her emotions under control and they'd both retreated to their respective ends of the rock shelf, there wasn't a whole lot to do in the flooded grotto. Alaric kept an eye on the waterline and dwelled on his grim thoughts. He occasionally caught Talasyn toying with the wedding band on her ring finger. Perhaps out of boredom, yes, but also perhaps wishing to be free of it. He couldn't blame her. She wouldn't be in this situation if not for him, if he hadn't ignored Jie's warnings in his eagerness to get away from a castle that had felt so empty.

The already wan daylight weakened even further when more rain poured into the cracks overhead, accompanied by the growls of thunder muted through stone. The lake sloshed worryingly within its banks, the cascade at the grotto entrance picking up speed. Alaric squinted at the ceiling, their only means of escape.

"If I bring it down," he said, "would you be able to shield us both from the debris?"

"Yes," Talasyn replied without an ounce of hesitation. "I suppose you'll use the same technique as Gaheris when he destroyed the rebel stormship."

"I've never actually tried," Alaric admitted. "If the lake overflows, then we'll see if I'm my father's son."

"You're not, though."

She said it so quietly beneath the faint susurrus of the gale whistling through the world above. When he turned his head to stare at her, she bit her lip, as though regretting her words, but she soon plowed ahead with the stubbornness that he knew so well by now.

"You're nothing like him. You would never hurt your own child the way he hurts you."

How deep such a simple statement cut. A blade through the heart. With the pain came the anger, and he opened his mouth to tell her off, but something about the way she was huddled against the wall, so small in his tunic, her brown eyes faintly luminous in their earnestness, even as she seemed to steel herself . . . but for what?

Alaric momentarily stopped breathing.

Talasyn *expected* him to retaliate. Every time she brought up the subject of his father, he only ever responded with rage and threats. The way she watched him carried echoes of the way his mother had watched Gaheris, waiting for the inevitable explosion.

I want to be better than the past, Alaric thought. *In this, and in so many other ways.*

He quirked a brow. "My own child?" he repeated dryly. "That's in our cards then, Lachis'ka?"

This had the desired effect of reducing Talasyn to indignant sputters. Alaric blithely continued: "Come to think of it, our respective courts *would* appreciate some heirs. Shall we while away the hours picking out names?"

She stood up, her face pinched like she'd swallowed a whole calam-lime, no longer expecting to bear the brunt of his darkness. Her apprehension forgotten.

"On second thought," he said, relieved, "I shall take charge of the names. No son of mine will be called 'Watermelon Ossinast.'"

"That's—that's *not* what I meant, and you know it!" she snarled.

He cocked his head. "Were you planning on 'Guava'?"

"Argh!"

She tackled him. The hotheaded little Lightweaver actually *tackled* him. Alaric let out a grunt as his back collided with the damp, hard ground. By contrast, he held a warm, soft armful, one that was proclaiming him the worst sort of scoundrel in a breathless screech.

Perplexed by the uncharacteristically refined insult, he gave Talasyn's braid a light tug. She lifted her face from his chest and peered down at him, the dying light barely strong enough to reveal that her freckled cheeks were dark with embarrassment.

"Have you forgotten your Continental expletives?" he inquired.

"Oh, shut up." Her blush deepened. "*You* try living in a foreign country with a different language for nearly a year. I already called you an asshole earlier and I couldn't think of anything else—"

She broke off as it clearly occurred to her, at the same time that it did him, that there wasn't an inch of space between them from the neck down. Her legs were locked around his hips, his chest rose and fell underneath hers. His hand curled around her bare thigh, fingers grazing the edge of the tunic—the tunic that he never should have lent her, because she was sprawled on top of him and she was wearing his clothes, and her lips were all that he could look at, and she was all that he could feel.

"You have me on my back." Alaric was shocked by the hoarseness in his own voice. "Now what?"

"I don't know," Talasyn mumbled. Her gaze was also focused on his mouth. Her heart was beating a wild, violent rhythm in tandem with his. "I didn't think that far ahead."

"Pity." His fingers ventured higher up her thigh, caressing the silky flesh. She swallowed, her hand sliding down his abdomen in silent invitation.

A fresh torrent of water rushed into the grotto. The lake rippled and churned, and Alaric saw the wave form at the periphery of his vision. He clamped his arms around Talasyn, intending to roll to safety, but it was too late—the wave broke over the rock ledge. Drenching them both in the cold and the wet and the salt.

They sprang away from each other—rather, Talasyn thought sourly, like the tussling alley cats that the residents of Hornbill's Head would dump buckets on from their windows. They pressed themselves against the grotto wall, warily watching the waterline. It stirred precariously for a few alarming beats but then went calm, having risen by only a couple of inches. The cascade at the mouth of the grotto ceased.

The chill set in again, now that she was drenched anew.

Talasyn attempted to make a fire.

Alaric had brought along some kindling and flint. Now Talasyn piled the kindling atop discarded banana leaves, to insulate it from the soaked ground, and struck the flint shards against each other with gusto. But with the leaky ceiling and the lapping ocean, it was too damp in the cavern. Whatever sparks were produced soon petered out, and before long the kindling was soaked, too.

Still, she persisted, because it was a suitable enough distraction from Alaric. He'd retreated to the opposite end of their campsite, but as far as Talasyn was concerned, no distance would be too great. Not after that near-miss, that near-kiss.

About half an hour passed before he called out, "Lachis'ka."

She didn't look up from her task. If anything, she bashed the stones together even harder.

"It's not going to happen." Alaric's tone was stern. "You'll only end up hurting yourself."

And maybe that was true, maybe her pruned fingers *were* starting to ache, but there was something freeing about such a mindless task. She could channel all her frustrations into brute force. She could ask her stinging skin and each failed spark of resounding stone why she couldn't control her reactions to her husband, why her will could not seem to surmount her craving for his touch. Why he made it so easy for her to throw everything else away.

The answer is simple, really, surfaced from the mire of her racing thoughts, like a rotting carcass dredged from the depths. *The rebels were right about me. I'm a traitor.* Once Sardovia claimed victory, she would probably be executed unless she hid behind her grandmother's skirts.

Talasyn finally gave up on the fire, her hands scraped almost raw. She and Alaric sank into sullen silence, avoiding each other as best as they could in the narrow space.

When night fell, the grotto was plunged into total darkness, all seven of Lir's moons unable to penetrate the thick clouds. The temperature dropped even further. Talasyn's nose and the tips of her fingers felt as though they were made of ice.

She heard Alaric rooting around among his supplies, then the thud of something metallic on the rock shelf and the click of a lever. The grotto was illuminated in the warm, reddish glow of the Firewarren, emanating from a bronze lantern. The aether heart contained within its glass burned like a lone ember.

"You can see in the dark," Talasyn said.

Or tried to say, anyway. She stammered out each word, her

teeth rattling as she shook from the cold that she'd been enduring all this time.

"To an extent. It improves with more and more exposure to the Shadowgate's nexus points." Alaric laid out his bedroll. "We both need to warm up, so come here."

His intent was obvious. Her response was immediate. "N-n-no. I'm f-f-ine."

He pursed his lips. "*I* need to warm up, then." When she didn't say anything—when she continued staring mulishly at him while she shivered—he added, "Surely you won't let me freeze to death before we can stop the Voidfell."

It was a sham, but Talasyn was suffering too much to inspect his reasoning more closely. She went over to where he now lay on his side, holding the blanket open for her. She crawled under it, stretching out over the small bedroll, facing away from him. His arm draped across her midriff. They were in too much like the disastrous, compromising position they'd woken up in yesterday, but she was hungry for the warmth. She scooted back against him, soaking up the heat that emanated from his body, with the blanket drawn over her nose.

"Go to sleep," he ordered. "I'll take first watch."

"Wake me up in four hours so I can take your place."

"Six. I'm not tired."

"Yes, you clearly have enough energy to argue."

He squeezed her hip in warning. She made a face that he couldn't see, then burrowed deeper into the shelter of him. She watched the lantern cast flickering patterns on the grotto walls as she began to drift off.

And in that split-second before oblivion, the crystal imbued with the light of the Firewarren became a red sun, and the limestone surroundings morphed into a brilliant sky, and the Eversea was gliding below her again, just as it had in that vision from a month ago. This time scaled coils pulsed with breath, revolving over the blue waters, and that gnarled hand was reaching for the heavens as something roared like thunder—

"What's wrong?" Alaric asked.

Talasyn realized that she'd gone stiff in his loose embrace. It was difficult to come back from the vision, from the images of air and sky and her soul racing toward some nebulous precipice, but eventually she scaled that cliff and she was in the real world again, the firelight chiseling at the sinews of Alaric's forearm as he held her.

"Do you ever—see things?" She swallowed. "When you're not communing with the Shadow Sever, I mean."

"No," he replied. "What kind of things do you see?"

"Memories. I assumed for a long time that they were solely mine, that it was my magic connecting me to my past, but lately . . ." She told him about the rushing ocean, the wizened hand, the snowy mountain ridge.

Alaric was quiet for a while. Talasyn could practically hear the gears whirring in his head.

"I've never heard of anything like that among the Shadowforged," he finally said. "Visions might be a Lightweaver trait. There's no way of knowing."

Because your country killed them all.

Now they both went tense, as though the thought striking out from the darkness had assailed him, too.

No matter where they found themselves, the war was always waiting at every corner, dragging them back down. But perhaps these constant, bitter reminders were what Talasyn needed. Even as she lay here in Alaric's arms, sharing in his warmth.

She closed her eyes and let herself be carried off to an uneasy slumber by the beating of his heart and the distant roar of the storm.

CHAPTER NINETEEN

Talasyn would never admit it to Alaric in a million years—not even if they lived long enough for all lands to sink beneath the Eversea—but she dozed off during her shift. One minute she was staring at the lake, and then the next she was jolted awake by a droplet of water that had most likely collected along the tip of a stalactite before splattering on her cheek.

Panic came first, a bright flare. Her limbs seized and she half expected to be neck-deep in the flood, but instead she opened her eyes to morning light and the absence of the lake.

She cautiously peeked over the edge of the rock shelf. The walls sloped down into a pit about ten feet deep; there was still water at the very bottom, but the rest had drained through the other tunnels that ringed the pit and flowed back out to sea with the retreat of the storm surge, on the inhale of low tide.

The lantern had burned all night. Its aether core was flickering, the magic close to spent. Talasyn turned to Alaric, who was fast asleep, half of his face hidden in the bedroll. A gentle shake to his shoulder was not enough to rouse him. He *had* been tired, despite last night's proclamation. Stubborn man.

Granted, his profile looked more like that of a boy in this moment. His mouth was relaxed, rather than set in a perennial frown. A shock of black hair fell across his pale cheek, and her fingers twitched from how badly they yearned to brush it back.

I'm glad you're alive.

The thought nudged at her heart so quietly, like a little thief hopping some garden fence. She was thankful that the storm hadn't claimed him, thankful that the ocean hadn't taken its due. She didn't know what she would have done if . . .

He cracked one eye open.

Before Talasyn could back away, before she could come up with a plausible explanation for why she'd been staring at him all mooncalfed, Alaric smiled.

It was nothing more than a drowsy lifting of the corner of his mouth, offering only the briefest glimpse of a slightly crooked incisor.

It was *devastating.*

Talasyn was rooted to the spot. The sight of Alaric's lazy grin went through her like thunder. It was a lesson in being careful what she wished for. She had been curious to see that smile, hadn't she? And now her brain had stalled and her stomach was doing somersaults.

"Morning," he murmured, his voice raspy from sleep. He lifted one hand toward her face, but it froze halfway, the bliss in his expression replaced by something not dissimilar to horror.

She was slower to recoil. And that, too, was its own kind of defeat.

"Had a pleasant dream, did you?" Talasyn opted for flippancy as she began packing up their campsite. It had to have been very good indeed for him to smile like that.

"My dreams are none of your concern."

And who exactly had starred in them, eliciting such groggy tenderness from the fearsome Night Emperor? Who had he mistaken her for when he woke? Who had he wished her to be?

Because there was no possible way he'd been thinking of her when he smiled like that. She wasn't that person to him.

Talasyn kicked a piece of eggshell into the pit. Alaric had sworn to her, on Belian, that he would be faithful despite the solely practical nature of their marriage, but that hardly meant that his affections didn't lie elsewhere, even if he never acted on them. One of these days he was going to regret his vow. If he didn't already.

She shouldn't care. She shouldn't. But she couldn't figure out how not to.

She made him turn around while she swapped his tunic for yesterday's clothes. They were damp and somewhat stiff from all the salt, but they would do. She averted her gaze as he changed into a fresh black undershirt and kept it averted because the defined muscles of his bare arms and the way the fabric clung to his chest drove her to distraction.

"We ought to leave while the way's clear," Talasyn said, after she'd tossed Alaric's tunic into the leather pack that he was now slinging over his shoulders. "No telling if the storm will pick up again."

The Shadowgate whizzed past her in the form of a grappling hook, sinking into the wall by the grotto entrance. Alaric held out his free hand expectantly, only to blink as Talasyn forged her own radiant version.

"I had a good instructor," she couldn't resist teasing.

And it *wasn't* that she was holding out for some compliment on her prowess, but it would have been nice to hear. However, he just grunted, and the proffered hand swept out in a curt "after you" gesture.

She hastened to leap off the rock shelf and swing over the pit to the grotto entrance so that he wouldn't see how puzzled and put-off she was by his behavior. He had been free enough with his praise when she aethermanced that first solid shield . . .

Without the flood currents to carry her through the Mouth, Talasyn found the trek arduous, a combination of scrambling over rockfalls, crouching when the limestone ceiling hung low to the floor, and shimmying up narrow vertical shafts. Through it all, Alaric was a dour presence behind her, always there to give her a boost whenever she needed it but otherwise as stiffly silent as the grave.

The storm surge had left the cave system smelling like salt and fish. Tendrils of seaweed clung to Talasyn as she walked. Higher up, closer to the exit, there were shallow, overflowing pools where the ocean had not completely receded. They eventually led to the river trickling in from the cave entrance, which was now a peaceful, almost somnolent thing ringed in daylight.

The light didn't hurt Talasyn's eyes as much as she'd thought it would after spending so much time in the darkness of the Mouth. On the contrary, she had the sensation of soaking it up, as though she were a plant in the early morning. Her visits to the Light Sever had bestowed on her a higher tolerance of sun, in the same way that Alaric could navigate without it.

It made her think, with sadness, of Ideth Vela. All of the Continent's Shadow Severs were located on the Kesathese half, and the Sardovian Amirante had never been able to refine her shadow magic to the point of gaining that ability. An aethermancer was nothing without their nexus point.

Alaric and Talasyn walked along the river and out of the Mouth of Night. It had stopped raining and the wind was less bitter, although the heavens remained relentlessly iron-gray.

The Kesathese shallop, predictably, had been tossed onto its side when the storm surge flooded the beach and the gale tore through, and a mooring rope had come loose. The vessel was a limp, pathetic sight on the white sand, against a backdrop of uprooted coconut palms.

It was too heavy for two people to upturn. They would break their backs even trying. And Talasyn's moth coracle—hopefully still safe where she'd docked it atop the cliff—couldn't accommodate both of them in its well.

"I'll contact Lady Bairung for assistance," said Talasyn. Chal was House Matono's domain, and Bairung would be all too eager to ensure that the Night Emperor and the Lachis'ka were indebted to her—as well as to have another tidbit of juicy gossip to share with the other noblewomen.

At Alaric's nod, Talasyn hoisted herself up the shallop's now-horizontal mast, using it as leverage to clamber up railings flipped sideways until she reached the aetherwave transceiver on the quarterdeck.

"You're going to fall," Alaric called out, sounding markedly unhappy. He dropped his pack and readied to catch her.

"Bet?" From where she dangled on one arm, Talasyn reached out to turn a knob on the transceiver. "I used to climb all the time, this is hardly—"

The transceiver *sparked.*

Perhaps waterlogged, perhaps jostled within their nest of circuits or damaged in the crash, the Tempestroad-infused aether hearts within the device emitted a miniature lightning storm that flowed out through the hinges. A sharp shock shooting up Talasyn's right wrist jolted her, and suddenly, just like that, she was plummeting to the ground, the world a rush of sand and ocean.

Alaric seized her out of the air and pulled her to his chest, with one arm wrapped around her torso and the other tucked under her knees. It was as though the lightning had lingered in her system, spun out into threads of static. She felt small and safe in his grasp.

"Thanks," she said, breathless.

Alaric swallowed.

Then he *scowled*, hastily deposited her onto her feet on the sand, and stepped away.

"The transceiver's broken." Talasyn was stating the obvious, but she was rattled. He'd barely said a word to her after waking up. "We can use the one on my ship, but it's all the way up there." She gestured to the clifftop.

"Don't let me keep you." His gaze swiveled to the ocean, where it stayed. "After you make contact, you may go ahead. Back to Belian, or Iantas, or wherever you please. I'll wait for help to arrive."

"I *am* the help that arrived," Talasyn wryly pointed out. "Besides, don't you want company?"

"I don't need it," he said tersely, almost snapping at her. "And you have better things to do."

"I can't just *leave* you here—"

"You have managed to before. I've no doubt that you will again with little trouble."

Regret spasmed across his features the moment the words left his mouth. His hands clenched into fists.

I've missed something, she thought. *Something important.*

She stepped into his field of vision. He could have just continued looking over the top of her head, but he didn't. His gray eyes flickered to her face, as though he was surprised that she'd come near.

"Alaric," Talasyn said cautiously, "what's wrong? You've been in a mood all morning." He made no response. She brightened at a possible solution. "We haven't had breakfast yet, we should—"

"I'm not hungry."

Talasyn was fast coming to the unfortunate conclusion that she couldn't *stand* it when Alaric was mad and she had no idea what she could have done to goad him. At a loss, she recalled Niamha's lesson on how to make a man melt. She was hardly dressed for the occasion in her salt-encrusted garments, with her bedraggled hair and the cave grime sticking to her skin, but the Nenavarene Lachis'ka was still the Lachis'ka no matter what she looked like. She could do this. She could harness her people's legendary charm and soften her husband's temper.

"Maybe you'll be less cranky once you've had something to eat," Talasyn suggested. Remembering what Niamha had taught her, she allowed a vague smile to soften the corners of her lips as she peered up at Alaric through her lashes.

The stare that he leveled at her was one of abject confusion. "What's wrong with your face? Are you in pain?"

She had experienced her fair share of embarrassing gaffes where he was concerned, but this was by far the absolute *worst* of the lot. This went beyond the hot flush of humiliation and beyond the paralyzing stab of regret and all the way out the other side into the desire to immediately become one with the spirit world.

It was also the end of her patience. Not that she'd had a lot to begin with.

"Never mind!" Talasyn snapped. "You're impossible!"

Alaric's brow creased. "What—"

"You don't—you don't react appropriately to anything!" Her irate tone mingled with the beating of the waves. "I bandage your wounds and you kiss me, then fall asleep when I kiss you back and you forget it ever happened. I write you a letter and you have your aide reply. I go to rescue you and you call me asinine"—she was jabbing an accusing finger at him as she listed his transgressions—"and you get annoyed because we didn't discuss the time we humped each other while half-asleep, but when we finally *do* start discussing it, you talk about *other* women. I wake you up and you smile because you're dreaming I'm someone else, I show you how you've really been helping my aethermancy improve and you grunt, I thank you for catching me and you practically *drop* me, I offer a way out of our predicament and you tell me to *leave*, I invite you to eat and you get snippy, I flirt with you and you ask me *what's wrong with my face—*" She threw up her hands. "I've had it! Stay here and rot for all I care!"

Shaking, Talasyn spun on her heel and stomped away along the waterline, kicking up spray and wet sand. The wind picked up again, dragging brisk fingers over her form as a wash of dark clouds spread from the horizon. The surface of the Eversea was speckled with a million goosebumps as the clouds headed inexorably toward the coast.

Talasyn glanced over her shoulder with the intention of yelling at Alaric to get his fool head to shelter before it poured, but then she stopped walking and turned—he was running to her. The shifting sands made his frantic pace difficult, but he charged through with bullheaded determination and reached her just as it began to drizzle.

"*Now* what?" Talasyn grumped.

Alaric worked a muscle in his sharp jaw. "First of all," he said through gritted teeth, "I don't know *how* to react to you. You are infuriating and self-righteous and you get under my skin. Secondly, there have never been any other women—there was never *anyone* before you—and much to my dismay you have provoked me so much that you've wormed your way into my dreams. You are the *only* one who plagues them. And one last thing"—his voice lowered into a growl—"the next time I kiss you, I want to *remember* it."

Raindrops dotted his cheek as he bent down. Lightning streaked the sky as he pulled her to him. The Eversea's dark waves slammed against the shore as he crushed his lips to hers.

CHAPTER TWENTY

Very few aspects of Talasyn's life had ever been as lovely as this moment, Alaric's bear hug of an embrace keeping out the worst of the wind, his mouth so warm slanted over hers, the surf and her heartbeat pounding in her ears. At some point during the last few seconds, she'd looped her arms around his neck, clinging to him else the world spin away from underneath the soles of her worn boots. She deepened the kiss and he rumbled a sound of approval in the back of his throat, his fingers tracing the spur of her hip.

This kiss felt different from before. There was a lick of anger in the way they moved, yes, but there was also something that Alaric was trying to tell her with his lips and his tongue and his hands—something that her own body echoed back to him.

I need you.

Let's forget everything else for now.

Talasyn was certain that they would have stayed like that forever had the rain not started pouring down in earnest. A loud clap of thunder heralded the deluge that cascaded from the sky in heavy sheets, and she untangled herself from her husband with a sound strangled somewhere between a shriek and a laugh, with water dripping into her eyes and the spray from the turbulent waves pounding into her side. She glimpsed a trace of genuine amusement on Alaric's face before they broke into a run—back to his lopsided airship, where they shielded themselves from the downpour under the overhanging portside that now served as a roof.

He wasn't done with her. With a gleam in his dark eyes, he mouthed at the slope of her neck and her knees threatened to collapse as her toes curled. She leaned back against the shallop's battered wooden interior, running her fingers through his hair, the blood in her veins wild like thunder, caught up in the giddy delight of it all.

"You should never flirt again," he said. "It might be the end of me."

She'd have been far more embarrassed if his tone weren't so unsteady, if he weren't falling upon her like a man starved. "I don't know, *something* tells me it was a success."

He nibbled at her throat. "I wasn't being sarcastic."

Talasyn pulled at Alaric's hair and claimed his mouth with hers. As sheets of rain poured down on the deserted beach, his hands greedily explored her figure while she practiced this kissing thing with a concentrated enthusiasm that she usually reserved for learning new aethermancy techniques. She impatiently worked through the clumsy clacking together of their teeth and the inopportune gulps of much-needed air, forging ahead with a crazed determination that he matched until they rediscovered the rhythm from their wedding night. His large fingers ran over her spine, stroked her thighs, cupped her bottom—and eventually they latched onto the hem of her tunic.

And tugged it upward.

She let him, in service to some primal instinct that clamored for *closer, more.* The fabric bunched between her collarbones and her chest, and his fingers crept up her exposed ribs, leaving a trail of goosebumps in their wake, stilling once they reached the bottom edge of her breastband.

"Take this off, Lachis'ka," he whispered.

Talasyn should have bristled at being ordered around by the likes of him.

She shivered instead.

Alaric watched with hawklike eyes as Talasyn unwound the band that covered her chest. Even though the plain, practical undergarment was a far cry from seductive, seeing her take it off made every drop of blood in his veins rush south. He fought to maintain what little composure he had left, but when the band fell to the planks at her feet and—*gods, at last*—he had an unobstructed view of her chest, it was all he could do to not come in his trousers right then and there.

The woman he had reluctantly married was in possession of the loveliest breasts on Lir. Granted, his opinion was hardly that of an expert, but he would gut anyone who wished to posit the contrary. They were small and shapely and, to his never-ending delight, dusted with freckles here and there. He could have studied them for hours, and perhaps he would have had Talasyn not started to cross her arms, a nervous intake of breath parting her lips.

"No," Alaric said hurriedly, all dignity forgotten. He was going to die from anguish if he couldn't look some more. He caught her wrists and dragged her hands back to her sides. Even in the storm's gloom he could see that her dusky nipples had pebbled—perhaps from the cold, perhaps from the need to be touched.

Figuring that he might as well cover all his bases, he blew into his palms and then rubbed them together to create more heat, and Talasyn gasped when he cupped her breasts, a tremor running through her as though she couldn't make up her mind whether to jerk away or to strain further into his touch. She mercifully decided on the latter, and he tried to be gentle at first, of course he did, but it was just so—

—*fascinating.* The suppleness of her skin, the smooth swell. She fell forward with a sharp cry, clutching at his shoulders for support. This brought the most beautiful breasts in the world mere inches below his mouth, and he was suddenly struck by the greatest idea of his life.

He bent his head and took her right nipple between his lips. *Oh*, how she jumped at that, how she raked her fingers down the back of his neck as he sucked. This was the most amazing thing, the only thing, using his mouth to elicit such startled mewls of pleasure from his fiery little wife. He slid his hand over her neglected left breast, rolling the tight bead of her nipple between forefinger and thumb while he laved at its twin with the flat of his tongue, tasting ocean and sunlight on her skin. Her cries grew louder, the husky scrape of her voice forming the shape of his name while the monsoon raged all around them, sound and fury piercing through their little shelter of wooden boards and canvas sails.

By the time *both* her breasts were flushed and wet from his ministrations, Alaric couldn't take it anymore. He swept Talasyn off her feet, cradling her in his arms. She showed him exactly what she thought of his oafish maneuver by biting his bottom lip. It was the kind of pain that sang, and he snarled as he tossed her onto her back, there against the inward curve of the lopsided airship's hull. As good a bed as any.

Talasyn propped herself up on her elbows to glare at him. "What did I say about you manhandling me?"

"I'll stop when *you* learn to be gentler with your teeth," Alaric retorted, kneeling between her spread legs. He wiped at his mouth with the back of his hand, the smear of blood she'd drawn dark against his skin in the faded day.

"Little hellcat," he muttered, lost in her narrowed eyes flashing with hints of gold. "Claws out even while you purr."

"I don't hear any complaints from you," she said, with a pointed glance at the tenting in his trousers.

He bent down and stifled a sardonic laugh in the junction of her neck and shoulder as he peeled her breeches down her glorious legs. She kicked them off the rest of the way, and then it was a blur of sliding against each other, squirming together, lips catching in open-mouthed kisses, his hand fumbling until it found its way home between her thighs, thumbing the gusset of her underwear aside, a finger sinking in.

She was as tight as he remembered. Wet and warm, pulsing around the stretch, eager for him. *Let me have this,* he thought, through the intoxicating muddle of sensations, through the roar of the storm-tossed waves, through the pounding of blood. *Just for a while.*

Talasyn was well aware that she was digging a deeper and deeper hole for herself with every moment that passed. With each kiss, with each caress, some distant corner of her mind screamed that no good could come from this, that she was betraying Sardovia and Nenavar, that there were some things that would always be unforgivable in whatever light. But somehow she could not be swayed from responding to Alaric, the haze of desire clouding all considerations of the future.

The last time they'd done this, she'd climaxed so quickly, unused to being touched after a lifetime of loneliness. But now her body knew what to expect, was drinking it all in, demanding more. And Alaric, as in tune with her in this as he was when they dueled, kissed his way down to her breasts, his clever mouth latching on yet again as his finger prodded and *curled.*

She was so focused on the circuit of pleasure afforded by him lavishing attention on two different parts of her body that, when he added a second finger, she almost didn't notice until he started to thrust. How she loved it, though. How her hips canted to meet his wrist, how she clawed at his bicep, how—

"Ouch!" Talasyn yelped. Alaric had wiggled his fingers perhaps a bit too ambitiously within her walls, the sudden sting similar to that of a pinched nerve.

He raised his head from her chest, his expression a mixture of horror and guilt in the half-light. "Too much?"

"Your fingers are clearly bigger than mine, and it's not like I've ever had anyone else in there before you—" she started to rant, only for the rest of it to die in her throat as the swift understanding that dawned in his eyes gave way to a burning possessiveness.

He leaned in and slipped his tongue between her lips, rolling it underneath the roof of her mouth as his fingers moved more gently inside her, figuring out what she liked. Before long, her pleasure had mounted again as though it had never been interrupted in the first place. Another strong gust of wind sent a curtain of heavy rain thudding against the airship, the racket echoing the jagged drum that her heart had become as it beat frantically, in near-perfect sync with how she throbbed and ached for him. He'd tucked his ring finger against his palm and the cool golden edge of his wedding band brushed against her with every downstroke, adding another layer of debauchery that threatened to overwhelm. And surely she was almost there, surely just a little more—

"That's it, Tala." Alaric pressed a feverish kiss to her temple, then another one to her jaw. He sounded as broken as she felt, that deep rasp of a voice guiding her higher. "Come all over your husband's wedding ring."

Her hips rolled as she gave herself over to the cresting, to the light, clamping down on him, shuddering, her hoarse cry drowned out by the swirling tempest. And he watched her the way one watched a sunrise.

Somehow, it wasn't enough. Somehow, she needed more. After the pleasure tore through her, it left a space aching to be filled.

Alaric must have read it on her face, or guessed it from how she reached for him, limply, silently.

He sat back, leaning against the shallop's bulkhead, hauling her into his lap. Talasyn went willingly, straddling him, his arousal straining against his trousers, the friction making her gasp. Lightning flashed at the periphery of her vision, but it was nothing compared to the look in his eyes. He was gazing at her with such sheer hunger that he looked like a man possessed, and she didn't feel entirely like herself, either. Her breasts covered in love bites, her body bared to the howling skies and the furious ocean. There was a wicked wind blowing through her, through them both, through the currents of aetherspace, matching the intensity of the gale that beat at the walls of the ship.

Barely remembering how to control her limbs, her world floating in a blur of heated kisses and illicit touches, she helped him wrestle off her undergarments, then the bunched-up tunic. There was something primeval about being stripped down to only her boots in such an untamed landscape, her braid tossing in the wind, her man looking at her with fierce reverence. There was power here, sung to her by the swaying trees, by the crashing waves, by the rain that lashed at her exposed skin. She reached down, blindly, and it was the work of moments to free him from his trousers, to encircle him in half a fist. He was heavy in her palm, twitching, so long and thick that a spark of nervous delight rippled through her core. Her knees dug into the teak boards as she poised herself above him, and a shudder went through his broad frame as his tip grazed her entrance. He rested his forehead against hers, breathing harshly. His question unspoken, but unmistakable.

Yes, she thought, but couldn't say out loud. She was afraid that the word would crack and her vulnerability would come seeping through. She was afraid that he would see the full scale of it, of what he was capable of doing to her. She—

—had hesitated too long. Alaric drew his head back slightly, peering at her through half-lidded gray eyes.

"*Well?*" he asked, his voice gruff.

There was a flush to his cheeks that quickly spread all the way to his ears. *There was never* anyone *before you,* he'd told her. They were both new to this, and she should probably be more charitable, but—

"What do you mean '*Well?*'?" Talasyn snapped, her own face growing warm. "I'm the one spreading my legs right now, aren't I? If *you* don't want to—"

"Gods," Alaric muttered, through clenched teeth. He darted a quick, mildly vexed kiss to the freckles on her nose, and then his hands were on her hips, pushing her down, and she was gripping him by the base, guiding him in . . .

The breach of his first few inches was almost too much, despite how wet she was. It startled a cry out of her. One that echoed through the ship's wooden confines before it was whisked away by the pelting rain. Talasyn was utterly mortified, but Alaric looked *stricken.*

"Stop?" he croaked, holding her waist tightly so that she couldn't slide any lower. His sharp features were tense with fear. "We can stop."

She rocked her hips experimentally, regarding him with an

air of defiance as she sank down another inch. Something in his expression shattered and he gathered her close to his chest, the squeak that she let out at suddenly taking more of him muffled against his throat, and then he was scattering kisses to her temple, to the shell of her ear. Not to be outdone, she tugged at his hair and scraped her teeth along his jaw, and she swore that his eyes all but rolled into the back of his head before he buried his face in her collarbone. And drove forward the last few inches to hilt inside her.

At first, it was strange more than anything else. A pressure, a fullness. Talasyn's breath emerged in rough little hitches as she adjusted to the sensation. She was unsure what to do next, but a sort of—*wiggling*—seemed as good a place to start as any, and it felt somewhat nice. It took the edge off the discomfort, this gliding of him along her inner walls. Intrigued, she shifted upward, then slid back down.

"*Oh*," she moaned. And did it again and again, clutching at Alaric's shoulders for balance.

It wasn't long before she realized that those shoulders were strung as tight as halyards in the same gale-force wind that was roaring across the beach.

Her husband was a statue at first glance, his face still tucked against her clavicle. But closer inspection revealed that his every muscle strained with the effort of not moving, of not hurting her. Chagrined, she coaxed his head up—and found herself looking into silver eyes that *burned* with need.

"Tala." He sounded almost broken, her name as urgent as a battlefield hymn. "I want to—may I?"

"Yes," Talasyn breathed out. And this, too, was surrender. This, too, was letting go of fear. This, too, was free fall. "I think so. Yes."

And Alaric was kissing her again, and then he began to *move*.

⁂

Tight, she is so tight, so hot and wet and all for me—

That was the one semi-coherent line of thought that Alaric's mind had dissolved into; the rest was pleasant static, a whirl of beautiful sunlight girl.

Talasyn was mostly quiet as he rocked up into her with shallow thrusts, only the faintest sighs escaping her lips. She was more expressive with her hands, those nimble fingers digging into his biceps, tracing the sides of his face, disappearing beneath his shirt to scale the ladder of his ribs.

Soon she was grinding down on him, and he was delirious with the feeling. He had never felt anything like it before and wanted to feel only this for the rest of his life. He couldn't stop kissing every part of her that he could reach. It would have been concerning if he'd had it in him to have concerns beyond the snug warmth that had become his whole universe.

It would have been concerning, too, the whine that left his lips when she pushed him away, but it swiftly melted into a groan when her small, strong hands pinned his shoulders to the bulkhead and she *rode* him.

This was how Alaric was going to die. Talasyn was truly going to kill him, with her brow furrowed in concentration like that, with her breasts bouncing like *that.* Naked and golden in his lap, she rose over him and sank back down with each roll of her slim hips, as though he were the shoreline that her waves broke against, her eyes fiery like high summer, her kiss-stung lips curving into a winsome smile. A smile that—

—that was perhaps a little too *smug*—

"Ruin looks good on you, my lord." She had never looked more Nenavarene than in this moment. Or more maddening.

He pressed one hand to the base of her spine, holding her in place as he thrust roughly up into her. Her mouth dropped open in surprise and he gave that mouth no opportunity to scold him, kissing it as he palmed her breasts.

When she finally cried out, some dark and somewhat petty satisfaction swept through him. He clamped his arms around her waist, and she looped hers around his neck, and then they were moving together, the ship's boards creaking, blood and magic shrieking, the Eversea tumultuous, and the skies ablaze with lightning.

Outside, like the animals.

In the storm, like they were made of it.

"Careful, little wife," he murmured in her ear, for no reason other than to piss her off, "or I'll start to think you like having me around."

And the hellion bit him *again*, this time sinking her teeth into his shoulder. Hauling him dangerously close to the brink.

"I told you," Talasyn gritted out, "not to call me that when—"

"When what?" Alaric took her by the hips, setting a fevered pace that had her panting, and had him seeing stars. "When I'm bouncing you on my lap? When you're dripping all over me? You fuck the same way you fight, Lachis'ka, did you know that? No quarter. Chomping at the bit." He hit a spot inside her that made her *writhe*, her walls squeezing down on him. He did it over and over again. "Deadly. Magnificent. The prettiest thing I've ever seen."

Alaric could tell, from the way Talasyn bristled, that she was gearing up to say something, probably to call him a name, but whatever it was emerged as a sound caught between a sob and a scream as her eyelids fluttered shut and the rest of her went still. Thunder rent the air as she dragged him with her headlong over the precipice.

For him it was an unfurling, it was breathing out for the first time in years, it was the world going white at the edges and the soul rushing south. He came snarling like the wolf, spilling inside his wife as she collapsed against his chest. Thrusting up into the wet heat of her, making her take every last drop.

Allowing himself to believe, in this moment, that he would never be alone again.

I'm done fighting this. Another coherent thought, breaking through the fog of his mind. Here, at last, was something that felt right. Something real. *Whatever else happens, I won't fight it anymore.*

And if that made him a monster, made him a traitor—then so be it.

He kissed her again.

I'll never be the same.

The storm swept through and the waves spiraled up and Talasyn came down, Alaric's lips soft against hers through her aftershocks until she slid lower along his body, utterly spent.

I will always remember this.

An errant tear streamed down her cheek, and she hid it against his throat, pulling him close.

Just him and me and the monsoon.

CHAPTER TWENTY-ONE

They made it to the coracle on the cliff eventually, once the rain had slowed. An hour later, a ship from House Matano arrived to ferry them to Iantas, while some of its crew stayed behind to retrieve the Kesathese shallop on the beach.

At the castle, Talasyn waved off the concerned twittering of Jie and the Lachis-dalo and fled to the royal suite of rooms, while Alaric was busy assuring Sevraim that he had not in fact drowned at sea and come back to haunt him. She bathed, meticulously scrubbing at their combined release that had leaked down her thighs, while her mind turned over with all the possible ramifications, all the doubts.

A restlessness was gathering in her soul. After bathing, she drifted into her study and leafed through the messages piled on her desk. There were the agricultural reports and breakdowns of the state budget that Urduja always made sure were copied and sent to Talasyn from the Roof of Heaven, as well as a slew of invitations from the other noble houses to various festivities.

"Your Grace." A servant appeared in the doorway. "His Majesty requests your company for a late lunch. Or an early supper. 'However the Lachis'ka prefers to think of it,' he said."

Talasyn was famished, but her courage failed her. She and Alaric hadn't spoken a word to each other the whole journey home, and she didn't think she could bear to face him over something as innocuous as a meal so soon after what they'd done on the beach. She couldn't even meet the servant's eyes. "Tell him I'm busy."

The servant bowed and left. A long while later, Alaric strolled in, fresh from his own bath. He slouched against the doorframe, hands in his pockets, studying her with a quiet alertness. Talasyn very firmly cleared her throat and made a show of going through her files—even though the words on the parchments had lost all meaning—but he made no move to leave. Trust this man to be incapable of taking a hint.

"Ran from me again," he observed.

"Don't flatter yourself," she scoffed. "I have a lot to do, as it's plain to see." She held up one of the letters for his perusal, a boldly inked invitation to a parade that had been elegantly penned in Sailor's Common as a courtesy to the Lachis'ka's consort.

Not that said consort appreciated it. "Ah, yes, very important stuff. Not at all an excuse."

A growl of frustration formed low in her throat. "It's *not* an excuse, I—"

"Don't want to finish what wc startcd?" hc suggcstcd hclpfully. "Fear this pull that exists between us?"

A growing tightness tugged in her belly like a thread on a spool. It was the anticipation and dread that one felt before a battle. She crumpled the letter in her fist. "I don't have to listen to this."

"You're right. You don't have to." Alaric's maddeningly full lips curved into a smirk. "Feel free to make your exit, then."

The utter *gall*. He'd been the one who came barging in and he knew it, judging from how absolutely *smarmy* he looked and sounded right now. He was *taunting* her.

Talasyn dropped the hapless invitation to the parade and charged. There were too many emotions left over, too much had been building up, and she seized the first possible outlet for all of it by letting her temper spike in a sharp flare as she hurtled toward Alaric. "I was here first," she seethed, "you unbelievably *annoying* man—"

His arms opened to receive her and she crashed into his wide, solid chest, and then they were kissing. A hot, open-mouthed tangle of biting teeth and punishing tongues. There was no grace to it, but how could there be when they were both on edge, when he'd been spoiling for a fight and gotten this instead?

He spun her around and walked her backward, their lips still connected, out of the study and into their bedchamber. At some point over the last hour or so, the monsoon had regained strength. It lashed at the exterior walls of Iantas, a sonorous melody of raindrops pattering on wind-carved granite. The meager daylight spilling into the room veiled the angles of Alaric's face in silver as he deposited her onto the bed, as she rolled on top of him.

Fumbling, grasping, they worked together to unbutton his tunic, a process impeded by how loath they were to stop exploring each other's mouths. Once he was shirtless, he peered up at her through hooded eyes in something like challenge. She had no clue where to begin; there was just *so much* of him bared beneath her, his pale skin a fine contrast to the wine-colored sheets.

But Talasyn was never one to back down. Lightning flashed through the balcony doors in splinters of brilliant white as she lowered her lips to the curve of his jaw. She felt Alaric close his eyes, his lashes fluttering against her face, his hand stirring ever so slightly between her thighs in a way that spurred her on.

Soon she had embarked on the rather delightful journey of marking him up, biting and sucking, soothing the skin with her tongue as he bucked against her. Soon his neck and chest were littered with mottled red bruises that stood out like crushed rose petals against his skin.

There was a trace of desperation in the way he reached for her. And there was no small amount of mischief in the way she leaned back, out of his grasp.

His gaze darkened. "You know what I want, Talasyn."

"Haven't the slightest notion," she chirped, putting on her best Lachis'ka airs.

He flipped her onto her back, and as her head hit the pillows she let out a sound that was almost a giggle, and he swallowed it with his mouth, curved into what was nearly a smile. He covered her with his body and proceeded to demonstrate *exactly* what he wanted as rain beat against the windows in a drowsy lullaby.

Reluctantly opening her eyes the next morning, Talasyn found herself in Alaric's embrace—*crushed* in it. The man didn't know his own strength: his arms were wrapped around her waist, keeping her back snugly tucked against his bare chest, and he was holding her as a child would a soft toy, so tightly that it was difficult to breathe. She wriggled around as best as she could in an attempt to loosen his grasp, but he was having none of it, muttering a faint, unintelligible protest into her hair.

Talasyn froze as her ineffectual movements brought her into contact with something hard that grazed the curve of her backside. Alaric might still be asleep, but there appeared to be at least *one* part of him that was ready to face the day. She nearly snickered, but cold realization crept up on her, bringing with it a twinge of pain that gathered in the bottom of her heart.

She forced Alaric's arms away from her, panic giving her a surge of strength. She sat up, her legs dangling off the edge of the bed as she frantically scanned the room for her undergarments. Where had she tossed them last night—

"It doesn't have to be a big deal, Talasyn."

She looked over her shoulder. Alaric had also sat up and was regarding her with somber eyes, the blankets pooled at his waist. There were streaks of red across his defined chest, the marks left by her teeth and her nails. Whatever he saw on her face made something flicker across his—in the morning light, it was almost bitterness, almost resignation, but it was gone in a blink, before she could tell for certain. Replaced by his usual hauteur.

"This," Alaric continued, "doesn't have to be anything more than it is. There is obviously an attraction between us. While that *does* move our marriage beyond the merely political, I don't believe there would be much harm in acting on it from time to time. Until the attraction runs its course."

He held it out to her the way he'd held out the promise of a future where they worked together to build a better world.

But he'd meant *his* better world, not hers. Never hers. There could be no better world until the Night Empire fell—and when that day came, he was going to hate her.

So why not? came that inner voice, dark and treacherous. *If he's going to hate you anyway, why not take your pleasures while you can?*

Talasyn's head ached. She didn't want to think anymore.

"I don't know," she muttered. "You might end up falling in love with me."

It was a quip to distract him from waiting for an actual answer from her. It worked a little too well; he *recoiled.*

"That's not going to happen," Alaric said flatly. "Love is for poets and dreamers, not leaders of state. You and I have no such luxury."

It wasn't that she didn't agree with him, but his remark still hurt a bit. As though she had a splinter in her lungs. She breathed it out slowly, frowning to herself. Where was *that* coming from?

"Well, as long as we're clear," she said.

"You need to see a healer," he said at the same time.

They stared at each other.

"Your, ah . . ." He raked a hand through his sleep-tousled hair. "A preventive. Because I—" He swallowed. "You need to see a healer for a preventive."

Talasyn almost screamed. It had completely slipped her mind.

She stood up—only to wince, then plop back down on the mattress. She turned to Alaric again, this time with a venomous glare that was pure accusation. "I'm *sore*."

He blinked. The ghost of a smile spread across his lips and his gray eyes went glassy, faraway. "Really," he hummed.

Talasyn grabbed the nearest pillow and hurled it at her husband's head.

The storm's final burst of vindictiveness before it dissipated had left the first level of the castle flooded overnight. Alaric and Talasyn both spent the morning dealing with it, helping the staff move what supplies and priceless artifacts could be salvaged to the upper levels. Once the water had finished receding, his wife had thrust a mop into his hands, saying that it was all hands on deck.

Alaric had never held a mop in his life, but he liked to think that he'd done a capable enough job. He then spent the afternoon in his study, attending to the pile of messages that had accumulated during his sojourn to Chal—a pile that, now that the weather was clear, only grew as skua after skua glided in through the window. Through it all, he could think only of Talasyn, of how tight and soft she'd been, of the pretty sounds she'd made for him.

The woman was a blight on his peace. Alaric held out for as long as he could—which wasn't very long at all, only a few hours—and then left his study at dusk, in search of her. The servants directed him to the northern wing of the castle, to the library at its topmost level.

Iantas's library was a treasure trove of ancient tomes, beautifully bound and inscribed, arranged with precision on the towering shelves that lined the walls. As Alaric stepped through the arched doorway, he abruptly stumbled and almost lost his footing; the inside of his head reeled with a summons from Gaheris. Cold, dark fingers reached for him, pulling him into the In-Between.

Or *trying* to, at least. Talasyn poked her head out from behind a row of shelves, and the sight of her sent a surge of warmth through him.

Alaric went over to her, shrugging off the summons. His father could wait. Everything else could wait.

It seemed that Jie had been successful in taking sponge and soap to her mistress. Talasyn's complexion was still rosy from the heated bathwater, which Alaric realized as he drew near had been scented with the candied-lemon tang of elemi oil. She wore a dress of opalescent lavender and silver brocade, with geometric cutouts that exposed the willowy curves of her torso, tantalizing stretches of olive skin that he longed to dig his fingers into as soon as possible.

The neckline was revealing as well, dipping almost to her navel, and Alaric promptly cast all his previous grievances with that accursed tailor aside and thanked the benevolent universe for the gift of Nenavarene fashion.

"Finished with your work?" Talasyn inquired, returning the book she'd been reading to its shelf.

Alaric nodded, not trusting himself to speak just yet. He stepped closer and something gleamed in her lovely brown eyes—his own heightening anticipation, reflected back at him in the twilight.

"What about you?" His voice came out too low for such harmless small talk, and talking was indeed the absolute *last* thing he wanted to be doing right now, but the sense of propriety that had been drilled into him from an early age insisted that one did not simply attack one's spouse in a library.

"The Lachis'ka's work is never done," she dryly replied. "Particularly when the first floor still smells like sewage."

"I don't understand why your ancestors built a castle in a flood-prone area."

"It's a summerhouse, so of course it has to be by the beach."

"Madness." He took another step toward her. She tilted her chin upward, pink lips shaped to receive his kiss.

It was a sudden spark of mischief that prompted Alaric to go straight for Talasyn's neck instead. When he nipped at the sensitive spot below her ear, she laughed in both surprise and delight, and the sweet, unexpectedly sultry sound made him smile as he worked his way down. He longed to use his teeth but he doubted she would appreciate that. Unlike the high collar of his tunic, which hid the marks she'd inflicted on him yesterday, her dress left little room for subterfuge.

Her breathing grew unsteady as he lavished the valley between her breasts with feather-light kisses, his hands tightening around her waist. The air had become very warm, and the fragrance of promise jasmines wafting from Talasyn's chestnut hair drowned out the scents of ink and parchment and old wood.

Alaric became faintly aware of a faraway noise, like a creak, as though the door was being pushed open, but it failed to penetrate the desire clouding his senses. His mind, whittled down to nothing but the basest of instincts, instantly dismissed the sound as unworthy of concern while he kissed his way to the freckles atop his wife's left breast.

A throat was cleared. Loudly.

They froze as their eyes whipped to the library entrance. Prince Elagbi was standing there, arms crossed, a thunderous expression on his face.

Alaric Ossinast, the Night Emperor of Kesath, saw his life flash before his eyes.

CHAPTER TWENTY-TWO

Talasyn had always prided herself on being a capable individual. Her quick thinking and resourcefulness had saved her life countless times during the Hurricane Wars. There had never been an emergency that she hadn't dealt with using her wits, her gumption, and her ability to adapt to a rapid change in circumstance.

But she was drawing a blank on how to handle *this*—being caught in the act, or the prelude to the act, anyway, all wrapped up in her husband's arms with his mouth hovering at her chest while her *father* postured in the doorway, features contorted in wrath.

How long had Elagbi been standing there? How much had he seen?

Alaric and Talasyn sprang apart to put a good several inches between them, placing their hands at their sides to very emphatically show that they were *not* touching. After what felt like an eternity, Elagbi relaxed. He offered the imperial couple an elaborate, courtly bow before walking over to them.

"Dearest," he said to Talasyn, holding out his arm, "rumor has it that you had a bit of an adventure during the storm.

I had to set sail from Eskaya as soon as the skies permitted to make sure that you were all right."

"The flood earlier today *was* harrowing," Talasyn joked weakly, slipping her hand into the crook of his elbow. "All those beautiful carpets are a loss, I'm afraid."

Elagbi tutted. "That's not what I meant, and you are well aware. Gallivanting off to Chal while a northwester blows in—I never! But no harm done in the end, I suppose. Shall we proceed to supper?"

"Um . . ." Talasyn glanced at Alaric, whose eyes were as wide as the plates they were going to be eating off of. "Certainly?"

Alaric remained where he was, rooted to the spot, as Elagbi escorted Talasyn out of the library, but this changed when the Dominion prince called out in a booming voice, "After all, there is no reason that the three of us can't enjoy a nice meal," which sent the Night Emperor trailing after them.

Elagbi maintained a neutral, amiable expression on the way to the small dining room on the second level—the one on the first level being out of commission as it dried out. Jie and Sevraim were already waiting for them.

Then the most awkward meal in the history of Lir began.

"We had no idea where you and His Majesty had gone off to, Lachis'ka," Jie piped up. "I'm glad that Prince Elagbi found you without incident."

Talasyn's spoon clattered against her soup bowl. At the opposite end of the table, Alaric appeared to choke on a sip of wine, hastily putting down his glass and dabbing at the errant wetness on his chin with a napkin.

"They were in the library," Elagbi replied with a pleasant smile. "I spent many hours there as a boy myself. Quite the compendium of knowledge. I would venture to say that it is a *sacred* space, with many old and fragile manuscripts."

Jie blinked, appearing confused at the pointed emphasis of Elagbi's little speech, but Sevraim came to her rescue. "Yes, the staff here at Iantas have done an excellent job of maintaining the library. I have been unable to find any reading material in Sailor's Common thus far, but it is a lovely place."

"Emperor Alaric seems to think so as well, from what I've seen," said Elagbi.

Talasyn contemplated using the aforementioned spoon to dig a hole in the floor and burrow down into it, never to emerge again. Before she could try, however, Sevraim asked, "What were you reading today, Your Grace?"

At first, Talasyn couldn't for the life of her remember what book she'd been holding before Alaric walked in and started kissing her breasts, but the cover finally flashed through her mind's eye. "Sonnets. I hadn't encountered much by way of poetry during my time on the Continent. It's . . . interesting."

Jie looked at Alaric in an effort to include him in what, from her end, was merely social chitchat. "And as for His Majesty?" She was just doing her job, of course, there was no way the poor girl could have known, and so she understandably shrank back when Alaric's features rearranged themselves into a defensive scowl.

"Whatever Emperor Alaric was helping himself to, he undoubtedly found it edifying," Elagbi declared. "I should very much like to discuss it with him over a bottle of rum when we're done with our meal."

Talasyn momentarily evaporated from her body. She knew that Alaric couldn't refuse such a benign-sounding invitation from his father-in-law, not in front of Jie and Sevraim.

"Yes, let's," Alaric muttered, sounding about as enthusiastic as he would have been if Elagbi had invited him to walk barefoot over hot coals.

Although that was *normally* the way Alaric sounded in response to anything, so neither Jie nor Sevraim found it amiss. The conversation shifted to other matters.

But the reprieve was temporary. Once the last of the plates had been cleared, Elagbi made a show of smacking his forehead.

"Silly me, I have just remembered that I needed to speak with you, too, my dear," he told Talasyn. "It won't take but a moment."

Talasyn nearly mouthed *Save me* at Alaric as she and her father proceeded to the salon. The only thing that stopped her was the certainty that such a plea would be futile. Alaric couldn't even save himself.

"Talasyn," Elagbi said once they were in private. Studying her with concerned dark eyes, he visibly deflated, his brow wrinkling while he pondered how best to approach the issue.

Talasyn said nothing. She knew that what she'd been doing was wrong—she needed no sermons on *that* account—but it was also impossible to process this feeling of having disappointed her father.

"This entire situation has been . . . difficult," Elagbi finally confessed. They were standing by the windows that overlooked the beach, and he fiddled with the intricate carvings on their panes as he spoke. "Not just the alliance with Kesath, but everything else in general. For nineteen long years, you were a child in my memory. Tiny and precocious and energetic and so quick to throw tantrums. Did you know that you didn't like being hugged?"

"What?" Talasyn was so startled that she let out a disbelieving laugh. "I didn't?"

"You *hated* it. You kicked me and Hanan away whenever we tried to cuddle you."

"I wouldn't have," she said, her voice oddly thick, "if I'd

known what was going to happen." *I would have held every touch, every moment, to my heart.*

He reached out to pat her cheek. She had a vague recollection of someone else doing this, someone with slender fingers and eyes like hers. "What matters is that you're here now. And that's the thing, you see. You came back into my life full grown, so strong and confident and self-assured. I remember when you demanded that the Zahiya-lachis listen to you on the *W'taida*. A twenty-year-old in soot-stained, ragged attire, confronting the Dragon Queen of the Nenavar Dominion—I was so proud of you then, and that pride only increased as the months passed and you met every new challenge head-on. You are very brave, my daughter, and yet also very hardened by the life you led before we met again. That's why I have no desire to begrudge you whatever happiness is within your reach, but . . ."

Elagbi paused, still staring at her. Whatever he saw on her face brought a grim, steely look to his own, falling over his countenance like a shadow.

"This cannot go on, Talasyn," said the prince. "You know that as well as I do. It's an undesirable development in an already precarious situation. I must counsel you, not only as your father but also as a man who loves his country, to nip this in the bud before it affects your judgment. Your resolve. The war is coming and you will need to choose."

"I'm not going to give up the Sardovians' location, if that's what you mean," Talasyn retorted, not without some ire—but whether at Elagbi or at herself, she wasn't sure. "It's physical attraction, and that's all. It might be the close proximity, or whatever it is, but I can assure you that there are no real feelings involved."

"Well, that's a relief," Elagbi said faintly. "That's what every man wants to hear from his beloved only daughter—"

She pursed her lips. "What I'm *trying* to tell you, Amya,

is that it won't change anything. The end remains the same." Why did it hollow her out to say that, even though it was what she believed, what she knew to be right? "I will still do what needs to be done when the time comes."

"Ah." All trace of sarcasm left his tone. "Now *that* is something that the Zahiya-lachis would want to hear. I can't figure out if that's good or bad." He regarded her in somber silence for a while, then shook his head. "For now, I can only hope that you'll tread carefully, and that you won't forget that I'm always on your side."

In spite of her father's sweet promise, the mention of Urduja sent Talasyn into a miniature but full-fledged spiral. "Please don't—"

But Elagbi, already miles ahead of her, was making a locking gesture in front of his mouth. "I shan't breathe a word. Frankly, I doubt that your grandmother's heart could take it. Now send the Night Emperor in, Lachis'ka. We missed out on a lot of things, and that includes my opportunity to put the fear of the ancestors in your suitors."

"He's already my husband," Talasyn pointed out. "Besides, he's not the kind of man who scares easy."

"I know," said Elagbi. "That's why I worry about you."

"Do me a favor." Standing just beside the open doorway to the salon, out of Elagbi's field of vision, and speaking in a near-whisper so he couldn't hear, Alaric gently seized Talasyn's arm before she could head upstairs. "Rescue me in two hours. Say we have aethermancy training."

She blinked up at him. Those eyes were far from the worst sight a man could take to his grave, and that lifted his spirits slightly. "Should you return and discover that I have gone to the willows," he drawled, "well, it would be no great mystery who did it."

"You'll be fine." Talasyn looked at his hand on her arm, then back at his face. There was a ruefulness to the small smile that she flashed; it gave him the disquieting sensation that she was viewing him from some far-off shore. "I'll see you in two hours."

She left him then. Alaric took a calming breath before entering the salon, where Elagbi was retrieving the promised bottle of rum from the liquor cabinet, along with two crystal snifters, and placing them on a golden tray.

Alaric sat down, not saying a word as the Dominion prince claimed the chair across from him and poured them each a generous inch of the spirit, which had a brown hue so warm that it was almost red.

"Sugarcane rum," Elagbi announced, "from the endless fields of Vasiyas, and the finest liquor produced in Nenavar, in my opinion. One more thing that we cannot afford to lose to the Voidfell."

"Talasyn and I will do our best to save the rum." Alaric took a tentative sip and nearly spat it out. "On second thought, perhaps not."

Elagbi smirked. "It's potent, I'll grant you that. However, there is an intriguing sweetness, once you have grown accustomed to it." He raised his glass. "To your health, Emperor Alaric."

The way he said it—it was a prelude to a duel. Alaric wasn't about to back down. He clinked his glass against the other man's. "And to yours, Prince Elagbi."

The rum began to taste good somewhere around his fourth pour. The deep molasses note might have come through sooner if not for the fact that his father-in-law set a pace that offered little opportunity for the drink to be savored. As a result, His Majesty Alaric Ossinast of the Night Empire and His Royal

Highness Elagbi Silim of the Nenavar Dominion were—as the masses would say—three sheets to the wind.

"Two sheets," Alaric corrected his own thoughts out loud. "Perhaps one and a half." He was, after all, still in full command of his senses, even if these were drifting further and further out of reach.

Elagbi's brow creased as he poured himself another glass. "Beg pardon?"

"Never mind." Alaric looked down his nose at the shimmering droplets that Elagbi had clumsily spilled on the floor. "You're quite inebriated."

Elagbi snorted. "You're the one going on about blankets apropos of nothing, my good man."

Alaric finished off the remnants of his drink, hissing through the burn in his throat as he placed the empty snifter on the table with a dull thud. "I'm not a good man."

"Certainly not good enough for my daughter!" Elagbi cheerfully agreed. "This may be an important political alliance, but you do *not* have my blessing."

"I don't require it," Alaric declared with smugness. "I already married her."

Elagbi swore at him in the Nenavarene tongue, then scratched his head. "The translation escapes me . . . 'May lightning burn your milk,' something to that effect . . ." The quandary apparently robbed him of steam, for he slumped in his chair and tipped more rum into Alaric's glass. "Do you remember when we had wine on your stormship—ancestors, why are you and I always drinking—and I said you had good taste in vintages?"

Alaric nodded warily, squinting to see the trap, wondering where it could possibly spring from. Perhaps more rum would help him spot it. He downed a new mouthful.

"You reacted so awkwardly," Elagbi mused. "As though you weren't sure how to respond to such a small compliment.

And I found myself wondering then—when was the last time anyone had a kind word for this boy?"

It was scarcely conceivable how one sentence—one simple question—could unlock a door in the human heart. Alaric truly couldn't remember when his own father's praise had not been mingled with admonishment. His eyes watered and he scrubbed at them, horrified, but Elagbi was thankfully too busy taking another swig to notice.

"That was the only time I was ever sympathetic to you!" slurred the prince. "You . . . you—daughter-defiler!"

Alaric thought about the fading love bites on his chest, the scratches on his back. "If anything, *she* defiled *me*—"

The sun chose that moment to walk into the salon.

"Amya, I must insist on retrieving the Night Emperor, we need to get some more training in . . ." Talasyn trailed off, looking mystified at the sight of her husband and her father clinging to the furniture, a half-empty bottle of rum between them, as though it was the most peculiar sight she had ever witnessed in her twenty years of existence.

Alaric automatically rose to his feet. It was simple good manners, but it took more effort than usual, as did the act of turning to face his wife. His very beautiful wife. She made his world spin.

No, scratch that—the room was *actually* spinning—

Talasyn hurried over to him, subjecting his features to intense scrutiny. He smiled at her.

She reeled back in shock—which, in all honesty, hurt his feelings a little, surely his smile wasn't *that* bad—and then she rounded on Elagbi. "You got him *drunk*?"

"Nonsense!" Elagbi boomed. "He's sober as a prosperity clam! Big lad. High tolerance."

"Yes," Alaric agreed, because that seemed like the most intelligent thing to do.

Talasyn scowled. She looked distinctly put out—and also extremely kissable. Alaric doubted he'd be able to plant one on her and live to tell the tale, so he settled for draping an arm over her shoulders. She didn't shrink back from his touch, and he was so relieved that he nuzzled at her temple.

"You smell good," he mumbled, closing his eyes. He could fall asleep like this, on his feet and breathing in the mangoes and the promise jasmines and the warm, gorgeous wife.

"You smell like a distillery," Talasyn retorted. "Let's get you to bed. And *you*"—she pointed an accusing finger at Elagbi as she led Alaric away—"you sit there and think about what you've done."

"I shall ruminate on my sins!" Elagbi happily exclaimed, raising his glass to them as they left.

Castle guards and attendants alike were falling over their feet to help the Lachis'ka drag the Night Emperor to the royal chambers, but Talasyn turned them all down. It was late in the evening and she didn't want to give anyone more work after a long day. Particularly when this was no one's fault but that of the two men in her life.

Alaric was . . . well, he was managing to put one foot in front of the other, she'd give him that. He moved as though he was torn between leaning on her and not letting her take all his weight, brows drawn together from the sheer effort. He was a considerate drunk at least—and a quiet one, too. It wasn't until they were ascending the last flight of stairs that he spoke.

"Tala," he said, in something between a whisper and a sigh.

"Alaric," she said dryly.

When he remained silent, she slanted a quizzical glance in his direction, only to find him already peeking down at her. He smiled again—the same lopsided grin that had so taken her by surprise in the Mouth of Night and then in the salon. Bashful and boyish, crinkling the corners of his eyes. Her stomach went all . . . swimmy.

"I merely wished to say your name," he said.

"Oh gods," Talasyn muttered. Her husband was a *sappy* drunk.

His silliness was good for one thing, though: it lessened the underlying nervousness that tended to flicker at the back of her mind whenever she was around people in their cups. Her time with the Sardovian regiments and at the Dominion court had taught her that not everyone acted like the orphanage keepers when they overindulged, but it was still difficult for her to let go of past associations, to quell the irrational dread that lurked in the pit of her stomach at the smell of liquor.

One slow eternity later, they were in their room. "Your father," Alaric gravely pronounced as Talasyn coaxed him into a sitting position at the edge of the bed, "is a miscreant."

"He takes after his son-in-law in that regard," she countered, kneeling between his legs.

Alaric made a sound not dissimilar to someone choking on his own tongue. It was only then that the suggestiveness of her position dawned on Talasyn.

"*As if I would ever*," she said shrilly, making it a point to yank his left boot off his foot so that there could be no mistaking her intentions.

It happened abruptly. Alaric lurched forward with his hand rising up from out of the shadows, the pungent smell of rum wafting from his skin. Talasyn cried out, shrank back, a child again, raising her arms over her head to ward off the blow.

But it never came.

When she dared to peer up at him, he was frozen in place, his hand hovering inches from his other boot. He'd only been about to help her take it off, not . . .

Her heart rate returned to normal. She felt foolish and small. And hopeless, with the realization that she would never be free of the things she carried.

"Did—were you—" Alaric faltered, each word laboriously plucked out from his stupor. "Did you think that I . . . would strike you?"

Talasyn remained silent a beat too long. Long enough for him to confirm that her answer, though unspoken, was yes.

"I wouldn't—" He hit the floor on his knees and shuffled toward her. She straightened up with the intention of nudging him to do so as well, but he flung his arms around her waist. "Tala, I would *never*"—he buried his face in her midsection—"never when we're not sparring," he said fiercely. "Never when I'm drunk, never in our room—"

"I know." She carded her fingers through his soft hair, in a tentative attempt to soothe him. "Please don't tell anyone—not even my father is aware of this—but it's . . . I can't help it sometimes. I get tense when people drink. Because the ones in charge—they'd hit me and the other children, back at the orphanage, whenever they were foxed." He flinched, holding her tighter. "So my mind makes associations. It's not you. I know you wouldn't."

"Never," Alaric repeated. "Give me their names, I'll find them, make them pay—"

"It's likely that they all died the day Kesath attacked Hornbill's Head."

He looked up, a motion that caused her hand to slip from his hair to the side of his face. His eyes flashed silver with Shadowgate and fury even as he leaned into the curve of her palm. "Good."

She should have chastised him for that. She should have called him a monster. So many had died when the stormship came; *she* had nearly died. But it was like a siren song, his anger on her behalf. It unleashed her own vindictive streak, it made her think of how everyone who had wronged her then had long rotted away beneath dust and rubble, while she was still standing.

And perhaps that made her a monster, too.

What is one night of not caring about other people? Talasyn asked herself mutinously, stroking the pad of her thumb across her husband's cheek. She had carried that burden ever since she was fifteen and the Lightweave first sprang forth. She was tired of forgiving the past. *What is one night?*

Tomorrow I'll be good again.

She led him back to bed. Once she tucked him in, he lay perfectly still, as though nervous about making any sudden movements that might scare her again. She would have interpreted this as pity in the time before, and it would have rankled. But she knew him better now. Knew enough to tell the difference between his pity and his compassion.

He had offered to find Khaede, and he'd eventually brought Talasyn news and some much-needed hope on that front. He hadn't hesitated to help the villagers who lost their homes and livelihoods to the Void Sever's flare. He had stopped the torture of the apprehended rebels, when Vela could not save them.

Talasyn changed into her sleep clothes and then slipped beneath the covers on her own half of the mattress. The minutes crawled along while lace curtains fluttered in the evening breeze that poured through open windows, moonlight glinting on the tapestried canopy over the bed.

"Here is something no one else knows." Alaric's hoarse, liquor-glossed rasp broke the silence. "My mother spoke to me the night she left Kesath. She'd timed it perfectly; my father was away, and in the sennights leading up to her escape she'd made a habit of evening strolls so the guards wouldn't think anything was amiss. There was a ship waiting for her at the docks, but she took a detour to my room and begged me to come with her. I refused."

"Why?" Talasyn asked in a near-whisper, afraid that too loud a voice might shatter the air of secrecy that hung around them.

"Because I was the heir to the throne. I had a duty, even if she would so willingly shirk hers. And because—" The sentence broke apart on his tongue and he tried again. "Because I thought that, if I didn't go, she would stay."

Talasyn's hand inched toward him. Alaric must have heard the rustling silk, or he must have glanced down to see it moving in the moonlight. He met her hand with his own, whatever the case. The tips of their fingers touched, more tentative than anything that she had ever known before.

"When you left . . ."—his hand twitched against hers—"when you left, it brought me back there. That was why I needed to go somewhere else, to clear my head. It wasn't your fault. But my mind makes associations, too."

Talasyn's heart squeezed within her chest, so bitingly that there was room for little else but a solemn, gray-eyed child, molded by loneliness and duty, who had still hoped enough to bet on his mother's love and lost—and the guarded man that child had become, ruthless and terrifying in battle and yet capable of concession, too, and of gentle touch whenever it was just them and the starlight.

She laced her fingers through the gaps between his. He clasped her hand tightly, now without an ounce of tentativeness, his thumb tracing the inside of her wrist.

Somehow, such a simple act was more intimate than anything else they'd done to each other, their palms curling together there in the dark.

CHAPTER TWENTY-THREE

Urduja Silim returned to Iantas in all her pomp and splendor four days later to observe the last practical demonstration of the shield amplifiers. Aside from the fact that Alaric was sailing back to Kesath tomorrow, there would be no more eclipses before the sevenfold one on the night of the Moonless Dark; this was the last chance to fine-tune, to get it right.

So, no pressure, Alaric thought wryly as he and Talasyn headed down to the shoreline after Urduja wished them luck. He could feel the Zahiya-lachis's flinty stare boring into his nape from where she and Elagbi stood at the front of the crowd of spectators that had gathered on the castle steps.

Ishan Vaikar and her Enchanters, busy arranging the glowing metalglass jars on the smooth white sand, were all smiles for Talasyn when she approached. By contrast, they afforded Alaric the barest hint of acknowledgement, clearly still miffed by his outrage a fortnight prior.

Not that Alaric cared. As far as he was concerned, he'd been well within his rights. He greeted the Ahimsan Enchanters with frosty sarcasm, and he smirked when Talasyn shot him an admonishing look.

"This is really it this time," Ishan proclaimed. "If it isn't, I'll cover myself in thornfruit and vanish into the woods."

The daya's resolve was commendable. And as darkness washed over most of Lir's seventh moon, leaving behind only a glimmer of silver, and the shield went up, hope stirred within Alaric that it wasn't out of place.

Light and shadow covered the whole island, stemming from where he and Talasyn stood. The newly modified aether cores groaned but the jars and wires held, and those glimmering nets of black and gold skirted around the shoreline, over the treetops, amidst that starry night.

The barrage began. The smattering of warships brought over from Eskaya for this purpose that were currently surrounding the island all fired at the same time. Streams of amethyst magic roared through the night air, one by one harmlessly vanishing the moment they crashed into the barrier.

Through the haze of combined Lightweave and Shadowgate, Alaric watched the void blasts spark and flare and fade, and he remembered fireworks blazing over Eskaya. He remembered that rooftop in the Dominion capital, the feel of Talasyn's bony shoulders as he dug his fingers in, as he lowered himself enough to almost plead.

Whatever better world you think you'll build, she'd told him then, *it will always be built on blood.*

If they pulled this off—if they saved Nenavar and the Continent from the Voidfell—would it be the same as wiping the slate clean? Once the waves of death magic receded, would people be able to blink in the light of a new world, safe for another thousand years, and believe that it was possible to start again?

Alaric had no answers for that, but he had never been more sure of one thing: he had to try to make it so. If they emerged unscathed out the other side of the Moonless Dark, Kesath would not fight another war. It was a resolve that went beyond the awful pit in his stomach at the prospect of taking Talasyn's magic away. It was an earnest desire to live, finally, in a time of peace. To preserve this beautiful, enigmatic place that was his wife's nation—and to rebuild his own.

No more, Alaric vowed to himself from where he stood at Talasyn's side, the two of them holding back the amethyst bolts, holding back the rot, keeping their island safe. *I will go against my father to make it so. After the Sardovian rebels, no more.*

It was around the forty-minute mark that Talasyn began to flag. The warships had long ceased their simultaneous barrage and were now taking turns firing a cannon each; the Dominion was rationing its aether cores since no new magic could be extracted from the Void Sever until it stabilized. On the Night of the World-Eater, though, the Voidfell would *not* retreat, not until an hour had passed. She needed to hold on for that long.

Aethermancing nonstop for such an extended period of time was akin to climbing an endless flight of stairs. Effortless at first, the body going through rote motions of muscle memory. An action so intrinsic that the exact moment fatigue started sinking in was difficult to pinpoint, and before long limbs throbbed and lungs shrank, squeezing out air in splinters, a taste of rust in the back of the mouth, and there was no choice but to keep going because it was too late to turn around.

Talasyn felt all this and more. Rivulets of sweat ran down her spine. She ached all over. By some miracle, she managed to keep her focus, drawing on the spate of concentration exercises she'd done with Alaric, and she kept her strength, buoyed by the hours she'd spent tapping into the primordial thread of the Light Sever.

It was with ten minutes left on the clock that something began to go horribly wrong.

The feeling—Talasyn could compare it only to when the aether cores inside the jars burst, back during the month's first trial. But the shattering came from inside her. It was *her* body hitting a critical point. Her magic—pushed to the limit, amplified by rain and blood and tempest—redirected *inward.*

It had nowhere else to go within the barrier. A radiant blaze engulfed her outstretched hand, strands of Shadowgate clinging to it like smoke. Her arm burned and froze all at once, the sensation quickly spreading through the rest of her, pouring into the stitch in her side, into every fault line of her shaking frame.

Another bolt of void magic slammed into the shield. Beside her, Alaric let out a hiss. The shadows were wrapping around his own arm, threaded through with the Lightweave.

He looked at her, a question in his silver eyes.

He wanted to put a stop to the exercise. He wanted to bring down the sphere.

But he would only do it if she agreed.

Talasyn couldn't stand the thought of him getting hurt. But she needed to believe in him, and in herself, and in what they were capable of together. The fate of their world depended on that belief.

She shook her head. "We can't stop now." Her voice was strained, almost drowned out by the roar of magic, but the expression on his face told her he was hanging on her every word. "This is the last chance. If we really can't maintain the shield for an hour, then we have to come up with another plan. We need to know *now.*"

"All right," Alaric said softly. "Breathe with me."

And Talasyn did. The minutes wore on and she coaxed air through her body the way he'd taught her to at the Roof of Heaven and amidst the Belian ruins. She felt a calming, a centering. It took the edge off somewhat, at first, but the burning freeze never subsided and eventually grew worse.

No one knew they were in trouble. The Enchanters were controlling the amplifiers from a hovering ship, beyond the sphere. Everyone else was too far away to see what was happening to them.

Talasyn watched in horror as her splayed fingertips and Alaric's turned blue. Then their skin rippled with red blisters. She felt no pain from them, which meant that the nerves were deadened, but everywhere else in her body—everywhere else was ice and inferno. The eclipse magic was eating away at them both, even as amethyst cannon fire continued to ram into it.

Then, in a moment of double vision, she was looking at her hand afire with blackened light, but she was also looking at that gnarled, aged hand as it dug into the snowy ridge, as it unfurled beneath the sun. Had it been her hand all this time? Had she been seeing what was yet to come to pass?

She thought that she might understand now what had happened to Gaheris. The Shadowgate had consumed him, demanding its due in exchange for power. One could gaze only so long into aetherspace before something lunged from its depths.

This was the price for meddling with the unknown.

It went on and on, the waves of black and gold and amethyst, and just when Talasyn couldn't take it anymore—

—just when she was fit to collapse, to lose herself in this ice-tinged death of a sun's scorching heart—

An hour had ticked by.

The void blasts stopped coming. The Ahimsan Enchanters brought down the amplifying configuration's nets, and the sphere of eclipse magic dwindled in size, receding from the space around Iantas until it eventually collapsed into nothingness as Alaric and Talasyn cancelled their aethermancy.

They stumbled together, catching each other with their uninjured arms, and swayed over the moonlit sands. People were cheering in triumph, but for her there was only exhaustion and inferno and the broadness of him, his arms clasped around her waist, cooling the fever in her bloodstream. Her face was buried in his shoulder, but out of the corner of her eye she watched her right hand. Watched the blue fade from its fingertips, leaving behind only the angry red blisters on her palm.

"I think, perhaps," Ishan Vaikar said much later, in the dining room, "we must prepare for the possibility that the aftereffects will be . . . long-lasting."

The table's other occupants—Urduja, Elagbi, Talasyn, and Alaric—stared at her blankly. Talasyn was famished after the taxing exercise, but she paused mid-chew, willing the daya to admit that her statement had been made in jest.

A vain hope, as it turned out.

"The amplifying configuration has clearly influenced Their Majesties' aethermancy on a molecular level," Ishan went on to explain. "I believe that our experiments have magnified your connection to each other."

"Connection?" Alaric repeated, frowning.

"Whatever it is that enables your magic and the Lachis'ka's to merge, Emperor Alaric," Ishan clarified. "If only there was a way for Enchanters to manipulate the Lightweave and the Shadowgate as well. Then I could study it better." She gave a wistful sigh. "But back to the matter at hand. The amplifier's effects could act like a poison, slowly leaving the system as they're processed. Or its effects could become a chronic condition in which the changes are more . . . permanent. It's impossible to determine which way they'll resolve at this time."

"But either option sounds positively delightful," Talasyn sniped.

"Well, let us hope that it is the former," Elagbi said with a scowl that matched Alaric's as the two men exchanged contentious looks.

"There is no help for it, I suppose," said Urduja. "It is the trade-off for saving us from Dead Season."

Like her father and husband, Talasyn felt a scowl tug at her lips. The Zahiya-lachis seemed rather cavalier about the prospect of her granddaughter accidentally forging a chronic connection with the enemy. Then again, having one more thing to hold over the Night Emperor's head nicely suited Urduja's plans.

Shouldn't they be my plans as well?

Another wave of guilt turned the food to dust in Talasyn's mouth. She and the Zahiya-lachis were supposed to be working together, pressing every advantage so that the Sardovian Allfold could take back the Continent before the year was out. It was the right thing to do, the only thing, and she still hadn't made up her mind where Alaric fit into it. She still didn't know if she could do what needed to be done when it came to him, when the time came for it.

"As for the injuries sustained during the casting," said Ishan, "there is clearly a threshold to this type of aethermancy. Aktamasok's crater is a little smaller than this island, but the amount of magic needed to repel the Void Sever will be tenfold. So I suggest . . . keep practicing." Ishan looked down at her plate dejectedly. "That's really all I've got."

Alaric opened his mouth, no doubt to give the daya another piece of his mind, but Talasyn placed a hand on his thigh under the table. An unmistakable command to stand down.

"It's too risky," Elagbi declared. "We should think of another plan to stop Dead Season."

"This is the best one we've got, Amya," Talasyn countered. She held up her right palm. "See? The blisters are already gone. Emperor Alaric and I have magical resistance on our side. We'll pull it off—especially now that we know what to prepare for."

Despite her words, Talasyn was nervous. Alaric was leaving tomorrow, and she would have to figure this out without him.

An attendant scurried into the room with a bottle of fermented pearl-barley wine and poured out generous amounts for Urduja, Elagbi, and Ishan, decorously bypassing Talasyn since her aversion to liquor was well known among the castle staff. As he hovered at Alaric's elbow and made to tip the bottle, however, gray eyes flickered in Talasyn's direction. Alaric covered the glass with his hand.

"Water," he told the attendant curtly. The latter bowed and went to fetch the jug from the other end of the table.

Some choices were cautious, arrived at after a lengthy weighing of pros and cons as meticulous as the dispersal of casongkâ stones. Other choices took hold with the fever of an impulse, unearthed like sparks that flew when a singular moment raked over the embers of the human heart.

Even if he hates me in the end—

The sparks swept through Talasyn as she sat there at the dining table, staring across at her husband long after he'd looked away, and channeling all her political training to not let an ounce of emotion show.

Even if they hang me for it—

There was fear, yes, but there was exhilaration, too. The defiant kind. The thrill of making a decision that was wholly her own.

I will save him.

CHAPTER TWENTY-FOUR

The next day the bright sun raged over a flurry of activity on Iantas's landing grid as the Kesathese delegation's bags were loaded onto the newly repaired shallop and its crew ran their usual preflight checks on ropes and sails and rudders and aether cores. The castle kitchens were busy, too, spitting out a parade of tall straw baskets stuffed with food that would soon join the larders of the stormship waiting at Port Samout.

"This is too much," Alaric remarked. He and Talasyn were observing the bustling scene from the balcony of their chambers. "What are my men and I to do with fifty cured pork legs?"

"Eat them," said his wife. "They're good with the sun buffalo cheddar and the dried mangoes."

"The twenty wheels of cheddar and the five sacks of dried mangoes, you mean."

She wrinkled her nose at him. "It's a three-day voyage. A lot can happen in that time. What if the ship crashes and you're marooned?"

"I'll build a raft from the pork legs," he deadpanned.

Talasyn clapped a hand over her mouth, transmuting a bark of laughter into an inelegant snort. Even as Alaric struggled not to grin, something in his chest lifted at the fact that he was able to make her laugh.

The truth was, he'd been feeling out of sorts all morning. Her laughter offered only a temporary reprieve once he realized that he wouldn't be hearing it—wouldn't be seeing *her*—for at least a month.

He had to sail back to Kesath. There was no question of that. He had to oversee preparations for the series of mass evacuations that would ensue before the night of the Moonless Dark. He'd been gone long enough as it was; his officers were getting antsy, and their written questions about the estimated date of his return were becoming more pointed. He'd already received a skua from Commodore Mathire with a list of meetings that required his presence, meetings that could no longer be put on hold. And always there was his father tugging at the edges of the Shadowgate, beckoning from the In-Between.

Talasyn had gotten her mirth under control and was now scolding him for being ungracious—she'd only been seeing to it that he and his crew wouldn't starve to death. She was wearing a dress that seemed chosen to punish him for leaving, with a bodice that clung to her trim figure like liquid bronze. Her chestnut hair was loose today, falling in soft waves over the metallic sheen of silk that Alaric's fingers itched to crumple.

You could stay. The treacherous notion intruded upon his thoughts. His mind conjured a fantasy of living here for good, in this castle by the sea, spending the rest of his days being scolded by a fiery slip of a girl. He pushed away the ache of such wishful thinking and drawled responses calculated to incense her further as they made their way out of the royal suite.

Iantas's corridors were deserted; most of its residents had gathered around the landing grid to see the Night Emperor off. Alaric found his and Talasyn's voices unnaturally loud in the stillness, their footsteps echoing. He barely registered what they were bickering about this time, too busy drinking her in, committing the placement of every freckle to memory.

"Just curious," he said, with a lightness that he didn't feel, as they descended the stairs. "How will you get through the next few sennights without me to harp on? I'd hate to deprive you of your favorite pastime."

Talasyn colored. "You certainly think highly of—*excuse me*—"

Alaric had quickened his pace so that he wouldn't have to look at those blushing cheeks and think about how much he wanted to kiss them. Talasyn stomped after him, but her skirt slowed her down. He reached the landing first and she grabbed his arm, forcing him to look back at her, at her irate gaze and her put-upon pout, and his restraint dwindled to nothing in an instant.

One month. It consumed all of the space in his head. A number of days abstract yet acute. *One month away from you.*

He seized the small hand that was digging into his arm and dragged her to a corner room, which—he discovered upon wrenching open the door—was *not* a room, but a supply closet stocked with cleaning equipment. He knocked over a mop as he hurriedly shut Talasyn and himself inside and flicked on the fire lamp, its soft glow painting her bewildered expression in splotches of gold out of the darkness.

He backed her up against the wall, concealing the tremor in his hand by flattening it over her head, leaning in. He was too big in this enclosed place, too clumsy, too desperate. But he didn't know how else to be.

"What"—Talasyn swallowed—"what are you doing?"

Alaric watched the gilded skin of her throat ripple. Wondered if her mouth had gone dry, too.

"I want a kiss for the road," he said hoarsely. "Should you deign to give it."

He captured her lips in a bruising kiss. She melted at once, swaying against him as he ran his black-gauntleted hands down her body, each caress a memory he could hold up to the lonely nights that lay ahead.

But Talasyn would always be Talasyn, no matter the situation, and she wasted no time in laying into him once he lifted his mouth from hers. "Everyone's waiting for us, you dolt," she snapped, although the effect was rather diminished by the way she was gripping his collar, pulling him ever nearer.

"Let them wait," Alaric growled, nibbling at her jaw, fidgeting with the pearlescent front clasps of her bodice until they gave way and his hand disappeared beneath the molten silk.

Talasyn scrabbled at the shoulders of his black tunic, then hiked up her skirt so that she could wrap one slim leg around his waist. Her response was even more enthusiastic than usual. Urged on by a sneaking suspicion, Alaric scraped the rough seam of his gauntlet over her breast, and something in his soul caught fire when she shuddered and canted her hips.

At least he wasn't wearing the clawed ones that constituted part of his battle armor that day. He had no wish to hurt her. And yet some dark intrigue blossomed within him at the thought of *that*, and he wondered if she'd be able to take it.

Talasyn yanked him toward her for another kiss, during which he thumbed at the fastenings of his trousers, driven only by the basest of instincts. Just once, before he left. Her fingers, wrapped around his hard length, were so warm they were almost burning, as though her magic was roaring out of her to devour him whole.

Alaric's head fell into the crook of Talasyn's neck. In his haste to close the distance, he accidentally kicked over a pile of the coconut husks that the Nenavarene used to polish their floors. As they clattered to the floor, he groaned into her skin, thrusting sloppily into her palm. It felt so good that he forgot about everything else—at least, until she huffed in his ear, "Well, I'm glad *you're* having fun."

He couldn't help chuckling at that. Neither could he help the rush of affection that made him finally, *finally* press his lips to her cheek. "I am honestly impressed by your ability to keep on mouthing off, Your Grace. Even when you have me in hand, even when I'm doing this—" The flowing fabric of her skirt was crushed between their bodies, and he slid a hand up her thigh.

"*Oh.*" She gave a start as his fingers curled around her, as he worked one in. "The leather feels different—"

"My gauntlet is going to smell like you." There was an undercurrent of anger in his tone even as he twitched in her palm at the debauched, forbidden thrill of it, and perhaps he *was* angry, at that. Angry that he couldn't stay away from her.

But his words had a fascinating effect on his wife. Her eyes narrowing in annoyance, her hips rolling a little bit more insistently toward his hand, she responded, "Don't say things like that."

"Why not, darling?" he asked, just to be contrary.

She tapped her fist against his shoulder in a halfhearted ghost of a punch. "Don't call me that, either."

"So many instructions," he grumbled, withdrawing his hand to arrange her other leg around his waist, the black gauntlet slick with her wetness digging into the flesh of her thigh. "I can hardly keep up."

He thumbed her undergarments aside and slid into her. The breathless cry that she let out, the way she stretched around him—it all combined to make him groan again, against her temple.

Shelves of pails and feather dusters and rags rattled around them as Alaric started thrusting in earnest, Talasyn's skirts bunched up between their bodies. She was louder than she'd been the first time, perhaps, he thought, because of the frenzied, illicit nature of the act: they were in a storage closet, still fully clothed, urging each other higher, stifling moans with each other's mouths, breathing expletives into skin. For him the specter of separation loomed like Dead Season, and he could only hope that some part of her felt the same.

The sobering reminder caused him to pick up the pace, in a burning need for her to feel him between her legs long after he was gone. "Look at you, Lachis'ka," he said, his voice gravelly and darkly teasing, the words conjured as usual from a heady mixture of bravado and sheer want. "Always scolding your husband, but you're still going to come all over him. You're still going to march out there—in front of *everyone*—and bid me goodbye while I'm dripping down your thighs."

"Bastard," Talasyn panted, her face buried in the side of his neck. Her nails raked through his hair as she unraveled around him. As she raised her head slightly and he saw the flare of golden magic in her eyes when she reached her peak. "*Alaric.*"

His knees nearly buckled at the sound of his name in her voice. By some miracle, he managed to keep standing, managed to keep pinning her to the wall until his own orgasm barreled through him, glorious and perfect.

He would have stayed inside her forever, if he could, but her right leg slipped to the floor and he made a growl of frustration as the movement eased him out of her. He wasn't done spending yet, and Talasyn solved his problem for him. She shifted the leg that was still around his hips higher and aimed him at the inside of her thigh. He hunched over her, the animal in his blood howling with the anticipation of marking her like this, while the more human part could scarcely believe that she would actually *let* him.

She had freckles there as well, a small cluster like a spiral constellation. He spilled all over those burnished little stars with a harsh exhale.

Talasyn bit her lip in the lamplight, arching back against the wall, and the sight of his come on her freckles was for Alaric a religious experience, was the taste of sugar, was peace after wartime. Ears ringing, senses cloudy, he held her thigh in place, fingers stroking soothingly as he wiped himself dry on it.

Her eyelids fluttered as the leather gauntlet roved over her skin. It was so interesting. It was another facet of their twisted dance that he was pathetically eager to explore.

But he couldn't. Not for a month.

He had to go.

After their breathing had evened out and they'd fixed their clothes as best as they could, Alaric succumbed to his worst impulses and drew his prickly wife in for another embrace, burying his nose in her hair.

"*Now* what are you doing?" Talasyn demanded, her words muffled into the front of his tunic. "Everyone's probably wondering where we—"

"Shut up, Tala," he said, without a trace of ire, with a foreign gentleness that was the most natural thing in the world where she was concerned.

And much to his surprise, she desisted, relaxing against him.

"I'll write," she mumbled. "But you'd better write me back."

"I will." His heart lurched inside his chest. "I promised, didn't I?"

After her husband's airship left, Talasyn went to the kitchens.

She hadn't bothered to correct Alaric when he brought it up, but in the Dominion there was little need to consult a healer for a preventive. The tree called wisewoman's lilac grew aplenty in the dense jungles, and every well-stocked kitchen had jarfuls of its bark on hand—for grinding up to use as a piquant seasoning and for brewing into a morning-after tea.

The tea was also an efficient treatment for menstrual pains, and that was the excuse Talasyn gave to the cooks. She gulped it down as fast as she could and then retreated upstairs. To send a missive to the Sardovian encampment in the Storm God's Eye.

CHAPTER TWENTY-FIVE

She lasted all of four days before writing her first letter to him.

In her defense, she had important news to share.

Talasyn was communing with the Light Sever on Belian for the third day in a row, folded into a cross-legged sitting position at the heart of the pillar of golden magic that suspended her a few feet above the ground.

She had learned, through a great deal of trial and error, that the Sever could be somewhat responsive to her thoughts when she immersed herself in it long enough, and this was the longest that the Sever had flared yet. For the last several minutes, it had been showing Talasyn her memories of her mother from a time when she should have been too young to remember anything. Aetherspace flowed into her and excavated the scenes from her soul. Whenever one scene started to fade, she snatched the threads of light that shaped it, willing them to lead the way to the next. Her mother singing her to sleep. Her mother laughing at a joke made by a younger Elagbi while Talasyn—Alunsina—cooed in her arms. Her mother leaning over the cradle, spirals of golden magic dancing between her fingertips while the room echoed with a child's squeals of delight.

Amidst all those idyllic memories, aetherspace kept spinning back to the conversation between Hanan and Sintan, and to Hanan in her gilded prison, knowing that she was about to die, holding her daughter for the last time. Perhaps that was the work of Talasyn's will, too—a subconscious desire, despite the heartache, to stay as long as she could in those final moments between her and her mother.

I will always be with you. We will find—

The Light Sever deactivated. The column of magic collapsed back into the stone fountain and winked out of existence, and Talasyn fell to the ground. And Hanan was gone—gone again . . .

Talasyn screamed. The sound echoed through the ruins, startling the birds away from their roosts in the grandfather trees. As they took wing all around her, she reached deep into the aether in her soul, desperate for more time with her mother, desperate to cling to the love she'd never known.

Radiance filled her vision. At first, she thought that by some miracle the Sever had flared again. Then she realized it was coming from *her*. The Lightweave was flowing from her fingertips, forming a golden dome around her about half the diameter of the Light Sever when it was active, but it was the largest magical summoning that Talasyn had ever managed to date that had a solid shape. It didn't break, it didn't burst, it didn't flare wildly into the sky. It was controlled. *She* was controlling it.

She finally understood how to.

In her longing for her mother, she'd ridden the currents of aetherspace, drawing out the connection to the past. Perhaps it was just wishful thinking, but she could almost feel Hanan Ivralis guiding her hand—could almost hear a voice in her head that she thought might be Hanan's.

This is how we build a wall.

This is how we save the things we love.

At Talasyn's whim, the dome grew and shrank, brilliant and flickering. She kept it up for as long as her concentration and energy held, then allowed herself a moment's breath before casting it again.

The first time hadn't been a fluke. The second dome was just as solid, just as malleable, and Talasyn pushed herself to maintain it for an even longer period of time, as Ishan Vaikar had recommended.

She could do this. She would not let eclipse magic consume her.

After a while, she sank to her knees on the sun-warmed stone, spent, heavy with exhausted hope.

There was only one thing on her mind. She wanted to share this triumph with someone.

She wanted it to be Alaric.

It wasn't that she *missed* him. Of course she didn't. But he was the only one who would truly understand this feat. Perhaps if he were here he might even smile that fleeting, crooked grin—

Talasyn put her fingers to her mouth and whistled. As her messenger eagle glided over to the campsite from where it had been patrolling the skies, she pulled out the stylus and ink set from her pack, along with a fresh sheet of parchment, and began to write, determinedly ignoring the stuttering of her pulse.

It's nothing, she told herself over and over.

At the edge of the Citadel, between the obsidian gates and the barren plains, thick plumes of shadow magic tore through the air.

The Sever wasn't active. All that raw, screeching energy was coming from the Night Emperor, who stood in the center of a protective ring of darkness that rose and dipped and flowed as though it were made of black fire. The ring stalwartly bore the attacks launched at it from all sides by a dozen legionnaires, growling and sparking silver every time a shadowy blade collided against it.

Alaric's strength was beginning to wane. The exercise had been going on for almost an hour, which was far longer than he'd managed in previous sessions, but it still wasn't good enough. His gaze remained fixed on the timepiece on the barren ground at his feet. Just a little while longer . . .

A vicious-looking greataxe broke through the ring. Its wielder, Nisene, swung the head at Alaric, who quickly dodged to the side and at the same time dismissed the barrier with a hiss of frustration. The axe and all the other weapons surrounding him winked out of existence, and the gray training grounds were still once more.

Alaric curtly ordered his legionnaires back to the Citadel. They turned and trooped toward the tall gates, Nisene shooting him a triumphant smirk over her shoulder. Soon only Alaric and Sevraim were left outside the walls, under the watchful eyes of the sentries posted above.

Alaric crossed his arms and arched a brow at the other man. "You are still here because . . . ?"

"Just wanted to tell you that none of us could have done better today," Sevraim quietly replied, "and it's probably all right if you got some rest."

"None of you carry the fate of entire civilizations," Alaric shot back. "For whatever reason, that burden has fallen to me. I'll rest after the Moonless Dark."

Sevraim grimaced. "If we return to Nenavar with you looking like death and too exhausted to hold back the Voidfell, your wife will—"

"*We* are not returning to Nenavar," Alaric corrected him. "You and the other legionnaires are staying here, to assist with the evacuations. And, on the night of reckoning, you will all be on the ships heading north, away from the blast."

Sevraim paled. "I can't let you go alone."

"I'm not asking for your permission. This is an order."

"But—"

Alaric held up an imperious hand. It was a command for silence that he rarely used on Sevraim, and the latter fell into a mutinous silence.

"Should Talasyn and I not be successful," Alaric said, "there is still a chance you and the other Kesathese will survive. If so, I need you to be with my father, to sway him from any warmongering, any rash course of action. I need you to get him to focus on rehabilitating the Continent after death magic sweeps through it."

"The Regent is not going to listen to *me*." Sevraim was aggrieved. "He still thinks of me as that initiate who organized a party in the barracks and got everyone foxed before the oathtaking."

"You will have to try." Alaric's tone was firm. "Should I not return from the Dominion, this is going to be the last thing I ever ask of you."

The legionnaire stared at Alaric, looking stricken. Alaric felt his own jumble of emotions rising to the surface, but he forced it back down with a clearing of his throat. "If I die and Talasyn lives," he continued, "I charge you with protecting her. From my father, and whoever else."

"You have to tell me why," Sevraim said with a hint of startling, uncharacteristic fierceness. "I deserve that, I think. You're asking me to abandon you—my commander, my *friend*—and carry out your bidding after you're gone. So, at the very least, tell me why you would still care about the Lightweaver's fate even from beyond the willows."

Alaric swallowed. What could he say beneath this gray sky, against these black walls? What did he owe to this person who had been by his side through everything since they were boys?

How could he even begin to explain what he felt whenever he thought of Talasyn?

How much he missed her?

Helpless anger flickered through him. He shouldn't even be in this situation in the first place. He'd gone soft, and Sevraim was taking him to task for it.

"Will you do it or not?" he demanded. "If you don't feel capable, I'll find someone else."

It was a bluff, and a pathetic one, at that. They both knew that there was nobody else he could ask.

"Fine," Sevraim conceded. "You can leave it to me." His dark eyes narrowed. "But you do realize that, for the rest of this month, the twins and I will be arguing with you over your decision to go back to Nenavar alone? You'll never know peace."

"I haven't known peace since I got married," Alaric retorted. "So—nothing new there, as far as I'm concerned."

A few days later, Alaric's father's eyes followed him through the mists of shadow magic that inked the hall.

"At last," said Gaheris, "my son shows his face."

A sennight had passed since Alaric returned from Nenavar, a sennight spent mostly shut away in council meetings or investigating rebel activity when he wasn't training with his legionnaires. A sennight of rebuffing Gaheris's summons with any convenient excuse that came to mind.

But *this*—Alaric could no longer let this lie.

There was a weak chirp from the lone sunlit corner. Tracking the sound to its source, he was pierced by shock and unease.

The sariman looked ill, its head tucked limply against its chest. Feathers littered the floor of the cage; what remained on its thin body had lost most of their iridescence.

"The weather doesn't suit it, I believe," Gaheris said lightly.

"Draining it of its blood on a regular basis certainly didn't help," Alaric snapped.

"The suffering of one creature in exchange for the greater good. You are well aware of that."

Alaric forced his thoughts away from the sickly animal. He'd come here for a reason. "I need to talk to you about the exclusion list." Commodore Mathire had presented it to him earlier that morning: a breakdown of the villages on the Continent that were heavily suspected of sympathizing with the Allfold rebels.

Gaheris smirked. "I wondered if that would finally bring you to me. What of it? Is it not simple common sense to deny Kesath's enemies passage on our ships?"

"It's cruel," Alaric stonily insisted. "These are not listed individuals but entire towns. I won't leave innocent civilians stranded on account of mere whispers."

"We're not stranding them. They're free to evacuate as they please. Just not on our vessels."

"*Whose* vessels, then?" Unlike Nenavar, where it seemed nearly every household owned at least one coracle, Kesath had allocated most of its raw shipbuilding materials to the war effort. Yet even coracles had not been able to save that village at the foot of Aktamasok when the Voidfell caught it unawares. The smell of rot, of all that death . . . As Alaric envisioned it spreading over his native land, he forced a surge of bile back down his throat, swallowing anger and frustration like a mouthful of thorns.

"Father, I've seen the destruction of the Void Sever firsthand. If the light-and-shadow barrier doesn't work," he tried to explain, tried to get Gaheris to see reason, "everyone left behind will die."

He searched the Regent's face, hoping to catch a glimpse of the man from before the war. The man who had sometimes smiled at a dry remark from his wife, who had sometimes ruffled Alaric's hair. But there was only ice and resolution.

"The Night Empire will not shoulder the burdens of those who conspire against us," Gaheris declared. "That is my order."

When it came to dealing with his father, Alaric knew that it was about picking his battles. This one wasn't a *total* loss; if anything, it gave him added incentive to succeed in holding back the Voidfell. But it still rankled.

"Very well." He looked at the sariman in the cage again, at this wilting reminder of those sun-drenched isles, and some helpless impulse, some shout into the endless abyss, made him add, "But if you don't want *this* creature to die, you will entrust it to my care until it is strong enough to withstand more experiments."

Gaheris sneered. "I doubt your meager talents extend to zookeeping, my boy."

Alaric stood his ground. "It needs fresh air, more light, and rest. You can't unlock its secrets if you kill it."

"Perhaps I can," Gaheris mused. "We've run all the tests we could on feathers and blood samples. Perhaps its bones are the key. Or its heart."

"*No.*" The Shadowgate roared through Alaric, his eyes flaring silver. But he caught himself, forced himself to speak more calmly as the Regent stared at him. "Father, don't waste the sariman the way the Sardovian guerrillas wasted their stormship. Don't burn it all to the ground before the endgame."

It was another way to buy time. He held his breath until Gaheris finally gave a measured nod.

"Have it your way. But if the bird ends up dying despite your efforts, it will be on *your* head."

"Naturally," Alaric muttered.

As he left his father's hall, it occurred to him that it had almost been too easy. Gaheris never backed down once the course was set. But perhaps his Enchanters had truly run out of ideas. Alaric could hope that was the case; for now, he'd gotten what he wanted.

Thus it was that he found himself locked in a staring contest with the sariman later that afternoon in his chambers. He'd had the cage placed by the window and its inhabitant was stretching its bald neck toward the sun. Studying him with copper eyes.

Now what? he could almost imagine it asking.

"I have no idea," he said out loud.

He turned to his desk to pen a response to Talasyn's letter, which had arrived the previous day.

Preparations were well underway throughout the Dominion archipelago for the sevenfold eclipse. As Aktamasok boiled over with increasing regularity, death magic shot into the air from its crater and spilled down its rugged slopes. Beneath the beating of its amethyst pulses illuminating the sky for miles around, the Nenavarene packed up their houses and loaded their vessels with as many supplies as they could find room for on board. Fields and orchards were stripped of seeds and grain, to be planted in case the ships returned to barren earth. Farmers picked out their best animals to acclimatize them to life on deck and in the holds; the rest would be left behind.

Talasyn helped whenever she could—readying Iantas alone was a slow process that would take sennights—but sometimes she slipped away.

To Belian, to commune with the Lightweave, making sure

that her magic was as strong as it could be on the night of reckoning.

To Eskaya, to visit her family, savoring every moment like it was her last with them—just in case it was.

To the privacy of her chambers, where she wrote letters to Alaric.

And on this night, to the Storm God's Eye. With Surakwel Mantes.

He'd insisted on accompanying her to the Sardovian encampment this time. "So," he said as they squeezed through the dark mangroves, "where are we on stabbing your husband while he sleeps, Lachis'ka?"

"Keep your voice down," Talasyn hissed. "The Lachis'ka isn't supposed to be here, remember?"

"It's not as though there are any patrols," Surakwel pointed out. "All the soldiers are busy with evacuation procedures."

"I wouldn't be surprised if the mudskippers themselves reported to Her Starlit Majesty."

He laughed, a flash of white teeth and merry walnut-brown eyes in the moonlight. Then he pushed his shaggy hair back from his wide forehead, a gesture that called attention to the ring on his finger, a large silver one embossed with the same serpent that adorned his yacht's sails. While it was the seal of House Mantes of Viyayin, the intricate metalwork was a signature of Lidagat. Niamha's domain.

"But Her Grace didn't answer my question," Surakwel pressed. "Will you stab him immediately after the Moonless Dark? He might be expecting that, though—"

"Maybe you should worry about your own relationships first," Talasyn sniped. "How you're naming yachts after Daya Langsoune and she's giving you rings yet the two of you *still* haven't declared for each other is beyond me."

Surakwel opened his mouth and then shut it again, as

though Talasyn's bluntness had demolished his repertoire of languidly caustic comebacks. Silence festered between them there in the swamp.

"Niamha is marrying someone else," he said at last. "A pact between her mother and his, kept secret all these years, as the possibility of marrying into House Langsoune is a powerful political tool. But they should be announcing it any day now."

"Oh." Talasyn swallowed. "I didn't—"

Surakwel cut her off with a brusque shrug. "It is what it is. The motherland cradles the family and family is where duty is born. That's the old Nenavarene saying, is it not? And who is Daya Langsoune to go against her late mother's wishes?"

Resentment laced his every word. Talasyn couldn't muster anything in the form of response, and fortunately she didn't have to; they soon broke into the clearing, and she locked eyes with the waiting Vela.

In the distance, the stormship *Nautilus* rippled with aether sparks on its grid. Its translucent metalglass panels were aglow as shipwrights worked on its inner modifications, their silhouettes hammering away and installing aether cores and circuitry long into the night. Another airship, a smaller frigate, was nearby and also being serviced. Its cannons were loaded with hearts that shimmered amethyst with the energy of the Voidfell.

"Nenavar's reserves of death magic are dwindling," the Amirante said. "We won't receive any more void hearts until after the Moonless Dark, when it's safe to harvest from Aktamasok again."

"And a very pleasant evening to you, too," Surakwel piped up.

Vela ignored him. "I have *some* good news," she told Talasyn. "General Bieshimma has secured an alliance with the Emberlords of Midzul. They're willing to send fifty warships. And twice that number of aethermancers."

Talasyn bit back a gasp. Midzul, the Land of Fire. Their help would be invaluable. But she had spent too many months under Urduja's tutelage to refrain from asking, "What's in it for them?"

"Aether hearts," Surakwel replied. "I've been there. Their soil runs too hot for crystals to properly form. Their nearest neighbor exports to them at a premium."

"And let me guess," Talasyn said slowly. "Bieshimma neglected to mention to the Emberlords that we blew up the mines on the Sardovian half of the Continent during the retreat and the Kesathese half has hardly any left to spare."

"It's *all* Kesath now," Vela countered. "That is the problem that we need to fix first."

"Nenavar has aether hearts aplenty, Lachis'ka," Surakwel reminded Talasyn. "I'm sure some kind of deal can be cut after we win."

After we win.

What was it about this optimism that carried some presentiment of doom? Perhaps her unease stemmed from not being able to see a clear way forward just yet.

"That's not all," said Vela. "Ornang has agreed to be a staging point. They are a tiny nation and can't offer ships or warriors, but our allies coming from the west may recharge aether cores and resupply there. As for what the benefit is to them . . . well, Kesath is too close for comfort. The Sardovian remnant is all that stands between them and a possible invasion."

Surakwel rolled his eyes. "More probable than possible, Amirante. The Night Emperor won't be satisfied with only Sardovia for long. He'll continue sending his stormships outward, occupying more lands, stealing more resources—"

"He wants to keep his people safe."

Both Vela and Surakwel turned sharply to Talasyn.

"He believes that the only way to do that is to wage war,"

she continued, remembering the wild look on Alaric's face and the barely concealed panic in his voice, his fear that the amplifiers had weakened his magic. She remembered a room in a black city, hot water and valerian, her wounded husband pleading, *Who am I if I'm not a weapon? What have you done to me?* "He sees Sardovia as a threat because of the Cataclysm and the Hurricane Wars. And the Nenavar Dominion sent ships to help the Lightweavers a long time ago. But a country like Ornang, which never did anything to Kesath, he wouldn't . . ."

Talasyn trailed off, the rest of the sentence dying in her throat when she registered Vela's expression. Even when she learned of Darius's betrayal, the Amirante hadn't looked like this.

"You're—you're defending him," Surakwel sputtered. "Lachis'ka, you're actually—"

"I'm *not*," Talasyn insisted, her heart dropping, her stomach hollowing out. "I'm just trying to explain that this is how Alaric thinks."

"Well, then, shall I have my envoy tell Ornang 'Never mind'?" Vela asked. Her tone was low, veering into scorn. It made Talasyn want to sink into the ground.

Talasyn shook her head. "No, of course not. I was only—"

Trying to convince Vela and Surakwel that Alaric wasn't like his father?

Trying to lay the groundwork for sparing his life?

She blinked rapidly at the mud-stained toes of her boots. She felt doomed. She couldn't see the way forward.

"I told you to be careful," Vela spat. "I told you not to have sympathy for him."

The Amirante sounded bitter and disgusted. She sounded like Urduja.

That was when understanding clicked into place for Talasyn. Her superiors saw her as a Lightweaver, as the Lachis'ka. As a means to win the war and secure the throne. They didn't trust her to make her own decisions. Whenever she showed the slightest sign of going against their wishes, they treated her like a child.

She had to do this on her own.

"I *am* being careful." Talasyn lifted her chin, meeting the Amirante's gaze squarely. "I haven't told Alaric anything. But how do you think it's going to look when our rebellion kills the man who saved Nenavar and the Continent from the Voidfell?"

"It is my personal opinion that there will be dancing in the streets," Surakwel said wryly. "Why should Sardovians mourn the Night Emperor who terrorized them?"

"After the Moonless Dark, he will be a hero in the eyes of the people," said Talasyn. "There's Kesath to consider as well. They're almost as insular a nation as Nenavar. All of their younger generation—every single one—grew up believing the rest of the Continent was out to get them. They look to Alaric for protection. If we kill him, the Kesathese will want vengeance, and a lasting peace will never be achieved. Somewhere down the line, yet another war *will* start."

Vela was looking at her strangely. She opened her mouth, as though to say something, then hesitated. "Is that one of your conditions, then, Talasyn?" she finally asked. "That Alaric Ossinast lives?"

Talasyn's nape prickled with a sense of wrongness. With the feeling that *that* hadn't been what Vela initially wanted to say.

But a question had been asked, and so she answered it. "Yes, Amirante."

"You do realize that he will never forgive you?" Vela pressed. "Even if we spare his life? I warned you about that before."

Even if he hates me in the end.

Even if they hang me for it.

"It doesn't matter whether he forgives me or not." Hearing herself say that out loud, Talasyn felt as though her heart had cracked in two. "This is the best course of action."

Vela nodded. "Then—I'll see what can be done."

Talasyn couldn't feel relief. Not yet. There was something the Amirante had wanted to say but for whatever reason hadn't. And Surakwel was looking at them both in disbelief, shaking his head.

"You *do* see my point, don't you?" Talasyn asked him.

He went still, his gaze growing cool. "No, I don't," he said flatly. "But I have thrown in my lot with the Allfold, and that means I must trust in their judgment."

There was a creaking sound in the distance as one of the *Nautilus*'s cannons swiveled into firing position. The shipwrights were conducting a weapons test, and Talasyn watched as a stream of pure lightning emerged, arcing up into the starry heavens.

"I will send you my instructions after the Moonless Dark," Vela told Talasyn. "Everything should have been prepared by then."

"You can count on me," vowed Surakwel, looking only at Vela. "House Mantes's private army is at the Sardovian Allfold's disposal."

Talasyn said nothing. The lightning cannon, freshly repaired, newly recharged, tore the night sky apart in fragments of white. Her eyes filled with tempest.

PART III

CHAPTER TWENTY-SIX

When Alaric returned to the Nenavar Dominion a month later, he returned to a land of ghosts. After exiting an otherwise empty port and then leaving the *Deliverance*'s hangars, the black Kesathese shallop had sailed alone over still cities, quiet villages, and the empty roads in between that once bustled with merchants' carts. The azure horizon was lined with the backs of ships, receding into the clouds, that carried the last wave of Nenavarene evacuees. They would journey on as far as they could before the Moonless Dark, their chances of survival measured by the distance they traversed through sky and over water as aether fumes bore them further and further away from the homeland that would spell their end should Alaric and Talasyn prove unsuccessful.

We'd be the first to die if that happens. The thought raked across Alaric's mind as he stood on the wooden deck above sprawling vistas of rainforest and white sand. He tried to ignore it—fear being anathema to the Shadowforged—but it gnawed at his heart with icy teeth. Grotesque images ran rampant in his mind—standing at the edge of the Voidfell's crater with Talasyn . . . being swallowed by the amethyst haze . . . the magic dissolving their two forms before spreading across their world . . .

Tonight. It all came down to tonight.

The spike of anxiety only served to worsen Alaric's black mood of the past month. Rebel activity had died down in light of the Continent's mass evacuations, but he would have preferred the simplicity of combat to the bureaucracy he'd had to endure. A month of squabbling with his officers, of dodging his father's verbal blows, of wrangling with the sheer logistics of moving millions of people and the necessary supplies . . .

They hadn't been able to move everyone in the end, not even all of those not on the exclusion list. There had simply not been enough ships.

A month of failures and dead ends, all while the sariman's song had echoed within the walls of his bedroom.

Freed from constant blood extractions and the darkness of Gaheris's private hall, the bird had regained its strength, as well as its fiery plumage. However, like most Nenavarene creatures, including Alaric's wife, it seemed to take vicious delight in causing him trouble, forever chirping and trilling and beating its wings against the bars of its cage when all Alaric wanted was to rest.

He'd named it Guava in the privacy of his own head. A little joke that only Talasyn would understand.

Not that he could ever tell her about it.

They'd written to each other somewhat frequently, the bulk of the letters carried across the Eversea by Kesathese skuas, which were better suited to long-distance flights than Nenavarene eagles or House Ossinast's ravens. Brief missives, formally worded, more argumentative than not, detailing little of consequence other than Talasyn's progress reports on her aethermancy. But Alaric had savored every line from her, spending hours trying to read between them and imagining how the words would sound in her voice, even as her horrid penmanship strained his eyes.

He couldn't wait to see her. It was a very strange feeling. Anxious and excited all at once.

As the shallop glided lower over the Eversea and Iantas's finer details came into view, Alaric spotted people on the landing grid waiting to receive him and others on the beach, either dragging fishing nets to shore or scaling the coconut palms to pick their woolly brown fruits. It could have been any normal day on the island, not the one with the potential to end everything.

Talasyn was conspicuously absent from the welcoming committee, though. Alaric felt a sliver of annoyance as he disembarked. This was a grave breach of protocol.

Jie stepped out from the throng to greet him, her dark curls bobbing.

"You're all still here." Alaric wasn't quite able to keep the question out of his tone.

"Oh, Her Grace urged the entire household to leave," Jie chirped. "The villagers' children were sent away at her insistence, but as for the rest of us—we rather felt that our place was with her." The lady-in-waiting's demeanor was as sunny as these shores and her eyes were bright, belying the difficult choice that she'd made. "The kitchen staff was particularly concerned that she wouldn't be able to eat her favorite meals in their absence. Prince Elagbi is here, too," she added as they walked into the spiny castle while the servants boarded the shallop to handle his luggage, "but he is napping, and Her Grace is occupied as well, so if I may escort His Majesty to the royal chambers—"

"You may escort me to her instead," said Alaric.

Jie turned her pert nose up at him. "The Lachis'ka is resolving a delicate matter in the aforementioned kitchens—"

"So take me to the kitchens."

Jie opened her mouth to argue, but Alaric's stern glare was an effective deterrent. There was a definite stomp in her gait while she led him to a wing of Iantas's first level that he'd never been to before.

Whatever Alaric had been expecting when he entered the kitchens, it was *not* the sight of his empress covered in thick, sticky pink liquid. Talasyn was standing, eyes squeezed shut, in front of a potbelly stove atop which perched an overflowing saucepan. Two similarly drenched cooks dabbed at her with hand towels while the rest hung back, looking terrified.

"Honestly, it's fine," Talasyn was attempting to soothe them, blindly gesturing in their direction, "it's all my fault, I'm the one who suggested the recipe, but who knew salamander currants would be so volatile—"

"*I* told her they were," Jie muttered to Alaric.

He clapped a hand over his mouth in order to suppress the chuckle threatening to burst from his throat. Cake batter plastered Talasyn's loose brown hair to her forehead; it dripped from her chin and trickled down the front of her sequined bodice. Although her eyes were closed, she stiffened at the sound of his aborted laugh and then his footsteps as he made his way over to her.

"Don't start with me," she growled.

Something in Alaric's chest began to thaw—an arctic tightness that he didn't even realize had been there in the first place, having lived with it for so long. The two cooks hastily backed away and he grabbed a fresh hand towel, using it to wipe the pink batter from Talasyn's face. This was not how he'd imagined their reunion going, but she'd always been something of an expert in throwing him for a loop.

"Dabbling in the culinary arts now, are we?" he quipped.

"We were testing dessert options for the masquerade," Talasyn grumbled. "The cake mix exploded right as you arrived."

Alaric frowned. "You were not scalded—"

"Not at all, we'd barely fired up the stove."

There was an edge to her assurance, the way there always was whenever he professed concern for her. As though she couldn't understand what he got out of it. He held back a sigh as he patted the bridge of her nose clean, as well as the skin around her eyes. Her lashes fluttered tentatively, and then brown irises were peering up at him from a face still smeared with pink batter at the sides. She presented an absurd picture, and yet—

"Um." Talasyn bit her lip. "Welcome back. Hi."

The moment spun through time in a thread of gold. As Alaric stared down at his wife, all of the stress that he had felt over the past month—all of his fears for tonight—melted away. "Hello."

The Talasyn of nearly a year ago, that war-torn orphan, would never have dared to let Alaric Ossinast move through a room while her eyes were closed and she wasn't aethermancing. That she did so now was an irony far from lost on her. After recovering from her embarrassment—she really *should* have left the cooking to the kitchen staff—she furtively watched her husband, reacquainting herself with his careful movements, his sharp features. Trying to determine if anything about him had changed since they last saw each other.

They sparred on the beach in the late morning, when the sun shone fiercely and the granite castle in the distance blazed almost the same bright silver as Alaric's eyes. Rather than being tired after the long journey from Kesath, he was as strong and agile as ever, not letting up in the least as they took turns shielding and striking. She noticed, though, that he clenched his teeth harder than usual, and she wondered if it was possible for someone to run on sheer determination alone. Or perhaps it was spite.

Finally they banished the last of their weapons and collapsed onto the sand, sprawled out side by side. Talasyn gazed up into the burning heavens, the surf crashing in her ears. She was winded, but not as exhausted as she would have been before her constant trips to the Light Sever. The sun's rays poured through her body as though embracing it.

She had changed so much here in Nenavar. Her magic had changed.

And speaking of things that were out of the ordinary, Sevraim should have popped up with some irreverent remark by now. Too many hours had passed since the Kesathese ship's arrival. "You didn't bring your better half, my lord?" Talasyn asked.

Alaric was red-faced from exertion, gasping like a sea creature wilting in the tropical heat, but he mustered enough energy to turn his head and glare at her. "*Better?*" he echoed stiffly, reddened cheek pillowed on the soft white sand.

She grinned. He blinked, as though taken aback, then his brow wrinkled in annoyance. Now *this* was a change she could get used to—being comfortable enough to tease him.

"I have no use for my legionnaires here," Alaric said. "Sevraim's fleeing north with the rest of them, although my father and a few of my officers were against it."

"They probably wanted you to have some protection," Talasyn surmised. "Just in case I kill you after we save the world."

The corner of his mouth twisted in a rueful half-smile. "To tell you the truth, I'm more interested in the officers who *didn't* put up a fuss."

There was no need for him to elaborate. She'd learned enough from Urduja to know what he meant. She pictured him back at that cold obsidian fortress that was the Citadel, surrounded by people he couldn't trust. Her gaze strayed to where his hand was mere inches from hers and she longed to reach for it.

But it wasn't as though he could trust *her*, either. She didn't want to take his hand with these thoughts in her head, as though to say she was better than his officers. She had her own hidden motives, too.

A shadow fell over them. It was Prince Elagbi, looking well rested from his nap. "I have marshalled the refreshments, Lachis'ka!" he proudly announced, indicating with a flourish the castle staff setting up a grand lunch beneath the coconut palms further up the shore. He peered down at Alaric with something like concern. "Not a moment too soon, it would seem."

"I'm fine," Alaric grunted.

"It's understandable," said Elagbi. "You were gone for a month, the humidity takes a toll on people not used to it—"

Alaric stood up. With some effort, but pointedly, he unfolded to his full height so that he towered over the Dominion prince.

Talasyn would have laughed at such a petty display of injured male pride if the sight of her father hadn't darkened her mood. "I still can't believe you stayed," she scolded Elagbi as the three of them headed to join the staff. "Do you not understand the gravity of the situation—"

It was an old argument, but this time Elagbi flapped his hand at her in the same manner one would shoo away a cat wailing for scraps. "I don't believe I shall be taking life advice from someone who thought it would be a good idea to apply heat to salamander currants, my dear."

Alaric *snorted*. Talasyn quickened her pace, leaving the horrible men behind in a flurry of sand. She glanced behind her in time to see Elagbi suppress a chuckle and lightly clap Alaric on the back. Alaric ducked his head while she shook hers in disgust. It figured that these two would start acting companionable only at her expense.

While Alaric and Talasyn were sparring, the remaining denizens of Iantas had brought out a feast. Rabbitfish grilled in bamboo tubes, fermented crabs wrapped in silverleaf reeds, clay-pot chicken, balls of rice and pig's blood—all laid out on trestle tables around the aforementioned pigs, which had been stuffed with lemongrass and roasted whole on spits. Everyone from the Lachis-dalo to the housemaids dug in with their fingers, making merry. As Alaric approached them, he was already resigned—for the chatter to stop and the staring to begin.

To his surprise, however, while there *were* a few uneasy glances, the majority of the crowd called out greetings, inclining their heads respectfully. A couple of people he vaguely recognized from the village rushed forward, passing him a clay pot and a coconut half-shell brimming with the sweet, clear liquid.

It was several beats before Alaric remembered how to move his hands in order to take the proffered items. "Thank you."

The villagers responded in Nenavarene. They didn't sound angry, or as though they were trying to poison him, so he gave a tentative nod and they melted back into the crowd. And soon enough Elagbi and Talasyn were leading him to one of the tables.

Elagbi pointed to the nearby roast pig in its bed of banana leaves. "I recommend the belly, Emperor Alaric. It's the best part."

Alaric stared at the pig. Its body had been carved up, but the head was intact and it stared back at him, lips curled into a frozen grin.

"Just grab a piece," Talasyn instructed under her breath.

"It's looking at me," Alaric replied in kind. "Why are we feasting, anyway? The world as we know it might end tonight. That's hardly cause for celebration."

"You should have realized by now that the typical Nenavarene response to anything is to throw a party," said Talasyn. "Remember when the Zahiya-lachis announced our betrothal?"

"Fair point."

His serving of the roast pig was a sumptuous chunk of crispy skin and sweet flesh that coated his tongue in a wash of fat. He enjoyed the other dishes as well, observing Elagbi and Talasyn out of the corner of his eye so he could mimic how they ate with their hands, food compressed in the palm, the thumb pushing it into the mouth. He could have done without the perennial breeze making a mess of his hair and the sand that stuck to his clothes, and some cynical part of him surmised that Iantas's residents were merely using up everything in the larders before they all died. Still, there was something idyllic about this gathering. It was the calm before the oncoming storm.

As lunch came to a close, Talasyn drifted away from the crowd and nearer to the waterline, nursing a half-shell of coconut juice. Alaric followed her with the air of someone who didn't know what else to do, and soon enough Elagbi joined them, good-naturedly bellyaching about having lost a casongkâ game to one of the castle gardeners. The heat had dissipated slightly as the sun sank lower in the sky. In a few more hours, the day would end, and then the night . . .

The night might be the last.

"Amya." Talasyn turned to her father. The relaxed smile that he flashed at her was so gentle, so utterly at peace, that the fear of never seeing it again sank in like winter's chill in this golden land. "You should have gone with the Zahiya-lachis. What if the shield doesn't work, what if—"

"It will," Elagbi said firmly. "I have faith in you."

"But *if* it doesn't—"

"Then I will sail with the ancestors," said Elagbi, "content in the knowledge that I didn't leave my daughter alone at the very end."

It was the same as it had been when he first saw her on her wedding day, when Talasyn was helpless, speechless, in the face of so much love. All their quarrels about this issue over the past sennight boiled down to this moment. She leaned into Elagbi's space, resting her head on his shoulder, and he stroked her hair.

Alaric was gazing stoically into the distance, affording them what privacy he could. He was even more subdued than usual after they retreated into the castle. Talasyn's own worries grew with the gathering dusk, restlessness haunting her every step, each fidgeting move. No one knew what would happen at midnight. They had all placed their faith in eclipse magic because hope was second nature, was the last good thing, but whether or not it would be successful, no one could actually say for sure.

Talasyn noticed a few of the servants hastily wiping away tears while they tidied up for the evening, and the sight brought her perilously close to the brink as well. Before Alaric could push open the door to their chambers all the way, she grabbed hold of the embroidered cuff of his sleeve, her fingers twisting into the skin-warmed silk.

"Do you want to go somewhere?" she blurted out. "A quick stop before the sevenfold eclipse?"

Gray eyes regarded her somberly. Glimmers of her own misgivings were reflected back at her, but she saw none of the wariness that she anticipated in response to her abrupt question.

Perhaps she wasn't the only one who was changing.

"What do you have in mind?" he asked.

Talasyn wanted to visit Eskaya before they went to the Void Sever. Alaric agreed readily enough; there were still six hours to go before midnight and he was restless, too. It also struck him as oddly fitting, on what might be the final night, to go back to where this odd marriage began.

First things first, however. They had to prepare for battle.

In his dressing room, he donned his armor meditatively, clearing his mind the way he always did before an impending skirmish. The stakes were just as high.

He hadn't been expecting his father to summon him, but there it was, the scrabbling at the edges, the thinning of the veil. Alaric entered the In-Between cautiously, wondering what Gaheris could possibly wish to see him about at this final hour. Silver eyes watched him from a throne of shadows, within walls of tremulous, staticky aether.

Gaheris seemed to be in no hurry to speak, so Alaric took it upon himself to break the silence. "You are well away from the Continent, Father?"

"We have sailed as far north as our ships would allow," Gaheris replied. "The rest is in your hands, my boy."

"I know."

The Regent's withered fingers twitched over the armrest of his throne. "If this is farewell, then it is farewell." His expression was contemplative. "And our souls will find shelter in the willows until all lands sink beneath the Eversea and you and I meet again."

It was shameful how these crumbs of affection went straight to Alaric's heart, rendering him temporarily mute. Shameful how he longed for more. There was a time when he might have deemed it enough and been content, but he'd seen how Elagbi treated Talasyn and couldn't shake the feeling that was what a father was supposed to be. Perhaps Gaheris could have been that, if not for the war.

Or perhaps Alaric was simply asking for too much.

"I won't fail you," Alaric vowed. "Or Kesath."

His father nodded. "Remember," he said, "when you turn your ship to home—bring your Lightweaver with you. Or don't come back at all."

The Shadowgate withdrew its icy claws, but the cold remained inside Alaric for a long while after.

CHAPTER TWENTY-SEVEN

The Nenavarene were determined to send their Lachis'ka to her potential grave in style. That was the only reason, Talasyn thought, for the ceremonial armor that Jie had brought out before she spent ages securing Talasyn's hair in a tight braid.

It was certainly the most practical of the garments that the Dominion had foisted on her thus far. A high-collared leather tunic, dyed blue, the bodice closely fitted, slashes running from thigh to knee to allow movement. Pauldrons that cascaded down her shoulders like laurel leaves. Pleated blue trousers tucked into a sturdy pair of gold-embellished boots. Talasyn almost felt like a soldier again.

From Iantas she and Alaric flew to the main island of Sedek-We, on the same pleasure yacht that the warship had fired void bolts at during aethermancy training last month. It was a narrow vessel with an asymmetrical mainsail that folded and rippled like a butterfly wing emerging from its cocoon; more style than substance, and slower than a coracle, it was completely devoid of weaponry. But they weren't defending themselves from anyone, nor were they running from anything—except from what midnight would bring, and they couldn't even run from that for long.

Elagbi, Jie, and the Lachis-dalo had wanted to accompany them, and Iantas's helmsmen had offered to crew a larger ship, but Talasyn had put her foot down in this regard. She wouldn't be able to concentrate with her people so near the eruption; at least on Iantas they would have a chance of avoiding the amethyst light, even if a slim one. While the Voidfell had historically left metal and mortar untouched, it slipped into the cracks of every building like the wind, like sound, rotting all living things within.

Stop picturing it, Talasyn chided herself. *It will not come to pass.* She had to be confident. She had to be centered.

As did her husband, but she was currently a little worried about him. Even though Alaric was wearing his wolf's-snarl mask, along with the rest of his battle armor, she could tell from the narrowing of his gray eyes that he had been scowling ever since he joined her on Iantas's landing grid. When Elagbi had shaken his hand and wished him luck, rather than dispensing some polite rejoinder, Alaric had merely grunted.

He had been in a decent enough mood during lunch. Then again, Talasyn supposed that even the fearsome Night Emperor was not above the occasional attack of nerves.

Talasyn landed the yacht on one of the empty docks that ringed the Nenavarene capital of Eskaya. She and Alaric set forth, on foot, in the general direction of the Roof of Heaven, its alabaster facade gleaming in the moonlight, as pristine as a statue of ice and snow crowning the steep limestone cliffs. They walked in silence for a while, both of them lost in their own thoughts, adrift in a deserted city. There were no patrols, no night markets, no ships streaking overhead, no strains of music and indistinct conversation, no drunks spilling out from the darkened taverns. Eskaya was so still that it seemed one wrong move could shatter it like glass.

Talasyn stopped walking halfway across a stately marble bridge that rainbowed above the city's main canal. She leaned over the railing, bracing herself on folded arms. Alaric followed suit, their elbows almost touching. Were this in the time before, she might have snapped at him to not stand so close to her, but it was a rather moot point now, after all that they'd done to each other.

The waterway sparkled with reflections: the rippling moons in full and crescent and gibbous, the stars like crumpled flecks of silver, the trees and rooftops flickering in the gentle current. And their own dark silhouettes, two people alone in an abandoned city.

But they weren't the only people left in Nenavar. And that was what weighed on Talasyn's mind.

"I keep thinking," she said, "about everyone who stayed. That Daya Vaikar and her Enchanters didn't leave I understand, even if I don't like it. We need them for the amplifying configuration. But my father and everyone else back at Iantas—they didn't have to. Even the refugees from the village stayed."

"They love you," Alaric said quietly. Her heart skipped a beat to hear the word *love* from his lips. "That's why. I think that's worth something. As is loyalty. Even Sevraim and the twins—" He cleared his throat with a hint of awkwardness. "They wanted to accompany me. I had to order them not to."

Talasyn had no opinion on the well-being of Ileis and Nisene one way or the other, but it *did* amuse her to imagine the kind of arguments Sevraim must have put forward. "Hopefully the Continent's evacuation went smoothly, despite those three's best efforts."

Alaric flinched. She saw it in the water. "We couldn't get

everyone out," he said, his tone brusque. "There weren't enough ships."

A pang went through her. "You should have asked Nenavar for help. We would have sent—"

"I floated such a possibility before Regent Gaheris." His broad shoulders dropped, as though in shame. "He had no wish to be beholden to the Dominion any more than necessary."

Brow knitting, Talasyn made to launch into her usual refrain that it was *Alaric* who was the Night Emperor—and maybe this would be the time that it got through his thick skull at last—but then he continued. "Most of High Command shared my father's opinion."

Now that she was all too familiar with. That maze of careful politicking to keep everyone happy—or at least content enough to not plot against you. That balancing act of considering all ulterior motives as you furthered your own goals. Urduja always had her hands full with her council of nobles, but she'd had decades of practice, whereas Alaric had only recently stepped into his role.

"I have failed them. My people." It was a hoarse confession. He looked so young in the moonlight. "I want to make a new world, but I share power with those who won't let the old ways go. Sometimes I think—I think it would be better to start over. Tear it all down." His eyes met hers. "And sometimes I think you and I could do that. If we make it through tonight."

His statement was so quietly spoken, but it seemed to ring throughout the abandoned city. It seemed to bring illumination with it—the way out of the tunnel, out of the labyrinth.

Join me, then. This was how a thought could strike like lightning, burning a path through the soul, shedding stark clarity on the next step to take. *Ideth Vela is alive. We have allies. We're ready to make our move after the Moonless Dark. Join us.*

Let's tear it all down.

And let's build a life together.

The words were on the tip of her tongue. She drew a breath to say it. She almost said it.

And then—

"We can stop all of this, this never-ending fight for power," said Alaric. "We'll crush the Sardovian resistance first, hunt down their leaders. Then we'll deal with the Kesathese old guard, who are opposed to progress. Once all threats to the Continent are stamped out, we can rebuild it together and truly begin to change things."

There was a horrendous, crushing pain in Talasyn's chest. She breathed through it slowly, secretly. As secretly as she'd carried her hope.

He shifted closer, turning his broad body to her, removing his mask. Determination flashed across his pale face as he leaned in.

He's going to kiss me, Talasyn thought.

She shouldn't let him.

But she couldn't will herself to move away. This might be the last time.

She stared at him as he bridged the distance. How the moonlight on the water caught in his gray eyes before he shut them, every hint of softness on his sharp features, every beauty mark—she committed it all to memory. There might never be an after.

Only when his lips met hers did she close her own eyes, surrendering to the feeling. Here and now, it felt like a glimpse of what could have been.

Halfway across the channel between Sedek-We and Vasiyas, there was a stirring in the water miles below. Talasyn cranked the lever that slowed the wind magic fueling the yacht, and she and Alaric peered over starboard. And down into a strange, strange sight.

The dragons were surfacing. Dozens of them, their frilled heads jutting out from the Eversea's dark depths on necks like rough-barked tree trunks, their serpentine bodies twisting amidst the waves. Their movements would have been reminiscent of the feeding frenzy of an eel farm if not for the fact that the dragons went still as soon as they saw the little yacht, only their jeweled eyes tracking its every movement.

"Simply another day in Nenavar?" Alaric ventured hopefully.

"No." Talasyn spoke out of the corner of her mouth, as he did. The alertness of the leviathans was unsettling. Even the smallest one was big enough to swallow their ship in one gulp. "I don't understand. I assumed they all started moving south last sennight, accompanying the evacuation vessels." She'd watched several flank the *W'taida*, Urduja's flagship, never leaving its side until the fleet disappeared into the horizon.

Alaric flexed his gauntleted fingers, preparing to aethermance. "Stay close to me."

"They won't attack anyone of Nenavarene blood," said Talasyn. "If anything, *you* should stay close to *me*."

It was at that moment that no fewer than four dragons elected to take wing and surround the yacht, and Talasyn gulped. Would the last words she ever heard in this life be a sarcastic *You were saying?* from Alaric Ossinast?

But no. The beasts slithered into a formation similar to that of their compatriots when they escorted the *W'taida* to safety. One flew overhead, one flew beneath the yacht, one flew on either side, and each took great care not to graze the vessel with their enormous wings. As Talasyn continued steering toward the shadowed ridge of the Vasiyas coastline, Alaric's gaze was uncharacteristically soft with awe, transfixed by the swirl of scales all around. The beating of leathery wings thundered in Talasyn's ears, the gusts of breath from fire-warmed lungs as sibilant as a hard rain.

And it wasn't long before this cacophony heightened, punctuated by the din of colossal bodies thrashing in the ocean, and she looked behind her to see the rest of the dragons rising from the Eversea. Trailing the yacht, keeping their distance as though in an effort to avoid colliding with it.

"Talasyn." Alaric's voice was raspy behind his mask. "What is this? What's going on?"

"I . . ." She made eye contact with the dragon to her left. A black slit of a pupil set amidst a field of amber, glowing like the sun even this close to midnight. Something unfurled within her, something far older than her magic. The creature tossed back its head and let out a roar, exuding a cloud of bright orange flame that drowned the stars.

It was a greeting, not a warning. The dragon's roar felt like her own heartbeat. She felt its fire as though it were the heat of the blood running through her veins.

The world had shifted yet again, as it did when she first stepped into the Light Sever. As it did when Alaric first kissed her and the air simmered with shadowed radiance.

Was it her fate to keep on changing, swapping one life for another like the coats of different seasons here in this land of eternal summer? Was she doomed to one day no longer recognize the girl from Hornbill's Head, the same way no snowy winter carried a trace of the scarlet autumn that came before?

"I think," Talasyn said, "that they're watching over me."

Not only did Ishan Vaikar agree with Talasyn's assessment, but Alaric found the daya remarkably unfazed by the host of dragons that rolled in like the tide along with the Lachis'ka and the Night Emperor's airship.

"I *thought* something like this might happen!" Ishan crowed. "The dragons will always protect the Nenavarene people, but some of us stayed behind, so it stands to reason, doesn't it, that some of *them* stayed behind as well? How did they decide who would migrate and who would remain? Fascinating beasts!"

Excited chatter came from the yacht's transceiver—it was Ishan's voice crossing the Tempestroad from her moth coracle. Each Ahimsan Enchanter present tonight, riding their own ghostly craft, was floating in a circle around the crater of Aktamasok.

Hovering directly over the crater—directly above its deep abyss—was the yacht.

It's a very small yacht, Alaric thought uneasily. And the amplifying configuration that had been laid out on the deck, the assemblage of jars and wires, seemed far too breakable when its backdrop was a yawning, bottomless pit.

He was Shadowforged. He shouldn't have been scared of the dark. But within *this* darkness lurked a horror that Alaric couldn't face alone.

Ishan was somehow still gabbling on, speculating about the dragons' method for communicating among themselves. Talasyn leaned well away from the aetherwave transceiver's mouthpiece. "Imagine if the Void Sever triumphs because of Daya Vaikar's unpredictable attention span," she muttered.

"At least it will be no fault of yours or mine," said Alaric, "and the survivors will remember us kindly."

Talasyn snorted. She shone in her blue-and-gold armor, in the moonlight, her dragons spinning above her. Some had dug their claws lower down the volcanic slopes, as though preparing to pounce at whatever emerged from the crater. Four of Lir's seven moons had already disappeared from the sky.

Ishan eventually stopped talking, perhaps realizing that no one on the other end was listening to her. And in the silence . . .

"I just wanted to say—" Alaric broke off. What *did* he want to say?

Talasyn blinked up at him. "Yes?"

I am sorry for everything.

I liked writing to you.

I won't let my father hurt you.

I know we agreed that it's simply physical attraction between us, but sometimes—sometimes I think—

Ever since we met, I have lived in a dream of what could be.

But he could never tell her any of this. Saying any of it would make dying tonight the *better* option. He could never confess about the stolen sariman and Gaheris's plans before he figured out how to fix all of it.

"If this is farewell," Alaric began, aping his father's words because that was affection as he knew it, and that meant something, too, "then it is—"

"It's *not* farewell," Talasyn interrupted fiercely. "You said so yourself, on Belian, remember? When I asked if you really thought we could stop the Voidfell, you said, *Yes. Otherwise, we're all dead.* You may have been a smart-ass about it, but you were right. We *will* make it through. We'll fight to live. You taught me how." Two more moons vanished, leaving only the Seventh, but all the light that he needed was in her eyes, the shards of gold within them fervent with conviction. "So stop moping and let's get this *done*."

Alaric smiled behind his mask. He reached out to tuck that particular strand of chestnut hair that was always escaping from Talasyn's braid back behind her ear, moving carefully so that the clawed tips of his gauntlet didn't rake into her temple.

She shivered at his touch, the seventh moon's wan silver glow dusting her freckled cheeks.

He drank it all in.

"If there's anything I believe in," he said, "it's your stubbornness. It annoys me quite frequently, but it can move mountains. I would have no one else by my side tonight."

Talasyn rolled her eyes. "I'll hold you to that the next time we argue."

Alaric shrugged. "I'm just glad that there will be a next time."

The aetherwave transceiver crackled to life. It was Ishan again, asking them if they were ready. Shadows were steadily creeping over the last remaining moon, like ink spilled from its bottle, over fresh parchment.

"We're ready," Talasyn confirmed into the transceiver's mouthpiece.

Ishan replied in Nenavarene before signing off. Alaric and Talasyn stepped closer to each other, facing each other within the amplifying configuration. "What did Daya Vaikar say?" he asked.

Talasyn's lips curved into a small, wistful smile as she translated for him. "'I'll see you on the other end of this, or in the Sky Above the Sky where our ancestors sail.'"

CHAPTER TWENTY-EIGHT

The seventh moon slid into place behind its fellows, forming for the first time in a thousand years a straight line that blocked sunlight and all its reflections from reaching Lir. Only the stars were left in the heavens, but they shone so faintly that the world was effectively plunged into shadow.

In the depths of the moonless night, the dragons growled and huffed and beat their wings. The primitive racket, speaking to magic much older than these islands, was soon joined by a low rumbling from the crater below Alaric's feet.

He glanced beyond the yacht. Embers of violet light bled upward in a slow and mesmerizing ascent from out of the darkness. In their glimmering multitudes, they shone like fireflies rising from the bushes in early summer as the dusk crept in.

But these "fireflies" carried death on their wings.

Alaric and Talasyn summoned their shields from aetherspace. Radiant light and black smoke, each other's mirror. He felt a twinge of pride at how solid her shield was, such a far cry from the days when she hadn't been able to conjure one at all.

I taught her that. Through the silver-flecked haze at the edge of his shield, he looked into her eyes, golden all over, blazing like high noon. *We're stronger together.* He'd told her that after the guerrilla attack on the Citadel, and he'd never meant it more than he did now.

They brought their shields together at the same time that the Enchanters hovering around the volcano seized hold of the magic in the metalglass jars. Aether cores blazed and wires sparked, and Lightweave and Shadowgate melted into each other. The two shields expanded, flowing from Alaric's grasp and Talasyn's to transmute into that familiar shimmering sphere, covering the entire peak of Aktamasok in a dome of black and gold.

From the belly of the volcano, the Voidfell came screeching forth, an eruption of molten amethyst, as hot and rich as lava. It crashed into the lower half of the barrier and—

—and truth be told, Alaric hadn't been expecting it to hit *that* hard. They could have trained for years instead of months, and he still wouldn't have been able to brace for the magnitude of it. Nothing could have prepared him. It was a thousand—no, a *million* void cannons all at once. The impact reverberated through the sphere, rattling his teeth, rocking the butterfly-wing yacht from side to side. The metalglass jars of the amplifying configuration swayed, coming dangerously close to tipping over.

Talasyn reacted quickly. Her hand slashed through the air, plucking out several threads of Lightweave from the interior of the sphere. She spun them into ropes, and at her command they wrapped around fore and aft, while she took care to control the magic so it wouldn't cut through the hull.

The other ends of the ropes, she connected back to the sphere. The yacht held still, tangled up in strings of golden magic that lashed it securely to the barrier's curved, glimmering walls.

Alaric blinked. "Good idea."

"I've been known to have them from time to time!" she snapped.

He hastily disguised a chuckle as a cough. Now was no time to be bickering.

The Void Sever flared brighter, pushing against the eclipse sphere with surge upon surge of raw, unbridled might. For the next several minutes, Alaric and Talasyn were kept busy reinforcing their barrier, channeling more magic into the weaker spots. It was a feat of immense effort and concentration. Talasyn was turning pale and Alaric was tiring far too fast. With each blow, the yacht strained within the bright cords that secured it.

After all the months of training, they were still so unprepared. Despite the amplifiers carrying their aethermancy to greater heights, they felt like they were trying to stand unmoved in the kind of howling wind that bent oak trees in half.

"Alaric." Talasyn forced his name out through gritted teeth. "There . . ." She pointed to a star-shaped whorl of violet pulsing into existence below them, spreading swiftly through the swirl of sun and midnight.

Alaric moved his arm—tendons nearly snapping in half at the effort—to pull strands of shadow magic over the crack in the shield. Talasyn followed suit with her light. The amethyst seam began to close up, but a second one appeared above it.

The sphere *groaned.*

He glanced at their ship's timepiece set into the control bridge alongside the transceiver. How was it possible that so little time had passed? His exhaustion had sunk deep into his bones, and his vison swam with lambent black dots.

"Forty-five more minutes," he said, as much for his own benefit as Talasyn's. The sound of his own voice came as a shock to him. It was almost his father's voice, cracked and worn. His throat hurt from the simple act of speaking. "Forty-five minutes, and it will be over. We have to hold on until then."

She gave a weak nod. She was covered in sweat, shaking violently, her eyes like fire. "Stay with me," she whispered.

His breath hitched. "You know I will."

The barrier rippled with several more splinters of amethyst light. They exchanged a look and then sent out another blast of combined magic, new waves of black and gold patching over the cracks. He could have screamed with the effort required to produce it. Both of them were drawing on their reserves of strength, and it was still only the beginning of the ordeal.

A wisp of Voidfell broke through the barrier. Bright and crackling, and yet no more than a wisp—but it traveled at the speed of lightning and lashed at the left side of Alaric's face. For a terrifying moment, amethyst was all that he could see. The pain was hot at first, splattering on his face like droplets of candle wax, and then it was a hundred sharp little teeth digging into his flesh, spreading beneath his mask.

It was the most human of instincts to clap a hand over that side of his face as he sank to one knee. The metal interior of his mask dug into the raw skin and he doubled over, and through the furious song of agony roaring in his ears he heard Talasyn screaming. Out of his right eye he saw a much larger current of Voidfell breaking through the sphere—

—and barreling directly toward him.

She was by his side before he knew it, one hand on the back of his neck, the other held out above him, fingers splayed against the oncoming amethyst glow. A section of combined Lightweave and Shadowgate peeled away from the sphere's interior wall and washed over the intruding void magic, driving it back.

Talasyn was controlling the eclipse barrier all by herself.

Her hand was incandescent at the edges, as though she were being eaten away by all that black and gold. The veins along her wrist and the inside of her forearm reddened and blistered, like the beginnings of frostbite, like burn marks, branching against her olive skin.

Alaric was in so much pain that he could barely think. But one thing was clear to him, the certainty of it anchoring him before he could drift away: he would not let Talasyn burn.

More splinters of violet collided against the pulsing sphere, cleaving to it, worming their way in. Alaric rose to his feet and Talasyn's hand fell away from his nape as their magic gathered around him. He took hold of the threads of it, and together they blazed beneath the sevenfold eclipse. Magnified by the amplifiers of rain and blood and tempest, another wave of Lightweave and Shadowgate engulfed the Voidfell, sealing the cracks.

No more appeared.

Just as Alaric was starting to experience a shred of relief, just as the pain shooting through the left side of his face was starting to cool—

—just as he was starting to think that the worst was over—

—the entire lower half of the sphere bent *upward*, as though some enormous fist were attempting to punch through it from underneath.

Alaric and Talasyn scrambled to fight off this new attack. Despite failing to regain its former shape, the barrier held fast against the blows that pummeled it. But—

"I—don't—like—this." Talasyn was wheezing, choking out her words. "It feels . . . the harder we push, the more it pushes back—like—"

"—like it's sentient," Alaric finished for her. "Like it's fighting us."

Ishan checked in with them. Although her voice was nigh

inaudible over the shriek and hum of magic, it was apparent that she was winded from the task of controlling the amplifiers' aether cores. "Your Majesties. I know you can't exactly respond right now, but something is *off.* The dragons are restless. And there are—*noises.* From inside the volcano."

Of course there are noises, Alaric thought. *The Voidfell is moving through the earth.*

Now that he knew to listen for it, however, he *could* hear something. Beyond the discordant notes of Lightweave and Shadowgate and Voidfell bleeding in from aetherspace, beyond the rumbling of the ground and the faint cries of the dragons, there was something else. A combination of breathing and snuffling, like a snake slithering over loose rock. He could tell from the look on Talasyn's face that she heard it, too.

How loud it must be if they could distinguish it from within the sphere, from amidst the maelstrom.

Suddenly, the Void Sever deactivated, its waves retreating into the crater. From afar it must have looked as though the volcano sharply sucked in its violet-plumed breath. Tendrils of amethyst death crawled back into the dark bowels of the earth from where they'd sprung. Alaric and Talasyn banished the sphere and collapsed onto the yacht's deck. Right on cue the cold swept through him, and he reached for her in desperate exhaustion, pressing his forehead to hers.

She cradled his face in her overheated palms. The after-effects of their combined magic receded slowly. Her fingers curled carefully, so carefully, over the metal mask and his skin, steering clear of where he'd been hit by the Voidfell. And that was how he knew that something was wrong. Even before she gasped out, "Alaric. Your face—gods—"

His heart dropped. It was instinct, too, how he made to twist away from her, but she held him in place, kissing the bridge of his nose, and then pressing her lips to the carved wolf's snarl of his mask. A balm, a blessing. Grace.

"I'm all right," he mumbled. It was true; the stinging was gone, leaving behind only a dull ache. "It's nothing . . ."

He trailed off as his gaze darted to her right arm.

The blisters had disappeared, smoothed away by her body's magical tolerance. But the pattern of her veins remained etched in bright scarlet, from her wrist to the inside of her elbow.

He couldn't even touch her arm in order to get a closer look. He was too afraid that the clawed points of his gauntlets would hurt her.

The world came flooding back to his consciousness, a rush of volcanic rock and humid air, and it was—

—still dark. Save for the light of the stars and the fire lamps of the ships.

The dragons had gone eerily silent.

"It's too soon." Talasyn crawled over to the aetherwave transceiver, checking the yacht's timepiece. "Daya Vaikar," she said, "there's still thirty minutes of eclipse left, why did the Void Sever—"

"I don't know," said Ishan. Her tone was hushed. Mystified.

"Maybe we scared it off," Alaric said with a grunt, which earned him a pointed glare from his wife. He didn't care, though. He never wanted to move again.

But when the rumbling began anew and Talasyn scrambled to her feet, so did he. They peered down into the crater, and Alaric saw with the eyes of the Shadowforged the open mouth and the rows of gargantuan teeth barreling toward them.

He dove for the yacht's controls, firing up its Squallfast hearts, yanking on the steering wheel.

"*What is it?*" Talasyn demanded, clinging to the guardrail.

He didn't bother to respond. She'd find out soon enough. He barked orders over the aetherwave, orders for Ishan and her Enchanters to get away. He pushed the yacht into a steep ascent, and behind him Talasyn swore loudly as the fire lamps on the bow illuminated what had risen from the belly of Aktamasok.

Their little ship cleared the crater, the fanged mouth chasing after it. The fanged mouth first, then the rest of the long, tapered snout.

Then the ridged brow, the curving horns, the violet reptilian eyes.

All of it unfolded from within the chasm on a white-scaled neck almost as broad as Lir's straits. The moons were gone and the stars spiraled on, and Bakun the World-Eater, the first dragon, vast and roaring and as old as time, raised its head over the volcanic summit, unhinging its jaws wide in a guttural scream of rage and grief that echoed through the very foundations of earth and sky.

CHAPTER TWENTY-NINE

The west wind sighs, all moons die.
Bakun, dreaming of his lost love,
rises to eat the world above.

The nursery rhyme that Talasyn had first heard children chanting in a hand-clapping game on the streets of Eskaya now beat an ominous chorus in her head. All those other dragons, she'd thought they were the largest creatures she would ever see, but they were nothing compared to this behemoth; while most of it remained submerged within the volcano of Aktamasok, the part that was visible could have crushed the whole of Iantas castle in a single constricting coil.

The pain in her right arm was still there, but she could barely feel it through the waves of adrenaline racing through her. Everything in her was focused on the World-Eater, on the myth come to life.

Bakun lunged for the yacht again. Alaric listed the vessel sharply to the right, and the colossal jaws snapped at empty air with a force that reverberated like a thunderclap. The Enchanters' moth coracles had made it to a relatively safe distance, and Ishan was pleading with Talasyn over the aetherwave to follow them.

Talasyn deactivated the transceiver, cutting the daya off. "If we flee, it'll take wing to chase us and we'll never be able to stop it," she said to Alaric. "We need to make sure it doesn't leave the volcano."

He arched a brow. "I'll just fly around its head like a gnat, then, shall I?"

"Yes, just be your usual irritating self," she retorted. As inappropriate as their bickering was for the situation, it had a grounding effect. It was something familiar to cling to—something *real.*

Alaric grumbled under his breath, but did as he was told. The yacht wove around the volcano in haphazard circles and Bakun's neck wove with it. The white dragon was fixated on the ship's every movement; it snarled and snapped, predatory and alert. One massive forelimb emerged from the chasm, its claws hooking over the crater's rim, tearing at earth and rock.

It was apparent that *this* dragon had no compunctions about harming anyone of Nenavarene blood.

But the others—the ones that had escorted the yacht to Vasiyas, the ones that had so far been hovering nearby or resting on the slopes—all rushed to Talasyn's defense. The night air filled with wings, and fear struck her heart when they started closing in from above; they were all so small compared to the World-Eater. She couldn't let any of them die.

She rattled off a hasty plan to Alaric. He looked markedly unimpressed, but he sailed them downward. Bakun's violet gaze followed them briefly, but then flickered to the host of oncoming dragons. It reared back its head and inhaled at the same time that they did.

A wall of orange flame lit up the night, shooting toward

Bakun, bigger than worlds and brighter than suns. Yet it was utterly dwarfed by the tidal wave of amethyst magic that burst forth with another scream from the white dragon's lips.

Fire and Voidfell hurtled at each other in what promised to be a disastrous collision. The air groaned with the rush of it, the veil between aetherspace and the material realm shattering. Half a second before the two energies could meet in the middle, however, a new shield of black-and-gold magic blossomed between them—from the yacht below.

The eclipse sphere washed over the volcanic peak, caging Bakun in.

The flames from the smaller dragons crashed harmlessly into the barrier and fizzled out. The void blast rebounded off the interior walls, and several splinters of it rained down on the yacht—pummeling the second sphere that Alaric and Talasyn had created within the larger one to protect themselves.

"And now we're locked in here *with* the bloodthirsty dragon that breathes death magic," her husband groused.

"Alaric," Talasyn said very sweetly, affection and annoyance warring within her, "shut up."

Bakun was thrashing against the barrier, crying out every time the combined magic scraped at its hide, but still determinedly searching for a way through, even as black gashes appeared across its snow-white scales, ichor dripping down like ink. Talasyn had no idea what the next step was. She and Alaric couldn't keep up the shield forever—only until the end of the eclipses. When she looked up, she saw that the edge of one moon was already visible, glowing a muted silver through the sphere's haze.

Talasyn made herself look away—only for her gaze to collide with Bakun's.

The World-Eater had veered to face her dead-on. Its snout

was now level with the yacht, at a distance that was much too close. The rest of its body went still as it tilted its horned head, as though trying to get a better look at her.

She felt it again, that same strange connection in the swirling depths of ancient, aether-touched eyes.

Something called out to her, some urge—whether instinct or compulsion, she couldn't tell. It tugged at her senses like the beating of battle drums.

Did she dare trust it?

What other option was there?

Alaric spoke, terse and deep. "I think we can kill it. Look at the wounds on its scales, from where it touched the barrier. If we attack it with eclipse magic—"

What he was saying made sense. Killing Bakun would mean cutting off the only source of the Voidfell in all of Lir, but it would ensure that Dead Season never happened again. What was the death of one old thing to save the lives of millions?

And yet—that urge. It grew more and more irrepressible the longer she looked the ancient dragon in the eye. It beckoned to her the way the Light Sever did.

How could she call herself an aethermancer if she didn't trust her magic? What if she and Alaric could save everyone—*and this one thing, too?*

Swallowing, Talasyn unraveled the Lightweave encasing the yacht. It fell away from the strands of its shadowy counterpart, and the smaller sphere winked out of existence.

"*You*—" Alaric broke off, as though too many choice reprimands had sprung to mind and he couldn't decide where to start. He stepped between her and Bakun, the outline of his war scythe materializing in his gauntleted fingers.

At the sight of the Shadowforged weapon, Bakun let out a warning snarl and faint plumes of void magic wafted from between its teeth.

Talasyn placed a hand on Alaric's arm.

"It doesn't want to fight," she told him, still locked into a staring match with the World-Eater. "Not really, I don't think. No beast *wants* to fight." It was all the primal need to protect territory, to perpetuate the species, to defend the self. Even wolves went for the easiest prey when they had a choice.

"You're asking me to trust this thing with your life," Alaric growled.

"No." Talasyn smoothed her fingers over his armguard. As soothing a gesture as she could make, given the circumstances. "I'm asking you to trust *me*."

He didn't banish his weapon, but he stayed where he was as she approached Bakun, her steps cautious over the yacht's wooden deck. Strands of Lightweave peeled away from the main sphere to gather around her like a cloak. Or a shroud. Her magic protecting her the best it could. Her hair stirred in an unnatural wind.

Talasyn stopped walking when the tips of her boots bumped against the yacht's interior hull and she could go no further. Bakun leaned in slightly, closing up another few inches of distance. She could see every ring on the ivory horns that curved back from its skull, every ridge of the scales that lined its crocodilian face, every crater in its irises. Every star in its slitted black pupils. Without the veil of eclipse magic to obscure it from her sight, something inside her was dragged headlong into whatever lurked in its amethyst eyes.

Aether and memory. It all came down to aether and memory. It was the same here, under the roof of swirling magic and sevenfold eclipse, as it had been that day on the sun-warmed beach when she felt one soul—or shadow of a soul—move through her and Alaric and the sleeping dragon.

Everything was connected, even if sometimes by the skin of one's teeth.

Within the circle of sariman blood and Rainspring and Tempestroad, everything was amplified.

Even the bleeding of the past into the present. Even an aethermancer's tether to the currents of what came before.

You know this, Alunsina, said an inner voice that was Talasyn's own but also not, that was one voice and yet hundreds upon hundreds of voices, a multitude of images racing together like star lines in the dark, their splinters spiraling backward into the rivers of time, red sun, seven moons, an unbroken line of Nenavarene queens who hung the earth upon the waters, speaking to her, speaking *through* her, from the Sky Above the Sky.

At the dawning of the world, you were there.

You have seen the first dragon's heart.

Talasyn fell into the same odd vision she'd sporadically been having, but this time the shape of it was solid and clear, the images at last clicking into place in her mind. What she saw wasn't the future, but the past. The Eversea, darker and deeper, its islands not as defined as they would become by her time. A winged shadow rippling over land and water, white scales undulating through the heavens. A stooped elderly woman, with emeralds woven through her long silver hair, clinging with one gnarled hand for purchase, not to a snow-covered mountain ridge, but to the rough crags of a dragon's brow. Her other hand rising in the air, fingers stretching shakily, reaching for the crimson orb of a younger sun.

"Not long now," the old woman murmured, closing her eyes as she soared over the world.

The dragon she was riding let out a harsh cry.

The memory lasted long enough to catch on Talasyn's heart. Long enough for her to understand.

Then she was back in the present, within the molten sphere,

and Bakun was staring at her, its dread jaws moving in a guttural approximation of human speech.

"*Iyaram?*"

There had been no eighth moon. That was a fairy tale spun by the ancestors to explain the vulana stone as much as the phenomenon of eclipse.

But there had been a woman. The first Zahiya-lachis, whose name the dragon had learned to say. Whose death had caused it to rage.

"No, World-Eater." Talasyn spoke in Nenavarene, in a voice that rang loud and clear within the shimmering black-and-gold walls. "It's not time yet. Go back to sleep."

Bakun screamed again. A sound that was somehow as deep as the caverns of night and yet so high that it made the hairs on the back of Talasyn's neck stand at attention. She was looking down the length of its forked tongue, set into the lilac membranes of its gaping mouth, each razor-sharp tooth that jutted out the size of a grandfather tree. Hot, sulfurous breath engulfed her.

And then the World-Eater *rose.*

More and more of Bakun emerged from within Aktamasok's crater. One glistening coil slammed against the side of the yacht, and as the shockwaves of the impact jostled them, the amplifiers burst. The cores within them, having strained for so long, dissolved in an explosion of metalglass and destabilized magic.

The dome of Lightweave and Shadowgate over the volcano flickered, then winked out of existence.

Two more shards of moons had returned to the heavens. In the wan glow they shed, Talasyn saw the wild light of freedom in its eyes as Bakun soared upward.

She didn't know whether it was instinct or madness this time, the thing that made her do what she did next. Perhaps it was fear—fear of what the creature would wreak if it was let loose over the land. Alaric was trying to re-form the shield, but she leapt from the edge of the yacht and onto Bakun's neck, using the ledges of the thick scaled hide to pull herself up. She scaled the dragon the way she scaled the ladders and bridges of the vertical mudbrick city where she'd once lived. Higher and higher, air and sky—

A rope of shadow magic wrapped around one of the great spikes running along the leviathan's spine, and suddenly Alaric was beside her. Beneath the waves of black hair blowing across his newly scarred face, the vein in his temple looked fit to burst. "I swear to the *gods*, Talasyn!"

"You didn't *have* to come along," she pointed out.

Together they climbed. They climbed the seesawing length of scaled ledges rolling unsteadily until they reached the top of Bakun's head, where they were in less danger of being thrown off. Clinging to the base of one horn while Alaric claimed the other, Talasyn looked behind and below to see white wings unfold from the crater and through the air. Bakun roared as it shot up into the sky, into the half-lit heavens, leaving behind the Enchanters' coracles, the smaller dragons, the barren ridge of Aktamasok. The wind currents almost blew Talasyn clear off, and she held fast to Bakun's horn, flattening herself against the curve of it.

With the creature's veins thrumming beneath her feet, with her arms around its horn, Talasyn could feel its desire for carnage—she could almost taste the Voidfell on her tongue. Bakun hadn't left its caverns since it went into its first long sleep. It had been content to wake every thousand years and push out its breath in a ceaseless exhale while still remaining underground.

Until tonight. Until it felt something push back.

Now it stretched its wings, unimpeded by rock and dirt,

its body burning like a gigantic furnace. It felt invincible, triumphant. It wanted to swallow the world, it wanted to see *her* again, it wanted to *breathe out*—

"No." Talasyn dug her heels into Bakun's hide. It huffed, then sailed higher. Higher than airships went. Higher than eagles could go.

It was like riding a mountain, or standing on top of it and feeling it grow, bringing one closer and closer to where the great ships of the ancestors sailed. The chill of the increasing altitudes slammed into Talasyn, quickly followed by . . . rain?

No—*mist*.

She spat out a mouthful of cloud. She had a feeling that Alaric would have laughed at her if he weren't similarly drenched. At first she could see him only in brief flashes of starlight, and then more clearly, the shape of him solidifying in the glow of the moons slowly returning to the sky. Their eyes met as they soared above the world, through pale crescents and silver mist, on ancient wings.

But there was scant opportunity to bask in the marvel of it all—Bakun tossed back its head, giving Talasyn a harrowing jolt that lifted her feet into the air before she tightened her grip on the horn, her teeth clenching from the effort. The dragon screamed again, unleashing a fresh wave of void magic that arced straight up. The clouds fell apart in pulsating streams of violet so bright that their flashes remained etched in her vision long after they had subsided.

Another scream. Another wave. Again and again, eternal. The Voidfell roaring through dragon lungs like chasms, spilling out of a throat that could wrap around the moons. The sky blazed with amethyst fire for miles around.

The World-Eater screamed until it was hoarse, then it kept on screaming, its neck lashing wildly with each new surge of void magic.

And even though the amplifiers were long gone, fragments of ancestral memory remained in Talasyn's soul. Amidst the cold and the stars they stirred, called forth by Bakun's cries.

By its lament.

Talasyn moved her scarred right arm as though in a trance. She stroked a shaking hand over the ridge of the creature's brow. Tears were streaming down her face. Were they hers—or Iyaram's? Perhaps it didn't matter. Back then, during the war, she'd never cried. Nenavar had changed that about her as well. And perhaps that, too, was all right.

"It's not time yet," she repeated softly. "I'm sorry." The dragon stilled, hearing her crystal-clear through the beating of its wings, through the howl of wind and the echoes of Voidfell. "Everything ends," she continued, "even the long night, even grief." She glanced at Alaric through blurry eyes, and he looked as though he could understand her—if not the words in the Dominion tongue then the tone in which she spoke them. Some things went beyond language. Some things, like loss and hope, were the same all over the world.

"One day all lands will sink beneath the Eversea," she told Bakun, in a near-whisper now, "and we will meet again. Go back to sleep, World-Eater. *Wait for me.*"

The dragon turned around, with a roiling of great scales. It tucked its wings slightly against its sides and plunged into a steep descent.

Talasyn's arms ached and she was bitterly cold, but she held on because she had no choice. They dived back to earth, breaking through the cloud cover. The sevenfold eclipse was almost over, and the moonlit panorama of ocean and islands rose up to meet them, vague shapes coalescing into their true forms with each second that rushed by. Specks became dragons and moth coracles, shadowy fields became rainforests, and the sea of darker black in their midst became the yawning volcanic crater.

And they were heading straight for it. Straight into it.

As Bakun began sinking into the abyss headfirst, Alaric conjured a grappling hook of shadow magic and flung its barbed ends at the crater's rim. He swung over to Talasyn's location, scooped her up by the waist, and then ran up the slope of curving, fast-falling ivory. He jumped off the tip of the dragon's horn, and then they were dangling from the high rope of his magic, her arms around his neck, the two of them rocked every which way in the mighty gusts of the World-Eater's passing.

Bakun descended and descended. The white dragon's return to the crater went on for an age. But eventually the last of it vanished into the darkness, the rumbling faded away, and all seven of Lir's satellites wreathed the sky above in their shining fullness.

Moonlit silence and moonlit stillness prevailed, broken only by the hum of approaching coracles, by dragons peering over the crater and then gliding away once they saw that Talasyn was in one piece.

"Never do that again," Alaric snapped.

"What?" Talasyn mumbled against his chest. "Ride a millennia-old dragon who tries to destroy the world every thousand years because it's still carrying a torch for my ancestor?"

He sighed. "This country is infuriating." His hand around her waist raked a claw down her hip, a clumsy caress. "Almost as infuriating as you."

She fought back a smile. They were still hanging precariously from the crater's rim, with nothing but miles of darkness below their feet, and yet somehow she wasn't worried. Alaric would never let her fall.

CHAPTER THIRTY

In bed afterwards, propped up against a mountain of pillows that Iantas's chambermaids had meticulously fluffed, Talasyn studied the scars on her right palm and inner forearm.

The pain was gone, but the discoloration hadn't faded in the slightest. Every vein in this region of her arm, from the tips of her fingers to the inside of her elbow, was outlined in bright red, as though cut open. Revealing the scarlet branches of a barren tree.

Her forearm looked grotesque. That was the only word for it. Talasyn had never set much store by her physical appearance, but the Nenavarene greatly valued beauty, and she had liked to think that her looks were tolerable enough for their standards.

Now, however . . .

The castle healer had given her a tin of salve that, if applied every night, might lighten the marks, but Talasyn wasn't optimistic, and neither was the healer. These were aethermanced scars, inflicted by a type of magic that the world had never seen before—not until Alaric and Talasyn spun it into existence. There was nothing else that the healer could do, because it didn't hurt.

Talasyn would just have to live with it.

It was stupid to be so bothered. She wouldn't have cared back when she was in the Sardovian regiments; everyone there had battle scars. But in the Dominion court everyone was smooth-skinned and beautiful, and she'd been here long enough now that something had shifted in her mind.

Alaric emerged from his dressing room. Talasyn stuck her arm under the covers, so self-conscious that it was almost painful.

He didn't approach right away. The fire lamps had been switched off, and only half of his face was starkly visible, palely etched in the moonlight streaming in through the balcony's glass panels. The other half remained cast in darkness.

The scarred half.

In the furor of the imperial couple's return to Iantas—on an Ahimsan airship provided by Daya Vaikar, because Bakun had apparently dashed the empty yacht against the crater's sides—Alaric had refused to have the healer see to him. He had vanished into his dressing room in full armor, his mask still on, and he had stayed there for a long while.

Talasyn thought about how he'd tried to flinch away from her back on the deck, after the Voidfell's initial wave had ceased. She imagined him looking at his reflection in the dressing room mirror, studying his scars the way she'd studied hers.

The Moonless Dark had irrevocably changed them both, but they didn't have to deal with it alone.

"Come lie down," Talasyn said. "You must be tired."

Alaric stayed where he was. "I can sleep in my study, if you—"

"I want you to sleep *here*."

Her tone brooked no argument. He walked over to her stiffly, like a man on his way to the gallows. He ducked his head as he clambered onto the bed frame, and he kept the left side of his face turned away from her as the mattress dipped beneath his weight.

Her heart caught in the crush of some uncaring fist, Talasyn took Alaric's face in both hands, forgetting all about her own marks. He resisted, but she managed to turn him toward her fully. And she saw, at last, the entirety of what had sprouted beneath his mask when that sliver of void magic hit him.

Whorls as black as midnight radiated from the base of his ear and all the way across his cheek, a few strands spilling over the bridge of his nose and up the outer corner of his eye. The overall shape was reminiscent of an oak leaf blowing in the wind; each inky line curled like a plume of smoke over the moon-kissed skin of his aristocratic features.

At first his gaze was determinedly trained on the sheets, but after a while his gray eyes met hers with sullen defiance.

"Does it hurt?" she asked hoarsely.

"No." His fingers curved around her right arm, barely touching the red marks there. "Does this?"

Talasyn shook her head. She smoothed Alaric's black hair away from his brow, then pressed a slow kiss to the scar at the corner of his eye. A shudder went through his powerful frame, his lashes fluttering against the edge of her cheekbone. She leaned into him, tracing the path of death magic with her lips.

"On second thought," he mumbled, "it does twinge a bit. You should—you should keep doing that."

The quip was so unexpected that she laughed. No, she *giggled*, a sound that she was making in his presence with worrying frequency these days. She kissed her way down his scarred face and then their lips caught somehow, and her mirth tapered off into a sigh.

The relief that he'd made it through the Moonless Dark surged within her like a volley from a stormship cannon. She'd kept it at bay the last few hours, distracted by practical concerns in the aftermath of a catastrophe averted, but now she seized on every sound he made, each rise and fall of his chest, and held them up to the hand of death, which retreated like a shadow dwindling as the sun reached its zenith.

Alaric had never kissed her like this before, so gentle and searching. It frightened Talasyn in a way she couldn't name, but she let it happen, too caught up in the feeling of his heart beating at her fingertips as she slid her palms down his warm, solid chest. They'd clawed their way out of one danger and many more lurked ahead, but tonight, beneath these silken tapestries, they were alive and that was *all* that mattered.

She helped him yank his shirt over his head. It was tossed to the floor, soon joined by her own, which he peeled from her shoulders, kissing every inch of skin as soon as it was bared. By the time the rest of their clothes were on the pile, she was shivering all over, her toes curling. What was it about this slowness that made it so unbearable and delicious all at once? She fell back against the pillows and he followed her down, their lips connected, his lean hips settling between her thighs. He was already hard, brushing against her in hot glides that made her clench with sheer need, but he acted as though they had an eternity of hours to draw from, mouthing at her throat, her collarbone, her breasts until she was squirming beneath him, flushed all over.

Talasyn's right arm collapsed against the pillow, over her head. Alaric glanced at it while he kissed the freckles on her chest, and that one glance was all it took for her self-consciousness to resurface, a cold and ugly thing cutting through the haze of desire.

He'd found her attractive. That had been the one thing stronger than their enmity, stronger than his hatred for Lightweavers. That had been the one hold she'd had over him.

And now it was gone.

She moved her arm, whether to tuck it against her side or shove it out of sight under the pillow, she wasn't quite certain, but he stopped her, clutching at her wrist.

"You don't get to be ashamed of these, either." He pressed his lips to her arm. "They're battle scars. Wear them with pride." He kissed each scarlet etching of her veins in the same fierce, hungry manner with which he'd kissed her neck. "You held back the Voidfell. You saved our world."

"You saved it with me." She laced their fingers together. Her free hand traced the spiderweb of black scars on his face. "I fought the way you taught me to out there."

When he slanted his mouth over hers again, it was a raking of slowly burning embers, sending up sparks. She was so far gone, she didn't want to wait any longer, she wanted to feel something that wasn't terror, wasn't the World-Eater's grief, wasn't a labyrinth of conspiracy and artifice. She kissed him and she kissed him, her fingers running over new scars and old, and then, wandering lower still, guiding him to her entrance.

Alaric slipped one arm between the mattress and her shoulder blades, his other hand coaxing her knee upward to get a better angle. In doing so, he broke their kiss, and Talasyn *growled*, which startled a raspy scrape of laughter from him. His smile flashed in the moonlight, before he brought his lips to her temple as he sank into her.

Skin to skin. Breath and magic. Alive, and no longer alone. She wrapped her legs around him, taking him deeper and deeper still, letting him open her up as he rolled his hips against hers, as he alternated between kissing her mouth and everywhere else he could reach.

"When you brought down your half of the sphere"—he sounded as shattered as she felt—"and when you leapt onto the dragon—I thought for sure—"

"It's all right," she said into his hair. "I'm all right, we're alive." How good it felt to say those words. How exhilarating it was to affirm that they'd cheated death that night. She could still see Bakun's amethyst breath pulsing in the darkness behind her shut lids every time she closed her eyes. "We're okay."

She clung to him as they moved together, as they brought each other higher, as death drew back its hand. It was so achingly gentle, so unlike anything they'd ever been to each other in the past. The metal of his wedding ring rubbed against her hip and she pressed kisses to his temple and it was so—

—*so* dangerous, that fluttering thing in her heart again, the swimminess in her stomach having nothing to do with arousal, or perhaps heightened by it—

I think I'm falling.

No. She couldn't.

She couldn't do this to everyone.

Talasyn didn't even realize that she'd gone tense until Alaric stilled above her. "What's wrong?" he grated out. He tucked wisps of hair behind her ear in a careful manner that belied the vibrating tension of his body, almost utterly wrecked by the effort of maintaining control. "Whatever it is, I'll fix it, I'll . . ."

He nuzzled into her neck, and it almost felt like love.

Something they didn't have a right to, he'd said so himself.

Something that she didn't deserve.

If he knew—when he finds out—

Scattered thoughts, howling through her mind like a whirlwind. And yet, through it all, refusing to so much as flicker, was the flame of how much she needed him. Of how much she needed *this.*

Talasyn raked her nails across her husband's spine. Alaric hissed, twitching inside her, the mouth at her neck biting down in retaliation. But it was nothing more than a nip, mildly chastising, more playful than anything else.

"Harder," was all she said.

He raised his head, a slight frown to his kiss-stung lips. She bucked against him, a show of impatience that disguised the growing tightness in her chest. His eyes flashed silver amidst pale skin and black scars, and she bit back a whine as he rose to his knees, slipping out of her.

The separation should have cleared her head, but all she felt was loss. Alaric didn't keep her waiting long, however; he notched into her again, then lifted her up by the hips and slammed all the way in with a single forceful thrust, knocking an undignified squeak out of her lungs.

Too much, was her first thought, her head lolling back, shoulders flat against the mattress. *It's too much, I can't—* he withdrew by a few inches, only to bottom out again with another jarring stroke that had her clawing at the sheets. Her mouth dropped open to form a tattered groan, and the look that he gave her was feral and heated. The seven moons gleamed on every rippling muscle of his bare torso as he set a harsh pace, just as she'd told him to. He always gave her everything she wanted when they were like this—it was a bittersweet epiphany that tumbled in along with the rush of blood to her head.

A part of Alaric was clearly still there in the crater. His anger resurfaced, the lid that he kept on his emotions loosening with each thrust. "Never put your life on the line like that again, Tala," he muttered as he took her roughly. "I'll govern your impulses if you refuse to. Your safety matters, as difficult as it may be for you to believe."

"You can't tell me what to do," Talasyn retorted in between pants.

His scarred features darkened with frustration. And there was something of frustration, too, in the way he slammed into her next, hitting *that* spot, the one that made her back arch. A treacherous corner of her heart cried out for the softness of earlier, but she knew that this was the better option in a never-ending series of bad decisions. The brutal physicality of it a refuge.

Soon enough she couldn't speak anymore, all shattered gasps whenever he sped up, lewdly drawn-out moans whenever he slowed down, his fingers digging bruises into her hips. Soon enough she had retreated into an intense space where there was only her and her husband and the war between them. The orgasm was building up inside her core, and Talasyn snaked a hand down her body in a frantic bid for more stimulation, for that one final nudge that would send her over the brink.

Alaric's pace faltered as he watched her touch herself. His eyes burned like starlight, fixated on her ring finger sliding against the bundle of nerves at the apex of her thighs, the sheen of her wedding band's vulana stone reflected on his face like sunbeams on lake water, like phantom traces of the World-Eater's tears.

And it was almost that same light, constellations of it, that exploded across Talasyn's vision when she came, her body twisting in fierce undulations before she collapsed, boneless, over the sheets. The bed creaked obscenely as Alaric bent to close the distance between them, capturing her lips in a filthy kiss, folding her in half as he chased his own release, his large fingers tangling in her hair.

Too close. Too much. She should have shied away. She very nearly did, but then his hips stuttered and he was saying her name in a quiet grunt, the shape of it muffled into her neck. There was a rush of warmth as he spent inside her, followed by the full weight of him, briefly, making it impossible to breathe.

He rolled onto his back, and for a while the two of them did nothing but stare up at the tapestried canopy, shoulder to shoulder, their racing hearts calming and perspiration cooling on their bodies.

Eventually, his hand found hers. She was too tired to pull it away. At least, that was what she told herself.

His voice broke the silence, gruff at the edges, low with melancholy. "Sometimes I wish—"

He hesitated, and that in turn made her own courage falter. She'd faced down Bakun without batting an eyelash, but she was a coward when it came to this, when it came to what achingly tender kisses and caresses had unearthed.

She didn't want him to say any of it. Not when her judgment was clouded by near-miss and nearness.

Not when they'd both agreed that there was a certain point where they could go no further.

Talasyn turned on her side, flinging an arm and leg over Alaric's body. She'd banked on this move to surprise him enough to shut him up, and it worked a little too well. He shifted so that she could use his bicep as a pillow, gathering her close.

"Goodnight," she muttered against his skin.

He didn't say anything in response, but his fingers danced along her bare shoulder, tracing drowsy patterns, until she fell asleep breathing him in.

CHAPTER THIRTY-ONE

As one of the last Nenavarene to depart, Urduja was among the first to return. Talasyn saw this as a calculated act of statecraft: the Dominion needed to be assured that things were back to normal, and what better way than for them to find the Zahiya-lachis happily reigning from the Roof of Heaven when they got home?

But Talasyn was also of the opinion that things would never be normal again. Not when the Void Sever had turned out to be the breath of a gigantic dragon lying beneath the earth.

"Are *all* the Severs like that, I wonder?" mused Niamha Langsoune. "Wind and tempest and rain and the rest—have we been harvesting dragon breath all along?"

"I should hope not," said Kai Gitab, the Rajan of Katau. "Else I've no idea what we'll do if *they* wake up."

Urduja's council was in session, two days after the Moonless Dark. Talasyn had finally left her bed to attend, but she was still a bit drained. Alaric hadn't even so much as stirred when it was time to sail from Iantas to the capital. She hadn't had the heart to force him to accompany her to this debriefing, especially when he would need all his energy to deal with her court at the masquerade the next night.

"It's a kind of estivation, what the World-Eater is doing, I believe," said Ishan Vaikar. "A reduction in metabolic processes, perhaps to extend life span? Prior to this, the oldest dragon ever recorded fell just shy of nine hundred years . . . And I suppose that Bakun wakes once every millennium, only for an hour, but expelling more and more magical energy each time. Then the cycle begins anew. Although that wouldn't account for all the other instances of the Void Sever activating before then."

Ishan was trying her best to reconcile science with folklore. But Talasyn knew only what she'd seen in the World-Eater's eyes. "It breathes out the Voidfell every time it dreams," she said. "Of battle, and of her."

The other people at the council table looked uneasy. Lueve Rasmey, Surakwel's aunt and Urduja's right hand, wrung the opal rings on her fingers. "If there truly was a battle, how did our ancestors manage to drive such a beast into the volcano?"

"We had other aethermancers in Nenavar then," said Gitab. "Not just the Enchanters. That might be how." He pushed his spectacles further up the bridge of his nose. "Perhaps we should just kill it." He glanced at Talasyn, almost hopefully, in a way that reminded her of his promise of alliance back when they stood in that dim hall lined with portraits.

"Out of the question," said Urduja. "We need the Void Sever. It is our greatest weapon, unique in all of Lir."

"It is *hardly* unique anymore, Harlikaan," Gitab argued. "May I remind you that Kesath has gotten their hands on it—"

"We still don't know how they're maintaining their limited supply," Urduja countered. "What happens if the Void Sever disappears for good and Nenavar's aether hearts run out? The Night Empire will then be the only nation in the world that has that technology. I refuse to give anyone that advantage over us, ally or otherwise."

Especially since we're planning to betray the aforementioned allies, Talasyn thought but didn't say out loud. Gitab was the only noble present who didn't know about Nenavar's deal with Sardovia. It had to stay that way, or he and his faction of dissenters would use it against Urduja somehow.

The thought of the war to come hollowed out Talasyn's stomach. But her conversation with Alaric on the bridge before the eclipse had made it clear that he wasn't ready to consider peace with Sardovia, and it was likely that he never would be. The best she could hope for was to save his life.

A life that wouldn't include her, not after what she was going to do. Would have to do.

Talasyn willed herself to put Alaric in a little box in her mind and seal it shut for now. The important thing was to keep moving forward. There was a council she needed to get through.

"We don't have to kill anything," she declared. "We've learned that Bakun can be reasoned with. We just need to keep that knowledge alive for . . . for next time." Her voice wavered a little. A thousand years was so far away.

"But can it be reasoned with *before* it breathes on the night of the sevenfold eclipse?" Gitab asked, and it didn't escape Talasyn's notice that he addressed her more gently than he did Urduja. "Or will our descendants still need eclipse magic to stop Dead Season? There is no assurance that we will be in possession of *that* a thousand years from now."

"There could be *some* assurance," Ishan said tentatively. "Aethermancy is passed on through the blood. We don't know if the properties conducive to eclipse magic are in the blood of House Ivralis or House Ossinast, but"—her gaze dropped to her lap, as though she'd suddenly found her folded hands of great interest—"we can preserve both if Her Grace and the Night Emperor's line remains unbroken."

There was a collective swift intake of breath from Lueve, Niamha, and Elagbi. The Zahiya-lachis was too canny to show much emotion, although she tensed just the slightest bit. But the prince, who had been holding his peace throughout the meeting—while looking, frankly, somewhat bored—now looked utterly horrified.

And Talasyn, or the girl that Talasyn had been before, would have been horrified as well. She would have turned red and stuttered, she would have railed against the very prospect of bearing an heir with Alaric Ossinast when she'd already had to marry him and would one day destroy his empire.

But she had learned a thing or two from her grandmother. She was watching Rajan Gitab, who was studying the other council members' reactions with the faintest crease in his brow.

"One might hear a pin drop," Gitab remarked idly. "The Lachis'ka and the Night Emperor are *already* bound by matrimonial duty to preserve the bloodline. Surely this new objective isn't too far off from that?"

Talasyn forced her lips to stretch into a smile, vaguely amused, serene. "You will have to forgive my father, Rajan Gitab. He can't take this kind of talk when it comes to his only child."

Elagbi coughed. "I truly can't." He sagged against the backrest of his chair.

Urduja made a show of checking the wall clock. "Let us reconvene to discuss this further at a later date," she said. "Alunsina has her hands full preparing Iantas for tomorrow's festivities."

But the way she briefly held Talasyn's gaze made it clear: the next time they spoke on this matter, it would be without Kai Gitab in attendance.

*

It wasn't that Alaric expected or *wanted* the Nenavarene to prostrate themselves at his feet for saving them from the grim specter of Dead Season, but *some* gratitude from the royal tailor would have been nice.

However, when said tailor barged into Iantas in the afternoon, Alaric had to endure several minutes of little indignities, as usual. He would probably have handled it a lot better had he gotten enough sleep, rather than having been unceremoniously woken by the incessant screeching of a skua at his bedroom window, bearing the news that his stormship had returned to Port Samout after fleeing the Voidfell along with the Nenavarene vessels.

In addition, Belrok had turned quite pale upon first catching sight of Alaric's scar, and although the tailor had quickly composed himself, this reaction hadn't endeared him to Alaric in the slightest.

"I believe this concludes our last fitting, Your Majesty," Belrok told Alaric as an assistant carefully tucked the masquerade getup into a chest. "I shall conduct some final alterations and deliver the completed ensemble tomorrow."

"You mean it's not yet *done*?" Alaric snapped.

"I take pride," Belrok said with icy hauteur, "in the flawless quality of every garment that leaves my shop. There are a few minor details that could be improved upon. Of course, these are easily missed by all but the trained eye—"

Alaric knew exactly where Belrok could shove his trained eye, but he was eager to put this unpleasant encounter behind him as soon as possible. They left his study and were forced to walk together in awkward silence because they were both headed downstairs, Belrok's assistants trailing behind them.

As sheer luck would have it, they encountered Talasyn and Niamha in the foyer. Once the greetings were over and done with, Belrok turned to Niamha with an enthusiastic cry. "Daya Langsoune! My light, my muse!"

"Come off it, Belrok," said Niamha, but she didn't hesitate to take his arm with an enchanting smile. "Her Grace and I have just finished smoothing out the wrinkles in the masquerade's seating chart."

"You nobles are no fun," Belrok chided. "What's life without a diplomatic crisis every now and then?"

"Honestly, I doubt Daya Rasmey can take much more at this point," Niamha quipped, and Belrok burst into hearty laughter. "Although she was relatively refreshed at council earlier. The miracles that avoiding Dead Season can achieve!" She turned to Alaric. If the scar on his face bothered her, she didn't show it. "Incidentally, thank *you* for that, Your Majesty—"

"How are you?" Alaric blurted out, staring at Talasyn. Asked as though they hadn't seen each other in ages, as though they didn't live together.

Before he could take back his inane question, she said, "I'm fine." Her gaze was glued to her shoes.

"That's good," he said.

"And yourself?"

"I'm . . . good."

Alaric was dimly aware that Belrok was looking between him and Talasyn with horrified fascination.

"Shall we have tea, Master Belrok?" Niamha suddenly chirped, dragging the tailor away without waiting for an answer. "I shall see you at the masquerade, Your Grace, Your Majesty!"

"But—" Belrok was still protesting as Niamha ferried him out the castle doors. His assistants bowed to Alaric and Talasyn and then they, too, left.

"I actually *did* have tea prepared," Talasyn muttered, casting a somewhat forlorn glance at the empty spot where Daya

Langsoune had been standing. "I don't suppose you'd care to join me?"

It took Alaric a beat and a half to realize that his wife was talking to him. "Let's." He hoped he didn't sound *too* eager.

Talasyn led Alaric to the same seashell-studded pavilion in the hibiscus garden where he'd once interrupted her and the other Dominion ladies. Today's tea was a vivid cerulean color, brewed from pigeonwing petals. Niamha's favorite, but it was all the same to Talasyn.

Alaric poured the tea and they drank. As always, Talasyn tried not to furrow her brow or wrinkle her nose.

He cocked his head at her from across the table. "You don't care for tea at all."

"It's leaf water," she said defensively.

His lips quirked. "Then why serve it?"

"Because the lords and ladies expect me to serve it."

"But what *do* you like?"

Talasyn chewed on her bottom lip as she contemplated her answer. "Cocoa, I suppose."

It was Alaric's turn to make a face, but he beckoned one of the attendants over and issued clipped instructions for a pot of cocoa to be prepared. Talasyn decided not to inform him that it wasn't the done thing among Dominion nobility to have cocoa at this hour; in truth, she liked the show of consideration. She could bask in it. And she brightened up significantly when the steaming pot of sweet, rich liquid arrived.

"You're the heir to the Nenavarene throne," Alaric remarked as he drank his tea and Talasyn drank her cocoa. "You don't have to do anything you don't want to do. In fact, you could set a new trend."

"Not one that you'd care for, judging from the face you made earlier."

"Ah." He smirked in a way that somehow made the sunlight brighter. "You caught me."

"You caught me first," she said. "I thought I was getting better at hiding my distaste."

"It's this little thing you do. You sort of . . ." He scratched at his jaw, as though somewhat abashed. "You lift your chin a certain way when you're forging ahead through circumstances you don't like."

"Well, *your* eye twitches." She felt a shiver of unease at being known in such a small yet intimate way. She was unsure whether it made things better or worse that she knew him like that, too.

Today, in this moment, there was no eye twitching. Instead, there was a crinkling at the corners as he flashed a grin. She didn't understand why that would make the breath catch in her throat. As though he'd kissed her.

"Would my eye have twitched if I'd gone to council?" he asked. "What did—are you all right?"

Talasyn had choked on her cocoa. Before Alaric could fully rise from his chair to check on her, she held up a hand to indicate that she was fine.

"Both your eyes would have twitched," she said, voice strained, wiping her mouth on her sleeve—then wanted to smack herself when she remembered that was what table napkins were for.

She told him about Ishan Vaikar's suggestion that the Ossinast and Ivralis bloodlines be preserved in order to stop the next Dead Season. She told him even though it was awkward. She told him because he would have found out eventually.

And she told him because a part of her felt that this was the one thing she could be honest about, without risking anybody's life or safety.

Alaric received the news with a straight face. Neither of his eyes twitched.

"Today is the first I've heard of it," she hurried to add. "It never crossed my mind before. I took the preventive, all those times—"

"Talasyn." His tone was far too calm, in her opinion, but it served to put a stop to her rambling. He drew a measured breath. "In the back of my mind, I always knew that we would have to, eventually. Both our realms need heirs. As we get older, that need will only become more imperative to our respective courts. This new plan doesn't change what was already implied when we joined hands."

Her world tilted, grew parchment-thin. Children. With Alaric. A son for Kesath and a daughter for Nenavar. Such a future swam before her eyes in nebulous, faceless shapes.

"All I ask," he said, "is that we wait until the situation on the Continent has stabilized. If there is to be a child, I do not wish for them to grow up in wartime."

Like we did.

The unspoken words hung heavy in the air.

Talasyn wasn't looking at the Night Emperor in that moment. She saw only a boy who'd been sent to the front too soon, like her, and who understood what that entailed. She saw only a man who was determined to be better than the past.

It would be so easy to love you in a different life.

The thought bloomed through her in all its wistfulness. And then it *scalded*, and she pushed it away.

"Yes," she said. "I'm fine with waiting."

"As long as we're agreed, then."

Alaric looked around the garden. At the profusions of orange and red hibiscus flowers with their large petals draped like skirts, at the pebbled walkways snaking through green, green grass. It was picturesque. Idyllic.

Surreal.

"We reached this point, after all," he mused, echoing Talasyn's thoughts. "For the last five months, the Moonless Dark was the greatest thing on my mind. It was the foundation that our marriage treaty was built on. And now it's over."

And the treaty has served its purpose. The realization hit her like a blow. She gripped her cup tightly. The Sardovian remnant and the allies it had gathered would make their move. Alaric would find out that she'd always meant to betray him.

They would have to take him prisoner. That was the only way. Or perhaps exile—

"What's wrong?" His gray eyes had gone soft with a concern that she didn't deserve.

"I was just thinking about the seating chart." What was one more lie?

"The wrinkles that Daya Langsoune mentioned?" Alaric prompted.

"Yes," Talasyn said, over the cracks forming across her chest.

She continued telling him all about the problems that she and Niamha had pored over after council, such trivial things, and he listened attentively, injecting the odd wry remark here and there. The air was heavy with perfume and pollen, and the sky was as blue as his tea. There were moments, shards of moments, when she could almost let herself believe that these days would last forever. That there was no storm on the horizon, no tangled web to navigate. That it could always be like this.

CHAPTER THIRTY-TWO

Two hours before the masquerade, Alaric walked into his dressing room like a man en route to the gallows and submitted himself to Belrok's cruel and unusual form of torture with far less grace than he would have normally allotted to the peccadilloes of life at court. Belrok pored over Alaric for a damnable eternity, tutting and mumbling to himself in Nenavarene as he arranged the Night Emperor's hair and applied brushes dipped in various—worryingly *glittery*—pigments to his face. How in the name of the gods did Talasyn put up with this almost every day?

A while later, Alaric heard his wife and her retinue enter the royal chambers as a gaggle of footsteps and feminine chatter reached his ears, muffled by the walls. He made to stand up, with a vague notion of saying hello to Talasyn, but Belrok let out what could only be called a shriek.

"Your Majesty, with all due respect, this is a *very* delicate undertaking! Please do not move!"

This outburst prompted a dark glare from Alaric, but Belrok only sniffed and resolutely continued with his work, snatching another brush from his complex array of tools. "In any case, it is better for you and the Lachis'ka to see each other once you're both all done. To appreciate the full effect."

Dusk had dimmed the sky when Belrok pronounced himself satisfied and held up a hand mirror for Alaric's perusal. Alaric blinked at his reflection. It wasn't as bad as he'd feared. True, he *did* look as though someone had dumped a bucket of glitter over his head, but most of it was concentrated in his hair, gold dust woven through elegantly tousled black locks. The glitter that had ended up on Alaric's face was dusted along his temples and cheekbones and over the smokelike lines of his scar. His brows were flecked with tiny shards of gold, and midnight-hued kohl was smudged along the edges of his eyes. A strip of shimmering gold pigment ran down the middle of his lower lip.

"In traditional Dominion aesthetic, that is the mark of the consort, Emperor Alaric," Belrok said, noting where the other man's gaze had dropped to in the mirror. "It is meant to symbolize the Lachis'ka's kiss. It shows that you have her favor." The tailor cocked his head, bemused. "Astounding. His Majesty looks rather nice."

"You're merely congratulating yourself," Alaric pointed out in the driest of tones.

"Oh, to be sure," Belrok said loftily. "We must all take praise where we can get it. Otherwise, it would be a very sad life indeed."

Fully costumed, Alaric waited in the bedchamber for Talasyn to emerge from her own dressing room. He elected to remain standing, because he was in danger of pitching Belrok right out the window if the tailor admonished him one more time to be careful not to sit on his cape. The mask that had been foisted on him was the inverse of his usual armor, covering his eyes, nose, and upper cheeks, but it was just as heavy, made of solid gold and weighed down with a plethora of jewels.

An attendant bustled in—one of the younger girls, wearing her best dress and a long-snouted mask with thin, shiny whiskers. "Everyone's here!" she gushed in thickly accented Sailor's Common. "It's almost time, please do head downstairs when—" She did a double take once she got a closer view of Alaric. "Oh, His Majesty looks rather nice!"

She hastily dipped into a curtsy before scurrying off. Alaric scowled while Belrok seemed entirely too pleased with himself.

The door of Talasyn's dressing room slid open and she stepped out. Alaric was robbed of words and breath. Jie and the Nenavarene couturier and her assistants were trailing behind, but he had eyes only for his wife. There was no possible way he could have looked at anyone else in that moment.

Talasyn's chestnut hair was piled high atop her head and threaded through with delicate chains of mountain lilies wrought in gold, studded with tiny emeralds and diamonds—the same kind of gems that liberally embellished the ornate butterfly wings covering the upper half of her face. Her collarbones and shoulders had been left strikingly bare, but there was no need for necklaces, not when her costume bodice itself was one large piece of jewelry. It was nothing more than a skimpy band, made entirely of golden leaves, wrapped around her rib cage and barely covering the slight swell of her breasts. The leaves rested on graceful stems spaced apart to afford generous glimpses of her toned stomach before connecting to a lustrous green skirt, with a shorter hem in front, which showed shapely calves that ended in slim ankles surrounded by the diamonds dripping from the straps of her heeled shoes.

Alaric felt like his brain had turned to mush, not just because of the ethereal, sylvan silhouette that Talasyn cut, but also at the sight of so much *skin*. Skin that glowed, as if subtly lit from within. Practically speaking, he knew that they must have bathed her in goat's milk and pearl dust to achieve such an effect, but Talasyn carried her own light, was made of it, and her radiance would envelop him . . .

And everyone else at the masquerade, whispered the inner voice that dwelt within the ugliest corners of his mind.

He'd seen her in revealing outfits before, but he'd never had to face the prospect of sharing that sight with a ballroom full of Dominion nobles until today. A tight, burning feeling grew in his chest as he thought of all the other men who would be staring at Talasyn from behind their masks, who would no doubt be lining up to kiss her hand and dance with her and put their hands on her body. Gods, he even wanted to kick Belrok out of the room just for *looking* at her.

"You're not wearing that," Alaric growled.

Talasyn started, narrowing her eyes at him from within the gilded confines of her mask. "*What* did you say?"

Jie and the other women moved fast—they grabbed Belrok and fled out the door. Once Alaric and Talasyn were alone, his hands balled into fists. "You heard me."

"Then allow me to rephrase." Talasyn placed her own hands on her hips—the universal sign, Alaric thought sardonically, that someone's husband was in deep trouble. "What makes you think that you have *any* right to dictate what I wear?"

"It's not that," Alaric said, but he didn't know how to explain that things were different now, that he *felt* different, that he didn't want anyone else to even *think* of doing the things that she'd let him do to her.

"So what *is* it?" When he didn't immediately respond, Talasyn pursed her lips and continued, in a voice dripping with sarcasm, "I sincerely regret that my costume doesn't meet your standards, but it's rather too late to change into anything else."

"You have entire wardrobes full of dresses," Alaric shot back. "Surely there's one that's"—floundering for the right words, feeling put on the spot, he snatched the first word that came to mind and knew it was the wrong thing to say the moment he said it—"less obscene."

A vein throbbed in his wife's forehead. "I could march out there naked if I wanted to—"

"Please don't," he said, with feeling.

"—and no one would be able to stop me, least of all *you*," Talasyn snarled. "Now, we're already running late, so you can escort me downstairs, or you can stay here and rot! I don't care either way!"

She stomped out of the room, wrenching the door open to a chorus of startled cries from Jie and Belrok and all the other Nenavarene who had been pressed up against it, eavesdropping.

Alaric was rarely one for crude language, but today he cursed under his breath as he hurried after her. It was going to be a long night.

What is the matter *with him?*

Talasyn fumed all the way out of the royal wing and down the staircase to the second level of the castle. She and Alaric ducked into the ballroom's antechamber, where they were supposed to wait for the lights to dim before slipping into the crowd. Unlike other celebrations, there would be no grand entrance for any of the royal family, in order to preserve the illusion of a masquerade—the illusion that the Nenavarene would somehow fail to immediately recognize the Zahiya-lachis, her heir, the Night Emperor, and the prince, just because their eyes and noses were covered. It was all a bit silly, but then again, the Dominion court thrived on artifices such as this.

Urduja and Elagbi had gone on ahead. In the quiet solace of the antechamber, where it was just Alaric and Talasyn, she could practically *feel* him locked in some fierce internal battle with himself. She attempted to pay him no mind, but as always, he proved difficult to ignore.

She tried to see it from his point of view. She really did. Continental fashion required more layers, more parts covered up, owing to the climate. It therefore wasn't *too* outlandish that Alaric would be scandalized by Nenavarene attire, although she felt that this issue really should have cropped up much sooner.

But Talasyn's attempt to be understanding failed. All she felt was annoyance whenever she glanced at her husband. And what a pity it was, considering how he looked. Her heart had skipped a beat when she first saw him in costume earlier. Jutting out from the sides of Alaric's mask, slightly above the eye-holes, was a pair of golden antlers, kingly and resplendent. His crisply tailored tunic was the same deep, iridescent green as her skirt, cinched at the waist with a belt of gold silk that matched the trim on the high collar and wide cuffs. Embroidered on the front of the tunic, in shimmering gold thread, was a stylized tree pattern, the slender trunk slanting up the right half of his rib cage, the bare branches fanning outward to streak across his chest in burnished rays. Belrok appeared to have taken pity on Alaric in constructing his trousers, which were simple in comparison—just plain black silk of various weights—but his formal boots were a dark mulberry hue, as was the cape that flowed from his wide shoulders.

The colors were striking against his pale skin and sable hair. And Talasyn had rather liked the poetry of being the butterfly to his stag—but then he'd opened his fat mouth.

The opaque burgundy curtains that hung at the threshold of the antechamber, separating it from the ballroom, were eventually drawn aside by an attendant dressed like a beetle. Knowing that they had to keep up appearances, Talasyn grabbed Alaric's arm without a word, shoving her hand into the crook of his elbow. He scowled, before flattening his mouth out into a—a smaller scowl.

Iantas's dusty, little-used ballroom had been completely transformed. The air was sweet with the perfume of myriad rose-and-hibiscus arrangements, mounted on marble pedestals. The celestial patterns splashed over the hangings and tablecloths gave off a faint sparkle in the muted light shed by chandeliers of crystal and bronze. And the crowd itself was a thing of wonder, a sea of bejeweled masks and fantastical costumes. Some were helping themselves to the smorgasbord of finger foods and fine wines, others were conversing merrily in little groups, and others still were gliding with their partners over the marble dance floor to the airy strains of a string orchestra.

As they made their way through the glitzy throng, Talasyn could only hope that she and Alaric were doing a capable enough job pretending to tolerate each other.

They went over to Queen Urduja, who wasn't too difficult to spot: she wore a silver dragon mask and a scale-pattern dress with an impressively frilled collar. The hummingbird-masked noblewoman she was talking to paled in comparison.

The Zahiya-lachis greeted Talasyn first, then studied Alaric over the rim of her champagne flute. "Emperor. Welcome back to the land of the living."

"Apologies for missing council, Harlikaan," Alaric tersely replied. "Holding back the Void Sever was more taxing than I had anticipated."

"Completely understandable," said Urduja. "I claim no knowledge of aethermancy and can't even imagine." She inclined her head toward the woman in the hummingbird mask, finally including her in the conversation. "You remember Daya Musal."

"Of course."

Alaric's tone was so carefully blank because, Talasyn realized, he did *not* in fact remember the noble who had led the charge in giving him a hard time at the engagement banquet. She jumped in, eager to avoid an awkward situation. "How good that the two of you can become acquainted in happier circumstances! Let us hope, shall we, Daya Musal, that there will be no duels *this* evening?"

Ralya Musal let out a melodious laugh, her brown eyes glinting over her mask's needle-sharp bronze beak. "No one would have the audacity to duel the man who helped save Nenavar. Not even Lord Surakwel—and I'd wager he is hardly aching for another go after being so soundly trounced by His Majesty last time!"

You'd lose that bet, my lady, Talasyn thought.

As Ralya chattered away at Alaric, Queen Urduja took the opportunity to lean in closer to Talasyn and issue a whispered command in the Dominion tongue. "See to it that Mantes and His Majesty steer well clear of each other."

"If the former even shows up tonight," Talasyn mumbled.

"Oh, he will." Urduja took another sip of champagne. "That boy positively *lives* to inconvenience me."

How long, Alaric asked himself an interminable while later, *have I been standing in this room?*

Surely longer than it had felt casting the eclipse sphere against the Void Sever. Surely longer than Bakun had been sleeping beneath the bones of the world.

More and more nobles were coming up to him, talking to him and then *talking with one another.* Etiquette dictated that everyone, even those who splintered off into their own little groups nearby, use Sailor's Common, so that Alaric could participate whenever he wanted to. And he *had* to participate, or he would waste the Dominion's hard-earned goodwill. The talking never stopped.

To make matters worse, Talasyn had been whisked off to the dance floor some time ago and she had yet to return, as she was busy going through one eager partner after another.

"Not only did the Lachis'ka stop the Voidfell, but she has also pulled off quite a splendid party," remarked one of the nobles. "Her Grace is a woman of many talents, it seems."

Alaric tore his gaze from Talasyn and her dance partner to glare at the man who had spoken. Or the *boy*, really. He looked to be in his early twenties, with lips nestled between the razor-sharp fangs of a bat's mask and a teardrop-shaped peridot hanging from one ear. Alaric had no idea who he was, but he swiftly came to the conclusion that he loathed this person.

Alaric loathed the man Talasyn was dancing with, too, the pompous frog-masked noble who'd had the gall to just—just *go up to her and request a waltz*—when she had *obviously* just finished dancing and any decent person would have let her rest for a while. He also loathed the nearby trio of dandies who were making no secret of their admiration, commenting on the excellent sense of rhythm of *his wife* and the fine figure she cut over the marble tiles.

"I profess myself rather envious of Lord Yaltik," one of them said. "I do hope Her Grace will spare me a dance as well."

"She already smiled at you at the last formal dinner," his friend protested. "Let us have a turn—"

The third member of the group was the one who noticed that Alaric was frowning at them. He nudged his companions, and they all smiled politely and bowed in sync. Then they resumed their conversation.

Alaric tried his best to not feel insulted beyond belief, but it was hard going.

Prince Elagbi wandered nearer, lifting his glass in what to all outward appearances was a cheerful toast, but the words he spoke close to Alaric's ear were serious. "I realize that things are different on the Continent, Your Majesty. Here, it is expected for men to fawn over the ladies at these gatherings. It's simply another way to pass the time, and the women take it as their due."

Alaric was glad for the stag's mask hiding the flush of his cheeks. Was he being *so* transparent?

Elagbi flashed a wry grin. "That scowl speaks volumes when it's aimed at all the young lords, Emperor Alaric."

Taking heed of Elagbi's warning, Alaric attempted to relax the line of his mouth after the prince went off to mingle with more festive partygoers. To distract himself, he turned his attention to Urduja—just in time to see her stride onto the dance floor with an elderly rajan in a boar costume. There was a subtle change in atmosphere as the Nenavarene started whispering among themselves behind lace fans and gloved hands.

Lueve Rasmey promptly filled in Alaric. She'd been gossiping with him all night—or, to be more accurate, gossiping *at* him. He attributed the daya's chattiness only to her relief that they hadn't all died. "That is Rajan Birungkil of the Mist Terraces. He was a favorite of Queen Urduja's back in the day."

Alaric froze. "A favorite," he said, before he could think better of it. He knew what that actually meant in court parlance. One had a spouse, and then one had a *favorite.*

Lueve shot him a look of vague reproach. "The Zahiyalachis *was* young once, Your Majesty."

That wasn't the reason for his discomfiture. Despite those pretty vows that he and Talasyn had sworn to each other at the dragon altar, apparently marriage was as sacred here as it was in Kesath—which was to say, not at all.

Lueve continued defending her sovereign from what she

clearly thought was Alaric's prudishness, with the breezy affectations that came so naturally to all the Dominion nobles. "I'm sure I have no idea how it is in Kesath, but it's par for the course here, Emperor Alaric. Married people still need to form strategic alliances, after all. And just like marriage, it's simply another way to maneuver in the political landscape . . ."

Alaric tuned out Lueve, and his gaze darted to Talasyn in something not dissimilar to panic. She'd gone through two new partners since the frog-masked lord, and more than a few noblemen, waiting for their turn, were gathered at the edge of the dance floor.

Not wasting time excusing himself, Alaric walked away from Lueve, setting a brisk pace for the dance floor. He had some faint idea of cutting in. It might be a bit of a social gaffe, but *surely* he was well within his rights, *surely* a husband could rescue his wife from all these lechers who wanted to use her for political gain.

Isn't that what you *were doing when you married her?* queried his nasty inner voice, which he pushed to the back of his mind, but not before it left a sour taste in his mouth.

Before Alaric could reach her, Talasyn switched partners again, her old one having deposited her into the waiting arms of a shaggy-haired noble wearing an eagle mask and a feather-flecked brown-and-gold costume that showed off his sinewy frame.

Surakwel Mantes.

It was telling that all of the chatter rippling around Alaric was conducted in the Dominion tongue rather than Sailor's Common, even though he was in the vicinity. The Nenavarene knew when to be polite and when to be discreet. But their bouts of quietly suggestive laughter, the intrigued tone of their remarks, needed no translation.

Surakwel was holding Talasyn closer than was strictly

necessary, and she was leaning in, too, the two of them murmuring to each other as they danced. A sickening blend of rage and despair welled up inside Alaric until he could barely see straight. Perhaps he should have seen this coming the night Talasyn leapt in front of the Shadowgate for Surakwel and referred to him by his given name. Perhaps it had only been a matter of time since then.

The lights in the ballroom were too bright all of a sudden, and the noise of the crowd almost deafening. Alaric balled his hands into fists to stop the tremors that shot through his fingers, and before he could allow himself to think twice, he resumed a determined path toward his wife. *His.*

CHAPTER THIRTY-THREE

"I have checked in with the Allfold as per your request," Surakwel's voice was soft in Talasyn's ear as they waltzed. "The Amirante has bade me tell you that she sprouted a new white hair the Night of the World-Eater, but otherwise everyone is fine."

"Thank the gods," Talasyn muttered. The Sardovian remnant had not evacuated from the isles of Sigwad, purely because the risk of discovery by unallied Nenavarene was too great. She couldn't even imagine the terror that they all must have felt.

"You're in Nenavar, Lachis'ka. We thank the ancestors here." Surakwel said it with only the barest hint of teasing. He'd been markedly cooler after witnessing her bargain for Alaric's life. "I have your new orders, by the way."

Talasyn's skin crawled with dread. "And they are?"

"The Amirante wants you to go back to the Continent. Find out how Kesath is supplying their warships with the limited pool of void magic from the moth coracle that Ossinast stole." Surakwel spun Talasyn around in time to the music, her skirts swirling over the marble, and then he brought her close again.

"Vela has been discussing this with Daya Vaikar's people. They think that all of Kesath's void hearts are connected to a single power source that can somehow replenish itself. It would be very helpful if you could find a way to disable that source before Sardovia attacks."

"And how is she proposing I do that?"

Surakwel shrugged. "You're the Night Empress, and you're a Lightweaver. Use *that*, and do it fast, because Midzul and the other allies are en route. I'm only an eagle away if you need my help." He blinked at something over her shoulder. "I have to go now."

"Not much for parties?" Talasyn acidly quipped.

"I have been known to enjoy them on occasion," he said slowly, "but this hasty exit has more to do with the fact that your husband is approaching us with murder in his eyes."

With that, he deposited her at the perimeter of the dance floor and disappeared into the crowd with one last courtly bow. Talasyn whirled around; sure enough, Alaric was bearing down upon her, paying no heed to the numerous guests who hailed him as he passed.

"My lord," she said, through gritted teeth.

"My lady," he replied in kind.

His fists were clenched and his gray eyes were dark with barely contained anger. An anger that hadn't been there earlier. This wasn't a continuation of their current spat, but something new.

And because she had *just* finished talking to Surakwel Mantes about the Sardovian remnant, Talasyn was plunged headlong into white-hot terror. *Alaric knows. Someone overheard us and told him. Or one of Urduja's allies has finally turned against her and told him.* It was irrational, but she couldn't let go of it, that piercing *What if?* She was numb all over save for the tightening in her chest.

"Lachis'ka!" Ito Wempuq of the Silklands materialized at her elbow. The rajan had opted for a goat costume on his ample frame, and the horns protruding from his mask nearly poked Talasyn's eyes out when he bowed to her. He also bowed to Alaric, albeit with far less enthusiasm. Saving Nenavar from the World-Eater had clearly not endeared the Night Emperor to Wempuq in the slightest.

"I hear Oryal called on you a while back, with the other ladies," Wempuq said to Talasyn. "I hope it wasn't too much of a bother."

"Your daughter is as charming as you are, Rajan," Talasyn assured him.

Wempuq's chest puffed up with pride. "May I say, Lachis'ka, that you look heavenly tonight, a vision of resplendent loveliness—"

"Er, thank you," Talasyn said, more preoccupied with the wrathful way Alaric's brows had knitted at this interruption.

"Your butterfly costume is *divine*, and so fitting for a creature of sunlight and summer and heavenly grace—"

"You used *heavenly* twice," she couldn't resist pointing out. It was easy to banter with Wempuq whenever he laid it on thick; he was one of her father's oldest friends, and perhaps in a life where she'd grown up in Nenavar she might have considered him an uncle.

Wempuq slapped a palm against his forehead in mock chagrin. "So I did! Perhaps you could allow me to expand my vocabulary as we dance."

"She's already spoken for." Alaric shouldered Wempuq aside, grabbing Talasyn's arm.

Talasyn had enough presence of mind to glance back at the rajan with an apologetic smile as she was ferried away. And then she narrowed her eyes at her husband. "Harassing the guests at a party *we're* hosting is shockingly poor form, even for you."

"And shockingly enough, I don't care." Alaric led her to the antechamber through which they'd entered the ballroom. The orchestra struck up the opening notes of a popular, fast-paced jig, and as the younger nobles swarmed onto the dance floor, laughing gaily, Alaric and Talasyn were able to leave relatively unnoticed. It was a struggle for her to keep up with his long strides, and by the time the curtains swung shut behind them, she was *quite* put out. But at least a bit more rational than before.

There's no way he knows. She took a deep, calming breath.

He leaned down and kissed her so savagely it made her head spin.

Oh.

It was always a shock, that initial press of his soft lips against hers. But Alaric didn't give Talasyn time to luxuriate in the sensation—instead, he swept his tongue into her mouth again and again until it felt not so much like a kiss as a taking. She kissed him back, determined not to lose whatever new game this was, pouring into it all her grievances. Their heavy, elaborate masks were in the way, however, and it wasn't long before she had to pull back because the butterfly's gold filaments were digging into her cheek.

"What's gotten into you?" she hissed as she adjusted her mask.

Her husband's eyes flashed silver. "I don't want to share."

Now she was just hopelessly confused. "Share what?"

He frowned. "You really don't know?"

"It's not as if I can read your mind!" she cried, irate.

Alaric closed the distance between their faces again. Talasyn glared up at him. If he tried to kiss her again, *now*, after being so frustrating, she would kick him in the groin.

But he didn't—at least, not on the mouth.

He went straight for her neck instead.

"I don't want to share," he repeated, nipping at a sensitive spot below her jaw. "Not with Mantes, not with *any* of them." He held her by the waist, his fingers kneading at the exposed skin of her lower back. "I don't give a damn what your court says. I don't care if it's par for the course that you take favorites. You swore yourself to *me*."

"This . . ." She was having a difficult time stringing words together. It was the feel of his hand on her spine, the sharp shock of lips and teeth at her throat, the buckling of her traitorous knees. "This is all because I danced with—"

He tilted his head, all the better to lavish her neck with furious, biting kisses. The golden antler of his stag mask slid cool across the corner of her mouth. "I rather doubt *dancing* was all your suitors had in mind."

It was the unfairness of the allegation more than anything else that finally gave her the strength to push him away. "If so, that's their problem, not mine! What are you mad at *me* for?"

Alaric stumbled back. "I'm not mad *at* you—"

"Could've fooled me—"

"I'm *jealous*, Talasyn," he snapped.

"Then you're an idiot!" She stomped her foot, because *that* was what he had reduced her to. "Didn't we promise each other on Belian that there would be no dishonor between us? Why does my word mean nothing to you?"

She stopped short, a hook catching at the pit of her stomach. Her word *did* mean nothing when it came to him. Just not in the way he thought.

I will raise my armies in your defense.

I will stand with you against your enemies.

Talasyn had sworn all that, at their wedding and at her coronation. But it could never come to pass.

Alaric swallowed, his wide frame tensing. After an age, he spoke. "I'm sorry."

I'm sorry, too, she thought. *For everything that has to happen.*

And because she didn't *want* to be sorry, because she felt petty and mean and selfish, because her duty had been so clear to her but he'd messed her up and she wasn't sure if she could really save him, Talasyn took refuge in the lingering flames of her wrath, hoping that they would reignite his own. Hoping for another fight, because that was the language she understood.

"You *should* be sorry," she said. "Honestly, those other men out there wouldn't be such a pain in the—"

His mouth was on hers before she knew it. Punishing, *possessive.* Almost desperately so. Before she could make up her mind whether to return the kiss or follow through with kicking him, he pulled away, his gaze dark, a muscle working in his jaw. "Talk about other men again . . ."

"*You started it, Alaric!*"

And somehow she was shrieking that right in his face, somehow she was surging up on her toes and—

—the next series of kisses came hard and fast. It felt like a war in its own way. They kissed and bit and pulled until each was breathing harshly against the other's mouth. Their masks clacked together, and the metalwork dug into her skin once more. She wrenched herself away from him to remove her mask altogether, but before she could do so he took advantage of the pause to walk her backward, his hands on her hips, guiding her to the antechamber's sitting area, where he pushed her down onto the gilded chaise lounge until she was leaning against the cushioned backrest.

Alaric was a forest god as he fell to his knees before her, golden antlers gleaming in the light. He hooked her left leg over one broad shoulder, dotting a hurried kiss on the ankle peeking out from amidst the straps of her shoe. Then he littered more feverish kisses along her bare calf as his hand slipped under her right buttock to angle her center toward his wandering mouth.

Once he'd gone past her knee, Talasyn was shuddering, her undergarments soaked through. His first nip to her inner thigh caused her to cry out, and gods, if it wasn't the most exquisite form of torture as he took his sweet time sucking bruises into her flesh, the pain and pleasure forming a heady cocktail that made everything else melt away. She needed relief—needed it so badly that she felt as though she were back on the Great Steppe in high summer, craving water to slake the thirst parching her throat. She closed her eyes and the Sardovian sun burned in the darkness to the sound of string instruments emanating from the ballroom.

As the orchestra segued into the *tawindalen*, a dance tune as fluid as quicksilver and as light as air, his large fingers latched onto the sides of her undergarments and tugged so frantically that she was surprised he didn't rip them. She wiggled her hips to help, probably looking more comical than not, but it got the job done.

Alaric was impatient, though—he'd only just managed to wrestle the scrap of silk off one leg when he gave up and returned to the apex of her thighs. He afforded Talasyn no opportunity to be self-conscious, immediately sealing his lips over her—

—and it was firelight, it was music, it was static, it was open sky—

She'd often wondered what this would be like ever since she'd first heard of such an act, back in the Allfold regiments. Her imagination had fallen pathetically short of the real thing. His nose bumped against her bundle of nerves as he licked away at her, long and deep, his lips pressing together at the end of every stroke so that it felt like yet another little kiss, each sensation sending out rivers of delight that rippled through her until she was delirious, yanking at his hair, grinding against his lush mouth. Sometimes it was too much and sometimes it wasn't enough, but she didn't care, urging him on with whimpers of *there* and *yes* and *slower* and *more.*

Her husband was blessedly quick on the uptake. When he worked out the rhythm that made her tick and set to it with a ruthless determination, Talasyn all but *shouted*, her spine arching, her head tipping back. She saw herself in the antechamber's mirrored ceiling, her emerald skirts glittering against velvet burgundy cushions, her lips parted and Alaric's dark head between her thighs, their figures bathed in gold. The masks, butterfly and stag, added to the illusion of depraved glamour, and she looked and *felt* like a goddess being worshipped, her hips writhing in time to the *tawindalen* as the orchestra played on in the next room.

"We shouldn't," she panted out, ". . . anyone can . . . walk in—"

"So?" Alaric pulled off her with an obscenely loud smack. He stared up at her with blazing, hungry eyes, the gold pigment running down his swollen bottom lip slightly smudged. "Let the Nenavarene see their Lachis'ka ride the Night Emperor's face." There was a ragged edge to his deep voice. His breath was hot against her wetness. "Let them see me make my wife scream. Let them know, beyond the Shadow and the turning of the stars, that you are *mine*."

He bent his head over her again, lapping at her with his wicked tongue. Her body was caught between twisting away from him and chasing the bliss, and it decided on the latter when he began to *suck*. Her thighs clamped around his neck, the heels of her shoes digging into his back, and he groaned and redoubled his efforts. The *tawindalen* soared to its crescendo and so did she, her scream drowned out by the crashing symphony, her eyes flashing gold in the overhead reflection as she tipped over the edge and into the fiercest, most *glorious* climax of her life.

Still on his knees, Alaric reached up to hold her through the aftershocks, the unmasked lower half of his face buried in the crook where her neck met her shoulder. "Have I made my point?" he asked gruffly.

"You should stop talking so much," Talasyn replied, breathless. Dazed. "That mouth of yours can be put to far better use."

She felt him smirk against her skin. She moved one hazy hand to punch him on the arm, but instead her fingers carded through the waves of his hair.

A question occurred to her, lazily, in the pleasant drowsiness of afterglow. "Where did you get the fool idea that I'd take favorites?"

He had the grace to appear embarrassed as he relayed what Lueve had told him.

Talasyn was puzzled. "Daya Rasmey can usually be relied on for her discretion. It's odd that she would gossip about Queen Urduja's past."

"The wine loosened her lips, probably. You should scold her." Alaric nuzzled at her collarbone. "But—later?"

"Yes." Later seemed like a good idea. He was warm and she was content, and she wanted this moment to last just a little bit longer.

CHAPTER THIRTY-FOUR

When they rejoined the party, Talasyn was in the best mood Alaric had ever seen her in. She gave her smiles more freely to everyone and was even somewhat affectionate with him, leaning just the slightest bit into his side while they conversed with their guests and clutching at his sleeve whenever she addressed him. Before long he was emboldened to reciprocate, his hand resting on the small of her back as they moved from one group to the next.

I will have to do that *again,* Alaric thought, a smile of his own threatening to burst across his lips. Not only had the taste of her been incredible and addictive—*the way sunlight felt*—but he also couldn't recall any other time he'd made someone so happy. It was intoxicating.

The masquerade didn't start winding down until Queen Urduja had retired to one of the guest bedrooms upstairs in the early hours of the morning. Alaric and Talasyn positioned themselves near the ballroom's main doors, accepting farewells from tired-looking nobles. A considerable number of guests were still dancing or consuming what remained of the food and drink.

Talasyn had been casting longing looks at those tables for the past several minutes. "I'm going to get something to eat," she announced, and Alaric was not in the least bit shocked.

What *did* come as a surprise was seeing her peer up at him with those big brown eyes and add, "Do you want anything?"

"I've eaten my fill," he drawled.

She *blushed*. Again, he had to bite back a smile as he watched her scurry off.

On her way to the refreshments, Talasyn came face to face with Ralya Musal once more. The hummingbird-beaked daya had Kai Gitab in tow, dressed as a porcupine. Poor eyesight had prevented the rajan from wearing a mask, but his spectacles had golden quills attached to their frames in honor of the occasion.

"Oh, Lachis'ka," Ralya gushed, "Rajan Gitab and I were just discussing how brave you and His Majesty were on the Night of the World-Eater! You saved us all, and we really cannot thank you enough."

"Indeed," said Gitab. "My peers and I have long been at odds with the throne when it came to certain matters, but this near-catastrophe has highlighted what is truly important. From now on, all of my house's resources are at your disposal."

"As are mine," said Ralya, not to be outdone. "Tepi Resok stands with you, Your Grace!" Her feathered earrings quivered with the strength of her enthusiasm.

Talasyn thanked them, somewhat shyly, but also feeling somewhat proud of herself. She was gathering allies from unlikely places. Gitab had privately sworn his loyalty months ago, in the hall of portraits at the Roof of Heaven; his public declaration now showed that he'd meant it.

It took some effort to politely extricate herself from the two nobles, but Talasyn eventually managed, her stomach rumbling. No sooner had she started digging into the food laid out on the moonlit tables by the ballroom's large windows than another group accosted her—Jie, Niamha, and two of the other noblewomen who'd visited Iantas when Alaric first took up residence. They clustered around her excitedly.

"Lachis'ka, you and His Majesty have been particularly tender tonight!" Bairung Matono exclaimed. "I don't think his hand left the small of your back for *hours*."

"Attached, just simply attached," said Oryal, with a dreamy sigh that seemed to flutter through the rose-colored praying mantis wings that adorned her from neck to toe. Beneath the matching eye-mask, tiny flowers glimmered on her cheeks, painted on with shimmery red pigment. "Like a quill to Rajan Gitab's spectacles."

The others laughed, but Talasyn was trying very hard not to go red in the face. "I sincerely hope you ladies have had time to enjoy the party on top of all your gawking," she snapped, cheeks bulging with pork-stuffed mooncake.

"The gawking *is* part of the enjoyment," said Bairung. "Tell us, did this romance begin when you were marooned in Chal?" Talasyn nearly spat out her mooncake. "I would be so sad if my rescue ship interrupted anything."

Bairung could never know how close her teasing had hit the mark. Before Talasyn could cobble together a hasty reply, Jie suddenly elbowed Niamha. "The way His Majesty swooped in on Her Grace and Lord Surakwel! Were you *very* relieved, Daya Langsoune?"

"My relief stemmed more from the fact that Surakwel managed not to step on Her Grace's toes even once," said Niamha.

Oryal snorted. "Yes, I remember all those dancing lessons from when we were younger. He was the worst of us!"

Through the merriment, Niamha gave Talasyn a strange look; Talasyn didn't know whether it was because of Niamha's feelings for Surakwel or because *she* wasn't supposed to have feelings for Alaric.

Talasyn caught herself. *I* don't—*I* can't—*have feelings for him.*

There was an attraction, and that was all it was. All it could ever be.

Especially now that Vela had given her a new mission, one that would bring the secret continuation of the Hurricane Wars closer to an end.

At that moment, there was an almost imperceptible flickering over the noblewomen's costumes, a rain of tiny shadows, blocking out the moonlight. Talasyn turned to the windows with a puzzled frown.

Prince Elagbi and Rajan Wempuq had wandered over after Talasyn left Alaric's side. Alaric found that he couldn't quite look his father-in-law in the eye, given what he'd done to his daughter so recently, but the Dominion prince seemed determined to make Wempuq warm up to Alaric. The copious amounts of wine that the two older men had been imbibing all night served to grease the wheels, and the conversation was not as stilted as it could have been.

In the midst of Elagbi and Wempuq regaling him with a wild tale from their youth, Alaric noticed two masked figures slip into the ballroom.

Figures who shouldn't have been there at all.

He excused himself from Elagbi and Wempuq and strode over to the new arrivals, who swiftly turned at his approach and led the way to a secluded alcove in the corner.

"What are you doing here?" Alaric demanded without preamble.

"What are *you* doing," Sevraim countered, "in *that*?" He pointed at Alaric's shimmering gold-and-green getup with an air of utter bewilderment.

"Focus," Ileis snapped at Sevraim. To Alaric, she said, "We bear urgent news, Your Majesty. Regent Gaheris tasked us to bring you back to the Continent as soon as possible. He insisted we *personally* see to it that you sail home."

Gaheris could have summoned Alaric to the In-Between. All the legionnaires knew that. The fact that he had not—the fact that he'd acknowledged, even in this small way, that his son might need a more pressing incentive than his word—spoke volumes about the seriousness of whatever was unfolding.

Alaric's pulse raced. "What happened?"

"There was a prison breakout during the Moonless Dark," said Ileis. "The Sardovian guerrillas snuck into the Citadel, slit the guards' throats, and freed their comrades. All of them."

In hindsight, Alaric understood that had been no better time for the rebels to attack than on a night when there was only a skeleton force in the Citadel. And no Gaheris.

"What about the legionnaires who stayed behind?" he asked. "Why couldn't they stop it?"

"The Sardovians caused a diversion that drew the legionnaires further away," Sevraim said. "All the way to the other end of the Citadel. The rebels were informed of the prison layout, Emperor Alaric. Someone told them that their comrades were being held in the eastern wing. Commodores Darius and Mathire are currently rooting out the informant, while Nisene is leading the hunt for the escapees, but you need to be there. We need to leave *now*."

The one good thing about this directive, Alaric thought numbly, was that he didn't have to bring Talasyn to his father. He could use this emergency as an excuse for not having had time to convince her to come with him.

"Tell the shallop crew to prepare to set sail," Alaric ordered his two legionnaires. "And have a message sent to my stormship to expect us. I'll meet you on the docks. Let me just say goodbye to my—to the Night Empress."

Sevraim saluted. "Yes, Your Glittering Majesty! At once, my shimmering master!"

"I have one more instruction, Ileis." Alaric nodded toward Sevraim. "Throw this one into the ocean."

After Ileis dragged a cackling Sevraim away, Alaric looked around the ballroom until his gaze landed on Talasyn. She and her friends were gathered at the refreshment tables. Behind her were flickers of movement against the ballroom's moonlit windows that faced out to sea—a scattering of stones falling from the sky.

A hailstorm? In Nenavar?

That was odd. Alaric squinted.

The stones grew in size—they weren't falling from the sky, they were being hurled at the windows by unseen hands—

—and they were all uniformly rounded at the sides and conical at the base—

Shells.

Alaric broke into a run, making for the tables. Talasyn and her friends were too near the windows, too far from him. He couldn't move fast enough. The ceramic shells hit their marks and the vast chamber rocked with myriad explosions as every single pane of glass disintegrated, the shards raining down on the crowd.

Ambush situations were nothing new to the Shadowforged Legion. Years of training and the long war with Sardovia had equipped Alaric to deal with such crises, but in that moment it seemed that all his wits had fled. He was consumed only by one thought. By one name. A name that he shouted over and over again as he pushed his way through the frenzied mass of screaming nobles. Figures clambered in through the broken windows, shooting crossbow bolts at the ceiling and the walls. The great chandeliers came crashing down and the fire lamps were snuffed out, plunging the ballroom into darkness, but Alaric barely paid any mind to the chaos. He thought only of getting to Talasyn.

It was an uphill battle. The Nenavarene jostled and shoved and stumbled, their cries drowning out Alaric's voice as sheer instinct repeatedly tore Talasyn's name from his lips. He removed his unwieldy golden mask, letting it fall to the floor, strewn with the bodies of all those who had tripped or been knocked over in the stampede.

Talasyn had vanished. He scanned the ballroom frantically—and something in his soul snapped in half. The Shadowgate left him, leaving nothing in its place but an aching void. Alaric had felt this before and knew at once what it was: a sariman nullification field.

He'd ordered Nenavar to remove those cages from his presence a long time ago, and there weren't any in sight now, but still the effect set in harshly, causing him to stagger against a nearby pillar. Clutching it for support, he looked around in a belated attempt to make sense of the situation.

The horde of assailants moved purposefully through all the chaos. They were in leather helms and armor, and several carried void muskets in addition to hand crossbows. They weren't shooting indiscriminately into the crowd, a sure sign that this was no mere attack on the Dominion. Rather, they appeared to be looking for someone.

And it didn't take Alaric long to figure out who. Bolts of amethyst light zipped toward him.

"Stay here," Talasyn hissed. "Don't make a sound."

Jie, Niamha, Oryal, and Bairung nodded, arms around one another, eyes wide.

Talasyn had herded the four noblewomen under a table as soon as the windows shattered. Now she crawled out from under it and threw herself into the commotion, searching for Alaric and Elagbi.

The Lightweave vanished then.

Sariman, she realized with a sickening clench that made her freeze—for just a moment, but long enough for the stampeding guests to knock her to the ground. Someone started running across her torso as though she were the floor, and she reared up, knocking the other person off her before their weight cracked her ribs. *Sorry, whoever you are,* she thought with a twinge of guilt, kicking off her shoes and scrambling to her feet, upright again—

—and staring down the barrel of a Nenavarene musket, gleaming bronze in the moonlight.

Talasyn yanked off her mask and hurled it at the assailant. The man yelped as the large, jewel-encrusted butterfly hit him in the face, and she made a grab for the musket, twisting it around in his hands and firing it into his chest. The sound was echoed by several more in the distance, violet magic illuminating the gloom.

She liberated her new weapon from the man's corpse and charged toward the light.

Alaric ducked behind the pillar in the nick of time. The granite reverberated with the fury of a dozen void bolts, and then he was off, disappearing into the mass of bodies scrambling for the exit. Common sense dictated that he head there as well, but he wasn't leaving. Not without Talasyn.

More shots rang out behind him. Alaric used the shifting crowd to his advantage, going wherever it was thickest and most chaotic. Two of the flowering marble pedestals had been knocked over; as he neared, they reflected the Voidfell's amethyst glow and he dove behind them, lying flat on his stomach. The pedestals trembled as the magic made contact, and the sickly sweet smell of decaying roses filled the air.

Alaric crawled forward on his elbows until he reached the sitting area at the edge of the dance floor, where most of the tables and chairs had been overturned in the havoc. One such table was lying on its side, and a slim arm shot out from behind it and hauled Alaric close with surprising strength.

"Are you—are you okay?" Talasyn whispered.

"Yes." He ran his hands over her body in the dark, hardly daring to believe that she was alive, and with him. "You?"

"I can't aethermance," she said. "How are they doing this?"

Alaric went through the layout of Iantas in his head. "There's a terrace wrapped around the ballroom. If they put the sariman cages there . . ." He trailed off. Each sariman could project its nullification field only within a seven-foot radius. The attackers wouldn't be able to cover the whole ballroom, unless—

"They're amplifying it somehow," Talasyn finished his thought for him.

He sighed. "Hopefully Sevraim and Ileis are all right."

Despite the circumstances they were in, there was something oddly charming about the way she wrinkled her nose at the mention of his legionnaires. Or perhaps just Ileis. "Why are they here?"

"I'll tell you later."

They both peered out from behind the table. A large group of assassins was moving toward their hiding spot. She retrieved her musket and began to take aim.

"*Have you taken leave of your senses?*" Alaric hissed. "If you fire now, they'll *all* know where we are."

"They'll find out soon, anyway," Talasyn argued. "Going on the offensive is our best option at this point."

"I'd much prefer an offensive that doesn't end in our current location getting surrounded," he dryly remarked. "Here, I have a plan."

CHAPTER THIRTY-FIVE

As their cohorts fanned out across the rest of the ballroom, the ten assassins searched the sitting area in tight formation, muskets at the ready.

A panicked figure emerged from behind one of the overturned tables and made a mad dash for the exit. One assassin reflexively pulled the trigger, and the ensuing bolt of void magic outlined the figure's horned goat's mask in violet light before he crumpled to the floor.

Behind the table where she and Alaric were hiding, Talasyn clapped a hand over her mouth, biting a scream into the mound of her palm.

"Moron!" someone snarled. "You just killed Rajan Wempuq!"

The words were in the Dominion language. Talasyn had known, of course, that the assassins had to be Nenavarene, given their void muskets and sariman cages, given that the dragons hadn't risen from the sea, but the confirmation made her insides shrivel. And now Wempuq was dead, and there was no time to grieve. The people who had killed him were moving closer to the hideout where she and Alaric lurked.

Someone *was* screaming, though. From all the way across the ballroom, through the din of everything else. Broken wails of *No* and *Amya*, interspersed with wordless sobs.

Oryal. She had seen her father die.

"*Now*," Alaric said.

The rounded table was small enough to carry, with some effort, and big enough to provide some cover. Alaric picked it up and held the tabletop in front of them as he and Talasyn ran at their foes while she reeled off one void bolt after another. The table served as both shield and battering ram right through the middle of the enemy formation, throwing the assassin ranks into disarray.

Alaric and Talasyn managed to overwhelm several of the attackers, but the rest rallied and soon the table had splintered into pieces under the onslaught of crossbow bolts, leaving the two of them no choice but to separate. She knew that they had no chance of winning; their aethermancy was gone and they were vastly outnumbered. But Alaric was as fierce and defiant as a caged tiger, and that inspired her to new heights. She ducked for cover behind pillars and slid under fallen chandeliers, and when the musket's aether cores ran out, she didn't shy away from using her fists, her elbows, her *teeth*. She left a trail of bodies in her wake, but soon two of the assassins managed to outflank her. She dropped to the floor the moment they opened fire, and one fell victim to his comrade's void bolt. She wasted no time in tackling the other by the legs. They wrestled over the marble tiles, but he scrambled upright before she could and took aim—

Then he spasmed and went still, the musket slipping from his limp grasp, the tip of a sword protruding from his stomach. As the blade was retracted, the dead man fell away to reveal the kaptan of Talasyn's royal guard.

"*Where is my father?*" Talasyn asked as Nalam Gao helped her to her feet. The rest of the assassins closing in from all corners of the ballroom had been intercepted by the rest of the Lachis-dalo, and the sounds of furious combat churned the air.

"Prince Elagbi was safely extracted by his own guards," said Gao. "He is on his way to Eskaya, along with the Zahiya-lachis. The castle's soldiers have been poisoned, Your Grace. The attackers have surrounded the ballroom. We need to get you out of here—we'll fight our way out."

"Easier said than done," Talasyn muttered. There were only ten Lachis-dalo and countless assassins. Most of the party guests were flooding through the exit, but several remained, cowering behind furniture or frozen in fear, in plain sight.

She came to a decision. "Jie and some others are hiding by the windows," she told Gao. "Take them and the rest of the civilians somewhere safe."

Gao blanched. "Lachis'ka, my duty is to you—"

"That's an *order*, kaptan."

Talasyn sprang away from Gao before she could argue. She ran to Alaric, to fight by his side.

After the duel with Surakwel Mantes, Alaric hadn't exactly been anxious to wield a Nenavarene sword again. But one of Talasyn's guards had tossed him hers, and it was worlds more efficient than his bare hands.

A sword was also, in theory, more efficient than what Talasyn was currently using, but somehow that didn't appear to be the case. She'd picked up a broken-off table leg and was now using it as a makeshift club, which would have given Alaric pause had he not been fighting for his life. She cracked skulls with it, swung it at stomachs and kneecaps, put enemies into strangleholds with it.

Without the benefit of aethermancy, his wife *brawled*.

Alaric slammed his forehead into an assassin's, breaking the death grip the other man had on him as they both recoiled from each other in pain. When the dark spots stopped swimming before his eyes, the first thing he saw was the amused look on Talasyn's face.

"Where did you learn *that*, I wonder?" she quipped.

He bared his teeth at her. "Only from the best."

Alaric was facing the broken windows. Over Talasyn's head, he spotted one of Iantas's smaller fighting craft, a crossbow-laden sloop, gliding along the length of the castle, its square sails gleaming blue and gold against the black velvet sky.

Elagbi was at the wheel.

Talasyn followed Alaric's line of sight. Her jaw dropped. "He's supposed to be with his guards!"

Still wearing his crocodile costume from the masquerade, the Dominion prince fired the airship's crossbows at something on the terrace. *Several* somethings. The resulting explosion was identical to what Alaric had seen when the amplifying configuration destabilized during the tests, and once more on the Night of the World-Eater. A plethora of fiery suns, flaring to life, and with them—

—the return of the Shadowgate.

Her husband's eyes abruptly turning bright silver was all the warning Talasyn needed to cast a shield. The Lightweave poured out of her, hot and rich, and the golden shield that materialized in her hand trembled and sparked as waves of raw shadow magic crashed against it, flowing around her to engulf their nearest assailants. The screams of the dying mingled with the guttural shriek from aetherspace, a grating parody of an orchestra.

More assassins converged on Alaric and Talasyn's location.

Neither light nor shadow magic could stop the Voidfell if there was no eclipse. But the attackers wielding the muskets were flesh and bone, and as such easily cut down with radiant javelins and inky throwing knives, easily hauled every which way by searing chains. As Talasyn exulted in the return of her aethermancy, she tried not to feel too much vindictive satisfaction, but as she thought about her frightened guests and how close her family had come to getting killed, and about poor old Ito Wempuq, the burning rose within her. Her rage fed the Lightweave, fashioning it into a sword in her hands as she and Alaric broke through the enemy ranks.

Talasyn was too caught up in the maelstrom of slashing and stabbing to notice that the last attacker flanking her position had succumbed. When she detected a dart of movement and a whirl of aether to her left, she automatically swung around to meet it. Caught up in her fury, she didn't even realize it was Alaric until she was staring at him through the haze of their locked blades.

Perhaps the snarl on her lips should have faded away. Perhaps his fierce eyes should have softened in recognition at the sight of her.

But this, too, was memory. They were surrounded by the fallen, the floor a mess of bloodstains and broken glass, their clothes torn and their chests heaving, adrenaline pumping through their veins. Her instincts marked him as dangerous. Her body knew his from the Hurricane Wars.

In the mood they were both in, they could have easily slit each other's throat.

But he leaned in, over the intersection of their blades, and pressed a hard and bruising kiss to her lips instead. Then another stream of void bolts flared out from the darkness and they separated.

As Talasyn scrambled from out in the open to take a more defensible position, she spotted Oryal on her knees, hunched over Wempuq's corpse. Oryal had broken away from the throng of nobles fleeing to safety, and she'd crossed an ocean of combat to reach her dead father's side.

Something in Talasyn's mind snapped, pulled to breaking point by the horror of the last several minutes. Of the last several years. Suddenly she was looking not at Oryal and Wempuq but at the past. At Khaede on the deck of the *Summerwind*, Sol's head in her lap. Oryal's praying mantis mask, discarded over the marble tiles, became the crossbow bolt, slick with Sol's blood, rolling over teak boards and iron nails.

Everything ended, even pain, even empires. Everything but this.

War was the unchanging season, the eternal state. No matter what Talasyn did, no matter what crown she donned, no matter who she loved or didn't love, someone was always going to die.

Oryal raised her head. Her eyes locked with Talasyn's. And there was something—

For the barest split-second, there were white sparks in Oryal's eyes, flashing through her tears. But Talasyn had to be imagining it, or it had to be a reflection of the moonlight—but in any case she couldn't dwell on it. Several assassins had swarmed around her, all wielding blades rather than muskets. The void hearts had probably run out. This battle was almost over, even if war would never end. She conjured her golden daggers, slicing them through and across her assailants' forms. They all fell, one after another, and when Talasyn finally surfaced—

Oryal was gone.

Talasyn looked around wildly, her heart racing. She had to get Oryal out of here. She'd lost sight of Khaede at Lasthaven, leaving her to an unknown fate. But she wouldn't fail *this* person, she wouldn't let go of this one thing that could still be saved.

In the gloom, she spied a skirt of rose-colored wings disappear into the antechamber from which she and Alaric had emerged earlier. Talasyn ran for it, leaving the battle behind. Gao had mentioned that the assassins had surrounded the ballroom; they might be lurking outside the antechamber, too, ready to mow down whoever exited as ruthlessly as they'd mowed down Wempuq.

Right before she ducked into the little room, Talasyn chanced one last look at Alaric. His back was to her as he fought in formation alongside her guards. He had his aethermancy and he had help, while Oryal was alone. Talasyn had to go.

And yet, as she turned away, the oddest sensation rippled through the pit of her stomach. It was fleeting and illogical, but there all the same, briefly beneath her heart—the feeling that she was never going to see him again.

She'd felt this before, on too many occasions to count. It was a kind of paranoia rooted deep in her psyche. Back when an endless series of battles swept across the Continent, in the shadow of the stormships there was always a chance that you'd be looking at someone for the last time.

But that wasn't going to happen here. She'd usher Oryal to safety, then return to Alaric's side.

Talasyn rushed into the antechamber. It was empty, but the door leading to the hallway had been flung wide open. Bodies lay beyond the threshold—two of them, clad in assassin's armor. She was rather shocked that Oryal had managed *that*, but then again, even ladies fought when cornered.

As she stepped over the dead men, a vague suspicion gnawed at the back of her neck. The corpses were still holding their weapons. How had Oryal . . . ?

Squinting down the deserted hallway, where all the fire lamps had been shot out of their sconces, Talasyn heard muffled crying from up ahead.

Ito Wempuq's wife had passed away a long time ago. Now he, too, had set sail with the ancestors. His daughter was an orphan.

I had no one, Talasyn thought. *Back on the Great Steppe, there was no one to hold me when I cried, when I missed a family I never knew, when I felt I had nothing.*

She headed toward the sound, rounding the corner. Oryal was leaning against the granite wall and weeping, face buried in her hands.

"Lady Oryal," Talasyn said softly, touching her on the shoulder. "We have to—"

Oryal appeared to crumple at such gentleness. She turned to Talasyn, spreading her arms like a child begging to be carried. The little painted flowers on her cheeks had been melted by her tears and now ran down her face like streaks of blood.

Talasyn hugged her.

"Lachis'ka," Oryal said, through sobs that rang with desperate grief, "it's so difficult. You understand how I feel, don't you?"

Talasyn nodded mutely, rubbing Oryal's back even as she kept an eye on their surroundings for the approach of any potential threats.

"I don't know which of us is more unfortunate," Oryal continued, shaking in Talasyn's arms. "We both lost our mothers when we were young, and now—at least you still have Prince Elagbi, but—but at least *my* grandmother didn't kill my mother."

What?

There was a tearing of the veil between the material realm and aetherspace, and Talasyn heard a crackling, like oil dribbled into a hot pan magnified a hundred times over—a sound she recognized from whenever the Tempest Severs activated. Oryal's hand was on her spine, and there was a jolt, as though that hand had pushed her with all the resounding strength of a horse's kick. Bluish-white lightning filled her vision and shot *through* her body, the pain immense, like a million burning wires.

Her knees gave way, snapping like twigs as an abrupt, frightening numbness consumed her from head to toe. She dropped to the carpeted floor with a thud, a dark fog crawling along the edges of her sight.

Something sharp was jabbed into her neck. A blade—no, a needle. Talasyn barely felt it, on top of everything else, but soon another layer of pain—a different kind—blossomed underneath the lightning's shock. Thousands of tiny glass shards forced their way through her veins as—*something*—ate at her magic.

It was nothing like the abrupt loss of walking into the sarimans' nullification field. It was a torturously slow erosion. The light inside her faded. She struggled to hold on to it, struggled to stay conscious. Begged it not to go.

A glass-barreled syringe fell to the carpet beside her. It was empty, but a bead of liquid remained on the tip of the hollow steel needle. The droplet shone a bright turquoise, marbled with ribbons of crimson.

Sariman blood and rain magic.

Oryal loomed over her, a wraith in a rose-colored dress. Lightning crackled in her fist. Her eyes flashed white with the Tempestroad.

"You really don't belong here in Nenavar, Lachis'ka." Oryal's voice, coming from much too far away, was the last thing Talasyn heard—and that scarlet-streaked face twisted in contempt was the last thing she saw—before the remaining fragments of the Lightweave vanished from her being and everything went black. "No one in the Dominion court would *ever* have fallen for that."

Talasyn plummeted into that black space, as vast and deep as the Mouth of Night. She could almost be within those caverns again, with the wind howling and the water rising, with warm fingers trailing down the inside of her wrist like safe harbor in a storm.

Alaric, she thought.

She tried to hold on to him the way she hadn't been able to hold on to her magic, but soon even he, too, was gone.

And there was only darkness.

Acknowledgements

Between the publication of *The Hurricane Wars* and me writing this note, it has been—simply put—an incredible year. I didn't know what to expect as a debut author, but everything that happened was beyond my wildest dreams. And it is all thanks to so many beautiful souls across the world.

To my agent, Thao Le, forever my stalwart advocate and guide, and the source of the wisdom that I severely lack, and everyone else at Sandra Dijkstra Literary Agency who has helped me navigate the wild world of publishing.

To the fine folks at HarperCollins US who made my debut one to remember, with their enthusiasm and hard work behind the scenes: publisher Liate Stehlik, associate publisher Jennifer Hart, senior editor Julia Elliott (and Teddy the World-Eater), publicists Danielle Bartlett and Genessee Floressantos, marketers DJ DeSmyter and Samantha Larabee, production editor Jeanie Lee, production supervisor Gregory Plonowski, managing editor Jennifer Eck, editorial director David Pomerico, interior designer Jennifer Chung, and cover art director Richard Aquan. Talk about a team effort! Thank you all for bearing with me.

To the lovely people at HarperCollins UK who sent me off on my first-ever book tour and have always been unfailingly kind and supportive: editors Kate Fogg and Ajebowale Roberts, publicists Maud Davies and Emilie Chambeyron, marketers Sian Richefond and Sarah Shea, producer Emily Chan, the sales team—Leah Woods, Harriet Williams, Holly Martin, Erin White, and Montserrat Bray—and the art team, Dean Russell and Ellie Game.

To my ultra-talented cover artist, Kelly Chong (@after blossom_art), my friend from fandom to beyond, and mapmaker extraordinaire Virginia Allyn (@virginiaallyn)—the two of you took my words to new heights with your gorgeous art. I love working with you!

To Consul General Senen T. Mangalile and the Philippine Consulate General and Sentro Rizal in New York—Vice Consul Cathe S. Aguilar, Mr. Joselito P. Aguinaldo, and Ms. Nikka B. Arenal, to name a few—and Tita Dely Go and Sir Troi Santos, who pulled out all the stops to welcome me to the US and advocated for the overseas Filipino community to support my book.

To every librarian and bookseller out there who gave *The Hurricane Wars* a place on their shelves—it would never have reached so many readers without your passion and tireless efforts. I'm forever indebted.

To the journalists and podcasters who featured me and shared my story with their audiences—it was truly an honor, and I promise to work at being a less awkward interviewee in the future.

To the book bloggers on Instagram, TikTok, and more—where would I be without all the amazing content you guys made for my series? Every beautiful photo, every fun video, every thoughtful post was an act of love, and my heart received it as such and returns it to you.

To everyone who took time out of their day to attend my signings, who waited so patiently—it was such a pleasure to meet all of you. The energy in those rooms—from the UK to New York to Singapore to Manila—was unreal. I will treasure every second until my last breath.

And, of course, to my dearest readers who have made fan art for this series, from breathtaking illustrations to intricate cosplays to gorgeous crafts to steamy fanfics; who have taken the time to write to me with excited questions and reviews; who have recommended my book far and wide; who have created the most insightful meta and the funniest memes (mostly about how Alaric is a loser)—as an author who started out in fandom, I will never get over this feeling. You all mean the world to me.